I0539015

Other Titles by Cheryl Brooks

Cowboy Delight
Cowboy Heaven
Unbridled: Unlikely Lovers Book 1
Uninhibited: Unlikely Lovers Book 2
Undeniable: Unlikely Lovers Book 3
Unrivaled: Unlikely Lovers Book 4
The Cat Star Chronicles: Rebel
The Cat Star Chronicles: Wildcat
The Cat Star Chronicles: Stud
The Cat Star Chronicles: Virgin
The Cat Star Chronicles: Hero
The Cat Star Chronicles: Fugitive
The Cat Star Chronicles: Outcast
The Cat Star Chronicles: Rogue
The Cat Star Chronicles: Warrior
The Cat Star Chronicles: Slave
The Cat Star Chronicles Bundle: Slave, Warrior & Rogue
Sharing (Sextet Anthology)
Entanglements (Sextet Anthology)
Occupational Hazards (Sextet Anthology)
Mistletoe & Ménage (Sextet Anthology)
Dirty Dancing (Sextet Anthology)
Small, Medium, & Large (Sextet Presents)
The Lady Takes a Pair (Sextet Presents)
A Tale of Two Knights (Sextet Presents)
Midnight in Reno
If You Could Read My Mind (writing as Samantha R. Michaels

UNLIKELY LOVERS

Unbridled

CHERYL BROOKS

DERRYMANE PRESS

Derrymane
Press

Unbridled
Unlikely Lovers Book 1
by Cheryl Brooks
Published by Derrymane Press
Copyright © 2014 Cheryl Brooks.
Cover design by Dragonfly Press Design
Cover image by Shutterstock
ISBN-13: 978-0-9838081-6-9

All rights reserved. No part of this book may be reproduced in any form or by any electronic or mechanical means including information storage and retrieval systems—except in the case of brief quotations embodied in critical articles or reviews—without permission in writing from its publisher, Derrymane Press.

The characters and events portrayed in this book are fictitious or are used fictitiously. Any similarity to real persons, living or dead, is purely coincidental and not intended by the author.

www.cherylbrooksonline.com

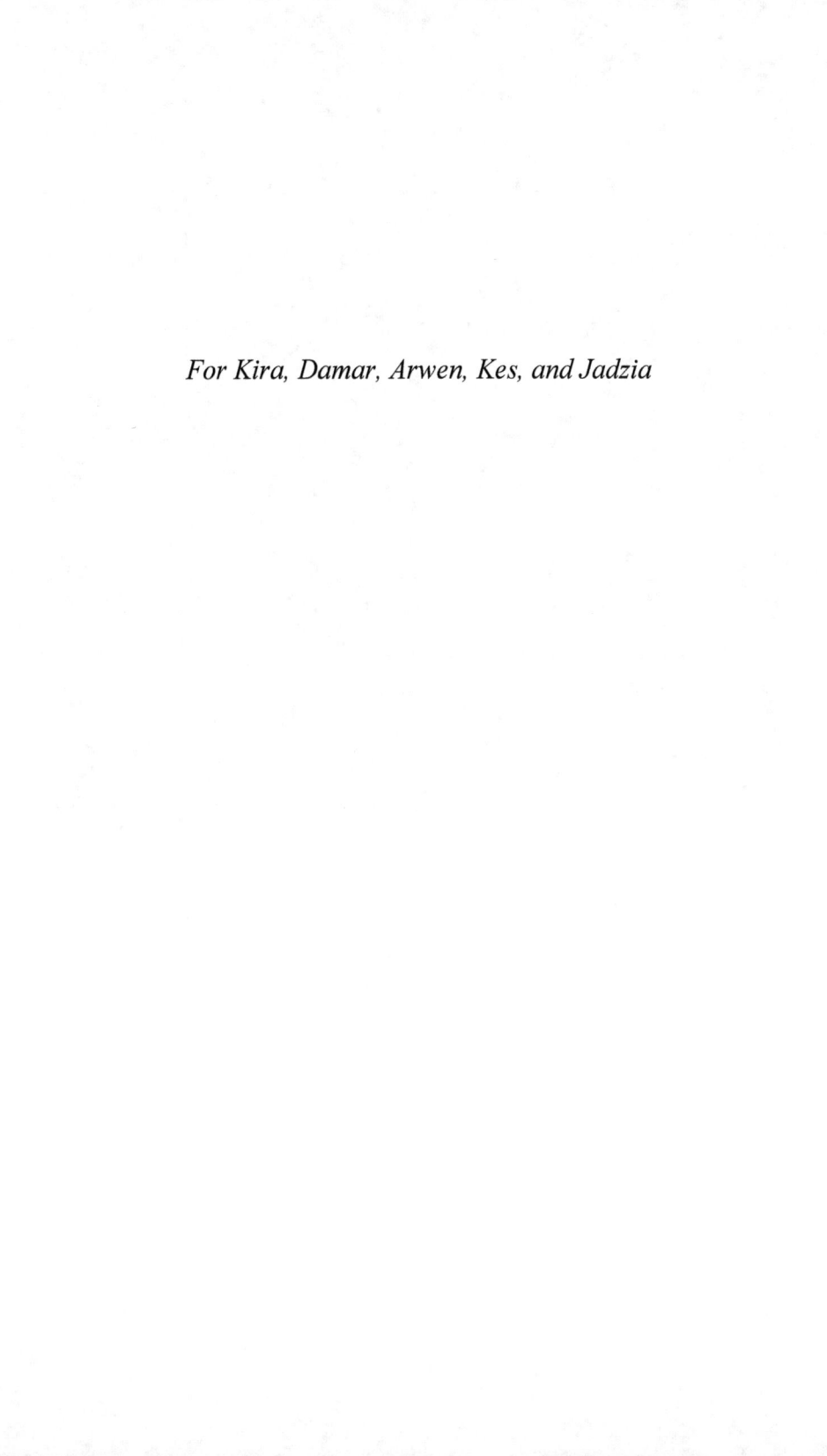

For Kira, Damar, Arwen, Kes, and Jadzia

ACKNOWLEDGEMENTS

My heartfelt thanks go out to:
My terrific critique partners, Nan Reinhardt and Sandy James.
My keen-eyed beta reader, Mellanie Szereto.
My pal and mentor in the self-publishing world, Marie Force.
My buddies in IRWA for their support and encouragement.
My friends and family for their love and understanding.
I couldn't have done this without you!

Chapter 1

When passion is given free rein...

ഇൻ‌ൽ

Miranda Jackson hadn't braved the chill of a late October cold snap for a riding lesson at Nigel Mirren's stable simply because she loved horses. Nor was she there to see Nigel—although the lanky Englishman never failed to make her laugh. No, the real reason was at the other end of the barn putting new shoes on Ghost, Nigel's sturdy Irish gelding. Miranda would have endured far greater hardships than cold weather for the chance to catch a glimpse of Travis York.

With the temperatures below freezing, Miranda's feet sat like two chunks of ice in the stirrups, and Kira's breath froze in the air as the mare trotted around the sandy expanse of the indoor arena. Still, Miranda considered it worth the discomfort. The sweet smile she would receive from Travis afterward would warm her all the way to her frozen toes.

Too bad a smile was all she would ever receive from him. He was completely adorable and one of the nicest men she'd ever met, but being at least fifteen years her junior, he would never see her as a potential girlfriend. In her experience, handsome young men had no interest in forty-five-year-old widows—aside from the fact that she suspected that the "interesting news" he'd hinted at earlier involved another woman. She'd asked Nigel about it, but he didn't seem to know a thing and quickly changed the subject to the loss of yet another fabulous horse he couldn't afford.

"You would have loved him, Miranda," Nigel lamented. "He

was big and bold and had a stride five yards long." He heaved a deep sigh of regret. "Absolutely beautiful."

"I'm sure he was," Miranda agreed. "Fifty thousand dollars worth of beautiful. Why do you even bother looking at those pricey horses? All it does is make you depressed." Miranda had stopped dreaming about Hanoverians and Dutch warmbloods a long time ago. Her nursing salary might've paid the bills, but it certainly didn't allow for major splurges.

"I can bloody well dream, can't I?" he protested. "And who knows? I might win the lottery some day."

"I wouldn't count on it. Besides, you have to play to win."

To hear Nigel tell it, he'd never had a dollar to spare for a lottery ticket in his life, and the slightly dilapidated nature of his stable and arenas proved it. Several of the arena's overhead lights were burned out, and feathery strips of disintegrating insulation dangled from the underside of the barn's metal roof, which also had a tendency to leak.

Miranda had done her best to contribute to Nigel's finances, seldom missing a lesson while at the same time hoping to provide him with a less expensive alternative to the type of horses he normally drooled over. "If you could just hang on until next spring when Arwen turns three, I'll sell her to you cheap and you'll be getting a nice horse for a lot less money. Then all you have to do is train her and she'll be ready for the next Olympics." At least, that was the theory behind Miranda's little breeding project—supplying crossbred horses for those who simply couldn't afford an expensive European warmblood.

"If I live that long." It was no secret that while Nigel had come close to making the big time often enough, he had been eliminated by some injury to either himself or his horse every time. Fate, it seemed, was against him. He sighed again. "Okay, Miranda. Get that big mare going. I'm ready to be impressed."

Miranda wasn't sure she'd ever impressed Nigel. Most of his students won ribbons for their riding, but it was never Miranda's intention to make a big splash on the show circuit. More interested in the breeding end of the horse business, all she really wanted to do was increase her skill as a trainer—and Nigel was one of the best. During the three years she'd been his student, she'd gotten loads of useful tips from him, and as she improved, so had her horses.

Even though she was hot and sweaty by the time her half hour was up, her feet were still numb with cold when she jumped to the ground. Shivering as the moisture cooled on her skin, she led Kira back to the barn where, to her delight, she heard the clang of Travis's hammer.

"Hey, Kira," she said, giving the mare a nudge. "Guess who's still here? Yummy Mr. Travis Adorable York. My day is now complete."

Kira turned her head briefly. *If you say so*, she seemed to say. *I could not possibly care less.*

"Oh, come on, Kira. Don't you think he's cute?"

The mare ignored the question as though it were beneath her to respond.

"You're no fun at all," Miranda grumbled. "If he was some hotshot Thoroughbred stallion, you'd notice him, wouldn't you?"

Kira glanced at her with a wrinkled brow and kept walking. That question didn't require an answer, either. Of course she would notice someone like *that*.

Travis might never see Miranda in a romantic light, but that didn't stop her from looking, which was a relatively new pastime for her. Her husband Kris had died in a helicopter crash while serving in the Marines, leaving her with a broken heart and their mildly autistic son, Levi. The horror stories of men abusing their girlfriends' children were enough to keep her from looking for a new man, even if she'd wanted one. Which she hadn't. Levi was the only part of Kris she had left. Risking his safety was not an option.

Kris Jackson had been the love of her life, and getting over his death had taken a very long time. She'd continued to wear her wedding ring not only as a symbol of their love, but also as a deterrent to would-be suitors. As the years passed and her grief waned, the ring became so much a part of her hand she didn't even think about it anymore.

Now that Levi was grown, she'd considered dating again, but

never seemed to find the time or the inclination—aside from the fact that no one had interested her at all—until she'd met Travis. Unfortunately, due to the difference in their ages, she didn't see him as a viable option. He was friendly eye candy, nothing more—at least, that was what she told herself. Quite often her imagination took her places she had no business going—and the fact that Travis ranked right up there with Godiva Chocolate on the eye candy scale didn't help matters.

She'd thought about having him shoe her own horses, but she'd been with David Sherman for years and didn't want to hurt his feelings by using another farrier. No, this way was much better. She could chat with Travis while he worked, and he would never even notice how much she drooled.

She led Kira through the enormous barn and up to the cross-tie area where Travis was shoeing a stocky chestnut gelding.

He glanced up as she approached. "How'd it go?"

Miranda shrugged, rolling her eyes. "I made Nigel scream."

"Is that good or bad?"

"I'm not sure," she replied, frowning. "Sometimes it's good, sometimes it's not. Today it was hard to tell. It could be that I'm not cut out to be a dressage rider."

"What makes you think that?" he asked, fitting a shoe in place. "I've seen you ride, and you look pretty good to me."

He drove in two nails before she answered him.

"I'm not disciplined enough," she finally said. "When I first became interested in dressage, I thought it was so cool and looked so easy. What I didn't realize was that beneath the facade of simply sitting on the horse doing nothing was a hell of a lot of hard work and total concentration. I don't think I have the right mindset for it, but I keep trying." After exchanging Kira's bridle for a halter, she snapped the cross-ties to it. "That's all I know, Travis. Are you ready to tell me the big news?"

His deep blue eyes twinkled with mischief, but that grin of his nearly stopped her heart. "I've got a date lined up. She's an obstetrician—supposed to be real pretty, too."

"Supposed to be?" Miranda echoed. "You mean you've never

seen her?" Why this absolutely adorable man would have to resort to blind dates was beyond Miranda's comprehension. Women should've had to buy raffle tickets for the chance to go out with him.

He nodded. "I know. I'll probably be sorry, but a client of mine is sure she'll be perfect for me."

Miranda let out a long sigh. She could have told him that he didn't need to look any further than the woman standing next to him to find a new girlfriend, but Miranda had no guts whatsoever when it came to such things.

"Well, she *could* be." He'd obviously misinterpreted the reason for her sigh. "It'd be stupid not to even meet her, wouldn't it?"

"I suppose so." Miranda resigned herself to yet another stint at playing Mother Confessor rather than the love interest—she'd even listened to the details of his brother's divorce—doing her best to ignore the twinge of regret nagging at her heart. *Forget it, Miranda. You're too old for him.* "Okay, then. Tell me all about her."

"I don't know a whole lot." He grunted as he clinched the nails. "She's about my age, pretty, and recently divorced."

"Does she like horses?"

"I don't know," he said after a moment's pause. "I guess that's something I'll find out when I meet her."

"Do you know anything about her divorce?"

"Not much." Switching to the rasp, he filed down the clinches on the nails. "Just that I'll be the first man she's gone out with since it was finalized."

Miranda giggled as she unbuckled Kira's girth. He was in for *so* much trouble…

After setting down the newly shod hoof, Travis straightened up, giving the horse a pat on the shoulder. "What's so funny?"

"Depending on the reason for her divorce, she'll either hold a grudge against you for being a man at all or she'll pounce on you."

Long dimples creased his cheeks when he grinned, sending Miranda's temperature skyrocketing. Her frozen feet were already forgotten. "Dunno about the grudge," he said with a lazy drawl, "but I wouldn't mind being pounced on."

The mere thought of being the one doing the pouncing made

Miranda's mouth go dry. Reaching for the bottle of water stashed in her tote bag, she took a long drink. If she'd had to guess, the amount of time an obstetrician had to spend on a boyfriend was probably comparable to what Miranda's lawyer friend Christina Minks had available, which wasn't much. "Good luck. Let me know how it turns out."

"Thanks," he said. "I'll do that."

Pulling off Kira's saddle, she watched him covertly from behind the big mare. Why would anyone like Travis need luck *or* have to resort to blind dates? He should have already been married with a cute little wife and a pack of children blessed with his good looks and sandy blond hair—and maybe even that birthmark at the base of his neck. She'd noticed it during the summer and had thought it was a hickey until she realized it never faded. Now all it did was make Miranda itch to give him another one to match it. Oh, yes, he could pounce on her anytime he liked. Too bad he would probably never get the urge.

Damn.

Already anxious to see him again the next week, Miranda packed up her gear, loaded Kira in the trailer, and headed for home. On the way, she stopped for gas at the convenience store where her son worked. At twenty-two, Levi had become much more independent, learning to drive and living in his own apartment, and though she did her best not to make it seem like she was checking up on him, she was still his legal guardian.

She never ceased to be amazed at her son's accomplishments, celebrating every triumph and cheering him on to the next. Her only regret was that his father hadn't lived long enough to see it, nor had he been there for much of his early childhood. Thanks to his excellent memory, Levi could still remember Kris, but the memories were few.

Miranda's own memories had faded. True, she still recalled her husband's smile, the sound of his voice, and almost everything they'd ever done together—the high school prom, the graduation parties, their wedding, the birth of their son—but the touch of his hand had grown quite distant.

In recent years, Miranda had been introduced to several men and hadn't accepted a date from a single one of them. Her friends' examples were quite enough to deter her—not to mention the horror stories she'd heard from her sister, Tracy. Mary Beth's husband had left her for another woman. Lola had been married three times in the years Miranda had known her, and they'd all been losers—helpful and kind at first, but then increasingly unreliable or controlling once the marriage was official. And those were just the first two that came to mind. No. It wasn't worth the trouble. Far better to stick to eye candy like Travis York than have to put up with *that*.

ℰℛ

Travis's father had often remarked that any man who would steal another man's wife deserved to be shot. Unfortunately, Travis had already been smitten with Miranda long before he'd spotted her wedding ring. The fact that she was a few years older than him hadn't bothered him a bit, and once he'd figured out that she had a riding lesson every Tuesday, he'd made a point of scheduling his appointments at Nigel's stable accordingly.

He'd spent every Tuesday in February trying to decide if she returned his interest or not. Finally, on a balmy day in March, he was all set to ask her out when she returned from her lesson and pulled off her riding gloves. The plain gold band on her left hand had dashed his hopes completely. He should have known it the moment he'd realized how much he looked forward to seeing her every week. The good ones were *always* taken.

He thought he'd done the smart thing when he married Janie Fredricks right after high school. The prettiest girl in their class, Janie was popular, an excellent student, and Travis adored her. Then he found out the hard way that marrying your high school sweetheart didn't always guarantee happiness—particularly when said sweetheart was sleeping with your best friend.

Travis had broken up with his last girlfriend not long before that first chance meeting with Miranda. If his attraction to her had been one of those rebound things, he thought he should've gotten over it once he realized Miranda was married. He hadn't. God knew he'd tried, but no woman had ever affected him as strongly, and now here she was again, looking every bit as good in those tight breeches as a woman half her age.

She'd been the star of his sexual fantasies for so long, he couldn't lay eyes on her without mentally tangling his fingers in her chestnut hair and pulling her down for a kiss. Although he'd never touched her, his hands seemed to know the contours of her body and the texture of her skin. He'd gone through the motions of dating other women, all the while craving the warmth of Miranda's smile and the touch of her hand.

Despite what he'd said, his hopes weren't high when he met Dr. Shelley Masters for dinner, though she turned out to be everything Dan Tolliver had said she'd be—attractive, intelligent, pleasant—if not particularly exciting. Still, three out of four wasn't bad, and he'd liked her enough to ask her out again. *Who knows, she might even turn out to be exciting.* Eventually.

Travis had been told he was too picky—which wasn't true at all. He'd liked every woman he'd ever dated; he simply hadn't fallen in love. Perhaps that was Janie's fault. He'd given her his heart, and she'd stomped on it. Unfortunately, that pattern had repeated itself. Frequently. He hadn't given up hope yet, but since he'd met Miranda, no one had measured up to her. Shelley was no exception.

He knew it was stupid; he'd never even dated Miranda and knew comparatively little about her. Still, she'd become the ideal woman in his eyes, an unattainable goal that made everything else seem pointless.

But it wasn't pointless. He would find her equal someday and live happily ever after.

Yeah, right. Like I'll ever get that *lucky.* Travis wouldn't wish the pain of divorce on anyone, but he had an idea that catching *her* on the rebound would be the best thing that ever happened to him. Unfortunately, he'd never heard her utter a single word of complaint about her husband—what was his name? Levi? Still, if Miranda ever needed comforting—or anything else, for that matter—he was her man.

Too bad he could never tell her that.

Chapter 2

The following Tuesday, Travis carried in his toolbox just as Miranda reached under her horse to catch hold of the girth, bending over to display one of the most succulent backsides he'd ever seen. His groin tightened as she glanced up at him and grinned. *Cool down, Travis. She's married. Remember?*

"How'd it go?"

He stood gaping at her for a moment before he realized what she meant. *Oh yeah. Shelley.* "She's a nice lady." He set down his tools and leaned against a nearby post, focusing his full attention on her and letting his eyes drink their fill. No one could blame him for *that*… "I'm not sure we'll ever find anything in common, but I do like her."

Chuckling, she gave him a wink. "Oh, let me guess. She's either allergic to horses or is terrified of them. Right?"

"Neither. In fact, she has no opinion of them at all, except that they're big." Too bad that wasn't the only problem.

"That's a start." She threaded the saddle billets through the buckles and pulled the girth up tight. Travis fought the urge to do it for her. "At least she wasn't kicked by one as a child."

"No, but she *has* been kicked, in a manner of speaking. Her husband cheated on her for years, and she finally found out and divorced him." Travis knew that feeling quite well, which was the one thing they had in common. Unfortunately, commiseration wasn't the best basis for love. Shelley had been fairly straightforward about it, but he was pretty sure he hadn't heard the whole story yet.

"Oh, *not* good."

Travis held his breath, his heart pounding as she reached around him to retrieve her bridle from a hook on the post he was leaning against. She lingered for a moment, temptation personified, her subtle fragrance taunting him despite the pervasive aroma of horse that filled the barn. Her full lips were moist and inviting. A single step and he'd be near enough to kiss her.

"How long since the divorce?"

He cleared his throat with an effort. "About a year and a half."

Quirking an eyebrow, she tucked her lower lip between her teeth and shook her head. "That long, huh? And you're the first?"

"Yep."

"Oh, you're in big trouble, Travis," she said darkly. "It's a good thing I wished you luck, 'cause you're gonna need it. Does she have any children?"

He shook his head. "No, and she doesn't want any. Says she doesn't have time for them."

Miranda appeared to consider this, pursing her lips as a frown furrowed her brow. "That's good, in a way—at least they won't come between you. Does it bother you that she doesn't want kids?"

"Maybe. I mean, I'd like to have kids, but the way things are going I'll never have the chance." He let out a rueful sigh. "I'd rather not do it without a wife."

"I see your point." Once again, her smile drew his eyes to her lips, making him glad she couldn't read the carnal thoughts racing through his head. "Is she a good kisser?"

"Okay, I guess." He'd kissed Shelley goodnight after their date, more out of curiosity than anything. She'd seemed to expect it, lifting her face to his, her lips slightly puckered. Truth be told, it was one of the least memorable kisses of Travis's life, but that could change. *Yes, and hell could freeze over.* Fires didn't start without sparks, and he hadn't felt a single one.

Miranda's bright green eyes danced with mischief. His cock tightened painfully as he imagined them gazing up at him, heavy-lidded with passion.

"So it's safe to assume she didn't pounce on you?"

A shiver ran up his spine at the thought of *Miranda* pouncing on him. He shook his head. "Nope. No pouncing—darn it."

"Poor baby." She smiled again. "Perhaps you should suggest it to her."

"I don't know if that would work or not." Shelley hadn't struck him as the pouncing type. He couldn't see her ever ripping his shirt off, but he could certainly see Miranda doing it—and then going for his pants. *The stuff of dreams...*

Miranda went right on bridling her horse, unaware of her starring role in his latest fantasy. "Maybe she's just biding her time and will grab you when you least expect it."

The fantasy continued as he imagined Miranda grabbing his ass when his back was turned. He'd be bending down to pick up a horse's hoof when her hand would slide down between his legs... "Lulling me into a false sense of security?"

"Something like that." Miranda pulled a pair of spurs out of her tote bag, then put her foot up on the old park bench that sat against the wall. His fantasy already had him hard as a rock, but it took a turn for the kinky when she buckled on her spurs. Did she like being fucked from behind? He could almost feel his cock sliding into her warm, wet pussy, his hands gripping her hips, helping him bounce against that ass...

The subject needed changing. *Now.* "She, um, likes fancy restaurants. Have you ever eaten in one of those places?"

"You mean the ones that charge you a fortune and you're still hungry when you leave?"

"Yeah. *That* kind." He raked a hand through his hair, trying desperately to regain control. "I liked some of it, but it was different from anything I'd ever eaten before. Although it *was*...colorful."

"I'll bet it was." She gathered up the reins. "Be sure to keep me posted. Have to ride, now." Heaving a sigh, she added, "I haven't practiced much this week because of all the rain, so Nigel will probably scream. Why is the weather only nice on the days I have to work?"

All Travis could do was shrug. The mysteries of the weather weren't anywhere near as interesting as wondering what it would be like to make *her* scream.

"See ya later." Waving her whip in farewell, she headed off toward the arena.

Travis had always made it a policy to avoid dating his female customers, and though one or two had flirted with him, he had never, but *never,* chased after a married woman. But as he watched Miranda walking away, the only thought in his head was that at least she wasn't a client.

ଛୠ

Nigel was already grumbling when Miranda reached the arena. "I certainly hope you're better prepared than the last one. It was hideous to watch. Simply *hideous.*"

As she mounted Kira, Miranda decided that her only hope for coming through the lesson unscathed was to distract him. "So, Nigel, have you made out your Christmas list yet?"

If anything, this made him grumble even more. "No point in it. I only get practical things for Christmas. Never anything frivolous or fun."

"Frivolous? Like what?"

"Oh, I don't know…a Jacuzzi, perhaps? Now, *that* would be a bloody great gift."

"Considering how often you get banged up, a Jacuzzi would be a *practical* gift for someone like you. I could probably use one myself." Miranda had lost count of the number of falls she'd had, and she'd been to the ER so many times she qualified as a frequent flier. "Who knows? It might even be a valid tax deduction since you could argue that it was an essential part of your business."

His expression brightened. "Really? You think so?"

"Well, no," she admitted. "Probably not. You'd have a tough time convincing the IRS."

His shoulders sank. "Oh, rot. Nice thought, though." Heaving a sigh, he waved her on. "Okay, then. Get out there and ride that big mare, Miranda. I'm ready to be impressed."

So much for trying to distract him. Miranda shook her head sadly. If she was ever going to impress Nigel, this probably wouldn't be the day.

The lesson went downhill from there. Kira simply wasn't in the mood to work and ended it by tossing Miranda on her ass. She wasn't hurt, but by the time she got back to the barn, Travis was already gone.

Then her phone rang. It was Christina.

"Where are you?" Miranda could hear the panic in her friend's voice.

"I'm just leaving Nigel's place. What's up?"

"I can't talk about it on the phone. Can you meet me for lunch?"

"Not unless you know a restaurant that serves horses."

Christina paused for a moment. "Oh, that's right. I forgot. Somewhere close to your house, then?"

Miranda chuckled. "Have you also forgotten where I live? There isn't *anything* close to my house."

"When can you meet me? It's urgent."

Miranda mentally calculated the time it would take her to drive home, drop off Kira, unhitch the trailer, shower, change clothes, and drive to Indianapolis. "Tomorrow?"

Christina's gasp of dismay warned her that tomorrow might be too late. "What about dinner?"

"Dinner I can do," Miranda replied. "Tell me where."

"How about—no. Can't go there."

"Can't go where?"

"Anyplace I've ever been with Mark."

Which probably ruled out every restaurant in town. "Somewhere in Greenwood, then. What about that Chinese place near the mall?"

"Never been there."

"Perfect. See you at about six?"

"Sure."

Miranda was halfway home when her phone rang again. This time, it was Mark. After hearing his side of the story, she had an idea that dinner with Christina was going to be dramatic, to say the least.

80C3

Despite red eyes and tear-stained cheeks, Christina still looked like a romance novel heroine. "Seven years." Her voice broke with sobs, and she paused for a sip of water before continuing. "We've been together for seven whole years. I loved him from the first moment I saw him. We got along great—the incredible sex was just the icing on the cake. Why would he do this to me?"

Having already talked to Mark, Miranda could have enlightened her, but decided that this might not be the best time. *His* slant on their relationship was that he'd felt more ignored than loved, didn't think they'd gotten along all that well, and had discovered that the sex could be just as good, if not better, with someone else.

"I don't know, Christina. Your law practice takes up so much of your time. Maybe he was lonely." Lonely enough to leave her for another woman. Not younger, not prettier, not sexier, not richer, just one with more time for him.

She nodded, sweeping a lock of dark, silky hair behind her ear. "I know I've been spending more time with my case files than I do with him, but I thought he understood."

"I'm sure he did, but that doesn't necessarily mean he liked it."

Mark DeVries had been a high school buddy of Miranda's late husband and had helped her out a lot after Kris died. Their friends all assumed that the two of them would get together someday—her sister, Tracy, had even laid bets on it—but she'd never felt any romantic interest in him whatsoever and had been relieved when he started seeing Christina.

"You'll find someone else, just like he did. I'm sure of it."

"But, who?" Fresh tears spilled from her doe-like eyes. "I don't want anyone but Mark. I'd take him back in a heartbeat, and I don't care what he's done—I still love him."

Miranda knew the feeling. She'd kept right on loving Kris after he died, even though there was absolutely no hope of ever getting him back. Placing a hand over Christina's trembling fingers, she gave them a reassuring squeeze. "He's moved on, Christina. I know it's hard for you right now, but you're sweet, successful, and beautiful. What more could a man want in a woman?"

"One who isn't working her ass off constantly and comes home once in a while?" Christina sighed. "Mark kept telling me he wanted to relax and enjoy life more—do some traveling, perhaps. But I wasn't listening."

Miranda nodded. "You'll know better next time—and it wouldn't hurt you to relax a little. One of these days you'll be as old as I am and realize you've never had any fun."

Christina stared at her, aghast. "You aren't *that* old."

"But I'm not getting any younger, which is why I'm doing stuff I've always wanted to do, like living on a farm and raising horses, planting a garden—all those things I never had time to do before."

"And a man? Do you finally have time for one of those?"

Miranda rolled her eyes. "Maybe, but I'm not a gorgeous chick with a perfect figure and a law degree. You're bound to have better luck than I will."

So far, Miranda hadn't been tempted, and her own sister's luck was even worse. Tracy had threatened to compile a "Not Safe to Date" list of local men to share with other single women, and Miranda's friends from the hospital had offered to contribute a few names. With the exception of Travis, Miranda hadn't found a single keeper, and she was beginning to believe she actually *did* stand a better chance of being killed by a terrorist than finding a husband— or even a steady boyfriend.

All through dinner, Miranda glanced up at each new arrival, hoping that the next man to walk through that door would be Christina's Mr. Right. She could see it now. Their eyes would meet, and the man would be instantly smitten and beg to be seated at their table. Miranda would take the earliest opportunity to depart, leaving him to astonish Christina with his wit while regaling her with tales of his rise to fame and fortune.

Chance meetings were usually best. In Miranda's opinion, playing matchmaker was a great way to lose two friends at once. Travis's client must not have seen it that way—nor had any of Miranda's buddies. Although she'd flat-out refused to be fixed up with anyone, she wasn't a man-hater. She simply hadn't met anyone she could love as much as she'd loved Kris, and thus far, she hadn't seen any point in settling for less.

On top of that, she was too set in her ways to cater to the whims of someone new. With her husband away most of the time, Miranda had become accustomed to her independence, handling the challenges of a special needs child and her nursing career with minimal assistance. She endured the separation by focusing on the *idea* that Kris would be coming home soon—a technique that also helped her to cope after his death. She simply told herself that he'd be home next month, and when that month arrived, she would imagine that his leave had been delayed, and then she would wait another month and so on.

She'd quit pretending after the first year or two, but she'd never stopped wearing her wedding ring, nor had she moved it to her right hand. Her matchmaking friends finally understood her reasons for not remarrying—or simply gave up.

Despite her empty nest, her life was full. She worked three twelve-hour night shifts in the ICU of a small hospital, and that salary, along with the money she'd received after Kris's death, had enabled her to buy a small farm and a few horses. Now that Levi had his own apartment, she had more time to devote to her animals.

No. She didn't need a man. All she needed was a bit of eye candy now and then, and Travis York provided that. And if he ever stopped coming to Nigel's barn on Tuesdays, why, she would simply look elsewhere—or reschedule her lesson.

Even so, she drove home wondering if a casual friendship with Travis was truly enough. Her house was warm and cozy, but the only welcome she received was from her dogs and cats. Levi had never been one to display affection—no hugs or kisses unless Miranda specifically asked for them—so that wasn't what she missed. The warm presence of another human being was what she needed, even craved, and that craving had only increased as she'd gotten older.

Christina had lived with Mark, and now that he was gone, her house must've seemed very empty. Miranda hadn't felt that echoing sort of emptiness since Kris left for the last time, but she felt it now. Perhaps she was more attuned to it in the wake of her dinner with Christina or even her chat with Travis. They had both lamented being alone, leaving Miranda to question her own decision to remain single. Had she been wrong to shun male companionship for so many years? Could she have found a man she could trust with her heart *and* her son?

She still believed her reasons had been valid in the beginning, but something had changed. Kris wasn't ever coming home, and all the cats, dogs, and horses weren't enough to fill the void. She wanted Travis, and not simply because he was nice to look at. Unlike any of the other men she'd met, she could see him fitting into her life—not dominating it or tearing it down to rebuild it according to his own needs—but enhancing it, adding richness and fulfillment.

If he'd been a few years older or had at least hinted he might want something beyond their current casual friendship, she might have tried to convey her interest. But he hadn't, and as matters now stood, she wasn't willing to take the risk. He'd awakened desires she'd thought were long gone. Giving up what little she had of him was unthinkable.

Chapter 3

Travis's truck was sitting outside Nigel's barn when Miranda arrived for her lesson the next week. "Ah, yes. Eye Candy Tuesday," she muttered as she backed her trailer into a parking space. Parking at Nigel's was always an adventure. The stable sat on a hill with a steep paved lot in front that always held an assortment of cars and trailers, which made parking an additional trailer difficult even on a good day. Add a few more vehicles, and it became a nightmare.

After three unsuccessful attempts, she finally got her rig parked reasonably straight, unloaded Kira, and led her into the barn. Travis was already hard at work, shoeing a big bay gelding. She didn't even have to see his face to know it was him. She'd seen him bent over so many times, she recognized the seat of his pants.

"Hey, there, Travis," she said cheerfully. "How's it going?"

The bay turned his head to look at Kira, who glanced at him briefly, then laid her ears back, clearly dismissing him as unworthy.

"I'm okay." He didn't *sound* okay—he was much too subdued for that. Something was wrong.

Nigel's working student, a slender blonde college student named Karen, walked by. "Whatever you do, don't ask him about his love life."

"Sad story?"

"*Sob* story," she replied with a giggle.

Travis dropped the hoof he was working on and stood up. He had his hoof nippers in one hand, a rasp in the other, and his shoulders sagged beneath their weight. His eyes were dull and for once, he wasn't smiling.

Miranda frowned. He looked terrible—more sick than lovesick. "Are you *sure* you're okay? You don't look so good."

Comparatively speaking, of course. Even on his worst days he outshone most guys.

"You see?" He waved his rasp for emphasis. "*You* believe I'm sick. *Nigel* believes I'm sick. Hell, Shelley's a doctor, for Christ's sake, and she didn't believe a word I said. I canceled a date with her last night and she called me all day long. *Six times.* All I wanted to do was sleep and she kept calling me to see if I was well enough to take her out."

"Are you sure she wasn't concerned about you?" Miranda asked, trying to put it in the best possible light. "Some people have odd ways of showing it."

He blew out a pent-up breath. "She might have been concerned the first time she called, but not the other times. She was sure I was with someone else and was checking up on me."

That didn't sound very promising. "I hate to admit this, but given her history, I can sort of understand that. She's been shit on for years and is probably expecting you to do the same. You know what they say, 'Once burned, twice shy.'"

"Yes, but I'm not her husband." He paused, wiping his eyes on his coat sleeve. "I'm not like that. When I'm dating a woman, I don't go out with anyone else."

"You know that, and I know that, but does she?" Miranda could see Shelley's side of it quite easily, whether she liked the idea of anyone treating Travis as if he were a liar or not. "She doesn't know you well enough to realize you're trustworthy, and she's been lied to for years. It's got to be very hard for her."

"I wish I wasn't her first boyfriend since the divorce," he grumbled. "I do like her, but I can't stand being constantly questioned. I'm willing to let her live her life and trust her—why can't she do the same for me? She's not the only one who's been lied to. Women treat me like shit all the time, but I keep trying. I'm willing to trust people until they prove me wrong."

Lied to and treated like shit? Miranda found that hard to believe. If he'd been hers, she would've treated him much better than that. "It's different with guys. You're made of sterner stuff."

He barked out a mirthless laugh. "If I were that tough, I'd have gone out with her whether I was sick or not—and it would've served her right if she caught the flu from me." He turned and started to pick up another hoof, but spun back toward her with a wave of the nippers. "And another thing. What's she going to do when she realizes most of my clients are women? I won't even be able to work without her questioning my every move."

Miranda shrugged. "I guess she'd dump you?" If Shelley hadn't shot her philandering husband, she probably wouldn't go after Travis with a forty-five, either, so getting dumped was the worst outcome Miranda could think of—not to mention the dumbest. Dump a guy like Travis? *Never.*

"You know, it would almost be a blessing." Shaking his head, he heaved a weary sigh. "I'm putting *way* too much energy into this."

"Need a lower maintenance woman?" Miranda knew precisely who she'd suggest, too.

"Not really. Everyone has needs. I just wish she would trust me. I don't think I can ever love her if it keeps on like this. I've never been so miserable with a woman in my life."

"Aw, poor Travis. Do you need a hug?" Miranda had been dying for an excuse to get her arms around him for ages. Now he was sick, sweaty, and upset because another woman didn't trust him. *Timing is everything.*

"Yes, I *do.*"

His emphatic reply should have come as a warning, but when Miranda took a step toward him, he flung his arms around her, hoof nippers, rasp, and all. Even though it *was* rather painful, she considered it worthwhile—maybe even worth catching the flu. She hugged him and patted him on the back, doing her best to ignore the tingling sensations zipping through every erogenous zone she possessed.

"I know Miss Right is out there somewhere," he whispered. "I just have to keep looking."

He was so close, she could have kissed him right on that cute little hickey birthmark—or given him another one—and his warm breath on her neck sent a thrill racing down her spine. She breathed in his masculine scent and squeezed her eyes shut.

Don't do it, Miranda.

It took a will of iron, but she let him go and backed away. "Sounds like you've already given up on this one."

He shrugged. "I think I may have."

"Well, good luck—and for goodness sake take care of yourself. I'm pretty sure you've got a fever." Miranda was dying to take him home, give him a nice warm sponge bath, tuck him into her bed, and feed him hot tea and chicken soup until he recovered. And after that…well, that was something she didn't dare think about.

Shivering, he crossed his arms over his chest. "Yeah. I feel sort of hot and cold at the same time."

"Take some ibuprofen when you get home," she advised, slipping into nurse mode. "That is, if you haven't already."

"I'll do that." Shoulders still sagging, he went back to work.

Steeling herself against urges she knew she'd regret if they were ever allowed free rein, Miranda focused her attention on Kira, vigorously brushing the mare's thick winter coat and trying desperately to avoid staring at Travis.

Travis picked up the bay's hoof and checked the fit of the shoe. It was a tad narrow, so he set it on his anvil and hammered it a few times. Normally a terrific way of venting his frustrations, this time, it didn't help at all. He still wasn't sure what had just happened. He'd actually held Miranda in his arms—too bad he was sick as a dog and they'd both been wearing heavy coats.

No, he decided, the coats were a good thing; otherwise she would've had bruises on her back. He could've at least put down his tools and hugged her properly.

Of course, with his hands free, he might've done something he'd regret. Miranda was a kind, caring woman. She didn't deserve to be groped by a guy with the flu who didn't have sense enough to stay home in bed.

A fleeting image of Miranda lying naked in that bed assailed him with the force of a horse's kick. He swallowed painfully, but his cock hurt even more. How could a man possibly feel so bad and so horny at the same time?

He finished nailing on the shoe and stood up, stretching his back. Miranda had already saddled her mare and had her spurs on.

Damn. I missed it.

Selecting another shoe from his toolbox, he put it on the anvil and gave it a few whacks with the hammer, keeping an eye on Miranda as she donned her gloves and helmet. He was trying to decide why watching a woman put things *on*, rather than taking them off was so overwhelmingly erotic when she looked up at him.

Smiling, she tucked a lock of hair under her helmet. "Just think, Travis. Maybe tomorrow you'll get a call from a nice single woman whose horse needs shoes, and you'll fall in love and live happily ever after."

He shook his head. "I doubt it. Besides, I don't date my clients." On the other hand, if Miranda had been a client—and single—he might've made an exception to that rule. In fact, he was sure of it. He wondered if she liked younger men.

"Then I guess you're screwed."

Travis somehow managed a chuckle when all he really wanted to do was cry. "I guess I am."

Ⅎ)ℴ℥

Nigel was screeching at a young girl on a bay gelding when Miranda opened the gate to the arena. If his current mood was any indication, her own lesson wasn't going to be pretty.

"What is *wrong* with you?" he shouted. "Why do you keep *doing* that?"

Miranda led Kira over to the mounting block and let down the stirrups, trying to see what had Nigel so incensed.

"Stop that!" he yelled. "Can't you hear me?"

Miranda climbed aboard Kira as the girl rode past. She still had no idea what was driving Nigel so crazy, but the poor girl looked like she was about to lose it.

Nigel let out a long, tortured scream and pulled his knit cap down over his eyes. "Stop!" he yelled. "That's enough. Get off the horse."

The girl dropped her reins, sobbing.

"You aren't in any shape to ride," Nigel said sharply. "When you feel like this, you should cancel your lesson and stay home."

It was good advice, of course, but Miranda understood why the girl was there. *She* didn't cancel a lesson unless she was dying. She'd ridden with raging headaches, sinus infections, smashed fingers, and a knee that had to be taped up. No matter how bad she felt, the lesson was important. Canceling was simply not an option.

Miranda began her warm-up, catching snatches of the conversation as she rode by. Apparently, the kid's grandmother was dying, and Miranda would've bet money that by this time Nigel was feeling pretty damn small. Head hanging low, the girl left the arena in tears.

Nigel sat huddled in the corner with his jacket pulled tightly around him and his hood up over his cap. He'd never truly acclimated to Indiana's weather, and Miranda hated to think how he would fare in Minnesota. In his opinion, Pemberton, Indiana was too cold in winter and too hot and humid in summer. There was no pleasing the man, and today was no exception.

Karen came out to exercise another of Nigel's horses. After giving her a few brief instructions, he yelled, "Okay, Miranda! I'm ready to be impressed!"

After that last lesson, it shouldn't be too hard. Shortening her reins, she leaned back, driving Kira forward into the bit with her legs. The big mare dropped her head slightly and surged forward.

"Good," he called. "But rounder, deeper, more leg."

She squeezed harder with each stride, but it wasn't enough.

"Both legs, Miranda! Get her rounder."

Tightening her legs to the point of pain, she worked the bit back and forth in Kira's mouth. Nothing happened.

"More leg!" he yelled. "More leg!"

There was a standing joke around the barn that no one would ever want to have sex with Nigel because he would be much too critical. Miranda could imagine him yelling, "More leg!" to his wife all the time. Small wonder she always seemed to be in a bad mood.

Turning her toes out, she used a tiny bit of spur.

"Yes, Miranda!" he exclaimed. "Good. Now keep her that way."

There's always a catch...

"Aaaahhhh... What happened? You had her and lost it. You've got to keep your aids coming. You go into neutral when you get her round and then you lose it."

If her concentration hadn't already been broken, Miranda would've lost it then. Nigel's screams nearly always made her crack up, and she found it impossible to concentrate on her riding while laughing her head off. At least he was in a better mood now. Undaunted, she tried it again.

"Yes, Miranda!" he yelled ecstatically. "Yes, yes, yes!" As she and Kira cruised by in a perfect frame, Nigel shook his fists in the air and stomped his feet. "Don't stop, Miranda! Keep on like that." He heaved a satisfied sigh. "Oh, *yeah*..."

Grinning broadly, she crossed the diagonal, still going strong, and thinking that sex with Nigel might not be so bad after all. If you ever *did* get it right, he would certainly let you know.

Chapter 4

After her lesson, Miranda let Kira walk for about fifteen minutes before heading back to the barn. Travis was still there, nailing shoes on a tall chestnut mare while Nigel furiously raked the barn aisle. Neither of them said a word while she unsaddled Kira and remained silent as she led the sweaty mare out to the wash stall for a quick sponge bath.

The same stony silence prevailed upon her return, and though she suspected that Nigel was itching to discuss that morning's events, so far, he wasn't talking. Having mulled over the scene with his young student, Miranda had some definite ideas about what he might have done differently, but she wasn't about to offer them unless he asked. Clipping the cross ties to Kira's halter, she covered the mare with a light fleece blanket, packed up her gear, and carried it all out to the truck.

Nigel rounded on her the moment she returned. "Could I have handled that better?"

"Yes, you could," she replied, pleased that he'd finally asked. "All you had to do was ask her why she was behaving so strangely—without screaming."

"She should have said something," he grumbled. "If I'd known she was worried about her grandmother, I wouldn't have yelled at her."

"She could have, but women usually don't volunteer that kind of information. Men will tell you up front when they feel like shit. You have to *ask* a woman, and you have to ask her nicely."

He shook his head. "I don't know if I can do that."

"It's not that hard, Nigel. A simple *Are you okay?* will usually do it. Not, *What the hell's the matter with you?*"

"I guess so." He blew out an exasperated breath. "It's these silly young girls, Miranda. I don't deal well with them."

"No shit," she said dryly. "You see yourself as their instructor, but they see you as their ticket to equestrian stardom. You're their hero, Nigel, and when your hero screams at you…well, let's just say it's not a good thing, especially for a young girl."

She glanced at Travis, who had stopped hammering and appeared to be listening.

"Now, me, I mostly laugh when you yell. You've never made me cry and I doubt you ever will. I'm too old to compete in the Olympics, but the young ones still have the dream, and it means more to them. Some days they can take the yelling and screaming because they know you can teach them what they need to know, and some days they can't. It's up to you to know the difference."

He shook his head. "I can't do that."

"Then you'll have to stick to teaching older women and leave the young ones to someone else."

"There's nothing wrong with older women," Travis chimed in. "They give really good hugs."

Miranda chuckled. "Yeah, right, Travis. Those young ones would probably cry when you hit them with your nippers."

His jaw dropped. "I didn't hit you, did I?"

"No," she admitted. "But you squeezed me pretty hard. I probably have nipper marks on my back."

"Let me see." He put down his hammer and walked toward her, a funny little half-smile lifting the corner of his mouth. "Turn around."

"Oh, Travis, I was kidding and you know it." Laughing, she held up both hands to fend him off. "I'm sure you didn't leave a mark."

Nigel snickered. "Maybe he wants to kiss it and make it better."

The mere thought of Travis kissing her on the back—or anywhere else—sent a quiver of anticipation running down her spine. Too bad he hadn't been the one to suggest it.

Giving herself a mental shake, she nodded at Nigel. "That's another thing men do. They always want to fix things. Sometimes a woman simply needs to talk about what's bothering her and all the man has to do is listen. Most of the time, she already knows what she needs to do. She's just reluctant to go through with it. Pointing out the obvious solution makes her seem stupid."

"Let me get this straight," Nigel said. "I have to ask what's wrong—nicely, of course—listen to the problem, and then *not* try to fix it? That doesn't make sense."

"I never said it made sense," she said patiently. "But if you're dealing with women, it's something you need to remember."

He shrugged and went back to raking. "If you say so."

Miranda rolled her eyes and went over to get Kira. She'd snapped a lead rope to the mare's halter and was unhooking the cross-tie when she felt a hand pressed between her shoulder blades.

"No nipper marks," Travis said, giving her a gentle massage. He seemed perkier than he'd been earlier, his funny little smile now a full-blown grin. "I figured you secretly wanted to know that."

"Thanks, Travis." Trying to ignore the flood of goose bumps racing over her skin, she resisted the urge to lean back against his hand. "I'm sure I would've lost sleep over it."

Laughing, he waved goodbye. "See you next week."

Although such a simple touch rarely affected her, she was still tingling as she loaded up her mare and went home. She probably *would* lose a little sleep that night, and it certainly wouldn't be from a sore back. Travis had the power to keep her awake all by himself.

೫೦೧೩

Travis knew he'd set a dangerous precedent. One hug—hell, one *touch*—would lead to another and another and before he knew it, he'd be kissing her. Then she'd probably slap the shit out of him, and she'd be perfectly justified in doing so.

He finished up at Nigel's and headed on to the next horse on his list, stopping for lunch along the way. He gave the cashier at the drive-thru a big smile, wondering if she would condemn him for lusting after a married woman. His family certainly would. He'd never hear the end of it, and his father would probably disown him.

His cousin might understand, though. There was something

different about Alan John. A cousin on his mother's side, the same taboos hadn't been drummed into him from birth. To hear him tell it, Alan had yet to find a woman who could stand as much sex as he craved, and he'd supposedly worn out more women than most men ever dated. Somewhere along the line, he'd probably fucked a married woman. *Or two, or three...* He might even have lined them up and done one after the other.

Travis didn't have that problem. With fairly normal sexual appetites and an upbringing that kept him from being indiscriminate, having an adulterous affair was completely out of character for him. Why, then, did he want Miranda so badly?

Miranda's husband was the farthest thing from his mind when she'd made him an offer he couldn't refuse. Then her comment about nipper marks had given him another excuse to get his hands on her. Too bad her reaction wasn't all he'd hoped for. Instead of moaning with pleasure, she'd simply loaded up her horse and gone home.

While Travis had no firm commitment to Shelley, Miranda had vowed to love, honor, and cherish another man—an incredibly lucky man, particularly in light of the fact that Travis respected those vows. Otherwise, he'd have been doing his best to talk her into having an affair with him.

No. An affair would never be enough. He wanted more than that. He wanted a home and a family. A woman he could love openly, without having to sneak around behind her husband's back. Unfortunately, having those things also meant he couldn't have Miranda.

Though he hated to admit it, maybe he *did* need to talk to Alan.

ॐ

Alan's advice was simple. "Don't do it. You'll regret it every day for the rest of your life."

After his last job of the day, Travis stopped by the health food store his cousin managed, all set to hear that he should flout convention and go after Miranda, no holds barred. He certainly hadn't expected Alan, of all people, to sit him down at one of the tables in the deli and tell him to forget about her.

"So you've done it, then?" Travis asked. "Had an affair with a married woman?"

Alan nodded, raking a hand through his disheveled locks. "More than once, and I've felt guilty ever since."

"Didn't stop you from doing it the second time, though, did it?"

"Actually, that second time was the cure." Alan didn't look cured. In fact, he looked about as miserable as Travis felt—hollow-eyed, unshaven, and thinner than Travis remembered. "I'm trying to give it up."

"Give what up?"

"Sex." Alan's hand shook slightly as he reached for his cup. "I'm trying to prove to myself that I'm not addicted."

"How long has it been?"

"Six weeks," he replied. "I'm doing okay, I think." He paused, frowning. "Of course, not having a girlfriend at the moment helps quite a bit."

Finding women had never been Alan's problem. With tousled curls and a face like a young Russell Crowe, he drew them like flies, and those that weren't attracted by his looks often took pity on his desperate need for sex. Unfortunately, he also tended to drive them crazy after a few months. Travis was pretty sure he'd never sent anyone to the loony bin, but he wasn't looking for a pity fuck, either. Not from Miranda or anyone else.

"It's not so much the sex as it is the physical contact," Alan went on. "I need it so badly." He let out a weary sigh. "Too bad no one else does."

The standard "Don't worry. You'll find the perfect woman someday" admonition probably wouldn't help Alan feel any better at all. Travis doubted there was a woman alive who could put up with him for more than six months, let alone a lifetime. "Maybe if you tried pacing yourself a little…"

Alan cut him off with a wave of his hand. "I *have* tried, and it doesn't work." He took a sip of his tea. "But you didn't come here to talk about my problems. So you've fallen for a married woman, have you?" He shook his head, chuckling. "Your old man will have a shit fit."

"Tell me about it," Travis muttered.

"Still, you *are* thirty-six years old," Alan reminded him. "Old enough to make your own decisions."

"Old enough to know better. And I do. I was hoping you could give me some insight."

"I did. Don't do it. You'll be sorry." He paused, frowning. "You know, most support groups recommend having someone to call when you're about to fall off the wagon. What you need is a buddy to keep you from doing something stupid."

"Want to be my buddy?"

Alan snorted a laugh. "I'm not sure I'd be the best choice. Maybe you should ask Stuart."

"Yeah, right. He's been walking around in a daze ever since his divorce." Travis's older brother had been happily married until his wife's bariatric surgery. Unfortunately, as her weight went down, her need for boyfriends had skyrocketed. "I doubt if I could spill my guts to him and not have the story leak out to the rest of the family. The whole adultery thing is a pretty sore spot with him—and you know my father's opinion on the subject. Sure you can't do it?"

Alan shrugged, giving Travis a weak smile. "I can see your point about Stuart, but with my history, I might end up doing the deed myself."

Although Travis knew Alan was joking, his comment kindled a flame of—what? Jealousy? Possessiveness? He wasn't sure, but it irked him. Nonetheless, he went along with the jest. "Over my dead body. Besides, I thought you were trying to give it up."

"I am, but temptation often strikes when we're at our weakest—like it did with you." He shook his head. "You and a married woman. Never thought I'd see the day."

"Yeah, well, you haven't seen it yet—and maybe you never will. I'm trying to be strong, but you know how it is."

"Oh, God, yes." Shuddering, Alan cupped his hands around his mug of tea as though craving its warmth. "This stuff is hot, sweet, and soothing—it's a chamomile blend—but I'd much rather be eating pussy."

Travis wanted to laugh, but for once, he was too much in sympathy with Alan to muster a chuckle. "Have you tried chocolate? I hear it's supposed to have the same effect as an orgasm."

"That might work if I didn't already know sex was a helluva lot better than chocolate."

Travis got to his feet and gripped his cousin's shoulder. "Hang in there, Alan. We'll get through this somehow. We're supposed to be the stronger sex, remember?"

Alan shook his head, his gray eyes as bleak as a winter sky. "That's a fallacy and you know it. They're the strong ones. They've got what we want and half the time they laugh at us. Compared to them, we're a bunch of pathetic fools."

Travis didn't argue. He'd never felt quite so weak and helpless in his life, and he didn't like it a bit. Still, there *was* an alternative. He could keep on dating Shelley and try to convince himself she was the one he wanted.

Yeah, right. And as soon as hell froze over, pigs would sprout wings and fly.

Chapter 5

Miranda had to cancel her riding lesson the following week to attend a mandatory class on ECG interpretation. In the interim, she decided that getting Travis married off to someone else would benefit them both. He would be happy and maybe, just maybe, she could get him out of her head.

In addition to Christina and Tracy, Miranda knew several single nurses that were about his age. Unfortunately, introducing them was something of a puzzle. Blind dates were nearly always doomed to failure—case in point, Shelley and Travis.

When she finally did see Travis again, it seemed that the inevitable breakup had already occurred. Shelley had given him an ultimatum of some kind—he didn't say what—and he had balked.

"It's not that I don't like her," he said. "I just don't think it's right for her to make me rearrange my life to suit hers. I've never met a woman yet who didn't think I needed improving. I'm not saying I'm perfect, but I am who I am."

Miranda went on brushing Kira while he talked, finally coming to the conclusion that Christina would be perfect for him. After all, if she didn't have enough time for Mark, she wouldn't have time to reform Travis. Miranda couldn't imagine anything that *she* would change about him, unless it was his age, and not even the most dedicated reformer could do anything about that.

He and Christina would make a striking couple and have lots of beautiful children—provided Christina ever found the time to give birth. Miranda's only hope was that they would move hundreds of miles away so she didn't have to watch.

The more Travis talked, the longer the list of Shelley's faults grew. "We don't even like to eat the same things. She likes fancy restaurant stuff and all I want is good home cooking."

"Yes, but home cooking takes time—which she obviously doesn't have. And not liking the same food doesn't necessarily mean you can't like each other. Levi and I hardly ever eat the same things. He likes it salty and I like it spicy. If he sees so much as a speck of pepper on his food, he won't eat it."

"I'm not *that* picky," Travis said. "I'll eat the fancy stuff, but I don't want it all the time."

Miranda laughed. "Levi eats the same things over and over. Finding a restaurant we both like is something of a challenge—he's the only person I know who actually *enjoyed* school lunches—but it can be done."

"What about Thanksgiving? Does he at least like turkey?"

"Yes, but he won't eat leftovers—not even turkey soup."

"My mom's turkey soup is the best part of the whole holiday—and before you ask, the answer is no, I'm not taking Shelley with me to meet the family. They'd probably be tickled to death to know I'm dating a doctor, but I'd rather not get their hopes up. I have a feeling it's over anyway."

"Really? Better tell me the rest of it."

"We're too different, and it's more than not liking the same foods—though it'd be nice if she'd come down to my level and go out for pizza and beer once in a while."

"Come down to your level?" she echoed. "Sounds like more than a slight difference in taste."

He nodded grimly. "She invited me to go out with some of her doctor friends, and I told her I'd rather not. I mean, what could I possibly have to talk about with people like that? Anyway, she said if I wasn't comfortable with her friends, we might as well forget it."

If he didn't want to hang out with doctors, he probably wouldn't feel comfortable with lawyers or nurses. *So much for my plans to marry him off.* "Doctors are people too, Travis. Some of them even have horses."

"I know," he said with a sigh. "That wasn't the only problem. It just wasn't working."

He finished shoeing the gray mare, and Karen brought out another horse—a chestnut mare that refused to stand in cross-ties and had to be held. Travis didn't say much after that, leaving Miranda to assume he didn't need to vent anymore. She chatted with Karen while she bridled Kira, and then headed out to the arena for her lesson.

Nigel was in a relatively chipper mood—that is, until he asked her to try that flying lead change thing again.

Miranda had gotten the canter figure-eight down to only one trot stride in the middle before picking up the opposite lead, and Nigel was sure she could get the flying change without much trouble, but no dice. She left the arena feeling discouraged, hoping that Travis could cheer her up—that is, if he hadn't left yet.

Karen was still holding the mare's lead rope, looking bored out of her mind. "How was your lesson?"

"Crappy," Miranda replied. "No matter how hard I try, Kira and I can't do a flying lead change. I feel like I'm beating my head against a brick wall."

"Beats standing here doing nothing," she said. "I'd rather be riding— or even cleaning stalls. Anything but *this*."

Evidently, she hadn't been looking in the right direction. Travis was interesting from any angle and the position he was in at that moment made Miranda long to throw caution to the wind and pat his hot little ass. Then an image of him doing farrier work while wearing only his boots and chaps flashed through her mind, and she nearly swallowed her tongue.

Travis put down the last hoof and gave the mare a pat. "She's done."

"Thank God," Karen muttered as she led the horse away.

Miranda giggled. "Boring the life out of the help?"

"I guess so." He tossed the hoof rasp into his toolbox. "She's not the easiest woman to talk to—unlike you. I could talk to you all day and you wouldn't say you were bored."

He was right about that. "Maybe she was bored because you *weren't* talking to her. Did you ever think of that?" Karen obviously hadn't imagined him without his pants. Miranda certainly could— hot ass, dangling balls, rock hard dick... She wiped her lips on her glove, convinced she was drooling.

"Aw, she doesn't want to hear about my rotten love life." He smiled sheepishly. "Thank you for listening, by the way."

"You're welcome. Anytime." *Yes, Travis, I'll be right here listening to you bitch and moan about women for the next ten or twenty years.* Maybe by then a woman fifteen years his senior wouldn't seem so bad. It would be a long wait—but worth it.

She had just pulled off Kira's saddle when Travis materialized right behind her, placing a hand on her shoulder.

"Here, let me help you with that." Not waiting for a reply, he took the saddle, set it on the rack, and zipped it into the carrying case.

"Thanks." She stared at him for a moment, puzzled by his unusual behavior, then gathered up Kira's blanket. As she spread it out over the mare's broad back, she glanced up to see Travis straightening it from the other side. *He's certainly being helpful today. Must think the old girl looks tired.*

A moment later, he was behind her again. "Don't suppose I could talk you out of another hug, could I?" He held up his hands. "No tools to hurt you with this time."

Despite his smile, pain lingered in his eyes. Refusing him was unthinkable. She'd barely lifted her arms before being enveloped in an embrace that robbed her of breath and reason. Her eyes stung with tears and her lips were already pressed against his cheek before she remembered he was only there to be comforted. Stolen kisses weren't part of the deal. She allowed herself a few brief seconds to savor the solid feel of him and let go.

"You'll be okay, Travis. It just takes a little time." She was lying, of course. It had taken her a *lot* of time to recover after Kris died.

He nodded, giving her a half-hearted smile. She suspected he'd liked Shelley more than he cared to admit, or perhaps he was simply tired of the game—always looking and never finding the kind of woman he needed.

Clearing her throat, Miranda patted him on the arm, then went back to packing up her gear.

Travis picked up her saddle. "I'll put this in the truck for you."

She was about to tell him not to bother when she finally realized why he was being so helpful. It was simply his way of thanking her for lending him a sympathetic ear. "Thanks. I'd appreciate that."

After tossing her tote bag into the truck, she returned for Kira. Travis stood next to the mare, speaking softly as he fed her a treat. Miranda hurriedly snapped a lead rope to the mare's halter and released the cross-ties, turning away before Travis could see the tears gathering in her eyes.

Barely trusting her voice enough to speak to him, she wished him a happy Thanksgiving and led Kira out of the barn, doing her best to ignore the growing ache in her heart. A chilly rain began to fall as they reached the trailer, and her numb fingers fumbled with the latch. "Don't suppose you'd consider telling me what he said, would you?"

A glance from her big, dark eyes was Kira's only reply as she stepped up into the trailer.

Miranda sighed and swung the tailgate shut. "I didn't think so."

Travis stood watching until Miranda's truck was out of sight, his cheek still tingling from her kiss. It might not have been the sort of kiss he craved, but it was better than nothing and far more than he deserved—especially after he'd done his best to follow Alan's advice and then fucked it up by asking for another hug. If Shelley hadn't given him such a hard time he might have been stronger, but between that and the disappointment he'd felt when Miranda hadn't shown up for her lesson the previous week, he was surprised he hadn't kissed her.

What would she have done if he had? His scalp tingled at the thought of her fingers threading through his hair, her hungry lips parting as he deepened the kiss.

"Stop it, Travis," he muttered. Grabbing his toolbox, he headed out to his truck. The rainy sky further dampened his mood. If the forecast was correct, the paddock at his next stop would be a sea of mud by the time he arrived. He'd already started the engine when a sudden impulse had him reaching for his phone.

Alan answered on the first ring. "I had a feeling I'd be hearing from you today. What happened?"

"Shit, I don't know. I'm about to lose what's left of my mind. You already know what happened with Shelley. If Miranda hadn't been so damned sympathetic, things might have gone differently, but stupid me, I asked her for a hug and she gave it to me. Even kissed me on the cheek."

"The slightest touch can be fatal," Alan warned. "Don't ever let it happen again."

"Tell me about it. I damn near kissed her back—and I wouldn't have stopped with a simple peck on the cheek." Grimacing, he shook his head trying to banish the thought of Miranda in his arms, urging him on with passionate, heart-stopping kisses. "Maybe I should come right out and tell her how I feel. Then she could tell me to go to hell and never speak to me again."

"I doubt it. She sounds too nice for that."

"You're probably right. Honestly, I don't know how much more of this I can take. It gets worse every time I see her."

Alan sighed. "There's a simple cure for that. Don't see her again."

Travis shuddered. "I practically had a stroke when she wasn't here last week. I've never wanted anyone so badly in my life."

"Cold turkey, man. It's the only way."

"I know. I can't help thinking if I stick around long enough, she might fall for me and leave her husband."

"And you'll feel guilty for breaking up her marriage for the rest of your life. I *know* you, Travis. Sooner or later, the taint would kill any chance of happiness."

Alan was right. Unfortunately, it didn't change a thing. "Yeah. Damned if I do and damned if I don't." He drew in a ragged breath. "Guess I'm better off keeping my mouth shut."

"Absolutely. Look, I gotta go now. Next time, call me *before* you see her. Maybe I can talk you out of doing anything stupid."

"I'll do that. Later." He switched off his phone and put the truck in gear, only then realizing he could have followed Miranda home if he'd left when she did. Of course, her husband probably would've killed him, but at least he'd be out of his misery.

8003

Rain was coming down in buckets by the time Miranda got home, and Kira's broad hooves left prints big enough to plant trees in as she trotted across the yard to the pasture gate. Although colder weather would undoubtedly cause other problems, Miranda could hardly wait for the ground to freeze.

The heavy downpour pounded the barn's metal roof with a deafening roar that masked the sound of their approach from the horses inside. "It's okay, guys," she told the startled animals. "It's just me and Kira. No need to get all bent out of shape."

Then it was her turn to get bent out of shape when she realized she was standing in the middle of a lake. Grumbling, she pulled off Kira's halter and blanket and sloshed her way to the tack room. Unlike the aisle, which had been packed down by the horses over time, the slightly higher floor of the tack room was still relatively dry. Miranda had raised the floor level in the stalls with rock dust and rubber mats. The aisle was another story.

Water tended to pool in the center where the ground was lowest and couldn't run out the front end and back down the hill without help. Digging a trench around the barn diverted some of the water, but Miranda's puny little ditch couldn't handle the deluge that ran down from the hill above the barn during a strong storm. Armed with a push-broom and a water pump, she trudged out into the lake to drain it before it turned into a muddy mess.

The horses were still too agitated to work around, so she opened up the stalls and let them in while she cleared out the water. Running an extension cord down to the trench she'd dug across the rear doorway, she plugged it into the outlet in the tack room, which was currently the only outlet in the main aisle that actually worked.

After flinging the drain hose out to the main ditch, she went to work with the broom, sweeping the water out of the front end of the barn. She'd tried digging a channel for it to run down the hill on its own, but the horses and the weather kept filling it back in. It was a never-ending battle—and Miranda was losing.

She had almost gotten all of the water out when the rain, which had slacked off while she was working, picked up again. She watched in despair as a vast sheet of water cascaded down the hill and came rushing through the door, sloshing her already soaked boots. She wanted to lay down and cry, but let out a frustrated scream instead. Kira nickered at her.

"Yeah, I know," she muttered. "When it rains, it pours, right?"

With a groan, she picked up her broom and started all over again. To make matters worse, she was scheduled to work at the hospital that night. "So much for my nap…"

Chapter 6

By 2 AM, Miranda felt as though she would keel over and die if she didn't get a little sleep. Lola and Mary Beth were working with her, which normally meant her shift would go smoothly—and it had— until they got a call from Adrian in the ER.

"We've got a patient with a blood alcohol level so high the doc's afraid he might have a seizure, so he's being admitted rather than going to jail." Adrian sounded apologetic, but Miranda knew she was probably tickled to death to be getting rid of the guy.

"Just what we need." Miranda's patient was on a ventilator and nicely sedated. The others were asleep. A loud drunk would wake up the whole unit.

"You shouldn't have any trouble with him," Adrian assured her. "He duked it out with the police at the bar where they picked him up, but he's been pretty quiet since he got here. He'll probably sleep it off."

"Okay. Let me give you to Mary Beth. She gets first admit tonight." Miranda handed the phone to Mary Beth with a grimace. "Sorry."

Mary Beth rolled her eyes as she took the receiver. She didn't say much as she wrote down the report, but looked like she wanted to cry by the time she hung up the phone. "This is *not* going to be fun."

Their new patient arrived on the unit quietly enough. Unfortunately, as soon as they slid him from the stretcher to the bed, he woke up. "Wha' ya' doin' tha' for?"

The alcohol fumes were so strong Miranda figured she'd get drunk simply from being in the same room with him. "Just moving you over to the bed."

"How come?"

"So you can get some sleep."

"How come?"

Miranda could already see where this was going, and after he'd said "How come?" for the umpteenth time, even Mary Beth, whose patience was legendary, seemed irritated. Lola, on the other hand, was giggling uncontrollably as she tried to take his blood pressure. Adrian had already fled the scene.

When the high-pressure alarm on her patient's ventilator went off, Miranda hurried from the room, grateful for the interruption. The same alarm that had been driving her crazy earlier was now music to her ears. Unfortunately, she could still hear the drunk saying "How come?" every ten seconds.

By the time Miranda had her man settled down again, Lola, who was normally level-headed and completely unflappable, had stopped giggling and was now tight-lipped and scowling. Sweet, kind, lovely Mary Beth had murder in her eyes. "I don't suppose we've got any sedation ordered for him, do we?"

Miranda flipped through the ER record and found the admitting orders. "Zero point five of Ativan every six hours—"

Lola let out a groan. "We might as well spit on him."

"—and he already had a dose less than an hour ago," Miranda continued.

Mary Beth shook her head sadly. "We are *so* screwed."

The drunk attempted to sit up, head lolling and arms flailing. "How come?"

Mary Beth pushed him back down without hesitation. "Please tell me we at least have an order for restraints."

Miranda grinned. "Yes, we do. Leathers if we need them."

"Thank God for small favors," Lola said. "Hurry up and get them before he falls out of bed. If he hurts himself, we'll have to keep him longer."

Miranda didn't hurry. She *ran.*

‮ℭ‬

Miranda came home the next morning to a flooded barn, and it took almost an hour to get all the water out. When she finally climbed into bed, although she still had ventilator alarms and "How come?" ringing in her ears, she had finally hit on a solution to the Travis problem. She would invite him to her Christmas party.

Every year Miranda threw a party for the hospital gang and several other friends—including Christina and Tracy. Travis wouldn't be the lone male, and he could meet her friends without any pressure—especially if she didn't tell him why she'd invited him. He would be free to pick and choose as he liked, although she hoped he wouldn't fall for Tracy. Miranda didn't think she could handle that, no matter how cute their names sounded together.

Christina had already called to make sure Mark wouldn't show up with his new woman. Although Mark had other plans for that evening, Miranda wished that having one of them as a guest didn't automatically exclude the other. Mark had been a good friend for years, and Miranda hadn't seen much of him since he'd found his new love. This year, however, Christina needed a party far more than Mark did, particularly if Miranda could talk Travis into coming.

℘ℚ

After working all night Thanksgiving Eve, Miranda came home, baked a pumpkin pie, put together a broccoli casserole to bake later on, stuffed the turkey, put it in the oven, and went to bed. The turkey was done when she got up, and Levi was already in the living room watching *The Muppet Christmas Carol*.

"Starting a little early, aren't you?" she asked. "We usually watch that after dinner."

"Yeah, I know, but I have to go home after we eat the turkey."

She stared at him, open-mouthed. "You mean you aren't spending the night?"

He shook his head. "I have to work tomorrow. I need to go home."

He'd had to say it twice before it sank in.

Home.

Home used to be her house, now it was his apartment. She

closed her eyes, biting her lip, trying her damndest to keep from crying. Now that he was older, he looked more like Kris than ever— same green eyes, same blond hair, same funny little grin. Although she rejoiced at his independence, at the same time, she wanted to keep him there with her forever.

"Okay, if you have to... I'm going up to the barn to feed the horses now. Everyone else should be here soon." She put the casserole in the oven, then changed into her barn clothes and headed out.

She trudged toward the barn while the dogs raced on ahead. She'd always known this would happen someday—the day when Levi left the nest for good—she just hadn't thought it would happen on Thanksgiving.

To make matters worse, it was raining again.

The rest of the family arrived. Her parents, Darlene and Stephen Richards, both in their mid-sixties, were enjoying their recent retirement. Tracy at least seemed happy, but then she usually did, even when she'd gotten herself mixed up with another jerk. The baby of the family at thirty—and in Miranda's opinion, the prettiest—Tracy's experiences with men were largely responsible for Miranda's continued determination not to remarry. The stuff that happened to her was enough to curl anyone's hair, and Miranda probably should have introduced her to Travis without further delay, if for no other reason than to prove to her sister there really was such a thing as a nice man.

She reminded herself that they would meet soon enough if they both came to her Christmas party. *Three weeks.* Three short weeks and she could kiss Travis York goodbye forever. Tracy was pretty and charming; men fell for her all the time, though not the right sort of men. Some of them had been certifiably insane. *She really can pick 'em...* She would be a better match for Travis than Christina. The idea should have made her happy, but it didn't. Not at all.

Miranda gave her mother a hug. "Heard anything from the guys?"

"They said they'd call in a little bit." Darlene sniffled. "I wish they hadn't moved so far away after they married. I still miss them."

Craig was in Fort Worth and Darryl lived in Tucson. Both her brothers were younger than Miranda, and she still couldn't picture them as being grown up with families of their own.

I'm as bad as Mom.

"Don't listen to her," Stephen said. "We're going to visit them—Craig at Christmas and Darryl at New Year's. Tracy's coming with us."

Miranda blinked. That meant she and Levi would be the only ones left in town for Christmas. "Why, th–that's wonderful. I had no idea."

"Spur of the moment," Stephen said with a casual wave. "That's the sort of thing we retirees can do."

Miranda didn't think either of her parents looked anywhere near old enough to retire. Her father was still fit and trim and his gray hair looked darn good on him. Darlene had picked up weight in recent years, but she still had the same sweet smile as always—something Tracy had inherited.

"Sounds like fun. Wish I could go with you."

Tracy's eyes danced. "I'm surprised I was able to go. I still can't believe they decided to close the clinic for the holidays."

Miranda couldn't believe it, either. Nurses *never* got off for the holidays, at least not those who worked in hospitals. Tracy worked in an outpatient procedure clinic, changing catheters, giving IV antibiotics, even putting in PICC lines. She hadn't pulled a night shift in years, and now she didn't have to work the holidays. "Must be nice."

"Sure is," Tracy said. "You ought to get a job there."

"I'll give it some thought."

The dinner went well—even though Miranda felt like a zombie. She was happy for her family, she truly was, but they seemed to be dissipating right before her eyes. She'd always prided herself on her independence and reminded herself that nothing ever stayed the same for long, but *still...*

To top it all off, here she was, trying to get Travis out of her life.

What was I thinking?

ഇരു

Thanksgiving with his family was the same as always—everyone else in the clan with their loving spouses and children, and Travis by himself. Except this year, he had Stuart to commiserate with. Shelley was the farthest thing from his thoughts, but Miranda was right there with him. He could see her fitting in with the crowd, and his mother would be so happy he'd finally found someone, she'd have overlooked the age difference entirely. Well…maybe for a little while.

The topic was bound to come up sooner or later. Still, if he was happy with Miranda, he doubted that anyone would object. Besides, it was none of their damn business who he dated.

Who am I kidding?

Everyone would at least have an opinion, especially his dad. He would have pushed for Shelley if he'd known anything about her, which was why Travis was determined not to mention her existence.

If he'd been strongly attracted to Shelley, he could've danced to her tune and probably wound up married to her, but the heat simply wasn't there. He couldn't imagine her as a lover—at least, not the kind of lover he wanted. Although settling for Shelley might get him a wife, he couldn't help thinking he'd end up being miserable, which was no way to feel about a potential spouse. He'd held out this long waiting for someone who knocked his socks off.

Too bad it happened to be Miranda.

Chapter 7

Travis seemed pleasantly surprised to be invited to Miranda's Christmas party. However, his expression quickly sobered when she gave him a quick overview of the guest list.

"Should I bring Shelley?" Judging from his pained expression, this prospect was about as exciting as a root canal.

"If you'd like. I thought you two had called it quits."

"Not officially. I could still ask her." Travis hesitated, then shook his head. "No. It's better if I come alone."

Miranda wasn't sure why he thought that and didn't particularly care. As she saw it, he had four choices. In addition to Tracy and Christina, Mary Beth and Dana were both single and about his age. Tracy was pretty, but Christina had her beat for beauty. Dana was cute and giggly, and Mary Beth was very nice, in addition to being totally hot, according to Rodney, who worked in Radiology. He always said he would marry her himself, if only his wife would let him.

The weeks leading up to the party were hectic, both at work and at home. Heavy rain continued to fall on a regular basis, with the result that Miranda's water pump and broom were in constant use. She put her Christmas tree up right on schedule, but was still engaged in the last-minute preparations when Travis came to the door with a bottle of wine and a heart-stopping smile.

"Merry Christmas!" Grinning, he gave her a hug that almost made her forget she'd only invited him so he could meet her friends.

"Yeah, well, here, let me put that wine in the fridge." Still reeling from the embrace and totally flustered at the thought of being alone with him, she turned away, pressing a hand to her chest as though it might calm her erratic heartbeat. She led the way to the kitchen, leaving him to follow.

"Is Levi here? I'd like to meet him."

Opening the refrigerator, she rearranged a few things and slid the wine bottle inside. "No, he's working this weekend. He doesn't care for parties, anyway. Crowds bother him—especially people he doesn't know very well."

Levi hadn't visited much lately. He seemed happy, which was the most important thing, but the way he'd referred to his apartment as home still bugged her. She closed the fridge and stole a glance at Travis.

A slow smile spread across his lips. "I guess that means I have you all to myself for a while."

Miranda stifled a gasp, turning it into a cough. "Funny thing about throwing a party. No one ever seems to show up on time. Obviously you don't believe in being fashionably late."

He shook his head slowly. "No point in that. If someone goes to the trouble of having a party, the least the guests can do is not leave the hostess twiddling her thumbs."

"No time for that yet." She forced a laugh. "I'm still cooking."

"Gives you something to do while you wait?"

"Something like that." She glanced around the room hoping a solution to the awkward moment would present itself. Then her hostess mode kicked in and she offered him a drink. "I've got hot cider, spiced tea, beer, wine, and stuff for mixed drinks."

"Cider sounds good. Smells good, too."

Ladling the cider into a cup, she passed it to him with hands that shook.

She could hardly wait to see him snuggled up on the couch with Christina and hanging on her every word. As beautiful as Christina was, he might not even notice her lack of wit or that she couldn't discuss her work. What *would* they talk about? Her breakup with Mark?

With that cheery thought, Miranda went back to making sausage-cheese balls—doing her best to ignore the fact that Travis was standing beneath a sprig of mistletoe.

He leaned against the counter, sipping his cider, no doubt oblivious to the temptation hanging above him. No one else would be there for at least another half hour. She could kiss him and no one would ever know. Hot, stolen kisses with Travis... She glanced down at the gooey mess of sausage, grated cheese, and biscuit dough she was mixing together with her hands.

My, how romantic...

"So, which one of your friends are you trying to fix me up with?"

Miranda's cat, Jade, strolled into the kitchen, her black coat gleaming and her tail waving gently. She looked up at Travis as though comparing him to some ideal, then took a few steps forward and sniffed at his pant leg before rubbing her head against him and purring. She turned to Miranda and blinked slowly. *Don't fix him up with anyone,* she seemed to say. *He smells nice. Keep him for yourself.*

Ignoring Jade's apparent suggestion, Miranda froze for an instant, her hands buried in the dough. "Whatever gave you that idea? You're simply here as a friend of mine, just like everyone else."

With a skeptical lift of his brow, he took another sip. "That's crap and you know it. Just tell me which one and I'll check her out."

Miranda stared at him for a long moment. *It's me,* she wanted to say. *Are you happy now?* But, of course she didn't. Jade gave her a disgusted look and sauntered into the living room.

"Come on," he urged. "Admit it. It's the only reason I get invited anywhere. No one can stand the fact that I'm not married."

Could be because you're so dammed cute.

She heaved a sigh. "Actually, there are four to choose from—Christina, Dana, Mary Beth, and my sister, Tracy. I'm not doing any matchmaking. I'm simply providing you with options."

"That's one way of putting it," he said grudgingly. "I've had enough blind dates to last a lifetime."

Miranda felt relieved, but at the same time, a bit let down. If he was that willing to meet them, he clearly had no interest in her whatsoever. "You see? It's perfect. None of them even know you're going to be here. I can introduce you to everyone, and you can take it from there."

"Or not." He speared an olive with a toothpick like he wanted to kill it. "I'm not sure I'm ready for another failed attempt."

"I only have this one party a year. It was either that or take you to work with me—although we'd have had to meet Christina for lunch. She's a lawyer."

He grimaced. "That's about as bad as dating a doctor. Does she at least like horses?"

"No, but she's really pretty."

"Yeah, well, looks aren't everything." He popped the olive into his mouth and chewed it slowly. She never would have imagined that simply watching a man eat an olive could be quite so fascinating. The play of muscles in his jaw drew her eye, and then when he *swallowed*... "If they were, I'd have stuck with the doctor. She was real pretty too."

Sighing, she blinked away her carnal thoughts. "I don't know what else to tell you. Just enjoy the food and the company and go home whenever you've had enough."

And get the hell out of my life so I won't feel so dammed miserable every time I look at you.

She began rolling the sausage mixture into balls and putting them on a cookie sheet. She didn't realize she was throwing them down until Travis came around the table and put a hand on her shoulder. He was so close, the scent of his cologne won out over the aroma of the pastry-wrapped olives baking in the oven. Her chest tightened and tears stung her eyes.

"I'm sorry, Miranda." His voice was soft and deep, making her pulse race when he clearly meant to be soothing. "I know you're only trying to help. I'll keep an open mind when I meet your friends, but I can't promise any more than that."

"I never expected anything else." Miranda hoped her lilting tone sounded more cheerful than she felt. "I want you to be happy, that's all."

"And I appreciate that. I probably shouldn't have said anything. I didn't mean to hurt your feelings."

At least he acknowledged the fact that she *had* feelings. Nurses were supposed to be tough—like the one referred to in Daphne du

Maurier's *Rebecca* with "all humanity washed away by years of disinfectant." Miranda was strong, but had managed to retain her humanity, and though she wasn't easily hurt, it did happen now and then.

"It's okay." She moved out from under his hand to put the tray in the oven and take out the olives. "But when I hear you going on about never finding the right woman, it makes me want to do something to help you."

"I know that, and I promise I'll keep my mouth shut from now on. The trouble is, I know what I want, but it's something I can't have." Travis paused, running a hand through his hair. "I just have to resign myself to it."

"What is it you want?" Miranda immediately wished she hadn't spoken. It was none of her business.

"I'd rather not say. I think it would be a mistake—one that I would regret for a long, long time."

She had no idea how to respond to that. Fortunately, a knock on the front door provided a welcome interruption. She held up her dough-covered hands. "Could you please get that?"

"Sure." He seemed almost as relieved as she was.

Judging from the babble of voices coming from the front room, several guests had arrived at once. Travis must've found someone to talk to, because he didn't come back.

Scared him off but good, didn't I?

Tracy breezed into the kitchen with a plate of cookies. "Merry Christmas!" She glanced over her shoulder and lowered her voice to a conspiratorial whisper. "Who's the hottie who answered the door?"

"That would be Travis York," Miranda replied. "He's a farrier—shoes a lot of horses at Nigel's barn. Nice guy, but he's had some woman trouble lately."

"You mean you invited him to the party to help him find a new girlfriend?"

Miranda shook her head. "I am *not* matchmaking. He's only here as a friend. If he hits it off with you or one of my buddies, then so be it." She finished her speech with a flourish of a sticky hand, tossing the last sausage ball onto the pan.

Tracy set the plate of cookies on the table and cleared her throat.

Miranda glanced up to find her sister scowling at her with arms folded and foot tapping. "Looks to me like there's a helluva lot more to it than that."

Crossing to the sink, Miranda pressed her lips together as she washed her hands. Tell Tracy the *real* truth and she'd never hear the end of it. "No, there isn't. Of course, he thought the same thing you did. He asked me who he was supposed to check out."

"Smart guy. Was I included on that list?"

"Yes, you were—along with some friends from the hospital. Christina broke up with Mark, so she's available too."

"Poor Travis."

Miranda stared at her with surprise. "What makes you say that?"

Tracy shook her head, her lips pursed in disgust. "I'm surprised Mark stuck with Christina as long as he did. That is one high-maintenance woman."

Which was true. "Maybe, but he might not like her."

"He'll be taken in by her looks. You wait and see."

Miranda didn't think Travis was quite that shallow, but men were strange. They would insist they wanted a woman with a brain and latch onto a bimbo in the next heartbeat. Christina wasn't a bimbo—far from it—but she was every bit as gorgeous as the average supermodel. "It's out of my hands. I'm not going to try to influence him in any way."

Tracy arched a skeptical brow. "Yeah, right."

"Seriously. He's only here because I thought he could use some cheering up. If you're interested, go talk to him."

"And I'd have your blessing?"

Miranda frowned. "Since when do you need that?"

Tracy blew out a breath, visibly exasperated, although Miranda was at a loss to understand why. "Never mind. Need some help in here?"

80Q3

Travis figured out which one was Miranda's sister almost immediately, but she was strictly off limits. No way was he going to take the chance of spending the rest of his life with the wrong sister.

The nurses were nice. *Too* nice. They deserved better than a man who saw them as the next best thing. Christina, on the other hand, was beautiful and shallow and still hung up on her ex-boyfriend. *Perfect.* She was a carbon copy of Shelley—though hopefully without the jealous streak. If he asked her out, the whole relationship could be over and done with in a couple of weeks. Travis could say he tried, and then Miranda could stop playing matchmaker and things could get back to normal between them—whatever *that* was. He wasn't sure. Either way, he'd be right back where he started.

As the evening progressed, he couldn't deny he'd enjoyed himself, although it would have been better if he could've spent more time with Miranda. Unfortunately, trying to catch another moment alone with her was like trying to catch a moonbeam. His conversation with Christina had yielded a date, and he was sure Miranda would be pleased. Still, those few moments alone with Miranda before the party remained stuck in his head, and he wanted to repeat them, even though he knew he shouldn't. Alan would be proud that he'd managed to get through the evening without dragging Miranda off to her bedroom and…

Don't even think about it.

But he *did* think about it. He liked her. Hell, he even liked her house. Granted, most places looked their best at Christmastime, but hers was homey, warm, and comfortable. Staying until everyone else left was easy; he'd been the first to arrive, and everyone else had parked behind his truck. He tried to tell himself he hadn't planned it that way, but he knew he had.

Miranda had introduced him as "my friend, Travis York" to everyone and then left him to fend for himself. She obviously didn't intend to hover, though he did catch her watching him from time to time. She gave him the occasional encouraging smile, but when he sat next to Christina, she'd averted her eyes before he could meet her gaze—obviously not wishing to interrupt him when he was doing exactly what she'd asked him to do.

No, she hadn't. Not really. She'd said she wanted him to be happy—and he knew exactly what it would take to make that happen. Christina had nothing to do with it.

When the last stragglers left, Tracy and Travis stayed behind to help with the cleanup. He'd made up his mind he would leave when Tracy did. That way he wouldn't be alone with Miranda again. Barring a call to Alan for support, that was the best strategy.

What he hadn't counted on was that Tracy would sneak out ahead of him. Travis had finished wiping off the kitchen table when he heard the front door close.

"That's it for another year," Miranda announced as she returned to the kitchen. "I'm beat. I'm sure you are too." She handed him his coat—obviously ready for the party to be over.

"I wanted to tell you, I asked Christina out."

"And…?"

"She said yes."

"That wasn't so hard, was it?"

"It's never hard to ask someone out the first time. It's the follow-up dates that are tough."

She nodded, stifling a yawn. "Yeah. The whole 'Do I invest more time in this relationship or not?' thing."

"That's right. I guess I'd better get going. Thanks for the invitation."

"Thanks for coming."

Travis knew he shouldn't do it, but when she walked him to the door, it was the most natural thing in the world to turn and give her a hug. He probably squeezed her too hard and held her too long, but she felt so good in his arms, he couldn't help it. At least he hadn't done anything *really* stupid. Like kissing her until her knees buckled.

Miranda watched him go, waving as he backed his truck out of the driveway. Travis had done exactly what she'd hoped he would do, which meant it was only a matter of time before he and Christina fell in love and set a wedding date. They'd live happily ever after, and

Miranda wouldn't have to wonder when he was ever going to realize how much he meant to her. Everything was falling neatly into place. She should be happy.

So why was she crying?

Chapter 8

Christmas came and went, and Miranda saw the New Year in with Lola and Peggy in the ICU, sharing a cup of sparkling grape juice with her only alert patient. After that, she found herself looking bleakly forward to another year without Kris and now, without Travis. He'd taken Christina out a few times and reported that things were going pretty well. At least, that was *his* side of the story. A bit later, she heard Christina's version, which was quite different. Travis had promised to keep his mouth shut and quit complaining. Christina had no such qualms.

"He's boring," she announced when Miranda met her for lunch. "He doesn't like anything I like, and I told him I didn't want to see him anymore."

"Boring?" Miranda didn't get bored when all she could do was look at him. Christina was either completely nuts, or all the time she'd spent with the criminal element had skewed her perspective. "He's never seemed boring to me."

Christina gave her shoulders a haughty shrug. "You've never dated him. He doesn't know anything about the law and doesn't even watch any legal shows on TV. I couldn't talk to him about anything."

"Not even the weather or politics or having babies?" *Where did that one come from?* Christina had never said anything about wanting children—at least not that Miranda could recall.

"Oh, sure, I could talk about those kinds of things." She paused, frowning. "Except the having babies part. He simply doesn't understand what it's like to be a lawyer."

"Who could possibly know that except another lawyer? I don't expect anyone to understand what it's like to be a nurse. No one would believe half of it, anyway. It's one of those things you have to experience firsthand."

"You at least like horses, so you'd have that much in common." She flipped open her menu and began reading, avoiding Miranda's gaze entirely. "I didn't like him, so let's leave it at that, shall we?"

Miranda heaved a sigh. "Okay, case closed."

So much for getting him married off. She couldn't blame Travis for not wanting to seem like a whiner, but whether he hit it off with Christina or not, he was still there every week at Nigel's for her to gaze at, dream about, and shed a few tears over. She'd been alone for a very long time. What was it about Travis that made her feel so *lonely?*

Christina peeked over the top of her menu. "Have you heard from Mark?"

So that's it. No wonder she thought Travis was boring.

Miranda would've thought Mark was boring if she'd tried to date him while she was still in love with Travis—which, she had to admit, she probably was. Somewhere along the line she'd gone from simply thinking he was cute and sexy to believing she couldn't live much longer without him. She still got her "Travis fix" once a week, but she needed more.

"Not since before the Christmas party when he called to say he'd asked his new girlfriend to go to Florida with him on some sort of fishing trip."

Christina nodded, tears welling up in her lovely eyes. "I heard that too." Her voice was barely a whisper. "I could never go on those trips. I was always too busy." She paused, dabbing her eyes with her napkin. "I wish I'd made more time for him. That's why he left me, isn't it?"

Miranda put down her menu, giving Christina her full attention. "He told me he wanted more than the little scraps of time you had for him. He wanted to do all of those things with you. Obviously, he got tired of waiting."

"I don't suppose there's any way he'd give me another chance, is there?"

Miranda knew exactly how she felt—hurt…empty…hopeless. She shook her head. "I think he's pretty much spoken for now. I'm sorry, but I have a feeling it's too late."

"Well, I guess that's that." She took a deep breath and sat up straighter, as though attempting to appear normal. "No one ever said life was going to be perfect. I've got my work and...not much else." Her face seemed to crumble and she slumped forward, sobbing.

Consoling her friend when all Miranda wanted to do was to cry was difficult. She still didn't understand how a beautiful, successful woman could seem so wretched. But, as Travis said, looks weren't everything, and neither was a good career.

Miranda let her cry until the waitress came to take their order. Christina pulled herself together after that. They went on with lunch, but Miranda doubted that she even tasted it. *She* certainly hadn't, and she could hardly recall what she'd eaten a few minutes afterward.

They parted with a hug, and Miranda drove home in the rain, the weather matching her mood. Three wet dogs came out to greet her when she arrived, as did her soggy cats. The horses stood waiting at the gate, seemingly oblivious to the rain, and she slogged up the hill through the mud only to find another lake where the barn floor used to be. The whole world was beginning to mildew, and as she swept away the flood, she couldn't help wondering if she wasn't getting a bit moldy herself—which was certainly the way she felt.

✄

Travis had been working on the gray gelding for fifteen minutes when Miranda arrived for her lesson. He knew precisely how much time had passed because he'd been checking his watch every three minutes for the past forty-five. He doubted he would even need to tell her he and Christina—who hadn't struck him as the type to suffer in silence—weren't seeing each other anymore.

Miranda responded to his wave with one of her own. "I heard you and Christina didn't hit it off very well."

"I thought we did. Apparently, *she* didn't." Seeing no point in making Miranda think he didn't like her friends, he at least tried to appear unhappy about it. "Too bad. She seemed very nice."

She hadn't seemed that way when she'd informed him that

they'd gone on their last date together. She'd sounded like a prosecuting attorney as she ran down the list of excellent reasons why they were a complete mismatch. Since he secretly agreed with each and every one of them, he hadn't bothered to argue.

"I can't say you didn't try." Miranda heaved her saddle onto the rack and left to get her horse.

"That's all of my news," he said when she returned. "What's new with you?"

"New? There's nothing new," she said bitterly. "Mud, rain, mud, rain, flood, mud, rain, and more rain. My barn is a quagmire."

He dropped the hoof he was working on and stood up. "Sounds like you need a ditch around your barn."

"I *have* a ditch around my barn." She snorted with disgust. "It's not big enough, but it's the best I can do with a shovel since Santa didn't bring me a backhoe for Christmas. I also asked for a concrete floor in the barn. Didn't get that, either."

"Dunno about concrete, but my brother has a backhoe."

She shook her head. "Can't afford it. I'd have hired someone a long time ago if I had the extra money." Her wistful smile sliced right through his heart. "Sorry. I just needed to vent a bit. I don't expect you to fix it."

He thought back to the lecture she'd given Nigel about dealing with women, but he didn't think it applied in this instance— especially since he really could fix the problem. "It wouldn't cost that much—just enough to pay for the fuel. I wouldn't charge you for labor."

"You won't get rich doing business like that."

"I'm not trying to get rich. I'm trying to do a friend a favor."

Her eyes narrowed, and Travis had the strangest feeling she could see right through him. "It's kind of you to offer, but I'm sure you've got better things to do than digging ditches—especially if you're not getting paid."

He shrugged. "Fix dinner for me sometime."

"I could do that. I hate mud with a passion, and there's so much of it, it's driving me nuts."

"I know what you mean." He was about to add further

encouragement when he remembered Miranda had a husband who might not approve of other men doing "favors" for his wife—or having dinner with her.

She gnawed at her lower lip as though weighing the pros and cons. "Okay. But it's gonna be tough figuring out when to do it. You've got to have the time and the ground has to dry out a little. Otherwise, you'd be stuck there until spring."

Travis couldn't help smiling. Getting stuck at Miranda's house until spring was akin to winning the lottery—as long as her husband was stuck somewhere else. "It's not supposed to rain again until the weekend. I could come over on Friday afternoon."

She nodded her agreement. "Okay, but I can't help feeling I'm taking advantage of you."

"Hey, you invited me to a party and introduced me to several new women. I'd say this makes us even."

She shot him a skeptical look. "Maybe—but only if you'd hit it off with one of them."

In Travis's opinion, any excuse to spend a few extra moments in Miranda's company was worth a few failed dates—plus the time required to dig a ditch. It might even be worth a confrontation with her husband. "Doesn't matter. I'll see you on Friday afternoon."

Right after I call Alan.

ℰℭ

Stuart was okay with the loan of the backhoe, particularly since Travis hadn't mentioned whose ditch he'd be digging. He helped Travis hitch the trailer to his truck, gave him a few pointers on ditch digging, and sent him on his way.

Travis stopped to refuel the truck and the backhoe, giving Alan a call while the tanks filled. Stuart might not have been the least bit suspicious, but Alan was worried.

"That is *not* the sort of thing you need to be doing," he warned after Travis explained the situation. "Going to her party was bad enough. This is *much* worse."

"True. I'll be on a backhoe digging in the dirt instead of

hanging out in her house with a bunch of her friends."

"You *know* what I mean. She'll feel like she owes you something. Do *not* accept any offers to repay you—especially not with sex."

Travis was thankful he was on the phone with his cousin rather than talking with him in person. Otherwise, he'd have been sorely tempted to take a swing at him. "She's not that kind of woman. If she was, I probably wouldn't be so crazy about her. She'd never suggest anything like that."

"Yeah, well, don't *you* suggest it, either. I told you to steer clear of her completely, and what do you do? You offer to dig a ditch for her." He blew out an exasperated breath. "Dammit, Travis, you're starting to remind me of me."

"If I was anything like you, we wouldn't be having this conversation. I'd have done something stupid already, and I haven't—yet. You're right, though. I can't leave her alone *or* stay away from her. I'm not that noble." The pump shut off, and he switched it over to the tank on the backhoe.

"Shit, man. You're worse off than I thought."

"Yeah. I know that, too." He tightened the gas cap on the truck. "Just wish I knew what *she* was thinking. Mind telling me how you knew those married women you had affairs with were willing?"

"The same way you know if a single woman wants you, dumb butt. They send out the usual signals—only they're more blatant about it."

Miranda had never given Travis the slightest hint that she was interested in him as anything other than a friend, and she certainly hadn't seemed willing to cheat on Levi. Or maybe it *was* encouraging. If she didn't want him, he could hang around and drool over her all he liked. Hell, he might even get *blatant* about it.

"Travis," Alan prompted. "You're too damned quiet. What's going on in that head of yours?"

"I dunno." He chewed on a thumbnail. He'd been doing that so much lately it was a wonder he had any fingers left.

"Has she been sending out signals?"

Travis couldn't think of a single, solitary one. "No."

"Not in private or not in public?"

"I mean, not at all." He paused, frowning. "What difference does it make where she does it?"

"Flirting in public means she likes you but isn't willing to take the plunge. In private…well, you get the idea."

"Yeah, I get it." The only time he'd truly been alone with Miranda, she'd been irked because he'd figured out she was trying to fix him up with one of her friends—or her sister. He was grateful to have dodged *that* bullet. Tracy was a nice girl, and she was very pretty, but she wasn't Miranda.

"Look, you've already promised to do this job for her, right?"

He hung up the pump and replaced the cap on the backhoe's gas tank. "Had to talk her into it, but yeah, I told her I'd be there this afternoon."

"Stay on the backhoe then. Do *not* go in the house. Do not accept anything from her."

"Not even dinner, or a handshake, or a hug?"

"No—especially not the hug. A simple thank you is enough. You weren't expecting anything more, were you?"

Travis winced. He hadn't expected anything, but he'd certainly hoped for more than a handshake—and not just the dinner she'd offered him. "No. Not really. But what about dinner if her husband is there?" He tore off the receipt and climbed back into the truck.

Alan laughed until Travis wanted to strangle him. "Do you really want to sit across the table from the man who actually has the right to fuck the woman you're nuts about? I may be a sex maniac, but even I have a hard time facing down a husband, particularly if he's a nice guy. Might knock some sense into you, though."

"I doubt if he'd do that." Nothing he'd ever heard Miranda say about Levi led him to believe he'd be the violent, jealous type. Then again, she hadn't really said very much about him at all.

"I don't mean he'd actually *slug* you. It's more of a reality check. When you see how happy she is with someone else, it…changes things. Trust me on that one."

"Okay, point made. I promise I'll be good. Talk to you later." Travis switched off his phone and leaned back against the seat with a sigh.

The weather forecast had changed slightly. The rain would be coming in sooner than originally predicted, and he had four hours of daylight left. If he was going to do this for Miranda, he needed to get his ass in gear.

Whatever happened after that was up to her.

Chapter 9

When Travis came up the drive, Miranda wasn't sure which looked better, him or the backhoe. "Damn that's beautiful," she said as he climbed out of the truck.

He chuckled. "You really *did* ask Santa for a backhoe."

"You bet I did. When I think of the jobs I've tackled with nothing but a shovel and a rake…"

"This time you can sit back and relax and let the heavy equipment do the work."

"Sounds fabulous." While he unloaded the backhoe, she went up to man the gate. The horses were already tearing around the paddock as though Earth was being invaded by aliens, and she tried not to cringe as he drove across the soft turf of her backyard. Telling herself that getting rid of the mud in the barn was worth a few ruts, she opened the gate and waved him through.

Miranda watched as he dug out huge sections of the existing ditch in a matter of minutes, not even wanting to think about the blisters and aching back she would have gotten had she attempted it herself. *That man deserves one helluva dinner.*

She was on her way back to the house to start cooking when she remembered he hadn't said what he wanted to eat or even when he wanted it. However, since Levi was coming home for the weekend, she decided to go ahead with her original plans. There would be plenty of food, and if Travis wanted to stay for dinner, he was more than welcome.

ಌ

The pie was almost done when the phone rang.

"Hi, Mom," Levi said. "I have to work tomorrow, so I'm going to stay here tonight."

Miranda took a moment to swallow her disappointment. "How come you're working so many weekends now? You never did before."

"Tabitha needs me to help her."

"*Tabitha* needs you? Who's Tabitha?"

"Oh, she's a girl who works at the store with me."

"I figured that," Miranda said. "What I mean is, have I met her before?"

"I don't think so. I like working with her. She's really nice."

Miranda knew this was probably the most information she was going to get from him for now. Too many questions tended to upset him. "I'll have to come and meet her sometime."

"Okay. Bye, Mom." Since his farewells were usually abrupt, she tried not to read too much into it. However, if what she suspected was true, this wouldn't be the first time he'd had a crush on a pretty girl. Hopefully, this Tabitha person was as nice as he'd said she was, otherwise he was in for a huge disappointment.

She hung up the phone, wondering whether to go ahead with the dinner plans or scrap them altogether. All she had to do was run up to the barn and check with Travis, but for some reason she was hesitant to do so. Inviting him to dinner seemed too…forward or something. Whatever the reason, her reticence kept her in the house, catching up on a few chores.

She didn't realize how long she'd been stalling until she heard the backhoe coming across the yard. Putting on her coat and boots, she went out just as he drove the backhoe onto the trailer.

"That didn't take long. Sorry I wasn't there to get the gate for you."

He climbed down from the trailer and raised the tailgate. "No problem. The horses wouldn't come anywhere near this thing." As usual, the man couldn't say anything without smiling. Miranda wondered if she would ever stop getting those warm, tingly feelings whenever he smiled at her. Hugs were even better. Unfortunately, she hadn't gotten one since the Christmas party.

"What do I owe you?"

"Nothing," he replied. "Like I told you, make dinner for me sometime."

"That's not what we agreed on, and you know it. I was supposed to at least pay for the fuel."

"Oh, yeah." He said this as though he'd just remembered it. "I'll let you know what it costs to fill the tank."

If he was that forgetful, she doubted he would ever tell her—which meant she would have to make him a really good dinner. "Would you like to stay tonight? For dinner, I mean." She wasn't sure which sounded stranger, what she'd said initially, or the fact that she felt the need to clarify it.

Travis didn't seem to notice. "Sounds good. I'm not exactly dressed for dinner, though—or what you'd call clean."

Miranda couldn't help laughing. Even splattered with mud, he was a dream come true. "If you smell too bad, I'll just throw you in the shower and give you some of Levi's clothes to wear."

Whoa, that was a mistake.

The thought of Travis in the shower sent a jolt of desire zipping from her nipples to her core.

Thankfully, Travis seemed oblivious to her reaction. "I'm okay with that, as long as he doesn't mind."

"No, he won't care. He called a while ago to say he wouldn't be home tonight. I'll go feed the horses real quick and then start on dinner. In the meantime, make yourself at home. There's beer in the fridge."

The horses were still agitated from their visit from the aliens, so Miranda waited at the gate until they settled down. After she fed them and cleaned the barn, she went out to inspect the ditch, which was now capable of handling a deluge of nearly biblical proportions. He'd even made a nice bank along the edge.

After doling out the hay, she gave Kira's nose a rub. "No more mud in the barn. Isn't that great? You probably don't care, though, do you?" Kira munched her hay as though mud was the least of her worries. "What do you think I should do with Travis? Should I give him dinner and then demand a kiss for my trouble? Maybe I should tell him the pie is extra and if he wants any, he has to spend the night."

Kira ignored her, but Kes shook her head.

"Oh, what would you know, Kester? Didn't you like him?"

Kes replied with a snort and went back to eating her hay, as well.

"You guys are no help whatsoever."

Upon her arrival at the house, Miranda's worst fears were realized. Travis was in the shower and his clothes were draped over the chair by the front door. All of them.

He must've stripped at the door and then walked naked to the bathroom. The mental image alone nearly gave her heart failure.

Does he think I'm made of stone? Had he raided Levi's closet for clothes or would he come strutting out of the bathroom wearing nothing but a towel?

Hurrying into Levi's room, she yanked open the drawers and pulled out a T-shirt, underwear, socks, and a pair of sweat pants. She was in the process of laying all of it in the hall by the bathroom when Travis opened the door. His groin was right at eye level, making the bulge beneath his towel very hard to miss. Straightening quickly, she handed him the stack of clothing, fighting the urge to rip the towel off him while his hands were full.

He smiled as though he half expected her to do it. "Don't look so surprised, Miranda. You told me to make myself at home."

"Yes, I did." She let out a nervous little laugh. "You're good at following directions."

And you look amazingly good in nothing but a towel. Then she made the mistake of taking that thought one step further, imagining him without the towel and almost choked. Her fingers itched to push that towel aside so she could see, kiss, taste, and caress every square inch of him.

"Miranda," he said gently. "You're staring…"

She took a deep breath. "Sorry. Can't help it. I may be a worn-out old nurse, but I'm not dead yet."

"Never thought you were."

Miranda didn't know what to make of that—or the accompanying twinkle in his eyes. "I–I'll just go back to the kitchen.

Put some clothes on if you don't want me to stare."

She was browning Italian sausages when he came up behind her a few minutes later, peering over her shoulder.

"What's for dinner?" His breath on her neck raised goose bumps that went wild, chasing each other across her shoulders and up and down her spine.

"That depends on how hungry you are." Her voice came out with a bit of a quaver, forcing her to clear her throat. "I'm fixing fettuccine Alfredo with Italian sausage and mushrooms. I can make a salad and garlic bread if you're starving. Plus, there's Dutch apple pie and ice cream for dessert."

"Hmm… That all sounds good, and I'm pretty hungry."

She tossed the mushrooms in with the sausage and put a lid on the skillet. "No problem. Have a seat. Want a beer?" She'd gone from quavering to speaking in short, abrupt sentences.

Calm down, Miranda.

"Sure." He sat down at the table, looking much more relaxed than she felt.

Pulling two bottles of Sam Adams out of the fridge, she gave him one, figuring he'd get up and go find a television. Pleased to note that he didn't, she went back to work. She paused after taking a sip of her own beer, realizing her mistake in drinking anything stronger than tea. She hadn't grabbed his towel earlier—which had required a significant amount of self-control—but with enough alcohol on board, anything could happen. She might even give him a hickey to match his birthmark.

Desperate for a neutral topic, she asked him about his brother. Inserting a question from time to time, she managed to keep the conversation going, but eventually the discussion turned to Travis and his efforts at finding someone to live with aside from Stuart. The beer must've loosened her tongue, otherwise she'd have never told him that the reason he was still living with his brother was that he was too damn picky for his own good.

"Picky?" His harsh, mirthless laugh took her by surprise. "Actually, I wasn't picky enough. I married a girl right out of high school and wound up divorced in no time. Now all the good ones are taken."

"No, they aren't. What was wrong with Christina?"

"It's pretty hard to get excited about a woman who only talks about her old boyfriend. I don't think I could ever measure up to him. Besides, she's too *busy*."

"You're right about the busy part, but I know Mark pretty well, and he's not *that* special. She would've stopped talking about him eventually. Maybe you should ask her out again."

Miranda knew why he wouldn't but saw no reason to let him know she'd been discussing him with Christina. She would certainly never tell him her friend had referred to him as boring.

"No, I don't believe I will. She's smart and beautiful, and I like the idea of a woman having her own career. But she seems more interested in her work than any mere *man*. That was all she talked about—aside from Mark." He frowned, taking another sip of his beer. "She couldn't care less about horses. We had absolutely nothing in common."

"Sort of like the obstetrician?"

He nodded. "Yeah—a *lot* like her."

"You never said why Dana and Mary Beth didn't interest you."

"No chemistry," he said with a shrug. "Very nice, intelligent, and attractive, but no spark."

"Sparks are a good thing. You don't need much else if you've got that." She dished up the fettuccine and set his down in front of him.

"I thought I might feel something for Christina at first, but it faded pretty fast." He leaned forward over his plate and inhaled deeply. "This smells great."

"Dig in." Miranda pulled out a chair and sat down. "Sometimes people sort of grow on you—especially those you're not sure about at first."

Travis had certainly grown on Miranda. Somewhere along the line he'd gone from being eye candy to being someone she cared for very deeply. What if he decided to give up farrier work or move to another state? The thought of not seeing him again almost made her sick.

Travis took a few moments to respond, savoring the first bite of his meal. "It's easier to get to know someone when you work with them or see them all the time. Then you can decide whether you like them or not without all the pressure."

"Which is why I invited you to a party rather than setting up a blind date." With a shrug, she picked up her fork. "I tried. I don't know of anyone else."

He gave her a sad smile. "Like I said. All the good ones are taken."

Miranda took that to mean that *she* wasn't one of the good ones. True, she was a good bit older than him, but being totally discounted hurt.

Travis was quiet after that, evidently preferring food over conversation. Miranda's appetite had disappeared completely. The longer she sat there watching that adorable man eat the meal she'd prepared for him, the more depressed she got. The beer had been a huge mistake.

He put down his fork and glanced at her plate. "Aren't you hungry?"

"Not as much as I thought," she admitted. "Are you ready for dessert?"

Smiling, he leaned back in his chair, rubbing his stomach. "Maybe a little later. I'm pretty full right now. Thanks, Miranda. That was the best dinner I've had in a long time."

"You're welcome." She smiled back at him, groaning inwardly. *Later?* That would be fine if he wanted to be with her, but if he was only waiting until he got hungry enough for pie and ice cream, she'd just as soon he left immediately.

She put his plate in the dishwasher and took her own uneaten dinner out to the dogs. The weather had turned sharply colder, prompting her to pick up a few sticks of wood, which she added to the fire in the woodstove.

Travis was washing his hands at the sink when she returned. She bit back a gasp as her eyes drank in the sight of him—the contours of his back and shoulders, the flexing muscles in his arms, the snug sweat pants accentuating every curve…

He glanced over his shoulder and smiled. What would he do if he had the slightest inkling of her thoughts? She had no idea, but that enticing birthmark was visible from where she stood, making her long to kiss him there.

Would it disappear if I licked it hard enough?

Giving herself a mental slap, she put the rest of the plates in the dishwasher, noticing that he wasn't washing his hands. He was washing the skillet. As if driving her nuts by wearing her son's tight pants wasn't enough, the man had the audacity to help out in the kitchen.

"You don't have to do that," she said. "You're being paid back for ditch digging—remember?"

He shot her a wink. "I wanted to help you get finished quicker. There's a movie on tonight that I wanted to see, and it starts in about two minutes. That is, if you don't mind me watching it with you."

Her heartbeat stuttered for a moment. *Easy, girl—it's not what you think.* "Hmm... Dinner *and* a movie? I don't know," she drawled. "You might have to dig a ditch along the driveway for that."

"Oh, come on, Miranda," he said, laughing. "That was a pretty big ditch I dug today—it's worth a movie too. Isn't it?"

It was worth a whole lot more than that. "Okay. What do you want to watch?"

"*The Bridges of Madison County,*" he replied. "You know, the one with Clint Eastwood and Meryl Streep? It's an older film, but I've always heard it was good. Have you seen it?"

Assuming he would prefer to watch an action movie, this particular choice came as a bit of a shock. "Yes, and it's one helluva a tear-jerker. You'll need a whole box of Kleenex at the end."

Reaching for a dishtowel, he dried the skillet. "Aw, no one dies, do they?"

"Yes, but it's natural deaths in old age—nothing violent or unexpected."

"I can handle that."

She almost wished she'd lied to him. Of all the movies in the history of cinema for him to want to see, that had to be the worst possible choice. Watching it with *him* sitting on the other end of the couch while Meryl Streep went on about how everything Clint Eastwood did was erotic—which was precisely the way she felt about Travis—would be pure torture. The only difference was that Meryl actually got to make love to her man. Miranda would never have that opportunity.

Chapter 10

Travis knew exactly what Alan would say to him if he called, which was why he'd turned off his cell phone and left it in his coat pocket. So far, he'd done almost everything Alan had told him *not* to do. But when Miranda had looked up at him with those beautiful green eyes and asked him to stay to dinner, how could he possibly refuse?

Even so, ditch or no ditch, he was a little surprised she hadn't booted him out yet. Alan would have told him to get his ass out of there and go home. Her husband probably would have done the same—if he'd been there.

The movie had simply been an excuse to hang around a while longer. What he hadn't realized was how much the story would affect him. A single man passing through, a wife left alone while her husband and children are out of town, and what happens when they give in to their passion. The pain of separation. The ache of knowing their love was something that could never be. The emotions were much too similar to those he felt for Miranda.

During one highly emotional scene, Travis stole a glance at her just as tears spilled over her lashes and slid down her cheek. The urge to take her in his arms and kiss those tears away was so powerful, he had to force himself to stay put and keep his hands to himself. Every scene struck a chord with him, and by the time the woman received the box of her lover's personal effects after his death, his tears were flowing freely. Miranda was openly sobbing.

When the movie ended, she left the room, but not before tossing a tissue into his lap. He understood how she felt. Turning off the television, he simply sat there, alone in the dark. Driving home in the rain held no appeal for him whatsoever. The warmth from the woodstove made him sleepy while raindrops pelted against the windows, making the house seem more like a safe haven than ever.

In another time and place, he could have stayed all night, sleeping with Miranda in his arms, making love to her and promising never to make her cry like that. Ever.

He heard plates rattling in the kitchen. She was serving dessert—his cue that his time with her was almost up. He could linger over a piece of pie only so long. But why prolong the agony? Better to get it over with and head for home.

Entering the kitchen just as the microwave dinged, he watched as she scooped out the ice cream. "You weren't kidding about that being a sad one. You probably think I'm a blubbering idiot."

She glanced up at him and smiled. "Not at all. I'd be more concerned if you hadn't shed a tear. No *normal* person could watch that and not be affected by it."

"I must be pretty normal, then. I know *exactly* how he felt."

Taking a seat at the table, he studied her for a moment, trying to gauge her reaction. Did she have any idea what was going on in his head—or in his heart?

"Wanting someone you know you can't have?" Her smile was wistful. "I think everyone can relate to that."

She was right. The feeling was probably as universal as breathing. "It would be tough asking a woman to give up her whole life for you. I'm not sure I could do it."

"Both lives change when two people get together. What about the life you'd be giving up yourself?"

He stabbed his fork into the pie with unnecessary force. "Who would want it? It's lonely, incomplete, and I'm *not* happy."

"And yet you're always smiling. I'd never have guessed." Reaching across the table, she squeezed his hand—a simple gesture that made him want to cry all over again. "You're too damn cute to be without a woman for long. One of these days when you least expect it, some sweet little chickie will snap you right up."

Despite his dismal mood, he laughed. "I'm not sure a little *chickie* is what I'm looking for."

"You didn't want doctors, lawyers, or nurses," she reminded him. "That sort of leaves the chickie type."

"What I want is somewhere in between—intelligent, but not so smart she makes me feel like an idiot. Pretty, but not so gorgeous I'd be worried she'd dump me for any handsome dude that comes sniffing around. Someone who has her own life and is willing to let me live mine. Two lives that are different, but with common ground. Do you understand what I mean?" He was describing *her. She* was the perfect woman for him, the one he couldn't have.

"That's pretty much what I'd want for myself if I were you." Her tone was neutral and diplomatic. Obviously she didn't understand—at least, not enough to take the hint.

"Tell me something, Miranda. Are *you* happy?"

She closed her eyes for a moment as though reviewing her life. "Mostly. But no one is happy all the time. Without a little pain, no one would appreciate feeling good, would they?"

"So what are you saying—that I should shut up and count my blessings?"

"No. I'm saying you need to keep an open mind and keep looking."

"You're right." With a sigh, he finished the last of his pie, then glanced up at the clock. "Guess I'd better hit the road. Thanks again for dinner. That pie was terrific."

"You're welcome," she replied. "And thank *you* for the ditch."

He made a half-hearted attempt at a smile. "Let me know if you need any more of them."

"Don't worry. With the rates you charge, you'd be the first one I'd call."

She set the dirty dishes in the sink, seeming relieved that the conversation had lightened up. Travis didn't think he could handle much more of the deep stuff himself, especially since it wasn't getting him anywhere. If nothing else, this evening had proved that while he could count Miranda as a friend, she wasn't about to offer him anything beyond that.

And he wouldn't ask it of her. Alan would be proud of him. He'd keep his mouth shut and go home—which was, after all, the right thing to do.

But why does it feel so wrong?

The temperature had dropped even further when Miranda went out to get more wood from the porch, and to make matters worse, it was raining—a cold, bone-chilling rain. Luke and Chewie came out of the doghouse, tails wagging. Toby trotted over from his bed in the garage, slipped on the bottom step, and smacked his nose on the concrete porch with a yelp.

She went over to help the little beagle, but he'd already scrambled up the remaining step and was frisking about with the others like he always did. She peered at the steps. Something didn't seem quite right, and a closer inspection revealed the problem. Evidently, while she and Travis had been watching television and eating pie, Mother Nature had served up one of her nastier surprises—freezing rain, which was the only thing Miranda hated more than mud. Everything was encased in a thick sheath of ice. She put out a foot experimentally and nearly slipped off the porch. "Oh, my *God...*"

Gathering up an armload of wood, she went back inside. "I don't know if you should be 'hitting the road' or not. It's really slick out there. You might end up hitting something besides the road."

Travis came down the hallway from the bathroom. "What?"

"I said it's getting pretty slick out there. I don't know if you should drive home tonight or not—especially pulling that trailer. There's ice all over everything."

He frowned. "I heard something on the radio about freezing rain, but they talked like it would probably be mostly north of here."

"Well, they were wrong." She dropped the wood on the floor and opened the door to the woodstove. "It's bad enough to pull down power lines now, and it's still raining."

Travis went out on the porch, returning just as Miranda was raking down the coals in the stove. "I don't even want to walk on it, let alone drive." After a moment's hesitation, he asked, "I don't suppose I could stay here tonight, could I?"

"Of course you can. I'd never forgive myself if you got hurt driving home." She tossed the logs into the stove one by one and closed the door. What she'd said was no more than the truth. She'd have felt that way about anyone, but if anything were to happen to Travis…

"I can sleep on the couch."

She shook her head. "No need for that. I've got an extra bedroom—two of them, actually. You can take your pick—although the one down the hall on the right has the best bed. I've probably even got a new toothbrush around here somewhere. Let me know if you need anything else."

She wished she could come up with some reason for him to sleep with her, but she didn't need that kind of temptation. The towel incident was quite enough.

"I'll get you a flashlight in case the power goes off—which it probably will. And if it does, the water won't work since the pump on the well is electric. If necessary, I can fire up the generator in the morning, but I don't like to use it unless I absolutely have to. I keep extra water for emergencies."

He nodded. "I'll go on to bed then. I'm kinda tired."

Miranda got a flashlight for him, and after a search of the vanity drawers, she found a toothbrush. She gave them to Travis, then went back to the living room and lay on the couch while she waited for the stove to heat up. No matter what happened next, this was going to be a *very* long night.

A few minutes later, she heard footsteps coming down the hall.

"I need to call Stuart." Sorting through the pile of clothes on the chair, he found his phone and slipped it into his pocket. "Aren't you coming to bed?"

The way he put it made it sound as if they'd be sharing a room. If they had been, he wouldn't have had to ask. She would've been there already.

"I'm waiting for the fire to get going," she replied. "I won't be up long."

"Okay," he said. "Goodnight, then."

"Goodnight, Travis. Sleep well."

Travis closed the door behind him. A cursory glance of the room revealed rough wood paneling, an old-fashioned dresser, and a bed covered with a patchwork quilt. Sitting on the edge of the bed, he pulled out his phone, along with the package of condoms he'd stuffed into the breast pocket of his jacket. He seriously doubted Miranda would have any reason to look through his clothes, but he wasn't taking any chances on her finding them.

He called Stuart and told him not to worry—about him *or* the backhoe.

Then he called Alan.

"And her husband isn't home? My, how convenient." Alan didn't bother to tone down the sarcasm. "You planned this, didn't you?"

"No, I didn't. Honest to God, I never thought this would happen."

"Mind telling me why you were there so late to begin with?"

Travis felt like a complete idiot. "Dinner and a movie?"

"Oh, so the two of you are dating now?"

"No, we aren't. I—it's hard to explain. I'd already told her to fix dinner for me sometime to pay me back for the work. When she offered to let me stay for dinner, I figured her husband would be home soon and there wouldn't be a problem. Then she told me he'd called and said he wouldn't be home tonight. That must happen a lot because she didn't seem upset by it—which makes me wonder what kind of work he does."

"Ask her in the morning, and then get the hell out of there. It's supposed to warm up overnight and be sunny tomorrow. The ice should melt off pretty quickly. In the meantime, keep your dick in your pants and your hands to yourself."

"I'm not going to—"

"I mean it, Travis. Don't do it."

"Okay. I hear you. I won't touch her. Not even if she wakes up screaming her head off in the middle of the night."

Alan snickered. "No need to be such a hard-ass."

Travis felt like strangling his cousin. "Look, I know you're trying to help me out here—and I appreciate it. But believe me, you aren't telling me anything I haven't told myself."

"It helps to hear it from the voice of experience, though. Trust me, I will never, *ever*, go after a married woman again. I've learned my lesson, and I'd rather you didn't have to learn yours the hard way."

"I won't. As soon as the roads are clear, I'm outta here."

"You do that. Sleep well."

"I doubt it."

Travis switched off his phone and set it on the nightstand along with the flashlight. He'd been miserable with Shelley, but that was nothing compared to this. After a few minutes of staring off into space, he spotted something he hadn't noticed before. An American flag folded up inside a wooden box with a glass cover—the kind given to the families of deceased veterans—sat in the shadows on the corner of the dresser. Curious, he got up to take a closer look but found no inscription, only the faded photograph of a Marine sergeant with a broad grin, blond hair, and lots of freckles. The picture wasn't old enough to have been taken during World War II or even the Korean War. It was more recent than that—the Gulf War, perhaps?

But who was he? Miranda's brother? He didn't resemble her at all. He could have been a relative of her husband's. Travis had never seen a picture of Levi or even heard a description of him. Puzzled, he put the picture back on the dresser and went to bed.

"Something else I'll have to ask her about in the morning."

Miranda wondered why Travis would care when she went to bed. She didn't have to work again for several days, and it wasn't as though she had to get up early for anything—except to feed the animals. Then again, perhaps he only wanted her to get up early so she could fix breakfast before he left.

She sighed miserably. She couldn't go on seeing him at Nigel's every week. It was too painful. All she had to do was switch her lesson to a different day, and she'd never see him again. She might even forget him.

Yeah, right. Like she'd forgotten Kris. Miranda didn't fall in love easily—the past fifteen years were proof of that—but when she fell, she fell hard. And she had fallen for Travis York. Trying to find another woman for him hadn't done her—or him—a bit of good.

There *was* another solution to the problem—one that required courage and a very tough skin—and was so simple, she couldn't believe she hadn't thought of it before.

I can tell him how I feel about him.

Given that the alternative was to never see him again, she had absolutely nothing to lose except her pride, and she doubted he would laugh in her face. He would be kind enough to let her down gently, and what happened after that would be his choice. Her regular lesson time was ten-thirty on Tuesday mornings. Avoiding her would be easy.

She went on with her bedtime rituals as though she'd been alone in the house. After washing her face and brushing her teeth, she turned on the fan in her bedroom, climbed into bed, and read Harry Potter until she got sleepy. It always worked. She *never* had trouble going to sleep. Tonight, however, was different.

Travis is lying in bed in the next room. He might even be naked.

Once those thoughts were in her head, they played over and over like a catchy, annoying song that no amount of tossing and turning could stop.

Then the power went off.

Without the white noise of the fan, Miranda not only had to listen to her own restless movements, but could also hear every move Travis made. He, at least, had the excuse of spending the night in a strange place. She'd heard somewhere that it took three nights to get used to a new bed. Travis only needed to stay two more nights, and he'd sleep perfectly well.

Yeah, right. I can really see that happening.

Chapter 11

The power came back on at daybreak. Miranda slept better after that, but not for long. As she awakened, her mind took off, racing from one thought to another the same as it had the night before. Was Travis awake yet? Should she let him sleep? Would the roads be passable? Would he be iced in with her for days?

No. If the power was on, most of the ice had already melted. It would be very slick, though. Melting ice was even worse than ice that was frozen solid. If she was going to tell him she was crazy about him, she had to be sure he could leave right away. She didn't want him stuck there after he told her she was out of her mind. A nasty little pain shot through her heart every time she thought about what he might say to her. His expression alone would probably break her heart.

She finally got up, noted that his door was still closed, and wandered out to the kitchen. Filling the teakettle, she set it on the stove. A glance out the window proved the ice wasn't gone completely, though it *was* melting. Water dripped from the trees and the deck railing. The rising sun reflected off the crystalline glaze, making the whole world sparkle. She fed Jade, and then put food out for the dogs, all of whom seemed to have survived the ice without further mishap. Even so, she'd be lucky to make it to the barn without breaking her neck.

The kettle was whistling when she heard Travis coming down the hall. She almost dreaded seeing his tousled hair and sleepy eyes. Hearing his yawn and the sound of water running in the bathroom was bad enough. It was too much like living with him or having spent the night with him as a lover—without any of the benefits.

Her resolve to tell him the truth was crumbling. She had to do something besides stand there waiting for the tea to brew.

Biscuits. Guys always like biscuits.

Since Levi used to ask for them every day, she didn't even need to look up the recipe. Having turned on the oven, she was collecting the ingredients when Travis came into the kitchen. His hair was too short to ever get messed up, but his clothes were wrinkled and had obviously been slept in. Barefoot, he stifled a yawn.

"Sleep okay?" she asked.

"Sure did." His voice was soft, drawling.

Her heart took a plunge when he smiled. If there had ever been a more adorable man, she had yet to lay eyes on him.

Travis was bound to have slept better than she had. After all, *he* hadn't been driven insane by the thought of her sleeping in the next room. With trembling hands, she fumbled with the mixing bowl. She hadn't been this nervous the night before, but then, she hadn't made her momentous decision until after she'd gone to bed. Clearing her throat with an effort, she asked him what he'd like for breakfast.

"Anything," he replied. "I'm easy."

If only that were true…

She glanced up in time to catch the smile that went along with his reply, and she wondered for the millionth time if he had any idea what that smile of his did to women. He was rather indiscriminate with it, so it was safe to assume that he didn't. But if he did, it was downright cruel of him to keep flashing it at her. Perhaps he thought she was old enough to be immune to that sort of thing.

Boy, is he in for a surprise…

"Bacon, eggs, and biscuits okay?"

"Sounds good."

"Looks like the ice is melting." Stirring milk into the flour, she tried to focus on the soft, white dough instead of staring at Travis. "You shouldn't have any problems getting home."

"I can probably get the truck down the drive. I might have to leave the trailer, though." He nodded toward her mixing bowl. "You don't need to go to so much trouble. Toast would've been fine."

She shrugged. "It's no trouble. I used to make biscuits for Levi every day." She could've made them in her sleep, which was a good thing considering how badly her hands were shaking. "Besides, I probably owe you more than one meal for all the work you did yesterday."

"No, you don't. And I didn't offer to do it because I expected to get paid."

"Does that mean you don't want breakfast?" The only upside to that was that he'd leave quicker and then she could relax and get back to normal or cry or tear her hair out or something. She should go ahead and tell him right now, but couldn't seem to find the words.

When it gets right down to it, I'm just plain chicken.

"I didn't say that. I wouldn't turn down breakfast if you're willing to fix it." There was that smile again.

"Perfectly willing." She dumped the dough out onto the board and kneaded it, grateful to have something to do with her hands. Patting it out flat, she had the biscuits cut out and on the pan by the time the oven finished preheating—something she'd done a thousand times before. That simple task calmed her nerves better than any drug possibly could. Breathing easier, she popped the pan in the oven, set the timer, and started on the bacon and eggs.

"Guess I'd better call Stuart and see whether he wants me to drive the backhoe home or not." He grinned. "He'd probably kill me if I let anything happen to it."

"His pride and joy?"

"Something like that."

"I'd probably feel the same way if it was mine." Her laugh didn't even sound forced, which was surprising. She relaxed even further. This was no different than fixing breakfast for Levi. "What would you like to drink?"

"Milk, please."

She suppressed the urge to roll her eyes. "I should've guessed that. A man doesn't get teeth like yours by shunning dairy products. You should be starring in toothpaste commercials." *Not sitting in my kitchen giving me fits.*

Clearing his throat, he gave her a sheepish smile. "You aren't the first to suggest that. Not my thing, though."

Miranda certainly couldn't argue with that. To be as handsome as he was, he was one of the least cocky men she'd ever met. She handed him a glass of milk just as the phone rang.

"Hi, Mom," Levi said when she answered. "Did the power go off last night?"

She couldn't help chuckling. "Should've known you'd ask me that. Yes, it was off most of the night, but it's back on now. Did it go off there?"

"Yes, and it's *still* off. I *hate* it when there's no power."

"I know, sweetie. You go on and go to work. They still have power there, don't they?"

"Yeah. I called. It's okay."

"Good. How are the roads?"

"They look okay. There's lots of cars going by."

"It's a good thing you park under that carport. Otherwise you'd be chipping ice all morning."

"Yeah. Well, I have to go now."

"Be careful."

"I will."

She hung up the phone, shaking her head. "Levi never could stand it when we lost power. Anytime there's a storm, he gets very upset—although it's better now that he's older. I used to think he was afraid of thunder and lightning, but that wasn't it. He just couldn't function without electricity. He's been like that ever since he was old enough to turn on a television."

Travis stared at her in disbelief. "You've known him that long?"

Miranda frowned. "Well, yeah. I mean, I gave birth to him and raised him and everything. It's not like I foisted him off on my parents."

Travis looked as though he'd been poleaxed—eyes wide and jaw slack. "Levi is your *son*?"

"Yeah," she said cautiously. "Who did you think he was?"

He didn't answer right away—simply sat there, gaping at her. "If he's your son, then who's your husband?"

Miranda's eyes widened in surprise. "My *husband*? I don't *have* a husband. At least, not anymore. Kris was killed in a helicopter crash about fifteen years ago."

"The Marine in the picture next to the flag. That's him?"

She nodded. "Levi was only seven when he died. I put those things in his room so he wouldn't forget his father."

"And you never remarried?"

The bacon started popping like crazy and smoke was rising from the skillet. Miranda hurried over to turn on the exhaust fan. She was flipping the bacon over when Travis came up behind her. His sudden nearness almost made her jump out of her skin.

"You didn't answer my question." He sounded irritated—almost to the point of anger.

"What? Oh—no. No, I didn't."

"Why not?"

She took a deep breath. "I–it's a long story."

"That's okay. I've got plenty of time. Start talking."

All of a sudden, she felt a teensy bit…apprehensive. "I thought you knew." She paused, frowning as she turned the bacon over one more time. "It was so long ago…"

"But you still wear a wedding ring."

"It took me forever to get over Kris's death. I didn't *want* anyone else at first, and later on, I wore it to keep men away for a different reason. Levi is mildly autistic and has some learning disabilities. You hear about stepfathers and boyfriends beating up on kids from previous marriages all the time. I couldn't risk it."

"Fair enough," he conceded. "But what about now?"

She glanced down at her ring and shrugged. "Habit, mostly. Everyone knows I'm a widow—and believe me, I know what it's like to have matchmaking friends. That's why I tried not to be too obvious about it with you. My friends nearly drove me crazy before they finally gave up."

"Why would you try to find a woman for me?"

She kept right on working, laying the strips of bacon on paper towels to drain. Cracking eggs in the skillet. Watching the edges turn brown as they sizzled in the hot grease. Sliding them onto plates when they were done. "Like I said before, you seemed…unhappy."

"*I* didn't know you were a widow. You never told *me*." He didn't sound angry anymore. He sounded hurt.

"It's not something I talk about much—and certainly not with someone…I mean, I don't walk up to people and introduce myself as the Widow Jackson." She added bacon to each plate and handed them to him.

"I can understand that. I just wish I'd known. Whenever you talked about Levi, I always assumed he was your husband. In fact, I've been dreading him coming home and finding me here." He put the plates on the table and came right back, standing so close she could've turned around and kissed him. "Why didn't you tell me?"

Tears stung her eyes and her vision blurred. "I didn't think it mattered."

"Why would you think that?" His voice was gentler now, almost a whisper.

"We're just friends—only a few months ago we were nothing more than casual acquaintances—it shouldn't matter to you whether or not I have a husband."

"That's all? Just friends?"

The timer went off. She took the biscuits out of the oven and put them in a basket. Her resolve to tell him the truth had failed her completely. "What's wrong with that?"

"Nothing. But when you were trying to find me a woman, why didn't you put *your* name on the list?"

"Because I'm too old for you." She was practically shouting. "I'm forty-five years old, and you're what? Thirty?"

"Thirty-six, actually."

"Oh, great. I'm only nine years older than you instead of fifteen. I—"

"You like me, don't you?"

"Of course, I do." She blew out an exasperated breath. "Look, let's just sit down and have breakfast. Then you can go home."

He crossed his arms and leaned back. "What if I don't want to go home?"

She glared at him. "Are you trying to drive me insane?"

A tiny grin lifted the corner of his mouth. "I certainly hope so."

She wasn't married and she thought the only thing standing between them was a nine-year age difference. He was about to show her exactly how negligible nine years could be.

Don't blow it now, Travis.

He put up a hand. "Okay. I'll sit down and I'll eat breakfast. But I want to hear everything."

She gave him an unreadable look and took a seat at the table. "There isn't much to tell. Kris and I were high school sweethearts. We got married after graduation and he joined the Marines. I went to nursing school, then had Levi. There were complications during the delivery, and he turned out to be our only child. One baby was more than enough for me, and with Kris away most of the time, I've always lived pretty much on my own."

"But you loved him."

She glanced away and let out a shuddering sigh. "Oh, yeah. He was the only one for me. Ever. Like I said, it took me a long time to get over his death. I used to pretend his leave had been canceled and that he would be coming home later. It worked for a while. Eventually, I had to face it, and by then, I was so used to being without him—or any man—I didn't feel the need to go out and find another one. Men can be so bossy and controlling. I'm too independent—too set in my ways. And then there was my son to consider."

Travis's heart gave a painful twist. That "ever" comment had him worried. "Tell me about Levi."

Her eyes grew misty. "I'm so proud of him. Everyone told me he'd never be independent, and he isn't completely—I'm still his legal guardian—but he has a job and an apartment. He even drives a car." The last word was more of a sob. She swallowed hard, giving him a watery smile. "He's twenty-two now, and I think he's found a girl he likes." Her smile shifted to a frown. "Of course, she isn't the first, and she'll probably break his heart, but at least he's out there meeting people. For a few years after graduation, there weren't any jobs to be had and he just hung around the house. He was a lot of help, but that's not the sort of life I wanted for him. This is much better."

"I'd be proud of him too. But what about you? Don't you get lonely?"

"Sometimes." She didn't elaborate, simply buttered a biscuit and took a bite. "Better eat that before it gets cold."

All Travis could hear was the clock ticking on the wall. She went on with her breakfast, obviously not intending to say anything else. He picked up his fork and did the same. When she'd finished eating, she took another sip of her tea and got up from the table in one swift, abrupt motion.

"Are you okay?" he asked.

"Yeah, I'm fine. I have to go feed the horses, and I'm not looking forward to going out in that mess."

"Do you want some help?"

She shook her head. "I do this twice a day, every day. Today is no different from any other."

She picked up his plate and set it in the sink. Travis got up and handed her his empty glass, then moved in behind her—so close he could feel the warmth of her body. Simply breathing the air around her made his groin tighten with anticipation.

He leaned in further. "When I said all the good ones were taken, I was talking about *you*, Miranda. But it turns out that you're *not* taken, are you?"

"Um, no. I guess I'm not." Turning on the water, she began washing the pan she'd used for the biscuits.

"You know, when you hugged me that day at Nigel's I remember thinking at the time what a kind thing that was for you to do. It kept me warm for a long time, but it left me wanting more, and the second time was even better." He reached around her and shut off the water. "I want to hug you again with my hands free and my coat off. Just once…" With a hand on her shoulder, he turned her around to face him.

She raised her hands in protest. "My hands are wet."

"I don't care. Dry them on me if you like."

Whereas the previous hugs had been quick and hard, this one was soft, slow, and sensuous. Smoothing his hands over her back, he realized she wasn't wearing a thing beneath her flannel nightgown, and that discovery sent even more heat rushing to his groin. His balls grew heavy and his cock pulsed with need as he lowered his head, inhaling her scent. Wrapping his arms around the small of her back, he pulled her up close, not caring that his hard cock pressed against her stomach. He wanted her to feel how much he wanted her. Her head fit nicely against his shoulder, her face nestling against his neck. When she turned ever so slightly, her lips brushed his skin— not precisely a kiss, but very, very close…

Sighing, he gave her a tight squeeze, then let his fingertips trail across her back, enjoying the intimacy. "I've wanted to do this again for a long, long time."

"It wasn't that long ago." Her voice sounded so normal, he was afraid she was unaffected.

"It seems like forever to me. You have no idea what it's like to have the woman you want more than anything try to fix you up with her friends. There was a *reason* I didn't fall for any of the others."

"I thought you were just too picky—that real women weren't good enough for you."

"No." He kissed the top of her head. "I wanted someone I thought I couldn't have. I wanted *you.*"

Chapter 12

Travis might have said he wanted her, but Miranda obviously had a hard time believing it.

"Maybe that's all it is—one of those forbidden fruit things. Now that you know I'm single, you'll probably lose interest."

"No possible way. You're so hot I can barely control myself as it is—and I don't think that's gonna change." Tangling his fingers in her hair, he tilted her head back until their eyes met. Her green eyes were streaked with gold, a detail he hadn't noticed before. But then, he'd never held her quite this close. "You know what *I* want. Now it's *your* turn."

She glanced toward his lips, hinting at the prospect of a kiss. What would it take to make her do it?

"I'll help you any way I can, Miranda, but I promise not to try to run your life. It's your life, your call."

When her mouth dropped open in surprise, he was sure he'd said the wrong thing. But in the next breath, she said the words he was dying to hear.

"Kiss me."

Travis wanted to shout with joy. Dipping his head, their lips met and hers parted, his tongue instantly filling the void. Delicious flavors mingled with the warmth of her tongue. The last thing she'd eaten was a biscuit topped with strawberry jam, adding flavor to a kiss that was already the sweetest of his life.

Her fingers threaded through his hair, and her back drew his hands like a magnet. The curves he'd caressed with his eyes he now caressed with his palms. As she slid her hands beneath his shirt, passion sizzled where she touched him, sending flames of desire racing up his arms, engulfing his heart before diving down to ignite an inferno in his groin.

Travis kissed his way across her face and down her neck as her head fell back in rapturous abandon. When his lips met the neckline of her nightgown, he longed for her to be naked in his embrace, allowing him full access to her body. His hands roamed ever lower, gliding over her hips, cupping her bottom and pulling her against him. Rocking her back and forth over the hard length of his erection, he ground his sex against her in a way that left no doubt as to where this kiss was headed.

Gazing up at him with heavy-lidded eyes, she trailed her fingers down his arms, then pushed up his shirt, exposing his chest and the taut nipples that cried out for her touch. Her hungry eyes seemed to devour him, their bright green shade now as dark as a raging sea. In an instant, she lunged upward, flinging her arms around his neck as she captured his mouth in a heated kiss.

This time, she was the aggressor, plundering his mouth as though intent on annihilating any resistance. She met none. He opened for her, a groan rising from his throat as she explored his mouth and dueled with his tongue. Moving on to the rest of his face, she cupped his cheeks in her hands, raining kisses everywhere her lips could reach.

Suckling his earlobe, she flicked it with the tip of her tongue, drawing a deep, shuddering sigh from him that seemed to escalate her desire. She kissed her way down his neck, then moved to the opposite side, sucking his skin so hard she nearly drew blood. His cock surged as he thought of her sucking him a little further down.

As if she'd read his mind, she hooked her thumbs on the waistband of his sweats and tugged, but they didn't budge. Only then did he remember the drawstring waist.

Damn...

Her attempt to get into his pants was all the encouragement Travis needed. Reaching down as far as he could, he fisted his hands in her gown and pulled. Miranda met him halfway, dropping to her knees and raising her arms. Tossing her gown aside, he let his eyes roam over her delectable body.

Oh, my God. She's actually naked.

Without a moment's hesitation, she yanked open the tie at his waist and skimmed his pants down so fast his dick sprang up and bounced off her face, leaving a glistening trail across her cheek. He was about to apologize, but her open-mouthed expression stopped him.

Sitting back on her heels, she stared at his cock. "Wow."

He got a brief glimpse of her succulent tits before she leaned forward, wrapping her hand around his shaft. Pressing the slick glans against her cheek, she let it glide over her skin in an exotic massage that made them both moan.

Much more of that, and I'll come right in her face.

Travis was perilously close to losing what little control he had left when she exhaled sharply and lurched forward with the force of an orgasm. Gasping as her forehead impacted against his groin, she clutched at his thighs and threw her head back, catching his cock with her lips. After one delirious moment of anticipation, she sucked him in.

Her hot mouth on his dick nearly had him spewing down her throat, but he held his breath, gripping the edge of the sink with one hand and bracing the other on the table. She teased his balls with her fingertips, pushing him ever nearer to the brink.

Oh, God...please, not yet... Though it *would* have been a first.

The point of no return was almost in sight when she let go, giving him an instant to gather his wits before her tongue swept over his scrotum. His cock pulsed, sending more pre-cum spurting from the slit. If he'd thought she would find this repellant, he'd have been wrong. With a low growl, she took a sip from the head of his penis, then bathed his scrotum with his own slick fluid.

Lost in the most intense pleasure he'd ever known, Travis didn't realize her full intent until her lips closed over a testicle. Sucking it into her mouth, she caressed it with her tongue, forcing a cry from him that fell somewhere between a groan and a whimper. She kept on with this exquisite torture until his head was spinning, then she switched to the other side. In his entire life, no one had ever licked his balls, let alone sucked them. His eyes squeezed shut as his knees gave way, and he staggered sideways, nearly tripping on the clothing looped around his ankles. Kicking his pants aside, he collapsed into the chair beside him.

Stroking his cock with one hand while circling the head with the palm of the other, she drove him even further toward the edge of his sanity. He could easily have come right then, but there were a few things he needed to do first.

Summoning every scrap of willpower he possessed, he grasped her hands and surged to his feet, draping her arms around his neck as he rose. With a firm grip on her buttocks, he turned and sat her on the table, shoving everything aside before easing her down onto her back. His beautiful Miranda lay stretched out before him, a cloud of chestnut hair fanned out behind her head. Glittering green eyes beckoned to him like a siren's song. Rosy nipples adorned full, round breasts, her chest tapering to a trim waist before flaring out at the hip.

Beautiful...

He stooped down and snatched up his pants, withdrawing a condom from the pocket. "Do I need this?"

A single shake of her head was the only reply he needed before sending the unopened packet sailing off in the general direction of the trash can. Scooping up her legs, he moved in between them, pulling her feet up to rest on his shoulders. Without another thought, he plunged into her.

Her tight, wet heat enveloped his cock, providing some relief at first, but the intensity quickly ramped up again as he rocked into her. He could hardly believe this was happening. The night before, he'd fallen asleep wondering what it would be like to make her moan. Now he knew, and it was far better than he'd ever dreamed.

But he wanted more.

Following several hard thrusts, he forced his own urgent needs aside to concentrate on her pleasure. Varying the angle, he finally found one that made her eyes roll back in her head and turned each breath she took into a moan. He closed his eyes to block out the visual, knowing that one glimpse of her would be the end of him.

Letting her response be his guide, he slowed the pace, stroking her with his cock, feeling his way toward her orgasm, hoping his own could hold off a little longer. In his haste, he'd already forgotten to do so many things that would have ensured her enjoyment. However, something told him this wouldn't be their one and only time together. He would have years to discover the best ways to make her scream in ecstasy.

As her inner muscles gripped his dick and a climactic cry erupted from her throat, he gave in to temptation and opened his eyes.

He'd thought Miranda was beautiful before, but the sight of her lost in the throes of orgasm ripped away the last shred of control. He slammed into her, drinking in her blissful expression and the gentle sway of her tits as they rocked to the rhythm he'd set.

Moments later, his back arched and his cock thrust forward with an ejaculation so powerful it seemed to lift him off his feet, leaving him gasping for breath.

Leaning forward, he planted his palms flat on the table, gazing at her with awe. "Oh, my *God*. Hot doesn't even begin to describe *that*. Where did you *ever*…"

The words had barely left his mouth when her face flushed red and he knew he'd said the wrong thing.

"I have to feed the horses." In her haste, she pushed him away so abruptly he almost fell on his ass. He had no idea what to say to her now.

She was halfway to the door when he finally found his tongue. "Miranda, wait. I'm sorry. I didn't mean that in a bad way. I'm just sort of…stunned."

Snatching clothes from a hook in the hallway, she put them on faster than he would have believed possible. "It's okay, Travis. I need to get some air or something. This is…I don't know…embarrassing."

"You don't need to be embarrassed. That was incredible. Hell, *you're* incredible."

She hesitated, frowning. "You really think so?"

"I *know* so."

The smile she gave him was tentative at best. "Okay. But I still have to feed the horses."

He wanted to tell her to stay put, that he'd do it all for her, but he'd already promised he wouldn't try to run her life. He had to let her go. "Be careful out there."

This time he got a grin. "You won't leave before I get back?"

He shook his head. "Trust me, I'll be right here waiting for you."

"Naked?" The accompanying flick of her brow reassured him more than anything else could.

"As a jaybird."

Laughing, she closed the door behind her.

Travis turned around to find a black cat sitting in the middle of the kitchen floor, gazing up at him with emerald eyes. Only then did he realize he was still wearing the T-shirt. "I must look damned silly," he muttered. "No wonder she was laughing."

With a wide yawn, the cat began licking its paw.

"Obviously *you* aren't impressed." He scowled at the cat. "I'm pretty sure *she* liked my dick, though. She even said 'wow' when she first saw it. That has to count for something."

The cat shook its head and sauntered away.

Great. Now I'm trying to impress her cat. I must be losing my mind...

Surveying the kitchen, he felt a smile tugging at his lips as he thought about all the wild, kinky things he could do with Miranda when she came back from the barn. Right after he stripped off her clothes, he was going to suck her tits and eat her pussy.

"Should've done that before. I knew I was forgetting something."

He glanced out the window and spotted her filling the bird feeder. She seemed to have decent traction, leaving deep footprints in the crusty ice as she made her way across the yard to the pasture gate. A yellow Labrador and a Golden Retriever trotted behind her while the beagle bounded on ahead. Her horses waited in the paddock, and she rubbed the nose of the chestnut colt before unlatching the gate. She must've had to shove it pretty hard because in the next second, her feet slid out from under her, and she fell, hitting her head on the steel rail before landing in a heap on the ice. The gray mare ambled over and gave her a nudge. Miranda never moved.

"Holy shit!" Racing to the door, Travis gathered up his clothes and got dressed even faster than Miranda had. He had to force himself to slow down. He'd be no help to her if he fell flat on his back. Fearing the worst, he started off across the ice, his heart pounding a rough rhythm he wasn't sure would ever settle back down.

හ)ශ

Miranda looked up into Kira's dark, fathomless eyes.

The mare blinked slowly. "Come on, Miranda. I'm hungry. I promise not to let you fall. Hold my tail and I'll help you up the hill."

Turning, she swished her glistening white tail. Miranda did as she was told and together they walked up the gravel path to the barn, Kira's powerful hindquarters pulling them both up the slope.

"Here you are, safe and sound," Kira said when they reached the barn. "You can let go of my tail, now." She walked into her stall, leaving Miranda standing by the tackroom door.

"Good morning, Miranda." Jadzia's voice was soft and breathy. "My back still hurts. You weren't planning to ride me, were you?"

"Don't be an idiot," Kira admonished her daughter. "It's too cold today, and the footing is terrible. Show some sense, girl."

Kes walked in briskly, her nose stuck out and her ears laid back. She might have seemed hateful, but Miranda knew she didn't mean anything by it. "Hey, Mom. Kiss me hello. I've missed you. Kira wouldn't let me in the barn last night and I've got ice all over me!"

She wasn't kidding. Icicles dangled from her mane and tail and there were even a few clinging to the long hair on her flanks. They clinked together like wind-chimes as she moved.

"Poor girl." Miranda gave the stocky mare a kiss on the hollow spot by the corner of her mouth. "Get in your stall where it's safe. Kira can't pick on you there."

As Kes whisked by and ducked into her stall, Arwen made a grab for her, ears laid back and teeth bared.

"Be nice, Arwen," Miranda snapped. "And get back in your stall."

"I *am* in my stall," the tall filly insisted. "It's not my fault I can reach that fat little cow from here."

"Now, now… Let's not be hateful," Miranda warned.

"Hey, who was that guy that was here yesterday?" Kes asked. "He was really cute. Did he spend the night with you?"

"Sort of," Miranda replied. "The roads were too slick for him to drive home, so he slept in Levi's room."

"Too bad," Kira said. "He's just the kind of stud I like. Not too big, not too small, just right."

Kes nodded vigorously. "Yeah, just right."

"Oh, what would you know?" Kira snorted in disgust. "You've never even been bred." She shot a stern glance at Miranda. "Don't run him off, Miranda. He's a keeper."

"That's funny. You never seemed all that taken with him before," Miranda remarked. "What made you change your mind?"

"Dunno," Kira replied. "Guess he's grown on me."

Arwen tossed her mane. "Well, *I* think he's too short."

Kira blew out a haughty breath. "Height isn't everything. Your dad was tall, but he was an ass. Now, Damar's father…" She paused as her eyes took on a dreamy cast. "He wasn't young and he wasn't tall, but that stud could fuck with the best of them."

Jadzia ducked her head down behind the stall door, visibly embarrassed by this frank sexual discussion.

"Kira!" Miranda chided. "Such language—and in front of your children!"

Damar danced with enthusiasm. "I want to do it with Kes. Please don't have me gelded before I get the chance."

Kes tossed her bushy black mane. "You're too young for me."

"You wait 'til spring, hot stuff. I'll be tall enough by then. Be ready for me, baby."

"Oh, shut up, you guys." Miranda went into the tackroom. She'd filled three of the buckets when Damar came through the door.

"Dammit, Damar, how many times do I have to tell you to keep out of here?" She picked up a training whip and waved it at him.

"Hey, watch it with that thing," he said. "No need to get all kinky on me."

"He probably wants you to put mineral oil on his dick again," Arwen shouted. "He won't admit it, but he loves that."

"I only do it to get the crusty stuff off his penis," Miranda called back. "It probably does feel good, though."

"What on earth are you talking about?" Damar demanded. "Are you okay?"

"I'm fine. Get out of the tackroom. No horses allowed in here, remember?"

"Uh-huh," he said with a touch of sarcasm. "How many fingers am I holding up?"

Miranda snorted a laugh. "You don't *have* fingers. You have hooves, and you can only hold up one at a time."

The girls must've thought that was terribly funny. Miranda could hear them snickering out in the barn.

"Yeah, right. Let me see your head." Damar nuzzled her temple. "You are *not* fine. You're bleeding and you're limping."

"Will you get out of here?"

"Okay, okay." His voice took on a patronizing note, like someone attempting to placate a mental patient. "Go ahead and finish feeding the horses, but after that, we're going to the hospital for a CAT scan."

"A CAT scan?" Miranda waved dismissively. "I've had scads of them and they're always negative. What would you know about stuff like that, anyway?"

"Enough to know you need one."

She laughed at the absurdity of Kira's nine-month-old colt giving her medical advice, but stopped abruptly as a sharp pain knifed through her side. "Dammit, Damar, you kicked me!"

"No, I didn't. You fell by the gate and hit your head. I'll bet you broke a couple of ribs, too. Come here for a second."

Turning her around, he kissed her—a slow, sweet, penetrating kiss that reminded her of something she thought she should remember...

Travis arched an eyebrow. "Now, do you *still* think I'm a

horse?"

Chapter 13

Miranda knew she was in for a tongue lashing as soon as she saw the tall, dark-haired nurse behind the glass partition to the ER.

"You didn't drive yourself to the hospital with a concussion again, did you?" Denise demanded. "You've obviously hit your head. What happened this time? Did a horse throw you or kick you?"

Miranda gave her an evil look. "Neither. I slipped on the ice and hit my head on the gate when I went to feed the horses this morning."

"I knew there had to be a horse involved somehow." With a smug smile on her baby-doll face, Denise didn't look like the sort of woman to have any intelligence at all, but sometimes she had way too much. "What else did you hurt?"

"Maybe some broken ribs, and my knee hurts, but I don't think it's serious." She knew from past experience what a *serious* knee injury felt like.

"Any memory loss or loss of consciousness?"

"I'm not sure." She touched the bump on her head. "I feel like I've missed something, but I have no idea what it was. Plus, my horses were talking to me."

"Uh-*huh*." Denise was clearly debating whether she needed to call in the orthopedic doc or notify the Behavioral Health Unit. "Hearing voices?"

Miranda gave her a cheerful nod. "Just lock me up in the psych ward. I'm sure I'll feel right at home with all the other nut cases."

"I think we need to take a few x-rays before we make any rash decisions. Come on back." She stopped and leaned over the desk, checking up and down the hall. "Dammit, Miranda. You *did* drive yourself here, didn't you?"

"No, this time I had a ride *and* a witness to the accident."

The last time Jadzia had thrown her, she'd been alone. She'd come away with a strained knee ligament, a concussion, and no memory of falling off *or* hitting the ground. Denise had been on duty that day as well, and she'd given Miranda hell for driving herself to the hospital. *She* thought she'd done pretty well to drive a truck with a clutch when her left knee didn't work right, but Denise had yelled at her.

There's no justice in this world...

"He's parking the truck," Miranda said. "He'll be here in a minute."

Her eyes lit up. "*He's* parking the truck? You've got a *boyfriend?*"

"Not exactly. Travis got stuck at my house last night when he came out with his brother's backhoe to dig a ditch around my barn. All this rain we've been having kept flooding it, and I guess he got tired of hearing me complain."

"Uh-*huh*," she said again, arching her brow. "The freezing rain didn't start until late, Miranda. Are you telling me he was out digging ditches in the dark?"

"Well, no," she admitted. "I sort of paid him for the work by fixing dinner for him, and then we watched a movie. He went to leave at about eleven and it was too slick by then, so he spent the night."

Denise was giving her that *yeah, right* smirk again.

"He slept in Levi's room! Don't look at me like that. Really, we didn't—"

She paused as a brief flash of Travis's face popped into her head—as if she was staring up at him from the middle of the kitchen table. She could even see the light fixture above his head. Then it was gone.

Weird.

"Poor Travis. Now everyone will think I've been sleeping with him, and all he did was dig a ditch around my barn. He probably won't ever offer to help me again, and I wouldn't blame him a bit."

Travis came up behind her. "Blame who for what?"

"Blame *you* for not ever wanting to dig a ditch for me again.

I'm sure you never bargained on having to stay the night and then take a crazy woman to the emergency room."

"Beats watching Saturday morning cartoons with my brother." He glanced at Miranda with a conspiratorial smile. "Much more exciting."

He seemed to be attempting to convey something significant, but whatever it was, she wasn't getting it. Truth be told, she wasn't getting a lot of things that morning. She hoped to figure it out eventually, but she also knew that memory loss was sometimes permanent. The fall she'd had with Jadzia still haunted her, mainly because she couldn't recall what had actually happened. All she remembered was Jadzia tossing her head and backing up. The next thing she knew, she was in the barn with a twisted knee and a splitting headache.

Miranda followed Denise into Room 6 and climbed up on the stretcher. Travis sat down on a chair in the corner.

Denise nodded at him. "Do you want him to wait outside?"

"He can stay if he wants to." She held out her arm while Denise applied the blood pressure cuff. "He might as well get his money's worth."

"The heat isn't working in the waiting room, anyway. It's freezing out there." After checking vital signs and making a few notes on the chart, she took Miranda's insurance card and went to get the doctor.

A few minutes later, Dr. Schwartz wandered in wearing rumpled scrubs and moccasins. "Well, let's see now…a bump on the head and a knee and rib injury." After studying the chart, he peered at her over his thick lenses, waggling his bushy eyebrows. "Looks like we need another CAT scan, don't we?"

"Very funny." The fact that Miranda had been scanned more than anyone else on the staff was a standing joke. One of the techs suggested she schedule them on a monthly basis, which was silly, since this was only her fourth in the past eight or nine years.

After checking her pupils, he poked around on her ribs. Then he wiggled her knee cap and tested the range of motion in the leg. "I guess we need some chest x-rays and one of the knee, too." He glanced briefly at Travis and then turned back to Miranda. "You're not pregnant, are you?"

Miranda sighed. She was tired of having to answer that question and wondered how old she would have to be before they finally stopped asking it. "Not a snowball's chance in hell."

Travis opened his mouth as though about to say something, but seemed to think better of it.

Dr. Schwartz simply nodded. "Okay, then, let's get those films and we'll go from there." He shuffled out of the room, leaving her alone with Travis.

"Why did they ask if you were pregnant?"

"X-rays can affect the baby during the first trimester," she explained. "They ask any woman of child-bearing age that question before taking any pictures. It's one of those cover-your-ass things."

He nodded. "I see. And you're sure you wouldn't be?"

"Oh, yeah. I haven't needed birth control since Levi was born." Aside from the fact that a woman actually had to have *sex* to get pregnant…

Rodney came breezing in wearing the same smug expression as Denise. He'd been the one to run her previous scan and often teased her about having seen her brains. Other men may have seen various intimate parts of her body, but *he* had looked into her mind.

Miranda groaned. "Oh, no. It had to be you, didn't it?"

"Ooh, *baby.*" He smacked his lips. "I get to look at your brains again—and your knee and your *chest*. I'm getting hot just thinking about it." Rodney didn't seem like the type to ever get hot about anything. Tall and skinny with a beak of a nose, he didn't have enough hair on his head to hold in any warmth whatsoever.

"If your wife knew how excited you get from looking at x-rays, she might make you quit and do something else."

He shook his head. "Nah. She doesn't mind. We all have to get our jollies somehow. Besides, isn't it thrilling to see a man enjoying his work?"

Travis frowned. "He's kidding, right?"

Miranda shrugged. "No clue. For all I know he might actually be telling the truth." Rodney was rarely serious about anything, though he did take a nice x-ray. She'd never had to go back for repeats whenever *he* took the films.

"Maybe I'd better go with you, just the same." Travis stood up and gave her a wink. "You might need protection."

Rodney clutched a hand to his heart. "We won't be alone? He doesn't *trust* me with you?"

"It's okay, Rodney." She laughed, then clutched her own chest. "Dammit, Rodney. Will you hush up? It hurts to laugh."

"Oh, please forgive me, dearest." Rodney's voice dripped with solicitude as he wheeled the stretcher through the door. "I wouldn't hurt you for the world. I promise to be on my best professional behavior from now on."

"I certainly hope so," Travis muttered.

"You've got to excuse these guys," she told him. "I not only work here, but I'm what they call a frequent flier."

"Meaning?"

"I get hurt a lot. My old chart must be into its second volume by now."

Rodney nodded. "Oh, at least. Your file here in x-ray is *huge*. Brains, knees, fingers, feet, ankles, and now, ribs."

"And my right hip," she reminded him. "Don't forget that one."

"How could I possibly forget that?" He heaved a sigh. "My only regret is that I wasn't here to do it."

"Me, too. Becky tried three times before she got it right."

Rodney sniffed. "She doesn't enjoy her work the way *I* do." Turning the corner, he bumped the stretcher into the door jamb.

Miranda let out a yelp.

"So sorry, dear. Allow me to apologize for my atrocious driving." He rolled the stretcher close to the table and she scooted over as best she could while holding on to her side.

Donning his lead apron, he nodded at Travis. "You should probably wait outside. You might want to father children someday."

"I don't think it matters." Travis gave her another wink, but stepped out of the room anyway.

After shooting the films, Rodney wheeled her over to the next room and parked the stretcher next to the scanning table. Miranda hitched over onto it, biting her lip as her broken ribs grated together. Settling herself on the hard, flat table, she heard Rodney in the control room doing his standard lounge lizard routine, putting a radiological spin on the theme from *Star Wars*.

"CAT scan...beautiful CAT scan. Wonderful CAT scan. Get one today."

The man truly did enjoy his work.

Having finished the scan, he danced out of the control room. "I didn't see any big, honking hematomas, but I did see *I love you, what's his name* scribbled all over your brains. What did you say his name was?"

She scooted back onto the stretcher. "Whose name? You mean Travis?"

"Yeah, that's it." He leaned over the end of the stretcher to adjust the pillow under her head. "That's the name I saw on your scan, dear. All over your pretty little brains."

"Nonsense. You didn't see anything of the kind."

"Did too."

"Did not."

"Did too."

"Dammit, Rodney. You're going to make me laugh again."

"Oops! Sorry dear—force of habit. I positively *adore* making you laugh."

She arched a skeptical brow. "Me and everyone else, so you can stop trying to make me feel special. I'm just another collection of bones and brains to you."

"Ah, but they're such *nice* bones. Some beauty is only skin deep, but yours goes all the way through."

She rolled her eyes. "For heaven's sake, don't start that again."

"But it's true," he insisted. "Don't you think so?"

This question was directed at Travis who had returned from the waiting area. "Think what?"

"That she's beautiful all the way to the bone."

Travis smiled. "Yes, I do. Even the broken ones are pretty."

Miranda scowled at him. "Has he been showing you my old x-rays? That's a breach of confidentiality, Rodney. HIPPA will get you for that."

"I didn't have to see the x-rays," Travis said. "I've got eyes."

Rodney gazed at him with newfound reverence. "Ohhh…x-ray vision! You are one lucky man."

"Shut up and drive, Rodney." Miranda growled. "I'd like to get home before I have to feed the horses again."

Travis patted her hand. "Let's wait and see what the doctor says about that."

She glared at him. "Oh, really?"

"Really. I've always heard that doctors and nurses make the worst patients, but I never believed it until now."

Miranda snorted a laugh. "Not true. Beyond a shadow of a doubt, the worst patients are the overdoses. The only kind that might be worse is a drunk with an upper GI bleed."

"She's got you there, pal," Rodney said with a nod. "You should try taking pictures of a drunk sometime. It's a real bitch."

Travis was undeterred. "If the doctor says you can't lift or he wants you to stay in bed for a few days, I'll feed the ponies for you. Just tell me what to do and I'll do it."

Rodney leaned down to whisper in her ear. "You'll never get a better offer. I've never said that to a woman in my life."

"Yeah, well, *you* wouldn't," Miranda drawled. "You'd dearly love for a woman to get hurt worse so you could take more x-rays of her."

He rubbed his chin, pursing his lips. "Hmm…hadn't thought of that."

She heaved a weary sigh. "Just drive, Rodney. I *really* want to go home."

Chapter 14

Travis held his breath as Dr. Schwartz flipped through the radiology reports. "The knee is only bruised, you do have a mild concussion, and there are three broken ribs—"

Miranda grimaced. "I knew that."

"I'm going to let you go home," he said with an inflection that suggested he would've preferred to keep her overnight. "But you have to take it easy for a few days. I've written an excuse from work for two weeks, and in the meantime, don't lift anything heavier than a bottle of water. In light of the concussion, I'd rather not give you anything stronger than Tylenol or Motrin for the pain. We'll give you an incentive spirometer to use every two hours to prevent pneumonia."

"Pneumonia?" Travis echoed. This was a complication he hadn't considered.

"The spirometer encourages her to take deep breaths," Dr Schwartz explained. "People with broken ribs tend to breathe more shallowly than normal, which can cause secretions to pool in the lungs and possibly result in pneumonia. You'll need to make sure she uses the spirometer as directed. Plus, you need to assess her neurological status every two hours for the first twenty-four and every four hours for at least another day after that. If you notice any significant changes in her level of consciousness, bring her back here immediately. We'll print out a list of instructions for you."

Travis nodded, not only relieved that the news wasn't nearly as bad as it could have been, but also pleased that he now had the perfect excuse to stay with Miranda for a few days. "No problem."

"So much for the trip to the ER," she muttered after the doctor left. "Guess I'd better take my note up to the unit."

"Want me to take you in a wheelchair?"

She scowled at him, but she didn't refuse, which seemed a little out of character. *She must be in more pain than I thought.*

As he wheeled her into the ICU, although Travis felt completely out of his element, Miranda seemed right at home. "Holy cow, Lola! What on earth did they have to pay you to get you to work the day shift?"

The tall blonde grinned as they approached the desk. "Night shift differential, time and a half, plus the call-in bonus. You better believe I did some wheeling and dealing before I said yes." Her smile disappeared as she leveled a disapproving glare at Miranda. "What happened to you *this* time?"

"I fell on the ice when I went to feed the horses this morning." Miranda held up the note from the doctor. "Is Jeni here? I need to give her this."

"She's on break." Lola blew out an exasperated breath. "Those horses are going to kill you someday—either that, or you'll wind up permanently crippled. *Then* what will you do?"

Miranda shrugged. "Retire on disability, I guess. Just remember, I can out-walk you even with a brace on my leg."

"True," Lola admitted. She glanced at Travis. "I've already had one knee worked on, and it took so long to heal I didn't have enough sick time left to fix the other one."

"Unlike me, who's one of the walking wounded whenever I get hurt," Miranda said. "I've had to wear leg braces and use crutches, but I've always been mobile."

"You *still* need to be more careful."

"I *am* careful. I can't help it if Mother Nature is always slamming me with mud and freezing rain."

"And evil horses," Lola added.

"They aren't evil," Travis said. "One of them helped her up after she fell."

Miranda twisted her head around to look up at him. "Really? You mean I didn't imagine that?"

"No. Kira nudged you a couple of times and then after you got up, you held onto her tail while she walked to the barn. I'd have thought she would've kicked you, but she didn't seem to mind at all."

Lola's eyes narrowed with suspicion. "And where were you when this happened?"

"Watching from the kitchen window. After she fell, I got dressed and went up to the barn to check on her."

She arched an eyebrow. "Got *dressed*?"

Travis didn't blush very often, but his face suddenly felt very hot. "Well...I did have to put on my coat and boots."

"It's a long story." Miranda handed over the doctor's statement. "Give this to Jeni when she comes back, and I'll tell you about it later."

Lola chuckled. "I can't wait to hear *that* story. Call me when you get home."

"I will." Miranda glanced up at him again. "Okay, Travis. I'm ready whenever you are."

He drove her down to the emergency entrance, parking the wheelchair inside the sliding glass doors. The weather had warmed up even further, and the ice was melting rapidly.

"Great," Miranda grumbled. "Just what we need. More water."

Travis stifled a laugh. She certainly had a one-track mind when it came to rain. "Better wait here while I go get the truck."

"I can walk," she protested. "No one said anything about not walking."

"Yes, but that doctor told you to take it easy for a few days, and I had to go a long way to find a parking space."

Although he suspected she would've argued about it under normal circumstances, like riding in the wheelchair, she seemed to accept it and waved him on. "I'll wait right here."

Travis set off at a brisk pace, hoping she wasn't in too much pain, and also wondering why she kept downplaying the fact that they were lovers. He felt like shouting it to the world. Still, she'd been pretty embarrassed when she left for the barn. He wanted to kick himself for letting her go alone.

I would pick one that's too independent for her own damn good.

Even so, he wouldn't change a thing about her. She'd been badly hurt and had yet to shed a single tear. Smiling to himself, he realized something else. He was proud of her. She was tough, resilient, and one absolutely incredible lover. His balls tingled at the memory.

Of all the times to get hot and bothered...

Miranda watched Travis walk away, only then allowing herself to fully acknowledge the pain. About the only part of her that didn't hurt was her left arm, and she was very glad he'd talked her into waiting for him. Thank God he'd been there to drive her to the hospital—although, if she'd been alone, she might have stayed home and saved the insurance company a little money. She was happy to have the time off from work, though. If nothing else, getting that doctor's statement made the trip worthwhile.

Taking care of the horses would be the tough part. Although Travis had said he would feed them, she doubted he would actually be willing to drive back and forth to her farm twice a day. It would've been different if his house was right across the road, but she had absolutely no idea where he lived. Even so, as bad as she felt, she was willing to take him up on his offer—regardless of any inconvenience to him.

No, that isn't the reason.

Her accident had nothing to do with it. She wasn't totally incapacitated, and if she had to, she could do the chores herself. It was the fact that Travis was the one offering his assistance that made her willing to accept it. Having him visit twice a day was worth a few broken ribs. Still, she saw no reason to let herself get soft and vowed not to let him do anything that wasn't strictly necessary.

As he drove up to the loading dock, she got to her feet, amazed at how stiff her knee had become in the short time she'd been sitting in the wheelchair. He'd pulled up close to the curb, but when she opened the door and put her left foot on the running board, her right knee wobbled painfully, threatening to give way beneath her.

Travis hopped out of the truck. "Will you hold on a second and let me help you?"

She shook her head. "I should be able to get up there by myself."

Ignoring her protest, he gave her a boost into the seat. "That's why I'm here, dear. And don't worry, I won't think any less of you for being a wuss." Closing the door, he went around to the other side and climbed into the driver's seat.

"I am *not* a wuss."

Her indignant reply only made him laugh. "I know that, but right now, being a wuss is understandable. I saw the x-rays."

She blew out a sigh. "I don't know if I can stand to sit around and vegetate for two weeks. I'll go nuts."

"I promise to keep you well entertained." His wicked smile and sly wink made her wonder just what sort of entertainment he had in mind. *Oh, surely not....*

"Don't you have to work?"

"Yes, but my schedule is pretty light this time of year. It would be different if it was the middle of show season. I'm booked solid then." He paused, his concern evident in his frown. "I don't like seeing you like this. Just this morning you were—"

"Were, what?" Beyond a vague recollection that her horses had been talking to her, Miranda didn't remember very much about the state of her health that morning. "I mean, other than the fact that I probably had unscrambled brains and no broken bones."

With an odd little grin, he reached over and buckled her seat belt. "You seemed perfectly fine to me." He started the engine. "How about I take you home, run the backhoe over to my brother, and then come back? Do you need me to pick up anything on the way?"

She shook her head. "I went to the grocery yesterday. And don't worry. I managed to keep going with a concussion and my leg in a brace once before. I'm sure I can do it again."

This time his frown displayed more annoyance than concern. "Aren't you taking this independent woman thing a little too far?"

"I live alone, Travis. It's not like I have much of a choice."

Scowling, he took a deep breath and remained silent for a few seconds, leaving her to suspect that he'd counted to ten before opening his mouth. "I'm not denying you your independence, but I *am* supposed to check on you every two hours. Remember?"

She grimaced. "Oh, yeah, right…forgot about that."

"Apparently." He still seemed irritated, which was odd for a man who was usually smiling. Then again, she'd been surprised the night before when he'd claimed to be unhappy.

Which proves how little I know about him.

"Look, I'm sorry for being such a pain. I just don't like the idea of putting you to so much trouble."

If anything, this seemed to increase his irritation. "Do you really think I consider taking care of you as trouble?"

Anyone else would've considered it a royal pain in the ass. Obviously he had a different opinion. She threw up her hands in surrender. "Okay, you win. If you insist on being my caretaker, then so be it."

"And after a week or so, we'll reevaluate your, um, *need* for me." His slow, suggestive smile and the flick of his brow made those innocent words seem strangely seductive.

Miranda stared at him, convinced she couldn't possibly have read that correctly. Then again, there had been that funny little wink a moment ago…

My brains must be more scrambled than I thought.

Mentally reviewing the events of the morning, she couldn't recall a single thing that would've explained it. She'd been nervous as hell, had made breakfast for him, and then went to feed the horses. But before that, Levi had called, which was when Travis figured out she wasn't married.

Was that all it took? Surely there would have to be more to it than *that*. Was it something she'd missed or something she'd forgotten? She wasn't about to ask him to explain. That would be much too embarrassing, especially if romance was as far from his mind as it ought to have been. In the end, she simply agreed and tried to settle in for the drive home.

Unfortunately, she couldn't find a comfortable position, nor would her befuddled brain leave her in peace. She recalled her intention to tell Travis how she felt about him, but had she actually done it? He hadn't protested when her friends had assumed he was her boyfriend, and he was acting very strangely. Did he really consider himself as her new love interest? With that spin on it, his behavior made more sense.

There was no reason for him to pretend. Being the "significant other" of a patient in the ER allowed him to stay in the room, but that was about it. Besides, she'd told Denise he could stay, even after denying any romantic involvement with him. The only reason Rodney had asked him to step out of the room was to limit his exposure to radiation. Granted, Denise had said there was no heat in the waiting room, but he wouldn't pretend to be her boyfriend simply because of that, would he?

Should she come right out and ask him if they were dating now? She'd talked herself into telling him the truth before, and even then, she'd had nothing to lose—although she *did* have something to lose now. She'd lose his help for the next several few days, and whether she cared to admit it or not, she was lucky to have it.

The best she could do now was to follow his lead and see where it took them. If he continued to seem interested in romance, she certainly wouldn't complain. After all, she'd had the hots for him for months. Having him return those feelings would be a dream come true. She simply didn't want to risk jumping to any conclusions that would make her look like an opportunistic cougar.

Still, she did have a bona fide excuse for odd behavior, at least for the time being. Almost anything could be explained by the concussion or the pain—and it wouldn't be far from the truth.

All she had to do was be nice and not fuss at him when he tried to help out. Unfortunately, that attitude was a bit out of character for her and might make him suspicious. He might even be suspicious already.

Be yourself, Miranda.

There was only one problem with that. She wasn't completely sure who that person was anymore.

Chapter 15

Travis parked the truck as close to Miranda's doorstep as possible, set the brake, and unbuckled her seat belt. "Do me a favor and *wait* for me this time?"

Lowering her head, she grumbled a bit before replying, "Don't worry, I will."

He got out and opened the passenger side door, then helped her turn to face him. Her dogs were milling around, obviously anxious to see her. He looped her arm around his shoulder. "Try to land on your left foot."

"That's my plan." Nevertheless, she yelped as he slid her off the seat. Shifting his hold on her, he held her steady for a moment before starting toward the porch. Fortunately, there were only two steps and she took them one at a time, leaning against him while putting most of her weight on her left foot.

"At least I've got one good arm and leg—although the left side of my butt hurts as much as the right, and I didn't even fall on that side—at least, I don't think I did. Weird, huh?"

Travis could think of at least one reason why her hips might be sore, but opted to suggest a possible cause that was a little less provocative. "Must be from sitting in the truck for so long."

"Probably. My knee is really stiff, too." A sidelong glance accompanied her tight smile. "I'm pretty sure I can make it from here. You can let go of me now."

"Not a chance," he said. "If I didn't think it would hurt you even more, I'd carry you."

Her attempt at a chuckle came out as more of a gasp as she clutched her side. "You're such a sweet boy, taking care of a banged-up old woman like this."

Travis suspected that was the concussion talking rather than

Miranda, but he went along with the game anyway. "Aw, shucks, ma'am. It's no trouble at all."

He helped her across the threshold and into the house and gave her a gentle hug. To his delight, she kissed him on the neck, filling him with warm, fuzzy feelings that somehow managed to settle right in his dick. He gave her another squeeze. "That's my girl. Now, let's get you out of this coat."

He held her left sleeve while she pulled her arm out of it, then carefully pushed her coat off of her right arm.

She was panting by the time they'd finished. "How did we ever get this thing on me?"

"No clue." He tossed her coat over the chair by the door. "Do you want to go to bed or sit on the couch or what?"

"I think I'll just have a seat in the kitchen. I seem to feel better sitting straight up than I do lying down. Besides, I'm not sure I could take another step if my life depended on it."

She looked exhausted—the lines around her eyes were more evident than usual, and her face had gone pale—so he didn't argue, simply pulled out a chair and eased her down onto it. "Better?"

She heaved a sigh of relief. "Much."

"Would you like to change into your nightgown? You might be more comfortable."

She glanced down at her clothes with a grimace. "None too clean, am I? I'd at least like to get out of this bra. The underwire is sitting on my broken ribs."

"No problem." He went around the table and retrieved her gown from where he'd tossed it earlier that morning. Odd that he'd be putting it *on* her now, rather than taking it off. Undressing her had been much easier then—and certainly less painful. He tried to be gentle, but even pulling up the back of her shirt and unhooking her bra made her gasp. "You okay?"

"Oh, *yeah*." Her shoulders sank as she visibly relaxed. "*Much* better. You have no idea. Thank you."

"Ready for the nightie?"

She nodded. "Just strip me down and throw it on me."

With the image of her sprawled naked on the table still fresh in his mind, the urge to act on that suggestion was overwhelming. Even so, he was fairly certain she hadn't meant it literally.

Must be the concussion talking again.

"I can do better than that." Kneeling down, he pulled off her boots and socks, then helped her stand and slipped off her jeans. He'd have liked to dispense with her panties, as well—his original plan to suck her tits and eat her pussy when she came back from the barn was still on his to do list—but under the circumstances he thought it best to leave them on.

Standing behind her, he pulled her shirt off over her head, gathered up her gown, and dropped it around her neck. "I'll let you take it from there." No way was he going to take off her bra. The compulsion to do more than simply gaze at her fabulous boobs would be too much to resist.

"Slippers," he muttered. "You had on slippers… Ah, there they are." He had no clue how they'd wound up under the table, but then, he hadn't been concerned with footwear at the time.

"You know, for a non-nurse, you're doing pretty well," she said as he slipped them on her feet. "You must've taken care of sick old women before."

"Now, Miranda," he chided. "You're not sick and you're not old. You're injured."

She waved a dismissive hand. "Same difference. I certainly *feel* like someone's sick grandmother."

"Yeah, well, trust me, you don't look it." Generally speaking, grandmothers didn't make his dick hard, whereas Miranda could do it without even trying. "I'll put some more wood in the stove before I leave."

"That'd be great."

While he built up the fire, Miranda's cat strolled over and rubbed against his leg. He paused to pet her before adjusting the dampers. Getting to his feet, he went back in the kitchen. "What's the cat's name?"

"Jade. I named her for the color of her eyes."

"Nice cat," he remarked. "Very friendly."

"She loves to sit by the stove—probably considers anyone

who'll keep the fire going to be a worthwhile human being."

He glanced down at Jade, who was staring at him again. "Never knew cats were that easy." If only it were as simple with Miranda. True, they'd had wild monkey sex on the kitchen table that morning, but something told him that episode was only the first hurdle. "Can I get you anything before I go? A cup of tea, maybe? I won't be gone long."

She shook her head. "I'll be fine. Take your time and be careful."

While he appreciated her concern for his safety, he'd have felt a hell of a lot better if she'd told him to hurry back. "I will."

₨⌒

Miranda would've stayed right where he left her if she hadn't been in serious need of a potty break. Drawing in a fortifying breath, she braced her hands on the table and hoisted herself out of the chair, then shuffled down the hall to the bathroom, making full use of the chairs, doorjambs, and wainscoting along the way.

While there, she made the mistake of glancing at herself in the mirror. The huge, bloody bump on the right side of her head made her look like something out of a zombie movie. Denise had cleaned off most of the blood, but a cut that hadn't been deep enough to warrant stitches was still oozing.

At least I don't have a black eye. Yet...

Pulling up her gown, she inspected her ribs, finding a nasty-looking bruise, but no open areas. The knee wasn't too bad—only bruised and skinned. However, when she leaned over the sink to rinse the blood out of her hair, a bout of dizziness forced her to abandon the attempt. After popping some ibuprofen, she went back to the kitchen.

While brewing a pot of tea, she nibbled on a leftover biscuit. Someone—she wasn't sure who—had put them in a plastic bag. She couldn't remember doing it herself, and it didn't seem like the sort of thing a man would do, although Travis *could* have done it. He'd already surprised her several times, and the day wasn't over yet.

As promised, she gave Lola a call, regretting it almost immediately.

"That was the guy from the Christmas party, wasn't it?" Lola asked, sounding simultaneously suggestive and accusing.

Miranda had hoped she'd forgotten. "Um, yeah."

"I thought he was dating your friend Christina. What happened with that?"

Nope. Nothing wrong with her memory. "Not much. Apparently, I really suck at matchmaking. She thought he was boring, and he was convinced they had nothing in common."

"So you decided to keep him for yourself?"

If only it were that simple. "Not exactly. He offered to dig a ditch around my barn and wound up having to spend the night because of the freezing rain. He was here when I fell, so he drove me to the hospital—and that's all. Honest."

Lola snorted a laugh. "It didn't seem that way to me. He sure acted guilty when I questioned him about getting dressed—like he'd really had to get *dressed,* if you know what I mean. He seemed sort of possessive, too—the way a man is with a woman he's staked a claim on."

Miranda's eyes widened. "Whatever gave you that idea? He didn't say anything of the kind."

"It was his body language more than anything he actually said."

If Lola had noticed it, Miranda couldn't very well deny the possibility any longer—the way he acted at the hospital, then driving her home and helping her change clothes. If only she had something more to go on than body language... "I still don't know...he's so much younger than I am."

"And that makes it impossible? No, trust me on this one, Miranda. He likes you, and not just as a friend."

If only that were true. Miranda still couldn't allow herself to believe it—not yet, anyway. Perhaps later, when her brain wasn't quite so fuzzy. "I'm still not sure about that. If he was interested in me, why would he let me introduce him to my friends?"

"Did he know that was why you invited him to the party?"

"Well, no, but he figured it out right away. If he'd wanted me, he should have said something then."

"Maybe he thought you didn't like him if you were trying to fix him up with someone else," Lola suggested. "Did you ever think of that?"

"No, I didn't." She paused, frowning. "No, wait. I remember now. He thought I was married."

"Of course he did," Lola snapped. "And I know why. You should've taken that ring off years ago. Kris is gone. You need to admit that and move on."

"I know," Miranda groaned. "It just seemed so wrong to take it off at first. Then later, I used it as a deterrent. I never told Travis I was a widow because I didn't think it mattered. I never *dreamed...*"

"Well, maybe it's time you did." Her tone was softer now. "You've dedicated your whole life to raising Levi, and you've done a terrific job. You deserve to dream a little."

"Maybe. But you of all people should know how controlling men can be—and how unreliable. I've always thought Travis was a nice, handsome fellow, but—"

"Has he seemed controlling?"

"Not really, no."

"Or unreliable?"

"No. He said he'd dig the ditch on Friday afternoon, and that's exactly what he did."

"Sounds like a winner to me," she declared. "Is he still there?"

Miranda couldn't help chuckling. Lola's husbands had all been losers—the first guy left her for another woman, the second was a controlling asshole, and the third was a pathological liar. The fourth wasn't proving to be any better than the rest, which made Lola's opinion essentially worthless. In this particular instance, however, Miranda tended to agree. "He took the backhoe home and said he'd be back in a little while."

"He'll be back," she promised. "He's not going *anywhere.* Now, do me a favor and get well quick so I don't have to work with that idiot Sheila any more than I have to already."

"I'll be back in two weeks," Miranda protested. "How bad could it be?"

"She offered to work extra while you're laid up, and I was scheduled to work four nights with you. Now three of them are with her."

"Don't worry. I heal quickly." *Most of the time.*

"Of course spending two weeks off with Travis might make you want to stay on sick leave forever."

Miranda ignored the hint of suggestion in her tone. "I doubt it. It'll probably be very boring."

Lola began laughing hysterically and was still laughing when she hung up. Miranda's friends were always seeing things she couldn't. Nonetheless, Travis had said he'd be back, and he hadn't lied to her yet.

Yeah, right. I'll believe it when I see it.

Chapter 16

Travis returned an hour or so later with several bags of groceries and lunch from Dairy Queen. "I thought you might be hungry, so I brought you a cheeseburger, fries and—" Reaching into the bag, he pulled it out with a flourish. "A Dilly Bar."

Miranda had been sitting there wondering if he would ever come back at all, and he'd brought her a Dilly Bar.

The man is a prince. If she hadn't been giggling so hard, she would have cried. Of course, giggling made her ribs hurt so much, she still felt like crying.

"Thanks, Travis. That was awfully sweet of you."

He dropped the ice cream bar back in the bag and put it in the freezer. "I wasn't sure what you'd like. I thought about getting you a Blizzard, but I've never known *anyone* who didn't like Dilly Bars."

"I know someone who doesn't even like chocolate. She'd never touch a Dilly Bar." Sheila had a number of peculiar traits. The chocolate-hating thing was simply one of the more obvious. "I think she needs a CAT scan, myself."

He nodded toward her teacup. "I see you've been up. How'd it go?"

"Not too bad," she replied. "Walking seemed to help the stiffness in my knee."

"Maybe we can take a stroll after dinner." He set her lunch in front of her and sat down to eat his own. "I really enjoyed our little walk from the truck." He followed that statement with a quick wink and a significant flick of his brow.

The last time they'd been walking together, he'd hugged her and she'd kissed him on the neck. Not only had he come back afterward, he'd brought her ice cream. Maybe Lola was right after all. Maybe *everyone* was right.

Unwrapping her hamburger, she took a bite, only then realizing how hungry she was. "You weren't gone long. You must live pretty close."

"About ten minutes from here," he said. "I spent more time at Dairy Queen than I did driving back and forth." He paused, taking a sip from his cup. "It didn't take long to unhitch the trailer and throw some clean clothes in a bag."

Clean clothes? Why on earth would he need clean clothes? Then she remembered he was probably still wearing Levi's underwear. Even so, he could have brought those back anytime. There was no need for him to return them right away.

"You usually feed the horses at about four, don't you?"

She nodded, thanking God for a neutral topic. "Sometimes it's later, but in winter, they're usually waiting at the gate by three."

"That shouldn't be a problem. I'm home by five during the week. I can stop by my place on the way if I need to pick up anything." He studied her as though trying to gauge her reaction. "You don't mind if I stay here, do you? It would be a lot easier— especially since I have to check on you every two hours tonight."

Of course he did. *Why do I keep forgetting that?*

Concussion, Miranda... She shrugged in what she hoped was a nonchalant manner. "Sure, whatever works best for you."

You can stay forever if you'll kiss me once in a while and bring me Dilly Bars.

Swallowing hard, she sat up a little straighter as she suddenly remembered that he *had* kissed her. The horses had been talking to her, and she'd thought he was Damar until he kissed her—in a very *un*-horsey way. But that hadn't been the first time, had it? She couldn't actually remember another kiss, but it had seemed so familiar at the time...

She glanced over to find Travis staring at her, a French fry poised before his parted lips.

"Don't worry. I'm not having a seizure. I just remembered something—at least, I *think* I did." She rubbed her head and blinked. "It's hard to tell."

"It must have been pretty important," he said. "You looked like you'd seen a ghost."

"Not exactly. Tell me something, though. When you came up to the barn, what was I doing?"

He bit back a smile. "You were putting feed in the buckets and talking to me like I was one of the horses."

"Anything else?"

Chuckling, he picked up another French fry, dipping it in catsup. "You said it was pretty silly for a horse to think you needed a CAT scan."

Her withering glance didn't stop him from smiling. "Did you do anything to convince me you weren't a horse?"

His smile broadened. "You mean you don't remember?"

"I *think* I do, but I'm not completely sure."

"I kissed you. It seemed a better way of bringing you to your senses than slapping you. I mean, you'd already been hit on the head once."

"That's…logical." Apparently, it took having hallucinations to get a kiss from him. She could fake them, of course, but that kind of behavior was liable to get her committed if she kept it up. *Better not risk it.*

His brow rose. "What's the matter? Am I starting to look like a horse again?"

She rolled her eyes. "Not unless you've suddenly grown a tail."

Popping up from his chair, he twisted around to check the seat of his pants. "I *have* got a tail! You'd better kiss me again, quick."

"Now, Travis," she chided. "I'm the one who's been seeing things, not you."

Bracing a hand on the table, he leaned down until his wicked smile was a breath away from her lips. "Maybe it's contagious. You'd better kiss me again, just to be sure."

The twinkle in his eyes melted her resistance, luring her ever closer. Sighing, she yielded to the desire she'd held in check for so long. If he wanted a kiss, she would make it one he would never forget.

Reaching up, she slid her fingers through his hair and pulled him down. After the first tentative touch, her tongue slipped past his lips as she devoured him. The flavor may have been burger and fries, but the feeling was pure Dilly Bar—melting, chocolaty, delicious Dilly Bar. As she deepened the kiss, a surge of passion flooded her body before sinking down to pool in her core. A blast of searing heat followed, growing hotter as it neared the combustion point.

Suddenly their roles reversed and he became the aggressor, his kiss driving her head firmly against the hand he'd tangled in her hair. His intoxicating lips stole her reason, his tongue probing gently before penetrating her mouth to caress her from within.

Moments later, he broke off the kiss and glanced over his shoulder. "It's still there. Better kiss me again. Kissing you makes all the bad things disappear."

And all the pain vanish...

Cupping his cheeks between her palms, she feathered kisses over his softly parted lips. She'd wanted to do that for *so* long...

A groan escaped him as though wrenched from the depths of his soul. "Oh, Miranda," he whispered. "You have no idea what you do to me."

He had no idea what he did to her, either. She thrust in deeper, her tongue dueling with his until she couldn't stand it anymore and sucked it, hard.

Moments later, he drew back, his breath coming in short panting gasps. "I don't think I can take much more. I'm—oh, help me, *please*." His hand gripped his belt buckle, the inference quite plain.

She stared at the bulge in his groin, filled with a hunger that had her licking her lips in anticipation. Their eyes met for an instant as she nodded in reply. With a quick flip of the buckle and the grate of the zipper, his jeans fell to his knees, leaving his hard, drooling penis right there before her lips. A growl rose from her chest as she sucked him in, her own body awash with a need so powerful it shocked her far more than the sheer audacity of what he'd suggested—perhaps even expected—her to do. Without hesitation, she did the same things to his cock that she had done to his mouth—licking, sucking, nipping...

A brief upward glance triggered an overwhelming sense of déjà vu—like she'd done this before, or at the very least dreamed about it. Blinking back the vision, she sucked harder, coating her tongue with the slippery fluid that spilled out of him. She was drowning in his essence when his breath caught in his throat. He pulled away with an anguished cry, but his climax never came.

"I…can't." His eyes were dazed with some emotion she couldn't read. "Use your hands, *anything*. I never could—"

Miranda had no idea what it was he couldn't do, but putting her hands on him seemed like excellent advice. Lacing her fingers together, she slid his dick through the tight tunnel between her palms. Three strokes later, he doubled over, catching himself with a hand slammed against the table.

His semen hit her shoulder like a blast from a high-powered squirt gun. She'd heard stories about the occasional guy who could hit the ceiling but had never really believed it was possible until now. Kris had never even come close to producing that much force. Travis, on the other hand, could've fired a shot out of a second-story window from the basement.

Okay, so that's a slight exaggeration, but still…

She leaned back in her chair searching for a topic to lighten the mood. "It's a good thing you put the Dilly Bars in the freezer."

He gasped with breathless laughter, still holding onto the table for support. "I think I need one now. I'm about to burn up."

"My point, exactly. The heat you're putting out would melt a lot more than ice cream." She hesitated, unsure whether to delve further into the subject, but she simply had to ask. "So, when did you decide I was someone you had the hots for? I had no idea."

He gave her a puzzled look as he pulled up his jeans. "I would've asked you out last spring if I hadn't thought you were married. I've been fighting the attraction ever since I spotted your ring."

That explained a few things, but not why he thought he could kiss her and then expect her to go straight to cocksucking. Whether she'd been willing to do it or not, looking back on it now, it seemed a bit presumptuous. There were plenty of women who would've flat-out refused, no matter how much a man begged. Miranda wasn't one of them, and he *had* phrased it as a request. Travis wasn't the type to insist or use force, so she could have said no. The funny thing was, he hadn't seemed to expect a refusal.

Then there was that feeling of déjà vu. If she'd done it before, his behavior wouldn't have been remarkable in any way. She wished she could ask him, but it would've sounded too ridiculous, something along the lines of *Hey, Travis—I forget—have I sucked your dick before? It seems sort of familiar…*

She was about to chalk the entire episode up to her rattled brains when she noticed Travis peering at her chest. "Did I, um, hit you?"

"With what?"

"With this." Chuckling, he pointed at her shoulder. "Sorry about that." Snatching a napkin from the table, he wiped his semen off her gown. "Do you want to put on a clean one?"

She shook her head. "It's not worth the trouble." Unsure of the proper etiquette for the situation, she did her best to seem nonchalant, as though she always had white stains on her nightie. She wondered what would be appropriate to say next. *Thanks for letting me suck your dick, Travis. I'll just finish my lunch now…*

Which seemed like a good idea, actually. Picking up the remains of her hamburger, she took a bite.

Travis winced. "It's cold, isn't it?"

"Kinda," she admitted.

"Guess I should've let you finish it first."

She giggled. "Oh, I don't know… It's probably best to do that sort of thing on an empty stomach, don't you think? I mean, what if I'd gagged and thrown up?"

He stood there for a moment, pensively chewing his lip. "I never thought of that. I've been fighting temptation for so long, I guess I lost my head. At least I didn't nail you on the floor."

"I probably would've raised a ruckus if you had. Lying on my back hurts like the devil. Those x-ray tables almost killed mc."

He frowned with concern. "How are you going to sleep?"

"I never sleep on my back, anyway. I should be able to lie on my left side. I'll be fine. Don't worry about it."

"I can't help worrying about you, Miranda. When I saw you fall this morning, I…I thought I'd lost you, just when things were starting to look up."

"Look up? I'm still in the dark here. All this time I've been listening to your sob stories and trying to fix you up with my friends, you never once hinted that you were interested in me. This whole thing has come at me out of the blue, so forgive me if I seem hesitant."

"I understand that, but why didn't you ever give me any hints? I didn't even know you were single. Why didn't you ask me for a date?"

She shrugged. "I'm not really sure. I guess I assumed you knew I was a widow—that maybe Nigel had told you—and you'd already ruled me out. I didn't want to make a blunder that would ruin our friendship. I should have stopped wearing my ring years ago, but there were valid reasons for it—at least, there were in the beginning." She knew it sounded lame, but then, most misunderstandings do once they're explained. "I thought about telling you or taking off my ring, but if I did and you still weren't interested…well, I didn't want to have to face that."

"I don't know why you'd think I wasn't interested. You're a beautiful, kind, intelligent woman. I'm surprised no one has tried to snap you up whether they thought you were available or not. Of course, most decent guys won't look past the ring."

"But you did."

"Yeah, well, I'm not proud of it." Grumbling, he ran a hand through his hair. "If my father had any idea I'd been lusting after a married woman, he'd pound me to a pulp. At least I waited until I knew you were single to make a move."

"True." And it had been one hell of a move. She blew out a breath. There was still one more obstacle to overcome. "Another reason I didn't say anything to you was because I'm so much older than you are."

"Honestly, the age difference doesn't matter to me." His lips curled into a grin. "Besides, you look incredibly hot—for an old girl."

She rolled her eyes. "Gee, thanks. In my present state that makes me feel *so* much better."

Travis had to bite back a laugh. "I thought it might. Can you think of anything else that might make you feel better?"

She shrugged. "I'll take a shower later. That usually helps."

The image of her wet *and* naked sent blood rushing back to his groin. *I will* not *shove my dick in her face again.* At least, not for a while. "Don't suppose I could wash your back, could I?"

She smiled as though she knew exactly what was going through his mind. "You can if you like, but I really don't think it'll be necessary. I can still function—as long as I don't make any sudden moves."

"You don't need me to do anything?"

She shook her head. "Just feed the horses and give me a Dilly Bar."

"No foot massage? No back rub?"

She raised a skeptical brow, no doubt imagining where that sort of activity might lead. "I'd like to finish eating *something*— something nutritious, that is. Your ding-dong is tasty, but if you keep this up I'll starve to death."

He hung his head in an attempt to appear guilty but simply didn't have it in him. He didn't *feel* guilty. In fact, he felt happier than he had in years. "How about if I nuke your hamburger?"

"Sure. If it'll make you feel better."

He gathered up her cold lunch and practically tripped over a chair in his haste to get to the microwave.

Great. Now she'll think I'm a klutz.

Fortunately, her microwave wasn't the type that required a book of instructions to operate. No point in making her think he was klutzy *and* stupid. When her lunch was nice and hot, he carried it over to her and sat down, resting his cheek on his fist, unable to take his eyes off her. She had no idea how wonderful she'd made him feel. None.

She must've been starving because she ate quickly, which made him feel even worse for having interrupted her meal. However, it wasn't until she swallowed the last French fry that he realized what her curious glances meant. He was staring.

"I'm making you nervous, aren't I?"

"A little," she conceded. "There's no need for you to hover."

"I'm not hovering. I'm…admiring you."

"Is that what you're doing?" Gathering up the empty wrappers, she stuffed them in the bag, turning away as though trying to avoid his gaze. "I feel like a bug under a microscope."

"You don't want me to look at you?"

She shook her head. "I didn't say that, but really, Travis, you don't need to be quite so attentive. I'm not going to die right in front of your eyes."

"Maybe not, but when you fell this morning, there for a while, I thought you had. Give me a chance to get over it, okay?"

Her eyes widened briefly before narrowing into a frown. "I'm sorry, I didn't realize it bothered you that much."

His heart took a rather painful dive and his eyes stung with unshed tears as he recalled seeing her head slam into the gate— perhaps the worst moment of his life. "You have *no* idea."

She searched his face as though she didn't quite believe him, then her expression changed, becoming more thoughtful. Glancing away she sat silently for several moments, the knuckles of one hand pressed to her lips. When she spoke again, her voice was barely audible. "I think I do, actually." A smile touched her lips so briefly he wasn't sure he'd seen it. "Don't mind me. I can be a crotchety old woman sometimes."

"And right now, you have every right to be crotchety, whether you're an old woman or not." He stopped short, closing his eyes. "I'm talking too much."

"Not really, but you do seem…different."

She was the reason for the change in him, even though she still didn't seem to understand that. "If I'm different, it's because of you." The corner of his mouth lifted in a smile. "I'm very sorry you got hurt, but aside from that, this has been the best day of my life."

She smiled back at him, but the slight tilt of her head conveyed her doubt. "Really? The best day of your life? How so?"

The incredible sex was only part of it, though the way she'd pounced on him that morning would remain permanently etched on his memory. The time they'd spent sitting in the emergency room would've been boring with anyone else, yet all of it seemed special, simply because they'd been together.

"I got to spend it with you."

Chapter 17

While Travis put away the groceries, Miranda made out a list of her barn chores along with a description of each horse and how they should be fed. Travis knew enough about horses to understand the dangers of overfeeding them, so she wasn't too concerned, which was a first for her. She'd rarely trusted the feeding chores to anyone, not even Levi, who was as meticulous as anyone with autism.

She brewed another pot of tea while Travis was gone and was sitting at the table, sipping from her favorite mug when he returned. "Any problems?"

He shook his head as he pulled off his jacket. "Not a one. I did notice a few broken windows up at the barn, though. I can fix them if you like."

Miranda practically had to bite her tongue to keep from telling him not to bother when she remembered her intention to be more accepting of his help—plus the fact that this was a task she'd already given up on herself. "Go right ahead. I fixed some of them, but only the sections that slide. I couldn't figure out how to replace the glass in the stationary windows."

"I know how," he said with a wink. "I can pick up the glass on Monday."

"Thanks. I'd appreciate that." She thought she'd handled that rather well—until his amused grin proved her wrong.

"Didn't cut your tongue to say that, now, did it?"

She set down her cup. "Damn it, Travis, I'm trying. Give me a break."

"I was all set to argue with you, but I can't say I'm disappointed. I'd much rather kiss you than waste time arguing." Toeing off his boots, he padded into the kitchen, his stocking feet barely making a sound. "Although that 'kiss and make up' stuff is sometimes worth it."

"If you say so."

Kris had rarely been around to fight with, and she sometimes wondered what their marriage would've been like if he hadn't joined the Marines. He'd been content to let her manage the household in his absence, but if he'd been home, would he have felt the same way?

Miranda had become even more independent after his death, and now that Levi had left the nest, all she wanted to do was to raise a few horses. Her nursing job provided her with income, and though she enjoyed her family and friends and was always there whenever Levi needed her, she'd striven to avoid needing anyone herself.

Leaning on Travis was a luxury she couldn't afford. She'd relied on Kris and he'd left her—not intentionally, of course, but the effect was the same—and she never wanted to feel that bereft again. Being gracious and thankful was fine as long as she didn't allow herself to become complacent. It was too dangerous.

With that in mind, she thought it best to retreat to a safer topic. "Glad the horses behaved themselves for you. They can be a little rowdy at times."

"They went right into their stalls, just like you said they would. You've got them pretty well trained. I'll have to get you to train my horse—if I ever get one, that is. I haven't had a horse of my own since I was a kid."

"I'll be happy to sell you one of mine," she said. "Nigel wants Arwen, but I don't know *what* I'm going to do with Jadzia. Her back is always sore and I haven't been able to ride her much. She might do better with a smaller rider, but I'm not sure I'd trust her with a child. She needs someone with more experience. Kes might suit you. She's like a sports car—very quick and responsive."

"I wish I could, but I don't have a place to keep a horse right now, and I refuse to board one. Do you have any idea what the monthly board bill is at Nigel's?"

"Yeah, and I wouldn't want to pay it, either. My horses don't cost me that much in *four* months, and there are five of them. Of course, I already have the land and I'm not trying to make a living raising horses—at least, not yet. Nigel has to make a profit." She paused, blowing out a breath. "I sure hope he buys Arwen. I know she'll make a great jumper, and I won't be sorry to see her go. She's really nasty to Kes and Jadzia."

"Any idea why?"

"She thinks they're too short." Pausing, Miranda took a sip of her tea. "She thought you were too short too."

Travis stared at her as though she'd just escaped from a psych ward. "Excuse me?"

She shrugged. "That's what she said this morning. Kes thought you were cute, Kira said you were just right, but Arwen thought you were too short. Jadzia was embarrassed by the whole discussion."

He laughed. "I suppose you'd have to have another concussion to hear any more of their opinions."

"I guess so. It was certainly interesting. You should have heard them giggling when I said you had hooves and not fingers."

When he sat down at the table, Miranda tried to ignore the feeling of closeness—as though he'd lived with her for years and actually belonged in her kitchen. "What did their voices sound like?"

"About the way you'd expect," she replied. "Kira's voice was deep. Damar's was high-pitched like a little boy. Arwen sounded like a bitchy teenager—that sort of thing."

"Well, if you ever hear them talking again, let me know and I'll run you back over to the hospital—in fact, I'm not sure I shouldn't do that right now."

She made a face at him. "You're no fun at all—although Kira thought you would be."

"Uh-huh," he said. "I'm not even going to ask what she meant by that. I don't think I want to know."

"It was just girl talk." She waved a dismissive hand. "You wouldn't understand."

His eyes narrowed. "You're only *remembering* all of this, aren't you? I mean, should I be concerned?"

She couldn't help laughing. "Careful, there, Travis. You're asking the crazy woman if you should be concerned about her sanity. Not sure I'm a very reliable source right now." Noting his uneasy expression, she reached for his hand and gave it a reassuring squeeze. "No, really. I'm okay—still a little fuzzy at times, but that's normal. Besides, *remembering* hallucinations isn't a bad thing. I've had perfectly lucid patients tell me all about the spiders they saw crawling on the ceiling when they were confused. The bad thing is *having* them."

He still seemed uncertain, his expression wary. "And you aren't hearing the cat talking to you or anything like that?"

"No. Nobody's talking to me except for this handsome fellow sitting at my kitchen table—though my vision is a little fuzzy." Squinting, she studied him closely. "You *are* real, aren't you?"

"*Very* real." Taking her hand, he raised it to his lips for a kiss. That brief contact felt more real to her than the pain in her side.

"Good. If I wake up in the morning and find you've disappeared, I'll know I need help."

He smiled. "Don't you worry about that. I'll be right here."

₭ℂℛ

Miranda went out to the living room and attempted to read after lunch, but her blurry vision and the sounds of Travis tidying up the kitchen distracted her from the story. If he hadn't been doing a better job than she normally did, she would've told him not to bother—especially when it occurred to her that he might be paying her back for sucking his dick. She already owed him for the ditch and figured that should have made them even—until she remembered that last night's dinner had been payment for the ditch. Perhaps he'd want another blow job for fixing the windows.

My brain is so *fucked up...*

Tossing her book aside, she turned on the television. The Weather Channel predicted rain. Again. She wished they'd lie once in a while, if only for the sake of variety.

She flipped through the channels, looking for something light and mindless—certainly nothing as emotional as *The Bridges of Madison County*. Sitting through that with Travis had been a huge mistake.

But he was her boyfriend now—sort of—and curling up on the couch to watch a romantic movie together wouldn't be quite so awkward. Or would it? She was still a little confused about the whole boyfriend/girlfriend thing. It was like waking up in Vegas after a three-day drunk to find yourself married to a total stranger.

She tried watching *Demolition Man*, but it was too loud and she'd never much cared for Stallone anyway. The History Channel was airing a program on the natural history of sex. *Not quite up to that...* She went back to the Weather Channel, thinking perhaps they'd changed their minds about the rain. *Not a chance.*

In the end, she opted for the episode of *Andy Griffith* featuring Aunt Bea's efforts at making homemade pickles. Unfortunately, all the laughing she did made her broken ribs hurt worse than ever.

When the show was over, she struggled up off the couch and went to see what Travis was up to. She paused at the threshold as her mouth fell open with surprise.

I'm hallucinating again.

The kitchen was spotless. Travis, on the other hand, had a smear of chocolate on the front of his shirt and was licking his finger, looking more adorable than ever.

"Brownies?"

"Aw, you spoiled the surprise." He popped the pan in the oven. "You were supposed to stay put for a while." Already irresistible, he added insult to injury by flashing that devastating grin at her again. What was it she'd vowed not to do? Become dependent on him? Fall head over heels in love with him?

That man is gonna break my fool heart...

She cleared her throat, recalling that Aunt Bea and her pickles had given her the perfect excuse. "I need some more ibuprofen."

"You should have asked me," he scolded. "I would have brought it to you."

"Yes, but I also have to go to the bathroom, and I don't need any help with that. I think I'll go ahead and take a shower while I'm there."

He sniffed as though pretending to fight back tears. "You're not even going to let me wash your back, are you? You never let me do anything interesting."

He was teasing her, of course, but she wasn't sure how to respond. She could think of a couple of "interesting" things he'd done that day—although perhaps he didn't count changing her clothes or getting his cock sucked as interesting.

I wonder what it would take...

"Sorry, Travis. Perhaps another time."

"Okay. Holler if you need anything. The brownies should be ready to eat by the time you're finished."

She shuffled off to use the restroom, popped two ibuprofen, and then gingerly pulled her gown off over her head, stifling a yelp as she raised her arms. Stepping beneath the steaming spray, she sighed with pleasure. After washing her hair, she reached for the soap but couldn't find it. Travis must've used up the last of it when he showered the night before.

"Travis!"

He burst through the door. "What's wrong? You didn't fall, did you?"

"No, I just need some soap." She tried to maintain a normal tone, but it wasn't easy, considering that she was wet and naked with only a shower curtain between them.

"No problem. I would have gotten it out last night, but I forgot to ask you where you kept it."

"It's in the cabinet above the toilet."

She could hear him rummaging around in the cabinet. "The sandalwood or the verbena?"

"Verbena," she replied.

She waited while he unwrapped the bar, putting her hand up over the curtain rod to take it from him—a position which offered him an excellent view of her bruised ribs when he pulled back the curtain.

"Whoa, that's one helluva bruise," he exclaimed, running his fingers over it. "That *has* to hurt."

Snatching the soap from his hand, she jerked the curtain shut.

"The rest of you looks just fine, though."

"Thanks, Travis," she snapped. "You may leave now."

She could hear him chuckling as he returned to the kitchen. At least they were even on that score—although she had yet to see all of him naked at the same time.

She finished showering without further incident and got out to dry off, catching a glimpse of herself in the full-length mirror mounted on the inside of the bathroom door. Frowning, she turned and peered at what had caught her eye.

There were bruises on her butt that looked for all the world like fingerprints. That explained the soreness, but not how they'd gotten there. As she stared at them, she suspected this might be something she would never remember, like the fall that had caused her last concussion. This wasn't the first time she'd found bruises she couldn't explain, but those were usually minor and could be attributed to general klutziness. These, however, were evenly spaced and were essentially the same on both sides. For the life of her she couldn't imagine what she could have fallen against that would leave marks like that.

How weird...

ৡৢৣ

The brownies were already cooling on a rack when Miranda returned to the kitchen wearing a clean gown and a robe, looking calm and refreshed.

Travis, on the other hand, was as hot and bothered as ever. The vision of her wet, naked body had made his dick so hard he was surprised it hadn't exploded. Nevertheless, he somehow managed to control his lust, simply smiling at her as he poured her a glass of milk. "Feel better now?"

She nodded. "Much."

"Glad to hear it." She certainly looked better. Her hair was soft and shining, rather than caked with blood, although she still moved stiffly as she took a seat at the table. "I didn't get any frosting for the brownies, but there's ice cream left from last night. I figured we could put that and some chocolate syrup on top."

"Chocolate syrup?" she echoed. "I don't have any—along with

several other things I've learned not to keep in the house. I only had pie and ice cream last night because Levi was supposed to come home for the weekend and I thought you might stay to dinner."

"Oh, come on," he argued. "Everybody has chocolate syrup."

"Not me, I don't—" Her expression suddenly went blank as she stared off into space, tracing her bottom lip with the tip of her tongue. Several moments passed before she tossed him an apologetic glance and a sheepish smile. "Sorry. I thought I remembered something."

He blew out a breath. "I sure will be glad when you're over that concussion. It freaks me out when you do that."

"Me, too." She shuddered, drawing her robe more tightly around her neck. "Imagine what it's like from my side—tiny bits of memories keep flitting through my head. It's like trying to remember a dream. The harder I try, the more it eludes me."

"Spooky," he agreed. "You don't remember falling, do you?"

She shook her head. "I don't even remember leaving the house."

"Weird." Cutting the brownies into bars, he put two of them on plates and then topped them with a scoop of the ice cream. "No chocolate syrup, huh? I suppose whipped cream is out of the question."

"Oh, no. That sort of thing is *way* too hard to resist. Just knowing it's sitting there in the fridge is enough to trigger a binge."

He arched a brow. "Really? You're prone to binges? I'd never have guessed that from the way you look."

"You'd be surprised. I can resist apple pie—up to a point—but chocolate is my downfall. I'll probably have all of those brownies eaten before morning."

"Sorry, I just wanted to do something special for you—something you might like."

"I didn't say I didn't like it—and it's not a problem as long as I keep that stuff out of the house. Once in a while is fine."

I've really blown it now... "Well...if that's the case, you'd better not look in the refrigerator."

"Why not?" Casting him a worried glance, she began chewing

her fingernail. "What else did you bring?"

"Cookie dough."

She whimpered as though tears would soon follow. "Chocolate chip?"

He nodded. "'Fraid so."

"Please tell me you didn't get peanut butter." Evidently, this was even more of a temptation than cookie dough.

I am in deep doo-doo now…

"Sorry," he said with a grimace. "Peanut butter is a staple at our house. Not sure I can live without it."

She snorted a laugh. "I hope you can live with a woman who's as *big* as a house. When it comes to peanut butter, I have no resistance whatsoever."

"Don't worry. I'll help you work it off. I can think of a couple of ways for you to get more exercise right off the top of my head." *Like fucking me senseless.* Or perhaps he could ration the peanut butter—and the chocolate syrup. Smeared on his dick, a little would go a long way. He almost came in his jeans at the thought of her licking him clean.

"I work out several times a week," she said. "But that's probably not what you meant."

"Not exactly. Look, don't worry about gaining weight for now." He gave her a plate along with a cheeky grin. "Once you're all healed up, I plan to give you a run for your money—and I promise you'll like it even better than chocolate."

Chapter 18

Snuggling up with Travis while they watched TV later that evening would've been wonderful, but since sitting bolt upright was her only comfortable position, "snuggling" was impossible. Eventually he wound up stretching out on the couch with his head in her lap, which was very nice, although it did make her wish his hair was long enough for her to play with. His short, sandy spikes suited him, however, and as long as they came with the rest of him, she really couldn't complain.

She sat there alternately dozing and eating the brownies he fed to her until her yawns became almost continuous.

"Think maybe it's time for bed?"

She nodded, yawning again. "Good idea."

Travis stood up and held out a hand. "I'll put some more wood on the fire and then take a shower."

Smiling up at him, she placed her hand in his. Even with his assistance, she was only able to get to her feet very slowly. "Thanks. This damned knee is still pretty stiff."

He threaded his fingers through her hair and bent to give her a quick kiss. "That's why I'm here...among other things."

Patting his cheek, she caught a glimpse of the cat just as she looked up from her perch on the back of the couch. Blinking with apparent approval, Jade let out a loud purr before curling up and going back to sleep.

While Travis built up the fire, Miranda made her way to the bedroom, wondering if perhaps sleeping on the couch might have been a better choice. By the time she'd crawled into bed and tried a dozen different positions, each one more uncomfortable than the last, she was sure of it. In desperation, she turned onto the side with the broken ribs, which felt better, although she was at a loss to explain why.

She was about to drift off when she felt a dip in the mattress and caught a whiff of a very sexy, masculine scent. Travis must have brought his own soap from home along with the extra clothing. Even so, his choice of soap wasn't the issue. What mattered was that he was obviously intending to sleep with her. "What are you doing?"

He cleared his throat. "Just following orders. That doctor told me to keep an eye on you, remember? Besides, you might need something during the night."

Which meant he'd probably wake her up every two hours. *Great. Just when I finally get comfortable...* Miranda fully intended to exact her revenge against Dr. Schwartz at her earliest opportunity. Stealing his moccasins seemed like the best plan. The ER nurses all hated those scruffy old shoes and would probably thank her. "Hey, how are you going to keep an eye on me while you're working tomorrow?"

"Tomorrow?" He paused for a moment, chuckling a bit before replying. "I'll call you every two hours to make sure you aren't hallucinating."

"What if the horses start talking to me while you're gone?"

He snorted a laugh. "Not gonna happen. You won't be anywhere near the barn because I'll feed them in the morning and again in the afternoon. Don't even *think* about doing it yourself."

"Hmm...Are you really planning to do neuro checks on me through the night?"

"Absolutely. I have my list of instructions, remember?"

"Yes, but you haven't done them all day. You should've been checking my pupils and hand grasps and orientation and all that."

"Well, except for checking your pupils, I believe I did."

"Oh yeah? What about the hand grasp thing?"

He burst out laughing. "You're forgetting something, aren't you?"

"What?"

"You had a pretty good grip on me in the kitchen earlier—strong enough to get white stains on your nightgown."

She punched him in the ribs. "Oh, shut up."

"Nothing wrong with your left hook," he said, clearly unperturbed. "Let's check your right hand."

Taking her hand, he guided it down to his groin. "Let's see how hard you can squeeze now."

His cock was like a steel rod. Hercules couldn't have put a dent in it. "Geez, Travis, how many times a day can you *do* that?"

"Oh, I don't know," he mused, "six or seven?"

"You're kidding me, right?"

"Dunno. I've never kept count." His voice deepened, taking on a sexy, drawling note. "Sounds like an interesting research project, though."

There were worse ways to spend a rainy weekend, and God knew there'd been plenty of them that winter. If only she'd screamed *I'm single!* at him months ago. No, he'd have never dug that ditch if she had because with him around, she probably wouldn't have noticed the floods *or* the mud. "I'll have to get back to you on that one. Right now, all I want to do is sleep, and you have to work tomorrow."

"It's not my fault you aren't asleep. I wasn't going to even wake you up, but you just had to fuss at me, didn't you?"

"If you were only going to sleep, then why are you naked?"

He laughed. "Noticed that, did you?"

"The way you checked my hand grasp made it fairly obvious. Do you always sleep in the nude?"

"No, I just wanted you to have something to do if you woke up and couldn't go back to sleep."

"A toy to play with, you mean?"

His chuckle was soft, seductive. "Something like that."

"I'll keep that in mind. Good night, Travis."

"Good night, Miranda. Sleep well. I hope you'll feel better tomorrow—*and* be better oriented. I'll be here all day to remind you that tomorrow is Sunday, not Monday."

She punched him again.

ഇറ

Travis had rolled over for the tenth time in as many minutes when Miranda finally spoke up. "If you're *that* uncomfortable, why don't you sleep in the other room? I shouldn't need anything during the night—except sleep, and I'm not getting much of that."

"Sorry," he said with a sigh. "I really thought I could do it, but I guess I can't."

"Do what?"

He blew out a pent-up breath. "Sleep in the same bed and not touch you."

"Hmm…let's see now…since we got home from the hospital, you've kissed me, seen me naked in the shower, I've sucked your dick, and then there was your peculiar method for assessing grip strength. What makes you think you can't touch me?"

"Because one touch wouldn't be enough—not even *close* to being enough."

"I never knew I had such a profound effect on you."

"Well, you do. Otherwise I'd have been asleep by now—part of me is sleepy, but another part is wide awake."

"Which part is that?"

"If you can't guess, we definitely have a problem. Let's just say you're making me drool, but my mouth is dry."

"Very clever."

"It's true." he insisted. "See for yourself if you don't believe me."

"I never said I didn't believe you."

"Check it out, anyway." That squeeze she'd given him earlier had been a mistake—setting him off to the point that his little head would *not* leave him alone. "It's bound to have been at least two hours since the last check. I need to make sure your hand grasps are equal."

"They never are. My right hand is a lot stronger than my left." Nevertheless, she reached down and wrapped her fingers around his cock.

His breath went out with a hiss.

"Holy shit! No wonder you can't sleep. It's a miracle you haven't passed out. Is there any blood going to your brain at all?"

"Probably not," he admitted. "I feel light-headed even lying down."

"Poor baby," she soothed. "But it's your own damn fault for coming in here in the first place."

He shook his head. "Trust me, it was like that all evening. Every time I looked at you or thought about you or thought about thinking about you or looking at you or—"

She cut him off with a dry chuckle. "I get the idea. You should have done something about it while you were in the shower."

He hated to admit it, but he had. The memory of her wet, naked body had him splattering cum all over the wall in record time. Unfortunately, the mere thought of climbing into bed with her sent blood rushing back to his groin, creating an erection even stronger than before. "It didn't do any good."

"Travis, I'd like to help, but I can't lie on my back. I hurt in practically every position, and when I move—"

"I've been thinking about that," he said. "You said that sitting straight up was the only comfortable position, right?"

"Well, yes."

"Good. This'll work, then. Trust me." He moved up closer and kissed her. "You just relax and let me do all the work."

"Pushy, insistent fellow, aren't you? Always wanting to do more work for me. Too bad I had to break a rib and get conked on the head to get so much attention."

"Oh, I wouldn't say that," he murmured. "I'm trying to make up for lost time."

"Time? I still feel like I've lost some of that."

Her kisses were soft, wet, and intoxicating. Travis would've liked to forget everything else, but he had a job to do. "Speaking of time, let's see what you remember, starting with your name."

Her breath was warm against his lips. "Um…Miranda. Miranda Jackson."

"Very good. Now, tell me the day of the week."

"Sunday—I think. It's past midnight, isn't it?"

Having glanced at his watch every half hour since he'd gone to bed, Travis could easily confirm that. "Right again. Let's see how well you can think while being distracted." Trailing kisses across her cheek and down her neck, he paused at the neckline of her gown. "Tell me the date."

"February 30th, 1491."

Oh, yeah...very distracted. "Close. Who's the President of the United States?"

"There *is* no United States," she murmured. "Columbus hasn't even discovered America yet."

"There's no such thing as February 30th, either." He drew in a deep breath, filling his head with her sweet, lemony scent. "And you have no business wearing a nightgown at a time like this."

"A time like what? I'm *so* confused...."

Pulling up her gown, he buried his face between her luscious breasts. "A time when I get to do things I've only dreamed about."

"Like what?"

"Like *this*."

Opening wide, he sucked as much of her left breast into his mouth as he could, which, considering her response, was probably a mistake.

"Ouch!" She caught him by the shoulder as he started to back off. "My fault, not yours...took too deep a breath... Oh, my God, that feels good."

Softening his tongue, he caressed her nipple, his cock pulsing with each sigh of pleasure that escaped her.

"You're going to have to get up early to feed the horses. Don't you think you should try to sleep?"

"Later," he murmured. "Right now, I'm too busy checking out your brain, making sure everything works. I can always come back to bed after I feed the critters. Don't worry about it."

"I'm not worried—well, maybe I am. This is all so sudden..."

He raised his head. Silhouetted against the glow of the clock on the table behind her, she was barely visible. "Don't you like it?"

"Well, yes I do, but—"

"No buts." He combed his fingertips through her hair. "Now, let's see how well you follow commands. Kiss me."

Miranda did her best to follow that command, kissing him the way she'd always longed to kiss him—a deep, sensuous kiss with all the passion she could pack into it. Her hand explored every curve and contour of his body—the hard muscles in his arms and shoulders, the smooth skin on his back, and the hollow dip along his flank. Each place she touched was warm, sexy, and utterly delightful.

Her sigh ruffled his chest hair as her fingertips circled lower, focusing on the soft, sensitive place where his torso blended into his upper thigh. "I love that spot."

Travis chuckled as she trailed the tips of her fingernails over his ticklish skin.

"I like hearing you laugh, too," she said. "Wonder what you'd do if I kissed you there?"

"Only one way to find out—but we'll do that later. Right now, I want your lips to stay exactly where they are."

His hands caressed her back as his lips melted into hers, his warm tongue slipping into her mouth. No one had ever kissed her quite like that before—as though he craved the taste of her. His reverent touch made her feel like a precious jewel—the most precious thing he'd ever held in his hands.

The same way I'm touching him. Reaching down, she let her hand glide over a cock so hot and engorged she was surprised he didn't cry out in pain. She knew the feeling. The sweet agony between her thighs begged for his touch, just as surely as his cock wanted hers.

Groaning, he rolled onto his back and stuffed a pillow beneath his hips. "C'mere and sit on me before I up and die."

Her stiff knee made maneuvering somewhat difficult, but he finally got her positioned facing away from him, straddling his right leg. With most of her weight resting on her left knee, her right leg hung over the edge of the bed.

"Now, aim me in the right direction and sit down."

As she followed those simple instructions, he filled her with every succulent inch of him. The ache in her core eased, drawing a sigh from her lips. "Oh, wow. That feels wonderful—and my ribs don't hurt at all. Neither does my knee."

"Glad you like it. All you have to do is sit there. I'll do the rest."

His first upward thrust pushed buttons she didn't even know existed. "Oh, God…"

"Good?"

"You have no idea."

A cry of ecstasy bubbled up in her throat, and Miranda had to bite her lip to keep from screaming. He might think he was hurting her if she screamed—and no way did she want him to think that, much less stop what he was doing.

"Don't stop." Her words came out in a ragged whisper. "No matter how loud I scream, please don't stop."

Travis's only reply was a quick thrust followed by a slow, grinding rotation of his hips that set off a wave of pleasure so intense she had to brace her hands on her thighs to keep from falling over. The weight of her body drove his cock into her with a shocking degree of penetration. As her hips mirrored his movements, her mouth fell open and her eyes rolled back in her head. A slight forward tilt of her pelvis had her clit brushing against the hair on his balls. "Mmm…"

"I wish I could see you…" He shifted beneath her, grunting with the effort. Suddenly the room flooded with light as he turned on the lamp. "Much better. Oh, Miranda… You should see yourself…your beautiful hair hanging down your back…that incredible ass sitting on my dick."

His breath caught in his throat and he gripped her hips, holding her firmly against him as his cock pulsed inside her. Miranda had never heard a man make a sound like that—like a gasp, a groan, and a yelp all rolled into one. She was nearly there herself; one more thrust and the scream she'd been holding back burst from her like water from an earthquake-weakened dam. She fell forward onto her hands, nearly losing her hold on him.

Jade jumped up on the bed, her tail brushing Miranda's arm as she passed by. Purring, she rubbed the side of her head on Travis's leg, her jade-green eyes gazing out from beneath blissfully narrowed lids.

"I like him too," Miranda murmured. "Kira's right. He's a keeper."

"What?" Travis gasped.

"Nothing. Just talking to the cat."

Travis stiffened beneath her. "She didn't talk back to you, did she?"

"No, she's only purring."

"Okay…just checking."

Easing her hips slowly from side to side, she savored the thick heat that still filled her, his semen adding its creamy texture to an already incredible mix. An aftershock struck her, causing her to suck a breath in through her teeth. Amazingly, her ribs still didn't hurt.

"You okay?"

"Never better." Pushing off from the bed, she sat upright, gasping as his cock penetrated her fully. "Just wish it hadn't taken broken ribs to get me to try it that way." She glanced over her shoulder. "Got any other brilliant ideas?"

"Oh, you bet." His slow, wicked smile matched his lazy drawl. "I've been saving some of them up for years."

"Don't suppose you know any more good broken rib positions, do you?"

"There's one that might work—we can try it next."

"Next?" He made it sound as though he meant in the next five minutes. "Define *next*."

"Later. You need to get some sleep, and so do I." He twisted sideways, craning his neck to see the clock. "Let's see…it's a little past three now…six o'clock maybe?" Yawning, he added, "Gotta do another neuro check on you then."

Miranda groaned. "Now I know how my patients feel when I wake them up every two hours." Dropping onto her hands, she rose up on her knees, feeling suddenly bereft as he slipped from her body. She crawled over to her pillow and was about to lie down when she remembered the mess she'd left behind. Snatching a box of Kleenex from the nightstand, she pulled out several tissues and tossed them to Travis.

"Thanks."

"Goodnight, Travis." She eased down onto the bed with a contented sigh. "See you at six."

A few moments later, he switched off the light and pulled the blankets up over both of them. This time, he didn't bother trying to keep from touching her, but snuggled up beside her, resting his hand on her waist. Her last thought as she drifted off was that if he could make her feel this incredible now, what mind-boggling things would he do when her ribs healed up?

Chapter 19

Travis was up early, but Miranda was sleeping so peacefully, he didn't have the heart to wake her. Easing from under the covers, he went out to the kitchen, figuring he'd wake her after he fed the animals. Thanks to the cat pawing at the door, he found the cupboard where she kept the cat and dog food.

"Thanks, Jade."

The cat merely blinked at him, but Travis could've sworn she said *you're welcome*.

He stared at her for a moment, then shook his head. "Miranda's hallucinations must be rubbing off on me." Having fed the cat, he got dressed and checked the weather before heading out. It was cold enough that the ground would be frozen, but, thankfully, there was no ice to contend with.

Scooping up a large portion of dog food, he carried it out to the porch. All three dogs were jumping up and down as though they were glad to see him—or starving to death, which he seriously doubted. Like all of Miranda's pets, they appeared to be quite healthy. While they wolfed down their food, he filled up the bird feeder before heading up to the barn.

So far, he liked all her pets and he felt surprisingly at home on her farm, almost as though he belonged there. He didn't, of course—at least, not yet—but he could easily see himself slipping into the pattern of Miranda's life. He hadn't forgotten his promise not to run her life, but that didn't stop him from longing to be a permanent part of her world.

Still, there were obstacles to overcome—chief among them the fact that she'd avoided men for years in order to retain her independence. Allowing him into her life was difficult for her. He'd seen that in the way her attitude toward him shifted back and forth.

She obviously liked him, and she was trying to accept his presence and his assistance, but he still had to watch his step.

Travis wasn't a stubborn or a particularly high-handed man, and even though issuing demands, ultimatums, or commands went against his nature, he had his opinions the same as everyone else. Miranda, however, seemed more sensitive than other women in that respect and might see his opinions as more than they actually were. A few careless words could easily ruin everything.

Having finished their breakfast, the dogs raced on ahead, cavorting with each other as they went. The horses were waiting at the gate, and Travis patted the gray mare as she walked beside him up the hill to the barn.

"I've never felt like this about a woman before. I am *not* going to screw it up."

Kira gave him a nudge in reply. He'd have liked to think it was encouragement of some kind, but what it truly meant was left to his imagination. Miranda's hallucination led him to believe that Kira was fond of him, but somehow, he didn't think he ought to put much stock in that source.

She's probably just hungry.

Although they were as well-behaved as they'd been the day before, the horses had obviously spent a fair amount of time in the barn during the night. He was cleaning the last stall when his phone rang.

Alan was pissed. "Since I never heard from you again, I figured I ought to call your place first. Stuart told me you were still staying with Miranda. Are you out of your fuckin' mind?"

Travis heaved a sigh. "Yes, I believe I am. That is, if falling head over heels in love qualifies as crazy." Somehow, he thought it might—but it was a really nice kind of insanity.

"You didn't do what I think you did. Please tell me you didn't."

"I did and I didn't," he replied, chuckling.

"What the fuck does *that* mean?"

"It means I slept with Miranda, but I'm not having an affair with a married woman."

For once in his life, Travis had the satisfaction of rendering his loquacious cousin speechless—if only for a moment or two. "I don't get it."

"Miranda's husband died fifteen years ago. She's a widow."

"Oh, really?"

"Yes, really. I'm glad I was here too. She slipped on the ice yesterday morning and hit her head when she fell—even broke a few ribs. Sorry I never called you back, but I've been kinda…busy."

"I'll just bet you have. You slept with her? As in had sex?"

"Oh, yeah. Awesome, incredible, mind-blowing sex."

Alan made an inarticulate sound, somewhere between a sob and a whimper.

"Sorry," Travis said with a grimace. "Forgot you were on the wagon."

"You could've lied, you know," Alan grumbled. "Or at least left out the adjectives."

"Too late for that now." He paused as it occurred to him that if anyone would know the best ways to have sex with an injured woman, it would be Alan. "It, um, hurts her to lie on her back. My first position worked pretty well, but I don't want to bore her by doing it the same way all the time. I've got some other ideas, but you're the Jedi master of sex. Any suggestions?"

Alan's snarl was so loud Travis jerked the phone away from his ear. "You're killing me, man. Absolutely killing me."

"Yes, but do you?"

Heaving a sigh as though resigned to his fate, Alan relented. "Of course I do. Got a pen? You might want to take notes."

෨Ꮯᎃ

For once in her life, Miranda was awakened by the heavenly aroma of bacon frying rather than the incessant prodding she usually received from Jade. Opening one eye, she spotted the cat curled up beside her. Travis must've fed her already because she barely moved when Miranda sat up.

Sliding her feet off the edge of the bed, she dug her heels into the side of the mattress to pull herself upright, somehow managing to accomplish this task without using her upper body or causing much in the way of pain. She shuffled her feet into her slippers and stood, surprised to find that her knee felt almost normal. Walking wasn't too difficult, and after quick stop in the bathroom, she followed her nose into the kitchen to find Travis standing in front of the stove. Naked.

Unless an apron could be considered clothing. She'd once imagined him shoeing a horse while wearing only his boots and chaps, but having witnessed this particular scene, she was convinced that her eyes had her imagination beat all to hell and back. His tight, rounded buns were on full display, along with that slight hollow she'd felt the night before—and another birthmark similar to the one on his neck.

"You didn't feed the horses dressed like that, did you?"

Apparently unperturbed, he continued frying the bacon, turning it over with a pair of tongs. "The mares seemed to like it, but I don't think Damar was very impressed."

"He *is* bigger than you are."

"Longer, maybe," he conceded. "But I bet I've got him beat when it comes to circumference."

"Give him a year or so and he'll catch up." Still staring at his perfect ass, she'd almost managed to tamp down the urge to squeeze it when she realized she didn't have to fight it anymore.

He's my boyfriend now. I can grab his butt whenever I like. Moving in behind him, she slid both hands down until the fullest part of his buttocks rested in her palms. Biting back a groan, she sank her fingertips into the firm muscle.

"I see you've got a good, strong grasp this morning."

"Mmm hmm..." Letting go of his bottom, she slipped her arms around his waist, pressing her cheek against his back. "What's for breakfast?"

"Bacon, eggs, and toast á lá Travis."

Sounds interesting... "Does that refer to the way it's cooked or the way it's served?"

"Both." He nodded toward the table. "Actually, I was hoping you'd still be in bed."

Following his nod, she spotted a tray with a glass of orange juice and a plate sitting on it. She took a step back. "Is that a problem?"

He shrugged, pulling the skillet off the burner. "Not really—but as long as you're here, how do you like your eggs?"

"Scrambled—or over easy if you prefer. I can go either way." She couldn't help wondering what it was he'd planned to do. There was only one way to find out. "Maybe I *will* go back to bed," she said, stifling a yawn. "I'm curious to see this á lá Travis method of serving breakfast."

"Waiters generally don't wear aprons—although telling you that may have spoiled the surprise. I'll have to think of something else."

She gave him a quick hug from behind. "I don't know…a naked waiter sounds pretty good to me." Was he always this much fun in the morning? If so, she couldn't understand why he'd never met another woman who didn't like it. Was the obstetrician that stuffy? Or was Christina a total prude? Had he even gotten to the naked waiter stage with either of them? Christina certainly couldn't have thought he was boring if he'd done it for her. Could she?

"Okay, then, you go on back to bed. I'll be there in a minute."

"I'll be waiting." She paused briefly as she turned to go. "Should I pretend to be asleep?"

"Sure." He shot her a wink. "It'll add to the drama."

Giggling, she made her way to the bedroom and crawled carefully back into bed. She was still giggling when she heard him coming down the hall.

"You don't sound like you're asleep," he drawled.

"Sorry," she squeaked.

"No problem. It's time to wake up anyway. Breakfast is served."

Having lain down on her right side, she had her back to him when he entered, so it was with a significant amount of anticipation—and pain—that she turned over. "Hard to do with a rib fracture."

"I'll bet it is."

He stood holding the tray, waiting patiently while she sat up and got her pillows arranged. That he'd taken off the apron was fairly obvious, but with the tray blocking her view, she couldn't see much else.

Even when he set the tray in her lap, her big bolster pillow hid everything below his navel. Still giggling, she reached for a napkin only then realizing that there wasn't one on the tray.

"Did you bring a napkin?"

"Sure did." His stripper-quality pelvic thrust aroused her curiosity, making her lean over the pillow for a closer look. Peering down at his groin, she discovered a napkin neatly folded and draped over his stiff penis. Howling with laughter, she would've knocked over the orange juice if Travis hadn't caught it in time.

Snatching the napkin from its perch, she used it to wipe her streaming eyes. "That was definitely worth going back to bed for."

"I'm glad you think so," he said with a chuckle. "I had to think of something fast, and this was the best I could do." He held the juice glass to her lips. "Here, better drink some of this before one of us spills it."

After taking a sip, she reached for the glass, but he drew his hand back. "No, wait. I've got a better idea."

"What's that?"

"You'll see."

With an intriguing smile, he pushed the bolster pillow aside and sat down on the edge of the bed. Setting the juice on the nightstand, he picked up a piece of toast. "Here, have a bite."

"You're going to feed me?" Miranda had fed a lot of patients in her time, but no one had fed her since she was a baby.

He nodded, waggling his eyebrows. "But I'm not going to use a fork."

Good thing he scrambled the eggs... "Sounds interesting. Tell me something, are you always this much fun in the morning?"

Laughing, he offered her a piece of bacon. "Probably not—at least, not unless I'm with you."

"So...this isn't normal behavior for you?" She took a bite of the bacon, chewing it slowly.

"I've never had this much fun with anyone before." Shaking his head, he added, "I'm not sure why, but it's the truth."

"I'll have to admit, except for broken ribs and a concussion, I've been having a lot more fun than usual myself." She sighed, wondering how long what they shared would last. A month? A year? Forever would be nice, of course, but somehow she doubted it would last that long. Wonderful things so seldom did.

And he's such a sweet guy. Those other women he'd dated were idiots—and the one he'd married even more so than the rest. Complete, utter, and *total* idiots. And that included Christina.

Travis, boring? *Oh, hell, no.*

Placing some eggs on the toast, he held it to her lips. She took a bite, chewing it thoughtfully. He was so adorable. What would he look like when he finally got fed up with her and left? Probably still adorable because even hurt or angry, he'd still be Travis...

"How come you're not eating anything?"

He shrugged. "I ate some toast after I fed the horses."

"You couldn't be very full, then. There's enough here for both of us. Why don't you come over here and let me feed you, too. For once, feeding someone seems like fun."

He crawled up beside her and she put her arm around him, kissing him before offering him some scrambled eggs-on-toast. "Wouldn't it be nice if we never had to go to work and we could do this all the time?"

"I dunno...seems like more of a treat this way."

She sighed. "You're such a sensible fellow. What did I ever do without you?"

"Nothing like this, I presume."

"No, nothing like this. Ever." She'd never even *dreamed* about it. Travis was doing wonders for her imagination.

After they'd finished eating, he wiped her lips with the napkin. "Ready for dessert?"

"Dessert?" she echoed. "With breakfast?"

"Hey, if you don't want it..."

"Another surprise?"

He nodded. "Yeah. Something big and long and tasty with

cream filling—and a dash of secret sauce."

"Secret sauce and cream filling?" She frowned. "Sounds like a cross between a Big Mac and a chocolate éclair."

With a sly wink, he hopped up and collected the tray and dirty dishes. "Be right back."

He returned moments later with a huge jar of peanut butter and a spoon. "Secret sauce."

Miranda groaned. "Oh, God, not peanut butter! Once I get started, I can't stop eating that stuff. It's practically an addiction. That's why I don't keep it in the house."

"Don't worry," he said, grinning. "I'll ration it out for you. You can only have it as the topping on your dessert."

"It better be a really *big* éclair," she grumbled. "Although I never thought of putting peanut butter on one. I usually eat it right out of the jar."

His lips curled into a slow, suggestive, heart-stopping smile. "It's big enough. Not as long as Damar's, but bigger around—remember?"

"Oh, *my…*"

"If you have to lick it off of me, a little will go a long way." Scooping out a small spoonful, he dropped a dollop in the same spot her napkin had been hanging earlier.

Holy shit…

Travis *and* peanut butter? Two of the most addicting things in the entire world? Together? Her swift inhale yanked her broken ribs out of alignment, forcing her to cough in order to push them back into place. Feeding breakfast to each other had been fun, but *this…*

The mere thought of it would have been hot enough, but to actually watch him spreading peanut butter on his rock-hard cock went beyond erotic. Her core ignited with the power of a volcanic eruption, sending rivers of searing lava coursing through her veins.

Seemingly oblivious to the inferno he'd set off inside her, Travis kept right on smiling as he smeared that wonderfully addicting delight on his equally addicting self, making her very glad she'd shared her breakfast with him and saved room for dessert.

She cleared her throat, but her voice still sounded hoarse. "If that's the secret sauce, where's the cream filling?"

"Don't worry, it'll *come* to you. I promise."

Miranda bit her lip and tried her damndest to look severe. "Very funny, Travis."

"What, you don't like my warped sense of humor?"

She lost it then, dissolving into helpless giggles. *What is with me?* "I love your sense of humor—warped or not." She tried not to stare, but her gaze kept drifting back to his succulent cock. "So, are you gonna stand there icing that thing all day?"

If anything, his smile became even more devastating. "I want to make sure I don't miss a spot. I wouldn't want you complaining to the chef."

"Not much danger of that," she assured him. "My only complaint is how slow my waiter is."

"Well, you know, sometimes slower is better." He slid his finger through the peanut butter. "Isn't it?"

Nodding, she sat spellbound as a droplet of viscous fluid welled up from the head of his penis and dripped slowly to the floor. "You're wasting the cream filling."

"Don't worry, there's more where that came from." Finishing his task, he licked the remaining peanut butter from his finger. "By the way, you need to undress for dessert. Only naked women get to lick my peanut butter-coated dick." Catching a droplet of pre-cum with a fingertip, he spread it out, putting a shine on his swollen cockhead. "Next time I go to the store, I'll get some chocolate syrup so you can have Travis á lá Reese's."

Wincing, she tried unsuccessfully to stifle her whimper. "You're going to make me even fatter than I am now if you're not careful."

"No, I won't." Grinning like the cat that got the cream, he added, "Come on, take off your nightie, Miranda. You're keeping your waiter waiting."

Chapter 20

Travis watched as she pulled her nightgown over her head…slowly, seductively. He didn't think he would ever tire of watching her undress—the anticipation, the visual, and especially the fact that it was Miranda lying there naked. He wanted to dive into her so badly he could barely restrain himself. And now he had to wait until she licked his cock clean before he could do it.

What a peculiar dilemma…

Swallowing his lust, he did his best to sound smooth and in control. "You see? You're not fat at all. A little more weight on you wouldn't bother me a bit."

"Well, it would bother *me*," she grumbled. "I try so hard not to gain, but it's getting tougher all the time."

"Don't worry, I'll help you. I'll lock up all the goodies and only give them to you once in a while." Picking up the jar, he consulted the label and did some quick mental math. "Besides, there are only ninety-five calories in a tablespoon, and there's probably less than that on my dick."

She threw up her hands. "Okay. You've convinced me—not that you needed to." Licking her lips, she patted the bed. "Come over here and we'll see if I can eat my dessert without getting it all over the place."

Not needing to be asked twice, Travis hurried around the foot of the bed and hopped in beside her to lie flat on his back, his rather impatient cock standing straight up. "Here you go, Miranda. Chow down."

Shifting onto her side, she scooted closer. "Oh, my God, that looks good."

Expecting a tentative lick, she surprised him again, taking as much of him in her mouth as she could hold. He could even feel the head pressing against the back of her throat while her tongue massaged him from the side.

Travis had never come in a woman's mouth before—had never been able to—but this nearly pushed him over the edge. Still, he wanted to do something to her that would feel as good as her mouth on his dick—and do it while she was sucking him. Unfortunately, all he could reach was the back of her head. Groaning, he wove his fingers through her hair.

Would she ever get tired of him constantly shoving his dick in her face? Even though she did seem to enjoy it, he was doing that quite a lot. For now, her injuries limited what she could do comfortably, although he would've done anything she asked of him. Alan's suggestions had been useful, but Travis still couldn't wait to lay her on her back and lick her until she came in his face. Surely she'd like *that*...

Moments later, she raised her head, altering the angle enough that he could actually see what she was doing. Her lips hugged his cock as though they never intended to let go. If he'd ever envisioned anything quite so erotic before, he'd already forgotten it.

"Taste good?" It certainly *felt* good.

Although her "ummhmm" sent thrilling vibrations zipping through his cock, he almost wished he hadn't asked when she let go of him. "It's like eating a hot peanut butter popsicle—all melty and creamy and delicious. Mmm...." His dick pulsed as she ran her tongue along the length of his shaft, sending more pre-cum pouring from the slit. She took a sip before licking it off completely. "I love that stuff too. Yummy..."

Travis sucked in a breath as she went down on him again. He couldn't stand it anymore. If he couldn't get his hands on her he was going to lose his mind. "Can you move your bottom up this way?"

Easing slowly up onto her knees, she pivoted toward him. He couldn't see her sucking him anymore, but the sight of her heart-shaped butt more than made up for it. Running his hand over her round cheeks, he slipped his fingers between her thighs.

God, she's wet. Her dewy moisture drenched his hand, allowing his fingers to glide between her soft folds until he found the tight knot of her clit. Stroking it gently, he was rewarded when she moaned and pushed back against him, encouraging his caress. Her reaction sent even more heat rushing to his cock. He loved hearing the sounds she made. What was it she'd said before? *Don't stop, no matter how much I scream.* She had no idea what that scream had done to him. None. He had to tell her.

Unfortunately, telling her things like that had gotten him in trouble once before. What he'd said after that first round of wild, monkey sex on the kitchen table had embarrassed her. He didn't want to risk doing that again.

Then it hit him what it was he'd said that upset her. He shouldn't have told her how hot she was—any man could get excited over a sexy woman—he should tell her how he felt about *her*.

But not now. Later. He would tell her later—when she wasn't sucking his cock and he wasn't holding her pussy in his hand. He'd make her scream again first. That was something else he'd discovered he liked about her. She was vocal and not overly modest. *A screaming exhibitionist.* She'd probably slap the shit out of him for saying that, but he couldn't help it. She turned him on like no one else ever had. Like no one else ever *could*...

Curling his fingers, he used two fingertips on her clit, loving her every whimper, every moan. Rocking into his touch, she was still sucking him, but seemed to be losing strength. Moments later she let go, falling face first into his groin, his cock resting against her cheek.

His first thought was that the peanut butter was all gone and she didn't like him plain. But no, she'd liked him well enough before. That couldn't be it. Her body grew increasingly tense; she even held her breath for a moment. Seconds later her sharp cry and subsequent gasps broke the silence. *God, what an incredible sound.* His cock nearly fired off into the air simply from hearing her come.

He kept on teasing her clit until the thrusts of the tiny bud ceased—but he still wasn't done with her. Somehow his fingers found their way inside, and she pushed back against him again and again, fucking his hand. His cock was going wild—so wild it hurt. Suddenly, his fingertips slid over a small bump in an otherwise smooth, muscular wall.

Her G spot. Alan had told him how to find it. Travis had never even attempted to locate it on any other woman, much less use it to make her come. He'd already done it with her clit, but now the pitch of her cries climbed higher. She sounded almost like she was crying. He hesitated for an instant.

"Don't stop." Her voice sounded so strained, he barely understood her. "*Please* don't stop."

He didn't stop again until she told him to—not with words, but with a series of screams that left her panting and him with a craving impossible to ignore. Her hot breath ruffled the hair on his balls, reminding him of the time she'd sucked them. But that wasn't what he needed now. If he didn't fuck her soon, his dick was going to split apart.

"Did you lick off all the peanut butter?" He was so hoarse he barely recognized his own voice.

"Oh, yeah." Her voice was different too—high-pitched and breathy. "It was gone a long time ago. I love sucking your dick. Don't need peanut butter. But what you did to me…I couldn't handle both at the same time. Incredible…" Her voice trailed off only to come back stronger than ever. "Fuck me, Travis. From behind. I'm okay this way. Just need a pillow."

Travis tossed a pillow beside her and she shifted sideways to lay her head on it. Rising up on his knees, for a moment all he could do was stare. He'd practically drooled anytime he'd watched her saddling Kira. Tight breeches were one thing. Miranda's naked ass aimed right at him was something else altogether.

Wrapping her arms around the pillow, she spread her knees apart and hollowed her back, exposing her sex. He was dying to lick her there, and he would have if she hadn't already told him what she wanted.

Seeming to sense his hesitation, her pleas became more urgent. "Fuck me, Travis, Hard as you can."

"You're sure I won't hurt you?"

"No. Fuck me. *Please.*" The act of shaking her head made her ass wiggle—or had she done that intentionally? Either way, his swift intake of air nearly choked him.

Her labia were as wet and swollen as his dick, and her breath went out with a hiss as he slid inside her—or was that *his* breath? He wasn't sure. Her pussy enveloped him in a tight, wet hug as he gripped her hips and plunged into her. Her head snapped up, increasing the arch in her back, altering the angle to drive him in even deeper.

"Ohh..." Her open-mouthed sigh became a growl as she backed into him, her ass slapping against his groin.

It was happening again—like the first time. That complete loss of control. She drove him mad with desire, her thrusts and whimpers like whips urging him on. Lying on his back with her sitting on him, he hadn't been able to develop much momentum, but he certainly could now—and she clearly loved it.

He was beginning to understand why she'd been embarrassed after that first wild episode; *she'd* lost control too. He'd never expected fireworks like that, even though he'd been lusting after her like a randy teenager for months. That she was a very giving, loving person was obvious to anyone. The fact that she had searing passion buried deep inside her wasn't quite so apparent.

Then again, she hadn't had sex in fifteen years, which might have accounted for at least some of her exuberance. He was dying to ask her, but couldn't find the nerve. That niggling fear that the tiniest little mistake on his part could shatter everything kept him quiet. He didn't need to know that now. Right now, all he needed to do was fuck her as hard as he could—which was no hardship whatsoever.

Gripping her hips, he pulled her against him, drilling his cock deeply into her core. He didn't have to hear her words of approval; the way she met him stroke for stroke was proof enough of her enjoyment. However, when she ground her butt against him, rotating his dick inside her, *he* was the one yelping. Letting out a yell that echoed off the walls, he fired off an ejaculation that seemed to come from his toes and didn't stop until his balls were aching and empty.

She gave him one last bump and grind before rocking forward and keeling over onto her side with a groan. He was sure he'd hurt her until she murmured, "Holy moly... That was the best dessert *ever.*"

"Glad you liked it," he said, chuckling.

"The best waiter ever too." She sighed, snuggling into her pillow as though settling in for a nap. "Must come here more often…and leave really big tips…"

Travis sank back on his heels, feeling like he was about to keel over himself. Miranda was without a doubt the hottest woman he'd ever met, and he was nuts about her. But there was so much more to it than that. Did she realize it?

He'd been as close to loving her as a man could get long before they'd been intimate. It wasn't all about the sex. It was about how she made him *feel.* How he missed her when she wasn't with him. How much he enjoyed her company and the way she made him laugh. She'd been so kind to him, listening to him bitch and moan about his rotten love life. She'd hugged him when he had the flu. She'd been a good friend to him even when she'd thought he would never be interested in her simply because she was a few years his senior. How little she knew about herself and how she affected others.

The funny thing was, he couldn't remember her ever saying she wanted *him.* Her actions had certainly indicated it, but she'd never actually said she was in love, or even in lust, with him—at least not in so many words. Had he ever given her the *chance* to say how she felt about him? Did he dare to ask?

Still, after the way she'd pounced on him in the kitchen, didn't he have a right to *believe* she wanted him?

He rubbed his eyes, trying to remember. She hadn't said anything like that. She'd simply asked him—no, *told* him—to kiss her. What happened after that might have been the most incredible sexual experience of his life, but would she describe it the same way? She seemed to be having fun with him now, but would she toss him out on his ear as soon as she felt better?

Stop thinking, Travis.

Good advice, if only he could follow it.

Miranda let out a long sigh. "Think I'll nap for a bit if you don't mind."

"No problem. I need to run by my place anyway. You get some

rest and maybe we can watch a movie later." He crawled over to her and planted a kiss on her temple. "Be right back."

She replied with a nod. After tucking the blankets in around her, he sat gazing at her for a long time. He didn't want to go home. *Ever.* He wanted to stay right where he was and love Miranda for the rest of his life.

If she'll let me.

Chapter 21

Miranda awoke to a silent house. Even Jade, who lay curled up beside her, wasn't making a sound. Obviously, Travis wasn't back yet. With a yawn, she tossed the covers aside and sat up, noting that her ribs hurt less—either that or she was simply getting better at moving in ways that didn't aggravate them.

Padding barefoot into the bathroom, the first thing she noticed was the grocery bag filled with Travis's clothes sitting on the floor. To have his things stashed in a corner so unceremoniously seemed wrong somehow—as though he were an unwelcome guest. He was certainly not unwelcome, although putting his clothes in a drawer might seem…presumptuous. Would he assume that the next step would be for him to move in permanently?

Probably not. Although he lived with his brother, she had no idea whether they shared a house or an apartment. Leaving an apartment behind would be easy enough, but if they owned a house together, he wouldn't give it up to move in with her, would he? The fact that he didn't have room for a horse didn't mean anything. Even a house in the country might not have a lot of land associated with it.

She was still pondering this as she wandered back to her bedroom, her eyes landing on the dresser that still held some of Kris's clothes. Not many, of course—only a few things he'd worn when he was home on leave and the personal items she'd received after his death. Although most of the drawers contained very little, she'd never seen any point in throwing any of it away, thinking that Levi might want it someday.

She was surprised to discover that she could accomplish the task of emptying out the top drawer with only a passing wave of wistful nostalgia, rather than the grief she might have experienced in the early years. Still, it wasn't permanent; she could always put

Kris's things back after Travis left. He wouldn't stay forever—only until she was able to feed the horses again.

She could've easily resumed her barn chores that morning. Even so, she wasn't quite ready for him to leave yet—a fact that had nothing to do with any work he might do for her. Nor was she afraid to be alone. It was more a matter of how much she would miss him.

She gave herself a mental shake. Putting his clothes in a drawer wasn't all *that* significant. She simply didn't want him to have to live out of a grocery sack. There was no more to it than that...

With nothing better to do, she was in the process of gathering up her dirty laundry when she heard Travis come in. He must've been shopping again; she could hear the rustle of bags and the sound of bottles rattling in the refrigerator. Hoisting the laundry basket onto her hip, she headed out to the kitchen. "Got anything you want washed?"

"Maybe a few things." Frowning, he stared pointedly at the basket. "Should you be carrying that?"

"You're starting to remind me of Denise," she growled. "If it hurt, I wouldn't be doing it."

"And *does* it hurt?"

He already knows me much too well... "Maybe a little," she admitted. "I do lots of things that hurt. This is just one more."

He arched an eyebrow. "As I recall, you aren't supposed to lift anything heavier than a bottle of water. Better give me that."

She rolled her eyes, but relinquished the basket. "I'm not used to having anyone fetch and carry for me. I feel sort of restless—I needed something to do."

"Take up knitting," he said over his shoulder as she followed him to the laundry room. "It weighs less."

"I might if I had any yarn or knitting needles, but I don't." She'd never done anything that domestic in her entire life.

"You really aren't used to sitting around, are you?"

"Nope—wait, I can at least do that," she said as he began sorting the clothes into the washer.

Stepping aside, he waved her on. "Might even keep you out of trouble for a while."

"Trouble?" She could think of several things she'd done with him that might constitute trouble. Doing his laundry wasn't one of them.

"Yeah, you know, the stuff you keep getting into?"

A quick mental review of recent events took the steam out of any argument she might have made. *Ice storms, floods, concussions, men who put peanut butter on their dicks...* "For someone who's supposed to be keeping me out of trouble, you seem to be doing your best to corrupt me. No one who would bring cookie dough and peanut butter into my house could ever be classified as safe."

A lazy smile curled his lips. "Depends on what you do with it."

"You're a dangerous man, Travis York." With a wag of her head, she gave him a wry grin. "Go get your dirty clothes, and I'll wash them."

He departed with a wink, returning a few minutes later with an armful of clothing. Aside from Levi's laundry, Miranda hadn't washed a man's clothes in a very long time. Still, it seemed only natural to toss his underwear in with hers. After adding detergent, she closed the lid. *So much for that. Now what do I do?*

Almost as if he read her thoughts, Travis leaned over and whispered, "If you're looking for something else to do, I believe I could make a suggestion."

His tone was certainly suggestive. "Does it involve food or sex?"

"Food," he replied. "It's time for lunch."

"Aw, darn." She smacked her fist into her palm. "And I was so sure it would be sex."

"I'm always up for that, but I *am* kinda hungry."

She scowled at him. "You're always hungry and you always want sex. I believe I'm seeing a pattern here."

"No pattern, just normal male appetites," he said. "To tell you the truth, it's been a while since I felt like satisfying either of them."

She snorted a laugh. "What, you mean you don't eat?"

"Not like I have since I've been here with you. You make me hungry for everything. You're a pretty good cook too."

She eyed him askance. "Thank you—I *think*."

"I'm easy. Just feed me and fuck me and I'll be happy."

He might have been laughing, but at least he was honest. Miranda wasn't sure any man needed much else from a woman. The rest he could take care of on his own. "No beer, no TV, no football?"

"Don't need 'em as long as I've got you."

"If I'd known you were easy enough to want me, I'd have said something a long time ago," she said ruefully. "I could have saved myself the trouble of trying to fix you up with my friends."

He glared at her. "What do you mean, easy enough to want you?"

"I'm not your usual type, am I?"

He seemed surprised. "I didn't think I *had* a type. What type are you?"

"Oh, I don't know...older, sort of battle-scarred and cynical, but under it all, a hopeless romantic."

"Sounds like my type exactly."

"Oh, hush." She didn't believe a word of it—was *afraid* to believe it. "What do you want for lunch?"

"Hmm..." He tapped his chin thoughtfully. "Decisions, decisions...do I want sex or food?"

"We're back to that, are we?"

"I guess so. Actually, I'd like both, but I'll settle for food—for now."

"Good, because you're wearing me out."

Which brought to mind another line in *Rebecca*—the one where Jack Favell makes the comment that "a lovely woman isn't like an automobile or a motor tire, she doesn't wear out. The more you use her, the better she goes." Miranda hadn't had much opportunity to test that theory—until recently. Somehow she didn't think it applied when the woman in question had fractured ribs.

Travis was still snickering when she opened the refrigerator and nearly choked on her own spit. He *had* been shopping again. In addition to the two packages of chocolate chip cookie dough he'd admitted to buying the day before, there was now a package of peanut butter cookie dough and a huge can of whipped cream. *What would they taste like together?*

She had to close her eyes whenever she passed those sections in the grocery. Otherwise, her inner demons would take over, forcing her to throw package after package into her cart. And now, all of this was in her own home, in her own refrigerator. Her knees almost gave way beneath her when she spotted the bottle of chocolate syrup.

"What's wrong?"

Clearing her throat, she averted her eyes from the tempting syrup to the hot dogs sitting on the shelf below. "Nothing, Travis. Nothing at all, just give me a moment to recover."

"You've really got it bad, haven't you?"

"You have no idea." She took a deep breath and picked up the hot dogs. "I know it sounds ridiculous, but I can't help it. It's like putting a huge jar of cocaine in a junkie's medicine cabinet."

"Sorry," he said, looking a bit chagrined. "I'll get rid of it."

Jade stalked into the kitchen, gazing up at her with reproach.

Miranda hesitated as if the cat had actually issued a warning. Still, whether Jade had said anything or not, she was absolutely right. *He's a keeper. Don't run him off.* "No, maybe it's time I worked through this. Let's see how long I can leave it there without eating it."

"I might end up eating it first," Travis admitted. "I shouldn't, of course, but I felt like celebrating. Guess I should have gotten champagne, instead."

"Now, *that* I could leave alone. Too sour."

He smiled. "I'm not crazy about it myself. We should make out a list." He took the hot dogs from her. "You can close the door, now, Miranda."

"What? Oh...yeah. Close the door," she muttered. "Right. Shut the door. Just like that. Sounds easy, doesn't it? But it's not."

Travis gently removed her fingers from the door handle and pushed the door closed. "There now," he whispered in her ear. "Out of sight, out of mind."

His nearness sent goose bumps racing over her skin and a new flush of heat diving to her core. "I hope so. But I doubt it." She paused as a new thought occurred to her. "Is there anything you crave and can't live without?"

"I'd have to be pretty stupid to tell you that, now, wouldn't I?" He pulled a knife out of the drawer.

"And I don't suppose you're what anyone would call stupid, are you?"

"My momma didn't raise no fool." He sliced open the wrapper on the hot dogs. "At least I learn from my mistakes. After that first marriage fiasco, I had sense enough not to marry anyone I didn't fall head over heels for and felt I could trust, so, no, I'm not that dumb. And I'm not about to screw this up over cookie dough."

"Screw what up?"

"This," he replied, gesturing between the two of them. "You and me...together."

Miranda figured it would take more than cookie dough to screw it up, at least, from her standpoint, because the best she could tell, Travis was freakin' perfect. She barked out a scornful laugh. "Don't worry, I'll be the one to do that. I'll wolf down everything you bring home, gain fifty pounds, and you'll get over me in a heartbeat. Probably won't take long since I'm not exactly what you'd call thin to begin with."

"If your goal is to be rail thin, don't bother on my account. The anorexic look has never appealed to me."

"Funny how no one ever believes they're thin enough— especially actresses. Gorgeous women like Jane Russell and Marilyn Monroe are fat by today's standards." She shook her head, grumbling. "Women's magazines are horrible. They've always got *Miracle Weight Loss Diet* in bold letters superimposed over a close-up of the biggest, gooiest chocolate cake you've ever laid eyes on. Shit like that really pisses me off." Snarling, she glanced up to find Travis smiling at her in the most peculiar manner. "Sorry. Just having one of my soapbox moments. Feel free to ignore my rant."

"Not likely," he said, chuckling. "Besides, I kinda *like* hearing you rant." With a wink, he flashed that pearly grin at her—again— and her heart did a pirouette right there in the middle of her chest. *Can't be good for it...* "I'll let you know if I ever get tired of listening to you."

"You do that," she said, nodding. But would a perfect man ever tell you he was sick and tired of hearing you bitch and moan? *Maybe.* Sighing, she realized she had yet to find a single thing about Travis she didn't like. He was cute, fun, and helpful—hell, he was even willing to give up cookies for her.

Maybe that was it. He was too perfect. Perfect teeth, perfect body, perfect smile, perfect everything. Miranda was sure she could never measure up to him. For starters, she was too old. That crap about the difference in their ages not mattering was just that. *Crap.*

Most people were their own worst critic, and she was no exception. Still, in at least one respect, she knew she was right. She was too bossy. She was doing her damndest to let him do things without telling him the right way—her way, of course—and he was still hanging around. But it had only been two days. How much longer could she keep her mouth shut?

She told herself to give the guy a chance, to give *herself* a chance. With the exception of what must have been a very brief marriage, he'd been single all his life. But had he ever lived with another woman after that? His brother had only moved in with him a few months ago—she remembered him telling her about the divorce. Could he adapt to her ways? Miranda was used to making her own decisions—Kris hadn't meddled even when he was home. Would Travis be willing to compromise or would he try to rule the roost?

Telling her brain to shut the fuck up, she sat down at the table while he fixed the lunch she'd intended to fix herself. She had to bite her tongue when he grilled the franks in a skillet instead of using the microwave, which is what she would have done. She was dying to fuss at him for dirtying up a skillet unnecessarily, but for once in her life she managed to keep quiet. Jade gazed up at her, her slow blink expressing her silent approval.

"What do you want on your hot dog?" he asked.

"Barbecue sauce," she replied recklessly. She'd never eaten one that way, but it seemed like a good time to try it.

"Sounds great."

Oh, yeah, he was perfect. She caught herself wishing she'd said chocolate syrup. Surely that would've grossed him out. Or she could've said she wanted the bun soaked in margarita mix. *Nah, too soggy.*

Plopping her hot dog on a plate, he reached up on top of the refrigerator for yet another of her weaknesses. *Potato chips.* She hadn't noticed them before, but there they were, an enormous, tempting blue bag full of them. He pulled a bottle of barbecue sauce out of the fridge and squirted it on her hot dog.

"You want this on your chips, too?"

Oh, hell, why not? "Sure." As she watched him prepare his own lunch the same way, she decided it was no wonder he hadn't liked the obstetrician and her gourmet tastes. He was as down-home, all-American boy as they came—he even liked apple pie. The only things missing were pickles and beer. "We can have pie for dessert. At least, I *guess* there's some of it left." She scratched her head, frowning. "I don't remember having eaten all of it."

He grinned devilishly. "You can have all you want as long as I get to serve it."

"And just how were you planning to do that?" She took a bite of her hot dog, which was quite delicious. *I'll have to remember that.* "Á lá Travis?"

"Maybe. But I draw the line at topping it with ice cream."

"Too cold on your dick?"

He nodded. "Might make it shrivel up and hide—and we can't have that, can we?" Picking up another chip, he studied it as though he'd only just noticed it was splattered with barbecue sauce. "These taste great—makes me wonder why I never tried it before."

"Glad you like them, but you're right; shriveling would be bad." Aside from the fact that she could feel her waistline expanding at the mere thought of Travis covered with pie and ice cream. "Perhaps I should have you plain. You're less fattening that way."

He munched on the chip, his head tilted to one side. "Do you think we can ever get through a meal without having sex?"

Aha! That sounds like a complaint.

"Doesn't seem like it." Letting out a long breath, she shook her head with mock resignation. "You might as well take those jeans off right now." As she recalled, cock-sucking usually came sometime during the main course...although her memory *was* rather patchy.

"Maybe I need to ration that, too—along with all the other stuff you find so irresistible."

Nope, not perfect if he was going to make suggestions like *that.* Sex with Travis was fabulous, and the best she could tell, it was in no way detrimental to her health. She arched a skeptical brow. "Oh, really?"

He appeared to consider this idea for a moment, then shook his head. "No, that would be too much of a hardship on *me*. I can live without cookies, but now that I know what it's like, I don't have any intention of rationing when it comes to you." He swallowed the last bite of his hot dog and winked. "Hurry up and finish your lunch. We've got better things to do."

She cocked her head, frowning. "I thought you wanted to watch a movie."

His lips curled into a seductive grin that sent a flood of heat sluicing down to her pussy, setting her aflame with need. What this man could do to her with one smile was freakin' *scary*. "We can do that later. Right now, I want you to sit in my lap."

"No apple pie?"

He shook his head slowly. "Later."

Chapter 22

A loud purr from somewhere near his feet drew Travis's gaze downward to Jade's iridescent eyes. Her slow blink seemed to indicate approval, which was ridiculous. *Yeah, right, like the cat really cares what we do.* Still, he couldn't shake the notion that approval was exactly what she was attempting to convey. With a quick shake of his head, he glanced at Miranda. "You aren't hearing that cat talk, are you?"

"Not me." She crossed her heart. Twice. "I'm not crazy. Not so sure about you."

"I could have sworn…"

She laughed lightly. "Had any recent bumps on the head?"

Frowning, he peered at the cat again. Jade ignored him and began licking her paw. "Not that I recall."

"That's how it is with head injuries," Miranda said with a sage nod. "I could have conked you on the head with a skillet and since my brains are already scrambled, it's possible that neither of us would remember it."

"Spooky."

"No shit."

The ensuing silence made him wonder if he'd killed the mood. His dick was as stiff as ever, but that was only his perspective. Miranda was much too hard to read—which was one of the things he liked best about her. She kept him guessing.

Picking up a napkin, she wiped her mouth before taking one last sip of her tea. "So where is it I'm supposed to sit?"

Her reply seemed innocent enough, but something in her eyes and the way she licked her lips made his cock twitch and his balls ache.

I am so fucking easy.

"Hmm…" He tapped his chin, trying to tamp down the urge to yank her into his arms and kiss her senseless. He'd certainly be glad when she was a little less…fragile. "We've already done the bedroom and the kitchen. The living room is next."

"Every room, huh? Then what? The deck?"

"Oh, *yeah*. The deck." The notion of leaning her over the railing and nailing her from behind like he'd done that morning turned his mouth to dust. *Maybe when her ribs are stronger…*

She shivered. "Too cold. We'll have to wait until spring."

"Not even in a sleeping bag?"

"Maybe. Levi was a Boy Scout, so there might be one around here somewhere, but I have no idea where to look for it. He could probably tell you exactly where it is. His ability to remember where things are is uncanny."

"I can't wait to meet him. I mean, aside from the fact that he's your son, he sounds…interesting."

"He is that." She smiled fondly. "I don't know anyone who doesn't like him. He's such a hoot—his psychiatrist used to ask him when he was going into show biz. Just wish school hadn't been so hard for him. He can't read worth a darn, but he can recite dialogue from a favorite movie almost word for word—not a thing wrong with his memory when it's something he wants to remember."

"He's not alone there. My memory can be a bit selective at times too."

"Like most men," she said with a roll of her eyes. "Levi can tell you the names of the planets backward and forward, but ask him to read a simple sentence and he'll get so mad the veins pop out in his neck. On the other hand, repetitive tasks don't bore him the way they do other people. Once he gets in the habit of doing something, you don't ever have to tell him to do it again. I think that's one reason why they like him so much at the store."

"Does he visit you very often?"

"He used to come home every weekend, but lately he's been staying in town. He said something about a girl named Tabitha needing his help. I'm guessing she's someone he works with. I'm hoping to see him next weekend, but who knows?"

"Sounds like he might have found himself a girlfriend."

"If so, it's a first. He's cute, and he's had a few crushes, but so far none of them have returned his affections."

Travis knew exactly how that felt. Obviously he should've been more forthcoming about his own feelings—at least, with respect to Miranda. After mooning over her for so long, he still had a hard time believing he'd actually slept with her. *Thank God for flooded barns and freezing rain.* "And he's how old?"

"Almost twenty-three."

Which meant that, at thirty-six, Travis was only thirteen years older than her son. That fact didn't deter him in the slightest, but he suspected it might bother Miranda. He caught her watching him, a pensive expression in her eyes and her lower lip caught between her teeth.

"I can almost see the calculations going on in your head." Her gaze swept over his hair. "Levi is blond too. You could probably pass for brothers." She paused, running a hand through her own glossy locks. "At least my hair is different enough people won't automatically assume you're my son or my younger brother when they see us together."

"No one would think that," he insisted. "Besides, you don't look forty-five."

"That's nice to hear, but you could pass for a lot younger than thirty-six, yourself."

"That's beside the point—and nine years isn't a huge difference anyway. You see older men with younger women all the time. Granted, sometimes they seem a little ridiculous together, but I don't believe we'll have that problem."

"People will still think it's weird."

If he couldn't convince her that the age difference was a non-issue, their relationship would be over before it ever truly began. "Who gives a shit what other people think? As long as we're happy, it's none of their damn business."

Her breath went out with a sharp exhale. "True, but you know how people talk. Instead of the Widow Jackson, I'll be Miranda the Cougar."

Travis couldn't help smiling. "Ah, yes, but cougars pounce, and you know how I adore being pounced on."

"Just wish I felt more like pouncing." Wincing, she held out a hand and he helped her to stand. "So, where is it we're going? The living room?"

He stifled his sigh of relief. "I was beginning to think you'd forgotten about that."

She winked at him, her eyes sparkling with mischief. "Nope—momentarily distracted perhaps, but I certainly didn't forget."

"That's my girl." Tucking her hand under his arm, he led her into the living room. Quickly shedding his clothes, he pulled a wingback chair over to face the couch. "This is the other broken rib position I mentioned." Actually, it was one of Alan's suggestions. Travis would've given him full credit if he hadn't assumed Miranda would frown upon his having that discussion with his cousin. Somehow, he suspected she might. "It should work if your knee holds up."

"No worries. The knee feels fine now."

"Okay, then. I'll sit on the sofa and you sit in my lap and hold onto that chair." Lowering himself onto the couch, he leaned back, grinning as his cock saluted her. "You get to do the work this time."

"Aw, but I'm the one with broken ribs," she lamented. "Have a heart."

"Try it, and if it doesn't work, we'll figure out something different."

She caught her lip between her teeth. "Just hope it doesn't set my recovery back a week or two."

"Oh, I hope not… Try bending down to kiss me first—a trial run, so to speak." He gave her a quick wink. "And I'd appreciate it if you'd lose the nightie."

She started to pull her gown over her head, but paused to glance down at Jade. The black cat sat on the floor nearby, gazing up at Miranda with a firm, unyielding expression, her pose as regal as that of an Egyptian deity.

"You two are ganging up on me." Snatching off her gown, Miranda tossed it in the cat's direction. "Just remember, you're my cat, not his."

He probably should've been concerned about whether or not she'd actually heard the cat speaking to her, but the sight of Miranda's shapely ass distracted him completely. "My God, you're gorgeous."

"No, I'm not." Turning, she crossed her arms over her breasts. "I don't feel...comfortable doing this in broad daylight."

He let his gaze roam over her body, wishing he could move her arms aside with the power of his eyes alone. "From my perspective, this is a vast improvement over doing it in the dark."

Her gaze heated his skin as it swept over him, lingering on his cock before flicking back to his face. "When you put it that way, I'll have to admit, I like being able to see you. But I'm sure you look a damn sight better than I do."

"That's your opinion. I'd say we were about even in the looks department."

She huffed out a breath. "You need glasses."

"And *you* need a better mirror." His cock pulsed, sending a bead of pre-cum spurting from his slit. In another moment, he'd have to take matters into his own hands. "Now, would you *please* kiss me before I lose my mind?"

Travis met her halfway as she leaned closer, her full, succulent breasts swaying toward him. Her kiss was soft and wet as she delved deeply into the recesses of his mouth, drawing a groan from him as her tongue slid past his in a sensuous caress. She affected him like no one else ever had. One kiss from her was worth a thousand from any other woman—a nuclear bomb compared to a firecracker. Cupping her breasts, he savored their weight and the satiny smoothness of her skin, loving the way her nipples responded to his touch.

Trailing kisses down her neck, he moved on to the warm softness of her breasts, burying his face in the deep valley between them—licking, sucking, kissing—before capturing a nipple in his mouth.

The quiver of her body's response drove him on to suckle the other firm nub. His cock was on fire, but he'd already been selfish enough. Wanting nothing more than to make her moan, he also knew that licking her all over would be a treat he would remember for a long, long time.

Without warning, she turned around, presenting her shapely backside to him. His breath caught in his throat, and he had to close his eyes to regain control. Now was *not* the time to come all over her ass. Positioning her between his legs, he grasped her hips and eased her down onto his cock.

Smooth as silk and hot as melted butter, her pussy held him in a fervent embrace. His head fell back and his mouth dropped open as a sigh escaped his lips, turning his words into more of a groan than actual speech. "You feel *so* good…"

He hardly dared to look at her as he held her hips in his hands, her back curved in a delicate arch, tapering to her waist before flaring out to her luscious bottom.

Miranda is sitting on my prick, fucking me. He bit his lip, trying desperately to hang onto the last few shreds of control he possessed.

Bracing her hands on the chair, she rocked up and down on him, rising up until his cock nearly slipped out before slowly gliding back down—again and again, ratcheting the tension ever higher, ever tighter. When she sat down hard, circling her hips, grinding his cock inside her, he got the moan he was waiting for. *The first of many.*

Her voice was barely a whisper. "Oh, wow…"

"You like fucking me, don't you?"

She nodded, shifting into the opposite rotation. "*Fabulous* cock… Feels like it belongs there."

"That's because it *does* belong there." Wiggling his ass, he pushed upward, seeking the deepest penetration possible. "Fuck me, Miranda. Fuck my stiff dick and make me come. Then I'm gonna do it to you."

And she did. Up and down, back and forth, and sideways. Travis has never been so thoroughly fucked in his life. With his eyes riveted to her beautiful backside, he held her hips in his hands as she swiveled them in his lap, driving him inexorably toward his climax. Moments later, indescribable ecstasy engulfed him, his head snapping back as he came with a cry.

With a firm grip on her thighs, he held her against him as his cock flooded her core with spurt after spurt of semen. The added slickness served as a reminder that there was more to this than his own elation; she needed to feel it too. He allowed himself a few minutes to savor the blissful sensations, letting his mind clear before relaxing his hold on her. He could have sat there for days with her heat wrapped around his cock, but at last, she leaned forward and rose from her seat, her pussy glistening with his cum.

"Now it's my turn." Stretching out the full length of the sofa, he helped her to straddle his head, placing her left foot on the ground, while resting the opposite knee beside his shoulder.

"You don't *really* mean…"

"Yes, I do. Sit on my face."

Her cum-soaked pussy hung tantalizingly above his lips, and he pulled her down, drilling his tongue into her soft folds. He'd never done that before, never tasted his own juice, but Miranda's whimpers of pleasure would have made him even more adventurous than that—the sounds she made were worth anything. *Everything.* Her hot pussy caressed his face until he found her clit and suckled it, occasionally delving inside to moisten his tongue before bathing the tight bud with his cream. When she finally cried out, he felt the tiny nub thrust against his lips, surging with the power of her orgasm.

Her climax sent need rushing back into his loins, and he eased her backward until she was once again impaled on his dick. Pushing up into her, he bounced her on his groin.

"I like the way you think," she whispered. "Matter of fact, I like everything about you."

Jubilation swept through him with her words, but there was one detail he wanted to be certain about. "Even the fact that I'm such a young pup?"

"Even that. A guy *my* age probably couldn't do this again—not as quickly, anyway." Closing her eyes, she sank her teeth into the fullness of her lower lip, but she seemed unable to stop a smile from turning up the corners of her mouth. Her head fell back, and she moved her hips in a slow, sensuous circle as though savoring the feel of him.

He wouldn't ask her if she loved him. Not yet. It was too soon. Even so, there was no doubt in his mind that he would be the one to say it first. He had no inhibitions whatsoever when it came to this woman. When the time was right, baring his soul would be as easy as baring his body. His only hope was that she would welcome his love as easily as she accepted his cock inside her.

A moment later, she dismounted in a move that was surprisingly graceful, considering her injuries, only to perform another laced with even more elegant eroticism. Her pussy lips beckoned as she straddled his head once again, this time facing the other direction. He had a brief moment to savor the vision before his eyes snapped shut and he sucked in a breath as her lips pressed his cock in a salacious kiss.

"Mmm...my incredible, edible Travis..."

Teasing his cockhead with her tongue, she cupped his balls, sending shivers of anticipation rippling through him. She obviously didn't mind the taste of his cum, but could he actually do it this time? Would she even want him to? As his cock filled her mouth he gave in to temptation and eased her down until his tongue penetrated her wet core. If there would ever be a time when he could come in a woman's mouth, this ought to be the one.

She seemed to sense his problem—either that or she remembered the last time—because she backed off, using only her hands. A crescendo of delirious pleasure ripped through him almost instantly, and he fired off a round that had to have splattered her face.

He might've believed her subsequent shudder was one of revulsion had she not held onto his cock, massaging her cheek with the slick, swollen head. As her body contracted, he savored the burst of tangy wetness that followed.

To his surprise, she giggled—a sound that ended with what was surely a gasp of pain. "It figures. The one time I really *need* to collapse on top of a guy, I can't do it."

As she crawled forward and reached for the box of Kleenex on the end table, Travis scooted out from under her and sat up. "I don't feel much like moving myself. That was like…*wow*."

Wiping the cum from her face, she landed in a heap where his feet had been. "No kidding." With a groan, she keeled over onto his lap. "Stick a fork in me, Travis. I'm done."

"No apple pie?"

She waved a dismissive hand. "Later."

Chapter 23

Travis had never felt less like going back to work in his life—not even when he'd had the flu—and it wasn't because he felt bad. Aside from the fact that he'd miss her like crazy, leaving Miranda home alone all day gave her free rein to do everything her doctor had told her not to do. Knowing her, she'd probably get bored and start putting new siding on the house or give the garage a good cleaning. Then there was the whole food junkie thing.

She certainly didn't adapt well to idleness, which made him wonder if she'd still have the hots for him when she went back to work and had less time to kill.

Great. I'm making myself sound like an occupational therapy project.

He considered bringing her some knitting supplies to keep her busy—an idea he promptly rejected after concluding that, while she might use the yarn to tie him to the bed—certainly an interesting diversion—he didn't even want to *think* about any alternate uses she might dream up for knitting needles.

In the end, he left her sitting on the sofa with a book, a cup of tea, her phone, her computer, and the TV remote, but doubted that any of those things would keep her out of trouble for long.

"Remember, absolutely no heavy lifting," he warned after he kissed her goodbye for the third time.

"I promise I'll be good." Her grudging response made him long for a surveillance camera. Unfortunately, a phone call now and then would have to suffice.

Every chance I get.

His first client of the day was one he'd never met—the horse *or* the owner—and within five minutes of his arrival, he wished he still hadn't met her.

After her first admonition to "Call me Lorene" when he'd addressed her as Ms. Malford, he'd decided she was the type whose attractiveness increased with distance. Blonde hair showing nearly black at the roots, she wore far more makeup than the occasion warranted, and she had a sultry, used look about her, like a rodeo honey who'd spent too many nights in the back of some cowboy's pickup.

She'd told Travis who recommended him when she'd made the appointment, but for the life of him, he couldn't put a face to the name. In addition to suspecting her of making up the story, her horse was a real pain in the ass. Unruly and bad-tempered, the mare refused to stand still and nipped at his butt constantly while he worked. Lorene must've thought this behavior was cute, because she didn't attempt to put a stop to it, seeming content to simply apologize. "So sorry she keeps doing that. It's *such* a bad habit."

Travis nodded his agreement, biting back a retort as he clinched the last nail. *Thank God...*

"I should pay you extra for the trouble." Her hand grazed his back. "Or maybe I could take you out to dinner sometime."

The suggestive nature of her touch set off warning bells in his head, and he was about to trot out his standard *I don't date my clients* rule when it occurred to him that for once in his life, he had the perfect excuse. "No need. Besides, my girlfriend wouldn't like it." *And neither would I.* He was dying to add that Miranda would probably rip Lorene's bleached-blonde hair out by the roots if she even *thought* about taking him to dinner, but he left it at that. Still, overkill or not, it would've been fun to see her reaction.

"The jealous type, is she?" The woman's pout was almost audible.

Travis couldn't resist. Setting down the mare's hoof, he straightened up and turned to face Lorene, affecting a thoughtful frown as he scratched his chin. "Jealous? No. I wouldn't say she was jealous. I think *vengeful* might be a better word."

The way her eyes widened was downright comical. "Sounds kinda scary."

"Nah, she's a real pussycat if you treat her right." Actually, she was more of a tigress, but that was a detail Lorene didn't need to know. "And I make a point of doing that."

Before Lorene could say anything else, he picked up his rasp and filed down the clinches. Giving the mare a final pat, he announced, "She's all done."

"What do I owe you?"

Travis stated the amount as he gathered up his tools. The sooner he got back on the road, the better. After pocketing the check, he waved goodbye and climbed into his truck, hoping the mare would hold onto those shoes for a good, long time. Normally, he would've scheduled a follow-up appointment to reset them in six weeks, but for once, he didn't bother. Repeat business from Lorene and her nippy little mare was something he could easily live without.

Following a quick call to ensure that Miranda was behaving herself—*I haven't done a damned thing! Honest!*—he drove on to his next client.

Two more jobs later—both of which went far more smoothly than the first—he stopped in to see Alan for lunch. After selecting a sandwich from the grocery's refrigerated display case, he took a seat in the deli and waved at Alan.

If anything, his cousin appeared even worse off than the last time he'd seen him, making Travis wish he'd stocked Alan's fridge with junk food instead of Miranda's. "Dammit, Alan, if you lose any more weight, you'll disappear."

"And when I do, all the women who've ever told me to get lost will undoubtedly rejoice." Alan's riposte proved he hadn't lost his ready wit, but his smile lacked conviction.

In the face of his cousin's plight, Travis couldn't help feeling a little guilty about his own happiness, because for once in his life, he had a woman and Alan didn't. Somehow he doubted that Lorene would be the solution to anyone's problems, but he figured he could at least make the suggestion. "If you're looking for a quickie, I think I know where you could get laid."

Alan winced and flung up a hand, his jaw clenched in denial. "This is the longest stretch of celibacy I've been able to pull off since I learned how to work my dick. Do *not* tell me. I don't want to know." Closing his eyes, he took a breath so deep and deliberate Travis could almost hear him chanting a mantra.

"Guess I shouldn't mention Miranda, either."

Blowing his breath out slowly and completely, Alan opened his eyes. "I take it my instructions were of some use."

The memory of Miranda's luscious bottom bouncing in his lap triggered a smile. "Oh, yeah. Can't thank you enough."

"I'm glad you're getting some, Travis. I really am. Are you in love?"

"If I'm not, I will be soon. She is *fabulous*. The perfect woman—at least, she is for me." The wistful nature of his cousin's expression prompted him to add, "Your perfect woman is bound to show up eventually."

Alan snorted. "I don't think the right *woman* for me exists. I'd need a full harem to keep up with my needs, which is hard to come by in this day and age. No one woman can do it, and I've decided it isn't fair to even attempt monogamy when I can't be trusted. This is better. I've been working out to use up the excess energy."

Judging from Alan's super-lean frame, his caloric intake wasn't keeping up with the demand. Travis took a bite of his sandwich. Stuffed full of alfalfa sprouts and topped with a few slivers of avocado and a tiny bit of cream cheese, if this was the sort of thing Alan normally had for lunch, it was no wonder he couldn't maintain his weight. "You look like you could use a sack of cheeseburgers."

"I feel great," Alan insisted. "And I don't need cheeseburgers—although I *have* developed an insatiable craving for chocolate ice cream. I've been hitting that ice cream parlor across the street at least once a week."

"It's a wonder you don't freeze your nuts off eating that stuff this time of year."

"Might be a good thing if I did," Alan said. "Might help me keep my dick under control."

Travis arched a brow. "I doubt it. I've seen the cute girls scooping out the ice cream in that store. I'm surprised they don't bar the door whenever they see you coming."

"Contrary to popular belief, I *can* control myself in public."

Alan paused, frowning. "Usually."

"Uh huh." Travis couldn't help being skeptical. A wide counter may have separated the employees from the patrons, but, being a very popular place, the customers were often lined up together for extended periods while they waited for their sundaes. A woman stuck in line with Alan might never want ice cream again.

"How's Stuart taking all of this?" Alan asked.

"I don't know. He seems happy for me, but he's still kinda shell-shocked from his divorce. No matter what I say, I can't convince him that women don't hate him."

"Yeah, well, maybe we've all lost our marbles. You falling for a married woman shocked the shit out of me."

"Miranda isn't married."

"Yes, but you thought she was, which amounts to the same thing."

Travis couldn't argue with that logic, because he'd berated himself with it more than once. "I'd like to take her home to meet the family. Not sure what Dad will say when he spots her wedding ring."

"She's still wearing it?"

Travis blew out a breath. "Yeah. I'm not sure I have the right to ask her not to. Not yet, anyway."

"Might be best to let her decide that on her own."

Something else I can't argue with. "You know, for a self-described sex maniac, you possess a surprising amount of wisdom."

Alan shrugged. "I do my best to understand the feminine point of view. Hasn't done me any good so far, but it hasn't hurt, either."

"So you're saying you can understand why women don't necessarily want sex every hour of every day, you just can't use that information to help you stifle your, um, urges?"

Alan actually smiled—this time with a touch of genuine amusement. "Something like that."

"Like I said, you might find the right girl someday. Don't give up yet."

"I haven't. This is an exercise in self-discipline, not a permanent lifestyle."

Travis suspected that sooner or later Alan's control would snap. And when it did, the lady on the receiving end would be in for the surprise of her life. "In the meantime, the harem idea has merit. I'll keep my eyes peeled for volunteers."

"You do that."

ℰℭ

Despite the phone call to check up on her, Miranda had the strangest feeling that she'd seen the last of Travis, and she was at a loss to explain why. He'd given her no reason to suspect that he was unhappy with their current arrangement, but that niggling little doubt persisted.

Maybe I'm just bored. With Travis around, she'd certainly never had *that* problem. She needed something to keep her mind off him—*and* the contents of her refrigerator. Having decided that he might notice if she ran the vacuum, she took a shower, did a Web search on the length of time required for broken ribs to heal (three to six weeks), and posted her status on Facebook. *Ribs still sore and crunchy. Headache gone. Not hearing the animals talk to me...much*—which drew a phone call from Tracy.

"Hey, Sis. Saw your status update. What's all that about? Are you hurt again?"

Miranda hadn't bothered to inform her family about her accident, mainly because she knew they'd needle her incessantly. After the first few trips to the ER, she'd decided that only life-threatening emergencies needed to be reported. "A little."

"A little? Animals are talking to you and that's all you can say?"

"Okay, but please don't tell Mom and Dad. You *know* how they are."

"I'll grant you that, but you could've at least told *me*. What happened?"

Preparing for a lengthy conversation, Miranda sat down at the kitchen table and gave her sister a quick rundown of recent events, concluding with, "Travis has been looking after me ever since."

"Oh, ho! So that's why you didn't bother to call me. You already had a nurse—and a hot one, at that."

Miranda sighed. "He is *totally* hot, and you wouldn't believe how sweet he is to me. I really don't deserve him."

"You deserve a sweet guy and then some, so don't give me any crap about being undeserving," Tracy snapped. "I take it you've finally owned up to your attraction to him."

"Sort of. I'm still not sure I can admit it to myself, but he's bound to have picked up on the idea."

"You aren't telling me a whole helluva lot." Miranda could almost hear her sister's tapping foot.

"I don't *know* a whole helluva lot. I keep feeling like I'll wake up and find all of this is another hallucination."

"No, it isn't. It's something that should've happened a long time ago—and probably would have if you hadn't been so damn stubborn. Travis is a nice guy. Don't run him off."

Miranda rolled her eyes. "That's what Kira told me." She thought Jade might have said something similar, but she wasn't clear on that. Then again, it could have been Lola or Denise…

"At least your horse has some sense, even if you don't. Has he met Levi yet?"

"No, but I'm hoping that'll happen this weekend. I'm not sure what I'll do if Levi doesn't like him. You know how blunt he can be."

Tracy snickered. "No shit. I'll never forget the time he told me I had a big butt."

"Me, neither." Her son's tendency to say exactly what was on his mind could be embarrassing at times. Simply because she couldn't find any flaws in Travis didn't necessarily mean that Levi wouldn't. "Thank God Travis isn't a smoker. I'd never hear the end of it."

"Score two points for Travis," Tracy said. "Don't worry so much about what Levi thinks. This is *your* love life we're talking about, not his."

"True—although that may change. Evidently, he's taken a liking to one of the girls he works with. I don't mind telling you I'm a little nervous about the idea."

"Of course you are—and it would be wonderful if he found someone—but don't let yourself get so wrapped up in his romance that you forget yours."

Miranda couldn't help chuckling. "Damn, Tracy. Who are you? My sister or something?"

"Yes, I am, so don't think you can kid me. I know how your mind works, and I know how hard it was for you to take the plunge. Do you love Travis—or at least think you can love him?"

"I should," she said with a rueful laugh. "In fact, I should be counting my lucky stars that he's here with me at all. He's sweet, sexy, adorable, and fun. He takes excellent care of me and everything else, all of my animals seem to like him—hell, I even spotted one of my skittish little barn cats rubbing on his leg while he was filling up the birdfeeder."

"But…"

Miranda blew out a breath. "For some reason it isn't enough and it's bugging the hell out of me—more so when I'm alone than when I'm with him. When he's here, everything seems terrific. But after he left for work this morning, I started having doubts. I mean, why is he interested in me, anyway?"

Tracy actually growled. "Should I make a list of your stellar attributes? Or would a swollen head make your concussion worse?"

"Don't bother. And don't scream at me when I say this, but something's missing. I just can't seem to put my finger on it."

"I can tell you *exactly* what's missing. Your sanity."

"I know! He's such a great guy—he's even going to fix the windows in the barn. He did ask me if he could, so I can't accuse him of trying to take over—"

"Oh, my God. Don't start with that."

"Tracy, you of all people should be able to identify with that feeling—that loss of control."

"No shit, but I can also relate to wanting someone in my life to share the load and have fun with. You've been working your ass off your whole life. Even the things you *like* to do could be seen as work."

Miranda knew she was right. "The trouble is, he seems to be assuming a claim on me that I don't understand. It's like he knew how I felt about him before my accident, or he learned something that day—something I can't remember. Part of me wants to accept and enjoy him, but another part of me is still trying to figure out exactly how it happened."

"Couldn't you just ask him?"

"That would sound really stupid. I can hear me now—*Hey, Travis. What the hell happened between us? Was there something I missed?* It's like the moment he realized I wasn't married I suddenly became his girlfriend."

"Let me get this straight. You're pissed because your affair began without your stamp of approval or because it wasn't your idea?"

"Not really. I feel like I wasn't consulted. Like my wishes didn't matter."

"But you had the hots for him. I know you did!"

"So the fact that I got my wish justifies the means?"

"Did it ever occur to your twisted brain that you truly might have missed something?"

"There've been times when I thought I did, but how could I forget something that significant?"

Tracy snorted a laugh. "Come on, Miranda. You know better than that. Concussions don't differentiate between trivial memories and the really crucial stuff. You need to talk to him. Seriously."

"I know, but…"

"If this is bothering you enough that it might screw things up between you two, you need to swallow that stiff-necked pride of yours and ask him. I think you should believe him too. He doesn't strike me as a liar."

Since Tracy's experiences were a large part of the reason Miranda had avoided men after Kris's death, having her vouch for Travis's honesty actually meant something. Not that he needed anyone to vouch for him. *He's perfect, remember?* He wouldn't lie, especially not about something that important.

It was her own honesty she questioned—or perhaps having the

nerve to *be* honest with him. Despite her concussion, she recalled her shaky resolve to tell him how she felt about him. Evidently, she must've said or done something, otherwise none of this would've happened.

Or would it?

"No, he isn't a liar. He's a perfectly wonderful, honest, reliable man. The fact that he's still single is nothing short of a miracle."

"Then treat him like the miracle he is," Tracy advised. "Don't ruin the best chance for happiness you may ever have."

"Okay, okay…"

After a bit of catching up, Miranda said goodbye to her sister and switched off the phone. "Now what do I do?"

Glancing sideways, she spotted something lying on the floor beside the trash can in the corner. Curious, she got up from the table and bent to retrieve it, noticing two things. First, that she was able to reach it with surprisingly little pain, and second, that the object in question was an unopened condom packet.

Unable to recall ever bringing it into the house, she could only assume that it belonged to Travis, but how it had ended up in that particular location was anyone's guess. He must've tossed it in the general direction of the trash can and missed. *But why?* A quick check of the date stamped on it proved it wasn't expired, so there appeared to be no reason to have thrown it away.

Unless he knew he would never need it.

The subject had never even been mentioned anytime they'd been intimate. True, he knew that becoming pregnant was impossible for her—he'd learned that during the ER visit—but what about sexually transmitted diseases? He might have known *he* wasn't carrying any, but he couldn't have known that about *her*.

Trusting fellow, isn't he?

Great. Now she had another question that would make her feel like a complete idiot for asking. Granted, it was a little late to be worrying about catching anything from each other, aside from the fact that he might take her query as a sign of distrust. Given the trust issues he'd had with the obstetrician, she suspected that challenging his integrity would be an offense he wouldn't easily forgive.

She wanted nothing more than to keep her mouth shut and continue to ignore her concerns, but allowing them to fester to the point that they poisoned the relationship was unthinkable. Tracy was right. She *did* need to talk to him.

Now all I have to do is find the nerve.

Chapter 24

In the end, Miranda opted for the coward's way out of her dilemma. She simply left the condom sitting in the middle of the table in the hope that Travis would see it and make a comment.

It's certainly a conversation-starter. After that, she did her best to ignore the evils lurking in the refrigerator and started cleaning out closets. Bagging up old clothes to take to the Goodwill wasn't much different from doing laundry, but she figured if she left the heavy lifting for Travis, he wouldn't fuss too much.

She was in the process of cleaning out Levi's closet when she found two sleeping bags, only then remembering that she'd bought the extra one with the intention of accompanying Levi on his first camping trip with the Scouts. She'd wound up having to work that night and had never used it, nor had Levi seemed disappointed by her absence. Although that campout had been a giant step toward his current level of independence, at the time, Miranda had been worried sick.

Thinking back over all that had happened since then, she was once again amazed by how much he had achieved—and especially how much he had matured in the last three or four years. He'd gone from a kid who had to have an aide at school and a driver to take him out a couple times a week, to a young man who lived in his own apartment and drove himself to work. And now he seemed to think he had a girlfriend. How would he react to his mother having a boyfriend?

He'd come a long way, but he was still a creature of habit, disliking change far more than most people. Moving to the farm and then to his apartment in town had been difficult enough. If Travis were to become a permanent fixture in her life, Levi would have to adapt.

Permanent fixture? Sounds like I'm thinking about marrying him.

Almost as though it had spoken to her, the flag sitting in its display case on the dresser drew her eye. Crossing the room, she picked up the photograph of Kris that sat next to it. Although she could easily see his resemblance to Levi, no one would ever accuse her of falling for Travis because he reminded her of her late husband. Travis was drop-dead handsome by anyone's standards. Kris, on the other hand, was cute in a slightly goofy way, with big ears and freckles. The quality of the smile and the twinkling eyes were similar, though. Maybe that was it.

She tried to recall the first time Kris had smiled at her and couldn't do it. They hadn't known each other until their senior year when they were both aides for the same teacher. He'd been a Grateful Dead fan, and she could never hear one of their songs without thinking of the first time he'd played "Truckin" for her. Funny how she could remember that, but not the first time he'd kissed her. Even funnier was the fact that she was a little fuzzy about her first kiss with Travis.

However, she had no difficulty whatsoever when it came to recalling that first hug. All she had to do was close her eyes, and she was standing in Nigel's barn with Travis's arms flung around her. Biting down on her lip, she relived that rush of emotions—the sexual excitement, the wistfulness of knowing that a hug might be all she'd ever get from him, the battle with herself to step away when it was the very last thing she'd wanted to do…

"I should have kissed him," she whispered. "*Really* kissed him." Tears stung her eyes as she considered what might have happened next—especially since he'd thought she was married. Would he have kissed her back, or would he have pushed her away? He'd admitted to fighting his attraction to her because she still wore Kris's ring. What would've happened if she'd explained her reasons for wearing it then?

Her gaze shifted to the band of gold on her left hand. From the moment Kris had placed it there, she'd never taken it off. She remembered that moment with perfect clarity. A wedding chapel in

Jellico, Tennessee. The sunbeam that turned his golden hair to flame. The steady warmth of his hands in contrast to the chilly tremors of her own. She'd been so nervous, but so much in love her heart felt like it had grown three sizes that day.

Like the Grinch Who Stole Christmas, Kris had said when she told him about it later. She'd punched him for laughing and then ended up giggling right along with him.

She stole another glance at his picture. "It's time, isn't it?"

His smile never wavered as she pulled the ring from her finger. "I know just the place for this." Opening the back of the case that held the flag, she slipped the ring inside, positioning it in the center of the base of the triangular frame. She set the case back on the dresser with the photograph next to it. "Loving you doesn't mean I can't love anyone else, Kris. Took me a long time to see that, but I finally do."

In that instant, she realized that if she'd taken this step sooner, she might be in another place with a different man, rather than with Travis.

Kissing her fingertips, she pressed them to the wooden case. "Thanks for making me wait for the right one."

Her reverie might have lasted longer if the dogs hadn't started barking. Moments later, the back door slammed in a way that informed her that this wasn't Travis coming home early. It was Levi.

"Uh, hi, Mom," he said, dropping the mail on the kitchen table as she came down the hallway. "I'm home."

"I can see that." She studied him for a moment, trying to gauge his mood. "I wasn't expecting you until Friday. Is something wrong?"

"Aunt Tracy called me. She said you were hurt."

Leave it to Tracy to force the issue. "I fell on the ice Saturday morning and hit my head. Broke some ribs, too. I'm doing better now, though." She pointed to the bump on her head. "See?"

He stepped closer, scrutinizing the wound. "That had to hurt! Why didn't you tell me? I would've come home to help you."

"I didn't want you to worry, and I, um, already had someone here to help me." Averting her eyes, she spotted the condom sitting out in plain sight right next to where he'd laid the phone bill. Her only hope was that he wouldn't realize what it was.

He frowned. "Who is it?"

"His name is Travis York. He's…a friend of mine. He puts shoes on horses. I see him at my riding lesson all the time."

"Trabis?"

She shook her head. "No. It's Travis with a V."

"Travis," he repeated. "Is he your boyfriend now?" As usual, Levi cut right to the chase.

Miranda blinked and her knees lost some of their strength. "Yes, he is."

He glanced at the clock. "Is he feeding the horses? It's four o'clock, you know." A stickler for routine, Levi had always fed the cats and dogs at four while she went to the barn, and he fussed anytime she failed to lie down for a nap at precisely one o'clock if she had to work that night.

"Don't worry, he'll feed them when he gets here."

"I think he's already here. There's a truck in the driveway."

"Really? He must've gotten home just before you did and gone straight up to the barn." Either that or the dogs didn't see fit to bark at his truck anymore.

"I have a girlfriend." Evidently, Levi felt he'd discussed Travis enough. "Her name is Tabitha. I want to marry her."

Miranda took a second to steady her knees and pick her jaw up off the floor. "You mentioned her before. Are you sure she likes you enough to marry you?"

"She kissed me."

"That doesn't necessarily mean she wants to marry you. She might have only done it to be nice."

"She *is* nice, but she said she kissed me because she loved me."

This was going to be tough. Miranda had yet to hear of a girl who truly loved Levi, at least not in the way he wanted them to. Although every woman who worked at the school was crazy about him—from his kindergarten teacher to the ladies who worked in the office—none of them had ever kissed him. Then again, the taboos at school didn't necessarily apply to the workplace. She *really* needed to meet this girl… "Are you sure she meant it that way?"

"Why wouldn't she?"

"You're sort of different, Levi. None of the other girls you've known have wanted to be your girlfriend—or marry you." This Tabitha had probably been kidding around, not realizing that Levi took everything literally. He actually believed TV commercials and thought that all a guy had to do was smell good to get women to fall for him.

"Oh. Well, maybe she's different too."

His crestfallen expression nearly broke her heart. "I'm sorry, sweetie. Maybe she really does love you. I'll ask her about it later."

"Okay," he said. "Do you love Travis?"

She didn't see any point in complicating things or denying it. "Yes, I do."

"I love Tabitha," he said with conviction. "And I want to marry her. I want to have a boy baby and a girl baby. I *love* children."

Much more of this and she'd be crying her eyes out. "I know you do," she said gently. "We'll just have to wait and see how things turn out. Have you had supper yet?"

"Tabitha fixed me a hamburger and French fries to eat before I left the store."

"That was nice of her. I'm getting ready to make dinner for Travis and me. You can meet him when he gets back from the barn. I think you'll like him."

Levi frowned. "He doesn't smoke, does he? I *hate* it when people smoke."

"I can't say that I care for it much, myself. Don't worry, he doesn't smoke."

"Tabitha doesn't, either," he said. "I really like Tabitha."

She made a vain attempt to divert him to another train of thought. "How's work been lately?"

"Oh, fine."

So much for that.

By the time Travis had finished feeding the horses, Levi was already pacing the floor and talking to himself. Nevertheless, he snapped back to reality as soon as Miranda introduced him to Travis.

Leveling a stern look at Travis, he demanded, "Are you going to marry my mom?"

Travis didn't bat an eyelash. "Maybe. I don't know if she likes me well enough yet to say for sure."

"I'm going to marry Tabitha," Levi declared. "I think she likes me enough."

Travis grinned. "I hope she does. Is she pretty?"

"Of course she is," Levi said, rolling his eyes. "She's beautiful."

"Can she cook?"

Levi nodded. "She makes cookies for me."

"Good cookies?"

"*Delicious* cookies," Levi replied with his biggest, widest smile. "She's going to school to be a chef."

"That's nice." Travis shot Miranda a wicked grin. "I made brownies for your mom. I think she should marry me for that."

"Cookies and brownies are great, guys," Miranda interjected. "But they aren't a very good reason for getting married."

"I dunno," Travis said with a slow wag of his head. "I make pretty good brownies."

She glared at him, hoping he'd take the hint. "Can we talk about something else?"

Travis replied with a wink and a nod. "So, Levi, do you like horses?"

"Yes, but I don't know how to ride them. They're kinda scary, you know?"

Travis suspected he'd found a kindred spirit in Miranda's son, particularly in light of the fact that he'd all but proposed for him. "What else do you like?"

"I like Tabitha."

"And I like your mom. Did you know I've been staying here to take care of her?"

"Yes, she told me."

"I'm feeling much better now," Miranda said. "Although he still won't let me go to the barn." Her sidelong glance put Travis in mind of his comment to Lorene. She certainly looked vengeful. *And totally hot...*

Levi frowned, shaking his head. "But the horses will miss her. You should let her see them."

"She can see them tomorrow. She should be well enough by then."

Miranda rolled her eyes. "Finally! I was beginning to think you were going to keep me cooped up in the house forever."

Travis chuckled. "I'll admit to having an ulterior motive. You'll probably throw me out, now."

"Nah, you're too handy to have around." Her flippant reply and dismissive wave had him worried until he realized what was missing.

Her wedding ring. Holy shit. Stunned speechless and completely overjoyed, he stood gaping at her with no clue as to whether to keep his mouth shut or squeal with glee.

Thankfully, he didn't have to make that decision because Levi beat him to it. "Mom! You lost your ring!"

Travis smiled at Levi, his respect for the boy increasing with each passing moment. "Don't miss much, do you, Levi?"

"No, I don't," Levi replied. "She never takes her ring off. Ever."

Miranda nodded toward her son, arching an eyebrow. "Have I mentioned how observant he is?" Although her tone was light and teasing, Travis could've sworn she was blushing. "No, I didn't lose my ring. I took it off and put it away."

"How come?" Levi seemed puzzled, and Travis couldn't blame him for that. He was a little puzzled himself—but hopeful.

"I should have stopped wearing it years ago. Your father is gone, Levi. I have to accept that and move on."

Levi stared at her in frank disbelief. "Of *course* he's gone. He died a long time ago. Didn't you *know* that?"

Evidently, Levi had a better grasp of the situation than his mother did. For an instant, her face seemed to crumble, then she lifted her chin ever so slightly and met his gaze head on. "Yeah, I knew that. I just never had a good enough reason to believe it until now."

Levi cocked his head, eyeing her askance. "You must've been really crazy, Mom."

His matter-of-fact tone had Travis biting back a chuckle as Miranda's hand flew to her lips, although not quickly enough to cover her smile. "You got me there, Levi. I probably *was* a little crazy. I'm over it now."

"Good," Levi said with a firm nod. "Now you can marry Travis."

Travis shouted with laughter. "I like the way you think, Levi. How about us guys have a talk while your mom fixes dinner?" With a wink at Miranda, he shepherded her son into the living room. If things turned out the way he was beginning to suspect, he'd be having the birds and bees discussion with Levi one day—possibly sooner than Miranda realized.

Might be a good idea to get to know him better first.

Miranda stared after the two men, still not quite sure what had just happened. Had Travis asked her to marry him, or did Levi do it for him?

Reviewing the conversation, she decided that while Levi had been the one to bring it up, Travis certainly hadn't tried to shoot down the notion—a pertinent detail that ignited all sorts of warm fuzzy feelings in her heart. He hadn't pressed her for an answer, though, which was probably a good thing. She wasn't sure how many momentous developments she could take in one day.

And I was worried about Levi...

After all this time, he could still surprise her. He'd gone off with Travis like they were old buddies—although the fact that Travis had encouraged him to talk about Tabitha was probably responsible for his easy acceptance. *He* hadn't been the one to burst the kid's bubble or try to let him down gently. He'd encouraged him to talk about the girl, even going so far as to prompt him for a list of her attributes. The possibility of a broken heart was never mentioned— although that discussion might be occurring now that they were out of earshot.

She'd been looking forward to their meeting, and yet dreading it at the same time. Obviously she needn't have worried. Levi was as blunt as they came, but Travis didn't seem bothered by it. Then again, he hadn't told Travis he was a terrible person for trying to steal his mother's affections from his late father. No, he'd bypassed the bullshit and told her *she* was crazy.

Another thing she hadn't anticipated was how cute they would be together. With very little effort, Travis had managed to bring out the fun side of Levi, and they were both so charming when they smiled. Miranda couldn't help being pleased by this, because the kid wasn't always happy. Sometimes he seemed downright melancholy, which made her wonder how he acted around Tabitha. Did he follow her around like a lovesick pup? Or did she make him giddy to the point that he couldn't stop laughing?

Despite having grown up quite a bit in recent months, Levi was by no means a typical twenty-two-year-old. Tabitha had to realize how immature he was. Surely she wasn't seriously considering marriage, and knowing Levi's blunt tongue, he'd probably already asked her. Miranda doubted his ability to deal with having a girlfriend, let alone a wife.

She hoped Tabitha had enough sense to realize that, and she also hoped that money wasn't the issue. Miranda had used most of Kris's death benefits to pay for the farm. Being naturally frugal, she'd managed to hold onto a nice little nest egg, which she'd been advised against putting in trust for Levi, since it would've rendered him ineligible for support services.

Therefore, there was no tempting trust fund for a spouse to siphon money from, and now that Levi had a full-time job, he wasn't even receiving Supplemental Security Income money anymore. If Tabitha was truly interested in Levi, she needed to be aware of that, plus the fact that Miranda was not only his parent but his legal guardian. She had to give her permission for him to marry, and it would take a lot more than cookies to convince her to do that.

Chapter 25

Travis hadn't expected to take an instant liking to Miranda's son. Nor had he expected the boy to make him laugh quite so much. And he especially didn't think Levi would turn out to be his best ally in his quest to win Miranda's hand. But damned if he wasn't turning out to be just that.

"Mom needs a husband," Levi insisted. "I don't know why she never found another one after Dad died. She's very pretty."

Travis nodded. "I know she is. I'm glad she didn't find a guy before me, though. I'd be pretty upset if I fell in love with her and she was already married." Actually, upset was too mild a word. Stronger terms like heartbroken, torn up, and devastated were more appropriate.

"Good point!"

Levi's style of speech seemed to put an exclamation mark after everything he said. Miranda had described him as entertaining, and perhaps he was simply "on" because Travis was a new acquaintance. He certainly kept the three of them chuckling for the greater part of the evening. If he'd been at Miranda's Christmas party, Travis would've had a hell of a lot more fun—and not only because meeting Levi then would've made it quite plain that he was Miranda's son, rather than her husband. Levi was a hoot.

He didn't even mind that Levi's presence curtailed the plans he'd had for that evening. There would be other opportunities to make love with Miranda, and the more he and Levi talked, the more he realized how much he was hoping to be in this for the long haul. He had every intention of marrying Miranda and looked forward to claiming Levi as a stepson.

The fact that a stepson would be all he would ever have should've bothered him, but it didn't. He'd told Miranda before that having children wasn't a high priority in his life, and he had an idea that there might be some grandparenting in their future. That is, if Levi and Tabitha could convince Miranda that marriage was appropriate for them.

He opted to reserve judgment on that until he knew Levi better—not to mention Tabitha—aside from the fact that Levi was Miranda's responsibility, not his. He had no claim to Levi unless he and Miranda were to marry, and perhaps not even then. There was also the possibility that they might not see eye to eye on such a touchy issue. After all, Miranda had known Levi since birth; Travis didn't have that advantage.

Although Levi was obviously immature in some ways, in others, he seemed very wise—particularly in light of what he'd said to his mother about moving on after his father's death. She'd had other reasons for remaining single, and Travis certainly couldn't fault her for wanting to keep her son safe. Still, he hoped she wouldn't flatly refuse to give her consent to the marriage if it ever truly became an issue. Like anyone else, Levi deserved his shot at happiness.

For the moment, however, he had no say in any of it. Levi was Miranda's son and she was his legal guardian. Travis was nothing more than a friend of the family.

Well...maybe a little more than that...

Should he stay the night if Levi didn't go back to his apartment? Miranda hadn't dated anyone before; therefore, Levi had no experience with any of his mother's boyfriends sleeping over. Sighing inwardly, he realized he probably needed to go, and not only because of Levi.

Although Stuart hadn't said anything about wanting Travis to come home, he *had* been pretty needy in the wake of his divorce. There was always the chance that if he got lonely enough, he might actually go out and meet someone new—a step he'd been very reluctant to take. Stuart hadn't done any dating since high school. Now he had an ex-wife in addition to a broken heart, two kids, and a mortgage, his marriage having taken several years longer to turn sour than Travis's had.

Given their collective experience, Travis was surprised he believed happy marriages were even possible. Stuart's attitude was still iffy, and although his self-esteem was at an all-time low, finding someone would probably be much easier than he thought. Girls had been drooling over Stuart since grade school, and as far as Travis could tell, they were *still* drooling.

In the end, he waited until ten o'clock and then kissed Miranda goodnight, not a bit happy knowing that a kiss would have to suffice.

Miranda, on the other hand, seemed to appreciate the gesture. With a nod toward her son, she smiled her thanks and gave him a hug that kept him warm all the way home.

Travis was halfway there before he realized he hadn't mentioned that condom he'd spotted on the kitchen table when he arrived—or the fact that it was gone when they'd sat down to dinner. Perhaps Miranda had already had the birds and bees discussion with Levi—maybe even while he'd been up at the barn feeding the horses.

Bet that was interesting.

ഗരു

For a first meeting, that didn't go too badly. Having been the other half of a two-person family for so long, Miranda couldn't have predicted how Levi would react to a new addition. She'd hoped he wouldn't see Travis as an intruder—and he hadn't, at least not yet. Perhaps he never would. "So, did you like Travis?"

"Yeah. He's nice. You should marry him."

She rolled her eyes. "Come on now, Levi. Marriage is a lot more complicated than that, and you know it."

"But if you love someone, you should marry them. It'll work out. Trust me."

Miranda suspected that he was simply parroting something he'd heard someone else say—perhaps even a line from a movie, since he had a tendency to do that. "Where'd you hear that?"

He shrugged. "I don't know. But it's true, isn't it?"

"Sometimes." She blew out a sigh. "And sometimes it doesn't

work out no matter how much two people love each other. There are other problems that make it hard."

"Like what?"

"Like the fact that I'm nine years older than Travis." The sharpness of her reply shocked her into softening her tone. "He's never had any children of his own and I can't have babies anymore. He might say it doesn't bother him now, but someday, it might. Aside from that, I'm not sure I can stand having anyone tell me what to do. I've been my own boss for too long." Travis might not seem like the controlling type, but that didn't mean he wouldn't turn out that way eventually.

"But aren't you lonely living out here all by yourself?"

"Maybe. I didn't used to be." Travis had probably already spoiled her. Likely as not, she'd think about him every time she climbed into bed, or fixed dinner, or smelled brownies baking in the oven. Then there was the whole peanut butter issue. She'd never look at a jar of peanut butter the same way again. "Are you lonely living by yourself in town?"

"Oh, no. I like it."

That wasn't too surprising. Levi had never had the slightest difficulty keeping himself entertained. On the other hand, Travis was the most fun *she'd* had in years. "Well... I do like having Travis here."

"Marry him, Mom," he urged. "It's the right thing to do."

His firm conviction made her smile. Everything had always been black or white with Levi—gray areas simply didn't exist. This was one area, however, that seemed pretty murky to Miranda. "We'll see."

৪০০৪

Tuesday morning, Travis parked his truck at Nigel's and hurried inside, itching to get the day over with. He only had one horse to do there and another job at one o'clock. After that, he was free until eleven the next day. Stuart had seemed pleased to have him home again, but Travis could hardly wait to get back to Miranda.

Nigel led out a chestnut gelding that was favoring his left forefoot. "He could barely walk on Thursday," he said as he snapped on the cross-ties. "He improved quite a bit over the weekend."

"Probably an abscess." Travis ran a finger around the coronary band, just under the hairline at the top of the hoof. Sure enough, there was a soft, open place where the pocket of infection had burst open and drained. After cutting the clinches, he pulled off the shoe, the dark hole in the toe plainly visible. "It's not in a nail hole, but yeah, it's an abscess. See where it blew out here?"

Nigel leaned down and nodded. "I figured as much. Can you still reset the shoes?"

"Sure. Now that the abscess has run its course, I can pack the hole before putting the shoe on. He might be sore for a few days, though."

"Not a problem," Nigel said. "His owner hasn't ridden him in ages, and she hasn't paid her board bill since November. I've been using him as a lesson horse off and on. The girl who rides him the most has canceled her lesson the past two weeks—it's been too cold and icy."

"No shit." Travis knew quite well Miranda wouldn't be riding today, but force of habit being what it was, he couldn't help glancing up as a truck and trailer pulled into the drive.

Evidently, Nigel had noticed that same tendency. He nodded toward the truck. "If you're looking for Miranda, she won't be here for a few weeks. She slipped on the ice Saturday morning and wound up with a concussion and some broken ribs."

Obviously she hadn't told Nigel who'd driven her to the hospital—or the details of anything else that had happened that weekend—when she'd called to cancel her lesson. Travis had been trying to figure out how to bring up the subject on the way over, but Nigel had given him the perfect opening. "Yeah, I know. I was there when she fell. Been taking care of her ever since."

Nigel's eyes widened, then his jaw dropped as the full meaning sank in. "You don't say."

"Oh, yes, I *do* say." Scowling, he added, "And would you mind telling me why you never mentioned the fact that she was a widow?"

"Bloody hell," Nigel swore, clearly aghast. "D'you mean to say you didn't know?"

"How the devil was I supposed to know when she was still wearing her wedding ring?" Travis snapped. "Jesus, Nigel. After all the carrying on I've done about women who were all wrong for me... I was nuts about Miranda! Why didn't you say something?"

"Dunno. I'm not very good with women, you know." He paused, rubbing the side of his nose in a contemplative manner. "Wait. Why didn't *she* tell you?"

"Because she thought I was too young for her."

"Well, you are, aren't you?"

"Oh, don't start that crap," Travis said, rolling his eyes. "She's only nine years older than me."

Nigel tipped his head to the side. "Is that all? Really? I'd have guessed more."

Travis snorted a laugh. "Better not let her hear you say that."

"Oh, I know exactly how old she is," Nigel said with a brisk nod. "She's forty-five. I remember that because she said something about having five years on me when I turned forty."

"Then what the hell did you mean, you'd have guessed more?"

"You're the one with the baby face. You tell me."

Travis bit back a snarl. "I'm thirty-six! I can't help it if I don't look my age."

"Yes, well, neither does Miranda." Nigel sniffed, pursing his lips. "D'you know, I believe you'd be perfect for each other."

Slightly mollified, Travis couldn't help but agree. Nevertheless, he was curious to hear Nigel's take on it. "How so?"

"She's such a sensible woman. Never gives me a bit of guff when I tell her she's doing something incorrectly. Always tries her best. Never argues."

Doesn't sound like the woman I know. "That's only true during a riding lesson. The rest of the time, she's pretty opinionated."

Nigel went on as though Travis hadn't spoken. "She never cries—just laughs at me when I fuss. Wish all of my students were like her." He hung his head, sighing deeply. "Love that mare of hers, too. Awesome ass."

"Oh, *yeah*… What? Wait a minute, whose ass are you talking about?"

"The mare's." With a dreamy look in his eyes, Nigel heaved another sigh. "Absolutely incredible. If Miranda could ever get her to engage that big engine, she'd be spectacular."

Travis cleared his throat with an effort as he recalled an even more spectacular ass bouncing up and down on his lap. "I'll take your word for it."

∞∞

Thankful that the horses had spent most of the night outside, Miranda did her best to take it easy while cleaning the stalls. While she worked, she listened closely, half hoping one of the horses would make a comment. However, after hearing only the usual snorts and nickers, she sighed with regret as she gave Kira a pat. "Too bad that wasn't permanent. I'd be one helluva horse-trainer if we could actually *discuss* how to do a flying lead change."

As the rest of the day dragged on, she tackled another long-overdue chore. Sitting on the floor in front of the woodstove with her file box, she went through old bills and bank statements, tossing any unnecessary documents into the fire. By the time Travis arrived, she'd sat there so long, her legs were completely numb.

"Damn, you must've really been bored to do that," he declared after she'd explained her task. "I take it Levi isn't here."

She nodded, holding out a hand. "He said he had to get back to work, but *I* think he just couldn't wait to see Tabitha again."

Taking her hand, Travis helped her stand, then pulled her into his arms for a long, slow, deep kiss that would've made her knees weak whether her legs were asleep or not.

"Believe me, I know the feeling." He kissed her again before adding, "I really like your son, Miranda. It's easy to see why you're so proud of him."

"He never ceases to amaze me. I didn't know what he'd say when he found out you'd been staying here with me."

Travis chuckled. "As I recall, he told you to marry me."

She rolled her eyes. "We had a little talk about that. Not sure I convinced him of anything, but—"

"I thought he had the right idea, myself."

Drawing in a ragged breath, she gave him a tremulous smile. "A little premature, don't you think?"

"Not really." He gave her left hand a meaningful squeeze. "Especially since you finally decided to take off your wedding ring."

"I knew that might be…awkward, but I didn't mean for you to think—"

He pressed another kiss to her lips, effectively silencing her. "Miranda. All it means is that you've decided you're ready to move on. Not that you intend to marry me or anyone else."

She nodded. "Levi obviously didn't see it that way. He's never been one to beat around the bush, but…" She paused, feeling the flush rising in her cheeks. "He thinks I'm lonely living here all by myself. And maybe he's right. I've been so busy with the horses and other things, I hadn't realized... Anyway, I want you to know, it's been wonderful having you here. I didn't think it was such a good idea at first, but now..."

"Why, Miranda." Clasping her upper arms, he leaned back slightly, his tone light and teasing. "Does this mean you want me to stay on?"

"That's up to you. I know you have your own home and other things to take care of. It would be selfish of me to expect you to stay forever."

"Not selfish at all. These past few days have been the best of my life, but Stuart *was* pretty glad to see me last night." He paused, shaking his head. "He just hasn't been the same since his divorce."

"Maybe he needs to get out more. I know of at least three women I could fix him up with."

"Yes, but if it turns out like your last matchmaking attempt, he'll fall for *you*—and then where would we be?"

"Not likely," she said. "Once he meets Christina, he'll never look twice at me."

"Maybe—although I can't see him having any more in common with her than I did." He shot her a sidelong glance. "And yes, I know she thought I was boring. Of course, the fact that I was only pretending to be interested in her might have had something to do with it."

"You were pretending?"

He shrugged. "I didn't want you to think I didn't like your friends, so I picked one."

"Yeah, the prettiest," she said with a wry smile. "I'm sure that was a really tough decision for you."

"She was the first one I met. It seemed sort of mean to make her think I'd met her first and then decided on one of the others."

At least he was considerate. "That was nice of you, even though you weren't entirely truthful. You told me things were going pretty well. Her story was completely different."

"I didn't want you to think it was my fault," he said sheepishly. "I wanted it to be her fault so you wouldn't get mad at me and never speak to me again—or hug me." He paused for a moment. "You know, that day at Nigel's when you hugged me, I thought you were just doing it to be kind, but there was more to it than that, wasn't there?"

She nodded. "I'd been itching for an excuse to get my arms around you for a long time." Taking a deep breath, she plunged onward. "It was tough feeling the way I did all the while believing you'd already ruled me out." If he'd had *any* idea what she'd been thinking back then... "I hadn't looked at a man in ages, and you never once looked back."

"Oh, yes I did. You just didn't see it. Hell, I scheduled all my appointments at Nigel's so I could be there when you had your lesson."

"Really?" *And I'd considered changing days so I wouldn't see him anymore.* "What would you have done if I'd quit taking lessons?"

"I have absolutely no idea. There for a while, I didn't even know your last name. I suppose I could have pumped Nigel for information—although after the Christmas party, I at least knew where you lived. I'd have found *some* reason to turn up on your doorstep." He ran a hand through his hair. "Even though I knew you were married, I couldn't help how I felt."

"Me, neither. You wouldn't *believe* the fantasies I used to have about you."

"I might," he drawled. "I had some pretty hot ones myself."

His slow, lip-curling smile made Miranda wonder if any of them involved getting his cock sucked during lunch—which might explain a few things. Not that she'd minded.

"Speaking of fantasies..." His eyebrows lifted suggestively as his long, sexy dimples began to emerge.

"What about them?"

"I've been having one all day." Moving closer, he placed his hands on her hips.

"About what?" *If it involves licking your succulent dick, count me in...*

"Remember when we talked about lying out on the deck in a sleeping bag?" Kissing her neck, he skimmed his fingers up and down her spine.

"That reminds me, I found two of them when I was cleaning."

He nodded. "I noticed them setting in the hallway last night." He pulled her against his groin. His hard cock was right there, straining against the zipper of his jeans, begging for her attention. "So how about it, Miranda? Wanna spend the night under the stars with me?"

"As long as we put lots of padding underneath the sleeping bags. I'm not so sure my ribs can take lying on the deck all night."

"I brought one of those inflatable mattresses from home. Stuart used to sleep on it when he first moved in with me. I thought it might come in handy sometime."

"You thought right. It's not supposed to rain tonight, is it?"

"Nope," he replied. "For once, it's not going to rain or be very cold. And I don't have any appointments until eleven."

His tongue grazed the side of her neck, releasing a flood of tingles.

"Ooh, *baby*..."

Chapter 26

Miranda awoke to the sound of birds chirping, the sun's heat on her face, and the solid warmth of Travis spooned up against her back. They'd fallen asleep in the same position they'd made love, her body still humming from the feel of him rocking into her from behind. A muted snuffle and a soft thumping nearby prompted her open her eyes to meet expectant gazes from all three of her dogs. She was about to nudge Travis when the dogs leaped up in unison and dashed down the steps, barking madly.

Rising up on her elbow, she cocked her head. "D'you hear something?"

"You mean aside from the dogs?" Judging from his tone, he hadn't appreciated the canine wake-up call. "Sounds like a car going down the road."

She hesitated, listening. "Holy shit, what day is it?"

"March first," he replied, yawning. "Please don't tell me you're disoriented again."

Sitting up the rest of the way, she unzipped the sleeping bag, praying she wouldn't jam it in her haste. "I am *not* disoriented and that is *not* a car going down the road. It's someone coming up the driveway. Probably the meter reader. She usually comes on the first of the month."

"So?"

Miranda got to her feet, gesturing frantically toward the meter on the wall by the door, which was less than six feet from where they were lying. "So, the meter is right *there*."

Travis scrambled out of the sleeping bag in record time, proving how quickly he could move when the need arose. They made it inside just as the car reached the house and came to a stop. Naked and giggling, they darted into the kitchen.

"Damn, that was close," Travis exclaimed as they heard the car drive away.

Hands pressed tightly to her side as she rested her hip against the edge of the table, Miranda could scarcely control her laughter enough to speak. "We probably would've given that sweet little old lady a heart attack."

"She's probably seen a lot worse," Travis said, chuckling. "Besides, if we'd been inside the sleeping bag, she might not have realized we were naked."

"True, but why else would we be sleeping on the deck when we've got a perfectly good bed in the house?"

"She still wouldn't have actually seen anything." With a low whistle, his heated gaze roamed up and down her body. "Unlike what I'm seeing now. *Wow.*"

Suddenly, Miranda felt more exposed than she'd ever been in her life, almost as though she'd been caught naked by a stranger. Fighting the urge to cover herself, she attempted a puzzled frown. "It's not like you're seeing anything you haven't seen before—is it?"

"Must be the morning light—or maybe it's because we're in the kitchen." The corner of his mouth lifted in a seductive smirk as he flicked an eyebrow. "C'mere and kiss me like you did the first time." His voice dropped to a low rasp. "Like you could swallow me whole."

A swift, downward glance certainly demonstrated the impossibility of swallowing his *dick* whole—*but I'm perfectly willing to give it a try.* Fascinated, Miranda couldn't recall that it had ever been quite so enormous before.

Guess it's that morning light thing...

Her brief attack of modesty completely forgotten, she hurled herself into his embrace. Winding her arms around his neck, she pulled his head down and devoured him, astonished at the unbridled hunger that made her crave even more. Sliding her hands down his back, she stroked his tight, muscular ass, seizing it with both hands, squeezing hard as she pulled him tightly against her.

His hard, drooling cock now trapped between them, she pushed his hips side to side, spreading his slick cock syrup over her skin.

Exhaling as her name escaped his lips, he thrust his tongue deep into the recesses of her mouth. As their tongues sparred with one another, Travis imitated her hold on him, pressing his fingers into her buttocks as he inched her backward until her bottom rested on the edge of the table. Pulling her leg up with one hand, he slid the other hand between her legs, soaking his fingers in the flood of moisture from her pussy.

Unable to maintain her grip on his ass, Miranda snaked her arms around him and held on, her fingertips roaming through the soft hair on the back of his head. With a ragged breath, he tore his mouth from hers and dipped his head to her breast. His tongue was warm on her nipple, and he laved it mercilessly while circling her clit with his thumb. Overwhelming sensations washed through her, leaving her too weak to hold on.

As her hands slipped from his shoulders, Travis let go of her leg and scooted her further back onto the table. Bracing her hands behind her on the smooth surface, Miranda's gaze locked with his astonishing blue eyes as he knelt down to bury his face between her thighs. She caught only a brief glimpse of the top of his head before her neck arched backward as he latched onto her clitoris.

Within seconds, her mind shifted to an image of Travis's balls dangling enticingly above her lips. As her body embarked on the steady ascent to the pinnacle of her climax, a scream rose in her throat, escaping only when her fantasy self sucked a testicle into her mouth. Torrents of an orgasmic storm thundered through her, wrenching more cries from her with each swipe of his tongue.

With a shuddering sigh, Travis let go of her clit to rest his head against her inner thigh. "I didn't forget this time."

Miranda had absolutely no idea what he meant by that and didn't care because, without pausing to elaborate, Travis surged to his feet and scooped her into his arms. Holding her close to his chest, he scattered fervent kisses over her face and neck before resting his head on her shoulder.

"Suck me, Miranda. *Please*." His voice was so deep and rough, she barely recognized it. "Put my dick in your mouth and suck it."

Needing no further encouragement, she slid off the table and sank to her knees, taking his cock in her hands. Pressing wet kisses along the length of his shaft, she opened her mouth when she reached the crown, savoring the slick sauce that spurted from his slit. As his dick slid past her lips, a deluge of moisture flowed from her core, drenching her halfway to her knees. She'd been hot before, but *nothing* like this.

With her orgasmic vision still fresh in her mind, she moved on to savor his balls, bathing the scrotal skin with his own slippery fluid until the glistening orbs seemed to beg her to suck them. His swift, gasping inhale as she allowed the first one to drop into her mouth seemed to herald his climax, but he held on, threading his fingers through her hair as she continued to devour him. Switching to the other side, she held his testicle in her mouth while caressing it with her tongue. Wrapping her fingers around his rock-hard cock sent a flood of lava rushing to her center, intensifying her aching need for him.

Letting go of his balls, she turned her gaze upward. The sight of his face there above her while his heavy cock rested on her cheek made her crave him to the point that she couldn't even be polite about it. "Come on, Travis. Fuck me. *Now*."

His response was so immediate, she barely had time to register the soreness in her bottom when he pulled her to her feet and clutched her buttocks to lift her onto the table. "Think you can lie on your back?"

"I'll try."

As he leaned over to ease her onto her back, the light fixture hung above his head like a halo. However, since neither of them had bothered to turn it on, there was nothing to compete with the fire in his eyes.

No longer resembling the sweet, adorable man she'd fallen in love with, Travis had somehow been transformed into raging stallion—a change that suited her mood perfectly. Suddenly overcome by an intense feeling of déjà vu, Miranda knew that somehow, somewhere, they'd done this before, and she shivered with anticipation as she awaited his next move.

Lifting her feet up to rest on his shoulders, he penetrated her tight passage in one swift stroke. His engorged cock filled her completely, and she grasped the edge of the table, holding on for dear life as he slammed into her. Although she had to hold her breath to stabilize her fractured ribs, she wasn't ready to complain about the position—yet. The pleasure totally eclipsed any pain she might have felt.

"Do you like that, Miranda?" Breathless with lust, he gazed down at her, his eyes heavy-lidded, yet aflame with desire.

Unable to speak, she could only nod in reply. Gradually, his thrusts slowed, becoming more deliberate as he lengthened the stroke. Her eyes widened as a tight knot formed deep inside her— growing, expanding—until it exploded with the power of an erupting volcano. Her eyelids snapped shut as every muscle in her body contracted in the wake of her orgasm.

"You are so totally hot." Travis ground out the words as he came with a cry and a push that nearly flipped Miranda's feet up over her head. The sudden pressure on her chest squeezed out a gasp, and he backed off immediately. "Sorry. Didn't mean to squash you."

A cough to push her ribs back into place drew a yelp from Travis and a giggle from her. "Feel good?"

"Oh, *yeah*. Do it again. Feels like—*wow*."

"Don't know if I can," she said breathlessly. "I gotta get off of my back. Help me up."

Gathering her in his arms, he set her on her feet. "Better?"

"Compared to what?" Barely able to stand, Miranda clung to him as semen ran down her leg. "Oh, my God, that was freakin' *awesome*."

Tipping her head back with a finger beneath her chin, he planted a kiss squarely on her lips. "Not quite as wild as the first time, but close."

"Oh, come on, now," she protested. "The first time was *nothing* like that. It was great, but..."

"Oh, yes it was," he insisted. "Only better."

"Maybe it was for you, but my ribs were hurting worse then."

Travis stared at her as though she'd lost what was left of her mind. "No, they weren't. You didn't fall until afterward." He blinked twice, then his mouth dropped open. "Holy shit," he whispered. "You don't remember, do you?"

She shook her head slowly. One of them had to be crazy, and she had a feeling it wasn't Travis. "You mean we had sex *before* I went to the barn?"

He nodded. "Oh, yeah. Crazy, wild, monkey sex right here in the kitchen."

For a moment, her mind went completely blank—a circumstance that undoubtedly showed in her expression—until the significance of that missing event finally sank in. "That explains a lot. *Damn...*"

"I think you'd better have a seat," Travis advised as he pulled out the nearest chair. "So, tell me, what *do* you remember?"

She sat down, gingerly rubbing the side of her head. The bump had shrunk considerably in the days since her fall. Unfortunately, her memory hadn't improved along with it. "I remember fixing breakfast and getting a phone call from Levi, which was when you figured out I was a widow. Then you hugged me—at least, I *think* you did. The next thing I remember is Kira telling me to hold onto her tail so she could help me up the hill."

"And you don't remember the sex at all?"

"Apparently not." *Great. Something I've dreamed about for months and I can't even remember it. How ironic...* "Did we have a good time?"

He laughed. "That's putting it mildly. It was without a doubt the best sexual experience of my life."

This is getting weirder by the second. "What on earth did you do?"

"Pretty much what I did this time—and you did a lot of the same things, too." He paused, scratching his chin. "Maybe I don't have much of an imagination, but the whole ball-sucking thing was something I'd never even thought of."

"Oh, come on," she scoffed. "I'm sure every man ever born has wanted someone to suck his nuts."

He shrugged. "Maybe so, but I never dreamed anyone would ever actually do it—and I certainly wouldn't have asked you to."

Great. He thinks I'm a ball-sucking slut. Her face tingled as a flush crept into her cheeks. *How embarrassing...*

He must've noticed her blush because he hastened to add, "Don't get me wrong. I loved every minute of it. I was just...surprised."

She frowned. If the first time was anything like the most recent episode, she'd enjoyed it quite a bit herself. The strange thing was, she'd never done anything of the sort, even with Kris. Surely she would've remembered if she had—then again, she'd already forgotten about it once. That enticing vision she'd had—which could only have been a momentary flash of recollection—must've been what prompted her to do it this time, but what the devil made her do to begin with? "Okay. Start from the beginning and tell me everything."

It was his turn to blush. Clearing his throat, he pulled up another chair and sat down. "We were here in the kitchen, and I'd just figured out you weren't married. I—we talked about why you never told me you were a widow and the difference in our ages. You were washing dishes and I came up behind you and asked for a hug." He paused, smiling wistfully. "I was beginning to believe a hug was all I'd ever get from you, but then you asked me to kiss you." He stopped again, running a hand through his hair. "It was one helluva kiss too. After that, I don't know...we sort of went wild. You tried to push down my sweat pants, and I pulled off your nightgown." He shrugged. "After that, it was a lot like what we did today—except for the broken ribs. You'd already sucked my balls once before, so it didn't have quite the same effect today, but that time, I couldn't even stand up. I about fell into a chair and I was about to come in your face when I grabbed you by the ass and put you on the table. I'd never fucked anyone so hard in my life, and you obviously loved it. Hell, we were *both* screaming."

No wonder sucking him had seemed so familiar later that day—and it hadn't been a dream or something she'd fantasized. It had actually happened. *Oh. My. God.*

"And after that, I just went out to feed the horses?" That seemed a bit odd. Perhaps he was making this up—although she couldn't imagine why he would do such a thing. Then again, she *had* found bruises on her butt that looked like fingerprints.

He nodded. "I said something about how I didn't think you'd be *that* hot, and you got all embarrassed and said you had to go feed the horses and started getting dressed. I'm pretty sure I had you convinced there was no reason for you to be embarrassed by the time you left the house. I was watching through the window and saw you fall."

"When I was at the hospital, I had a flash of memory like I was looking up at you from the middle of the kitchen table. Then when we actually did that a little while ago, I got this weird déjà vu feeling. As for the ball-sucking thing, when you were, um, licking me, I had this…vision…of your balls dangling above my mouth, and I came when I took it a step further and imagined sucking them."

He grinned. "I guess you liked that, too. Do you remember anything else—any other flashbacks?"

She shook her head. "Not a thing." Somewhere in her subconscious mind, she must've remembered everything, which would explain why she'd repeated the performance under similar circumstances, but— "Did you use a condom?"

"I had one, but you said I didn't need it, so I pitched it."

"That fits. I found it behind the trash can on Monday and left it sitting on the table, hoping you'd see it and say something."

"I saw it all right," he said with a chuckle. "I figured you'd been discussing birth control with Levi."

She shuddered. "Now, *there's* a scary thought. I haven't had to do that yet. I've mostly told him to keep his hands off the girls."

"You might need to have that talk with him pretty soon."

"No shit."

An awkward silence fell. Aside from making the obvious comment that she was getting cold from sitting there naked, Miranda couldn't think of a thing to say. Later, she would undoubtedly have loads of questions, but since he was the only one who could remember anything, she thought it might be best to let him talk.

His expression grew thoughtful as he tipped his head to one side. "You know, I was a little worried at the hospital when they asked if you were pregnant. You seemed pretty sure you couldn't be, but I still wondered about it. I mean, you were so sure even though we'd just done it that morning without any protection."

She rolled her eyes. "I was sure I wasn't pregnant because I knew I'd had a partial hysterectomy—aside from the fact that I hadn't had sex in fifteen years." Another thought occurred to her, bringing on a frown. "Wait a minute. If you thought I was married, how come you had a condom handy?"

"Because my dad taught me to always have at least two on me at all times." He hung his head, looking perfectly sheepish. "And also because Travis is a very bad boy. You've no idea how close I've come to losing control. I certainly lost it on Saturday morning." His lips curled into a wicked grin. "But then, so did you."

"Apparently. Geez, you make it sound like I attacked you."

"Attacked? I wouldn't put it that way. Actually, it was more like you...*annihilated* me."

Miranda's heart skipped at least three beats. "I annihilated you? That sounds terrible."

His ensuing shout of laughter didn't do much to reassure her. Taking her hand, he gave it a meaningful squeeze. "Didn't I just tell you it was the best sexual experience of my life? I loved being annihilated—or pounced on, or attacked, or whatever you want to call it. You can do it again anytime you like."

"Hmm...that might seem a little contrived. Maybe it was only first-time enthusiasm."

"Good God, I hope it was more than that—besides, today came pretty close."

"Maybe it was something you said or did that set me off."

"I dunno," he said with a slow wag of his head. "A lot of things happened that day. I might have trouble remembering it all."

"Well, if you think of anything, be sure to write it down or tell me. God only knows what it'll take to trigger my memory."

"Don't worry, I will. I've only been waiting my whole life for someone to knock my socks off like that." Releasing her hand, he cupped her cheek and leaned in for a gentle kiss. "*Now* do you see why you can't get rid of me?"

"I'm beginning to get the idea."

Now if I can just remember why I annihilated him in the first place...

Chapter 27

After breakfast, Travis accompanied Miranda to the barn with a fair amount of apprehension. Having taken over her chores for the past few days, he'd discovered that windows weren't the only things in the barn that needed fixing. Some of the lights were burned out and three electrical outlets didn't work at all. He'd stopped by the hardware store on Monday and picked up several items, but, preferring to visit with Levi, had held off doing any of the actual work until Tuesday afternoon. He'd also fed the horses that evening, with the result that Miranda had yet to see what he'd done—nor had he told her about it.

Prior to becoming a farrier, Travis worked in building maintenance, so replacing outlets was an easy task for him—he'd even had fun doing it—and he was happy to do whatever he could to help her out. Unfortunately, he'd only had her permission to fix the windows, and while most people would've been tickled to death to have their own personal maintenance man, Miranda wasn't typical. She could be rather prickly at times. He only hoped the great sex they'd enjoyed that morning softened her attitude a bit.

She didn't argue when he began cleaning the stalls. Nevertheless, he got the distinct impression she didn't think he was doing it correctly. More than once, she took a breath as though about to speak, but stopped before saying anything. Was there a *wrong* way to shovel manure?

Travis looked up to find her standing in the doorway of the stall he was cleaning, which happened to be the one that had required the most repairs. Since he'd flipped on the light—which was now fully functional—his interventions were easy to spot.

"I see you did more than fix the windows." She hesitated, taking a deep breath. "What do I owe you?"

He threw her a quick glance before dumping a shovelful of manure into the wheelbarrow. "Have I asked you for money?"

"No, but I feel like you should. I haven't even paid you for the ditch yet. I must be running up quite a bill."

"It didn't cost much—and I'd be more than happy to take payment in kisses." He paused to give her a wink and a smile. "Although, if you decide to pay me *that* way, you might wind up getting overcharged." Even in a ragged hoodie and patched jeans, she was still the answer to his every dream—and most of his prayers. He propped the shovel up against the wall. "You can make the first payment now, if you like."

For a second, he'd been sure he was in trouble. Her slow smile put his worries to rest.

"My pleasure." Pushing the wheelbarrow aside, she came into the stall, slid her arms around his waist, and laid a big one on him.

How many times had he seen her at Nigel's and wished she'd grab him and kiss his lips off? Too many. *I could* so *get used to this…*

One of the horses let out a snort and Miranda broke off the kiss, aiming a scowl at the culprit. "Be quiet, Kira. He's mine."

Travis's dick was already half-hard, but hearing Miranda stake a claim on him sent even more blood rushing to his groin. He was about to strip off her jeans and nail her against the wall when he remembered her broken ribs—and realized that she'd been carrying on a conversation with a horse. "Damn."

She drew back like he'd slapped her. "What?"

Oops. "Totally unrelated comment," he said quickly. "Never mind that, what did you just hear?"

"Nothing. She didn't actually *say* anything. It was her attitude."

"Oh." Travis couldn't decide if reading attitude into a snort constituted a hallucination or not. Then again, seeing her horse as a rival for his affections couldn't be good. Maybe he needed to introduce her to some of his more amorous clients—Lorene, perhaps.

No possible way.

Miranda arched a brow. "You seem almost disappointed that I

didn't understand her. Do you *want* me to be crazy?"

This was getting too complicated. "No, I don't want you to be crazy." Nor did he want her to feel like she had any rivals for his affections—equine or otherwise. Blowing out a breath, he tucked an errant lock of hair behind her ear. Shelley's jealousy and possessiveness had driven him up the wall. On the other hand, belonging to Miranda aroused him in ways he couldn't have predicted. "Unless you're crazy about *me*."

"Hmm… Don't know about that…" With a sly smile, she dug her fingers into the front of his jacket and pulled him in for a kiss that made his nuts ache. "What're the symptoms?"

"Not sure. Might be an overwhelming urge to pounce on me when I least expect it."

"Got that one," she said with a nod. "Although in my opinion, it's a perfectly sane thing to do—unless I were to tie you up and *then* pounce on you."

Travis had never ejaculated as the result of a mere thought, but this time, he came damn close. He cleared his throat with difficulty. "That might be considered crazy."

"True, but it's a different kind of insanity—the kind that makes perfectly ordinary women turn guys like you into their love slaves."

"Not sure I'd like it if an *ordinary* woman made me her love slave." He groaned as she ran the tip of her tongue up the side of his neck. "But then, there's nothing ordinary about *you*."

"So, you'd like it if I buckled a curb chain around your cock and balls and snapped a lead rope on it?"

His gut clenched as a gush of pre-cum soaked his briefs. Doubling over, he smacked his forehead against her shoulder. "Dammit, Miranda, you're gonna make me come if you don't stop."

"That's my plan." Her deep-throated chuckle sent even more fluid gushing from his slit. "I dearly love jerking your chain." Flicking his earlobe with her tongue, her warm breath on his neck set off a wave of tingles that had him quivering with anticipation. "Bet I could even make you come in my mouth if I tried hard enough."

In another minute, it would be a moot point. Sucking in a ragged breath, he shook his head. "Can't do it."

"I've noticed that. I don't suppose anyone's ever laid you down on a bale of hay and sucked your dick, have they?"

"Nope—especially not after they've been talking about ropes and chains."

"Think that might make a difference?"

With Miranda, anything was possible. "I don't know. I've got a pretty strong mental block against it."

"The teachings of childhood?"

Considering his father's strict admonitions, Travis was amazed that he could let a woman suck him at all. "Something like that."

"Aha! A *challenge*." Her eyes flashed with excitement, drawing him into their emerald depths. He'd be drowning in them soon.

My God, she's sexy.

She nodded toward the hay stacked behind a gate on the opposite side of the barn. "You go pick out a nice, comfy bale. I'll be right back." With a quick pat on his cheek, she left the stall.

His mind in a daze, Travis stared after her until a snort from Kira snapped him out of his stupor. "Yeah. Right. I'm going."

After pulling down a couple of bales from the top of the stack, he couldn't decide what to do next. Should he be sitting there waiting with his dick hanging out when she returned, or would she rather take his pants off herself?

In the end, he was glad he'd at least sat down when she sauntered over with two saddle pads and a Western-style rein. If he'd been standing, his knees probably would've given way beneath him.

"Thought this would work best." Tossing one pad onto the hay bale and the other onto the pallet, she held up the coil of thin leather. Stretching it out between her hands, she yanked it tight, the snapping sound marking the end of his hesitation.

Two seconds later, Travis had stripped off his jeans and was sitting on one bale while leaning back against the other, his stiff dick poised and ready.

With a mischievous grin, she looped the rein over his erection. Crossing it underneath his balls, she pulled it up for another pass over the top. "Have I ever told you what a fabulous dick you have?"

Travis gulped in a breath as she tugged on the rein, drawing his nuts up against the base of his penis. "The first time you saw it, all you said was wow. I'm surprised I didn't come in your face."

Chuckling, she tickled his balls before stroking the full length of his shaft. "From that, I can only assume I was on my knees at the time."

Travis nodded as more syrup welled up from his slit. "Yeah—and I'd just pulled off your nightie." If she didn't watch out, he was going to come in her face for real. "One of the more memorable moments of my life."

"Wish *I* could remember it." With a dismissive wave, she went on, "Best not to dwell on that right now—although I'm sure I was stunned speechless."

"Me, too."

Miranda settled herself on the saddle pad between his legs, taking one end of the rein in each hand. "No holding back, now."

"I'll try not to." Since he was already hovering on the brink, holding back wouldn't be the problem. The constricting rein had his dick so tightly engorged, the head was purple and veins stood out on his shaft like ropes wound around a fence post.

"I mean it," she said firmly. "Don't be thinking about baseball or anything else to slow you down. If you feel like you're going to come, let it go, you hear? I want to taste your juice."

Travis let out a strangled gasp as she pulled on each end of the rein, aiming his dick straight at her mouth. After an instant of breathless expectation, she went down on him, her warm lips closing over the head. His cock pulsed, sending a spurt of slick fluids into her mouth. Sweeping her tongue side to side, she spread the creamy liquid over the underside of his shaft.

I'm gonna come so *hard...*

Fisting the reins in one hand, she wrapped her fingers around the base of his penis, sliding up and down, using her saliva and his own lubrication for a smooth, frictionless glide. The sight and feel of her mouth on his dick, the stroke of her hand, and the frequent swipes of her tongue drove him quickly toward his climax. He was so close, so very, very close...

A heartbeat away from the point of no return, he sucked in a breath as the old taboo slammed into his brain, threatening to block his ejaculation. He could almost hear his father's voice. *You put your dick in a condom and then put it in the only place God intended. None of that disgusting, perverted crap, you hear?* In desperation, he tried to think of something else, *anything* to get those words out of his head.

As though she sensed the impediment, Miranda let go of his dick to massage his balls. That simple act, in addition to the strap around his junk and her tongue swirling over his cockhead, blanked out every coherent thought—and most of the incoherent ones. Within seconds, his head snapped back as his cock spewed out so much semen he was surprised it didn't run down her chin.

Gazing up at him with a triumphant expression, she backed away slowly, sucking off every last drop. Licking her lips, she swallowed. "Mmm…quite tasty. Must do that again sometime."

Travis gazed at her, scarcely able to believe what had just occurred. Granted, it wasn't a life-altering event, although given the circumstances, it was enough to make him at least *wish* he could give her the moon and stars on a silver platter. Gathering her up in his arms, he pulled her onto his lap and kissed her. "I can't *believe*… That was…you are…so incredible… I need to do a helluva lot more for you than fix a few windows. Got any other wishes? A new roof? Or maybe a new fence?"

With her wistful sigh and a glance over her shoulder as clues, Travis knew what she was going to say before she even opened her mouth.

"A concrete floor."

Thanks to the ditch he'd dug, the barn aisle was no longer a quagmire, but it was still a long way from being dry. He might have to call in some favors to get the job done, but he had every intention of making it his next project.

"You got it, babe. Even if I have to mix every square foot of concrete by hand, you got it."

ഉരഈ

When Levi came home late Friday afternoon, Miranda wasn't surprised to see that Tabitha had come with him. She'd followed him in her own car, which probably meant that she was only there for a brief "get acquainted" visit and wouldn't be staying the entire weekend.

Thank God.

Miranda had no idea what to expect, nor had she been looking forward to the meeting. She was protective of her son, which was natural, but Levi's history made the stakes even higher. Whether she gave her consent or not, he could still wind up with a broken heart, an outcome Miranda hoped to avoid at all cost.

As she stepped out onto the porch to greet them, she would've given a lot to have Travis there beside her.

Whoa. That's a first.

Having been Levi's advocate since birth, she'd dealt with countless issues, and she'd usually done it alone. Unfortunately, meeting Levi's girlfriend and discussing the possibility of their marriage was nothing like trying to decide whether or not Levi could tackle algebra. The emotions involved were entirely different. Miranda's wish for Travis's support proved that he was already becoming a part of her life, and, subsequently, her son's.

They both got out of their cars and Levi took the girl's hand, gazing at her with frank adoration before turning to face Miranda. "Uh, hi, Mom. This is T-tabitha."

Tabitha appeared to be no less smitten. The smile she gave Levi held no trace of indulgence for his stuttering introduction, only warmth and affection. "Nice to meet you, Mrs. Jackson."

"Nice to meet you too, Tabitha. Call me Miranda."

Levi had told Travis that Tabitha was beautiful, which, in Miranda's opinion, was an exaggeration. A nice-looking, girl-next-door type, Tabitha was rather thin with shoulder-length brown hair and appeared to be in her late twenties—a factor that Miranda hadn't expected. She couldn't help wondering if Tabitha knew Levi wanted to marry her.

After the introductions, Levi started toward the house, but Tabitha hesitated. "I'd like to see the horses first, if that's okay."

Miranda's heart sank. A private conversation with Tabitha was something she would've preferred to avoid. Nevertheless, it had to happen sooner or later. "Sure," she replied. "You go on inside, Levi. We'll be along in a few minutes."

Levi nodded. "Okay."

Miranda led the way across the yard to the gate where the horses stood waiting for their afternoon feeding. Miranda rattled off their names, and Tabitha petted each of them in turn before she finally spoke. "I suppose you're wondering why I'm here."

"Not really," Miranda said. "Levi talks about you a lot."

"Did he tell you we were dating?"

"Sort of. He said you kissed him because you loved him and that he wants to marry you."

"Sounds like something he'd say."

"Is it true?"

"Oh, yeah…"

Tabitha's heartfelt tone and accompanying sigh led Miranda to believe she was sincere. On the other hand, if she truly did love Levi, she was the first woman to do so.

"You know, most women treat him more like a younger brother than a potential boyfriend. He has a lot of good qualities, and I love him dearly, but let's be realistic. He has autism, which I assume you've realized. There are plenty of normal guys around. Why him?"

Tabitha's expression hardened. "Why *not* him? Being normal isn't all it's cracked up to be. Levi is the only man I've ever felt I could trust. On top of that, he actually *wants* to get married and have children. And I really do love him. When he first started working at the store, cleaning the parking lot and dusting the shelves, I thought he was cute and funny. Then they asked me to train him to help out in the kitchen, and I realized how much I enjoyed being with him. He grills hamburgers while I do the rest of the cooking, so we spend a lot of time together. I—I don't know—I sort of fell for him."

"I can understand that," Miranda said gently. "I love him too, but his children could turn out the way he did. Are you sure you want to take that risk?"

"Everyone takes a risk when they have children, and his kids might be perfectly normal." She gave Kira a pat on the nose. "I'm twenty-seven. I don't want to wait much longer. There are risks associated with older mothers, too. "

Until she'd actually met Tabitha, Miranda hadn't expected a ticking biological clock to be an issue. "True, and I doubt he would have any problems fathering a child. He's told me he wants a boy baby and a girl baby. I'm just not sure he's ready to be a father."

Tabitha sighed. "I know he's a little immature, but so are a lot of guys—and some of them are older than he is."

Miranda certainly couldn't argue with that. "He said you kissed him, but has he ever kissed *you*? Even when he was little, he never cared much for physical contact. Oh, sure, he'll give me a hug if I specifically ask him to, but he never initiates it. Can you handle that?"

"I think so," she replied. "And if I made it clear it was important to me, I believe he'd make the effort. I'm not sure he has any idea what to do with a woman. I suppose I'd have to teach him."

Miranda snorted a laugh. "He might understand how sex is supposed to work, but he's had no experience whatsoever. Other than telling him it's best to wait until he's married, I've never even bothered to stress the need for birth control. So far, it hasn't been an issue."

"And you'd rather it wasn't an issue now." Her inflection made it a statement rather than a question.

"To be perfectly honest, I don't think it's a good idea. He's still too young in so many ways. I hate to be the bad guy, but you'd better be damn sure you understand what you'd be signing up for. Sex is only the beginning. I have no idea how well he'd put up with a crying baby. He was around babies when he was in daycare, and he has a lot of fun with his younger cousins when they visit. But he never had a sibling, nor has he ever been responsible for the care of another child."

"My sister has a new baby. Maybe we could babysit and see how he does." She lifted her chin, her expression earnest. "Believe me, I've given this a lot of thought, and I've done some research. He's not the classic autistic, is he?"

"No, but that doesn't mean he'd make a good husband—or a good father. I don't know if he has the patience. And, yes, there are plenty of normal men who can't deal with marriage and fatherhood, but they can make their own decisions. I don't know if he's told you—or if he even realizes it—but I'm more than simply his concerned parent. I'm also his legal guardian."

Tabitha's face fell. "No. I didn't know that."

"I manage his money, I sign all of his legal documents, and that car he drives belongs to me. He doesn't even pay the insurance on it." Miranda knew she sounded harsh, but these were facts that needed to be considered. "Look, I think it would be wonderful if the two of you could get married and live happily ever after, but this isn't a fairy tale. I just want to make sure you realize that."

Levi came out onto the deck. "Are you all going to stay out there all day?"

"We're coming, sweetie. Give us a minute." She glanced at Tabitha. "See what I mean about him being impatient?"

"You should have been there the first day he worked at the grill. He got very frustrated, and he was so slow, I'm surprised we have any customers left, but he learned."

"Once he's decided how something is supposed to be done, he'll do it that way from then on, so be sure you teach him the right way the first time."

Tabitha nodded, smiling shyly. "Don't worry, I will."

Chapter 28

Levi had some questions of his own when Miranda and Tabitha got back to the house. "What were you all talking about?"

Knowing that his imagination would undoubtedly conjure up something much worse, Miranda told him the simple truth. "You."

"Oh, *really*?" His skeptical tone, crossed arms, and tapping foot were reminiscent of Daffy Duck's standard response—which wasn't surprising since he'd learned most of his social interactions from cartoons. Real people had been too inconsistent for him to mimic.

"Yes, really."

His arched brow dropped into a frown as his demeanor went from skeptical to accusing. He pointed at the refrigerator. "Mom, there's peanut butter and cookie dough in the house. You know you can't eat that."

"Yes, I know. Travis is helping me cure my, um, binging problem."

"And how is he doing that?" Levi demanded.

Sometimes it was best *not* to tell him the truth. "You don't want to know, Levi. Trust me on this one."

Although she'd been strictly forbidden to eat anything of that nature unless it was on his dick, Travis had never said what he would do if she pigged out while he was gone. Nevertheless, the suspicion that she might lose her cocksucking privileges kept her in line. She could think of several activities she could live without, but licking his dick wasn't one of them.

To her surprise, Levi let the subject drop. "So do you like Tabitha?"

He was nothing if not direct. Jade sauntered in and jumped up on the table, nudging his hand. Miranda glanced at Tabitha as she bit back a smile.

"Probably not as much as you do," Miranda replied. "But yes, I like her very much."

"Good," he said with a satisfied nod. "Now we can get married."

"Today?"

The swish of Jade's tail drew Miranda's attention. The cat's eyes narrowed as though warning her not to tease him.

Levi arched a scornful brow. "No, of course not."

"Well, then, when?" Miranda countered.

"Oh, I don't know," he replied irritably. "Maybe next week?"

Tabitha lost it. "No, Levi," she said between giggles. "Remember, I have to say yes first."

Levi hung his head. "Okay. I guess I'll have to wait a little longer."

"I have to think about it some more," Tabitha said. "I'm still not sure it's a good idea."

"Why not? If we love each other, we should get married."

If only it were that simple.

"Marriage is a big deal, Levi," Miranda cautioned. "Sometimes it doesn't work out even when you're sure it's what you both want."

He heaved a reluctant sigh. "Yeah, you're right. I guess I can wait."

Although devil's advocate wasn't her favorite role, there was another possibility Miranda felt needed to be explored. "What if Tabitha decides she doesn't want to marry you?"

His expression as he gazed at Tabitha was filled with such longing, Miranda's heart ached for him. "But I love you, Tabitha. More than anything!"

"I love you too, Levi," Tabitha said with a gentle smile. "But I still have to think about it for a while."

He nodded, then glanced at Miranda. "Can Tabitha have dinner with us?"

Tabitha shook her head. "I have to work tonight, remember?"

"Oh, yeah," he said with apparent regret. "You have to go now, don't you?"

She nodded. "Yes, but I'll see you on Sunday. Okay?"

"Yeah, I'll see you then."

To Miranda's surprise, he gave Tabitha a hug. He even had tears in his eyes. Miranda had never known him to be quite so demonstrative with his affections. This girl must have inspired him in ways no one else ever had.

Motivation. It was the one thing that could make Levi focus on reaching a goal. In that moment, she realized that while Tabitha's desire to marry him might waver, Levi's determination never would.

೫ಌ

Every time he turned onto Miranda's driveway, Travis felt like he was coming home. The mere thought of seeing her again made his skin tingle. Levi would be staying for the weekend, which meant that he couldn't spend the night himself—at least, he didn't think he could. He would take care of the horses and stay for dinner, but that was about it. Although he was well aware that he had no claim on Miranda, no clear-cut commitment, he was *so* ready to make a permanent arrangement.

Since the fiasco of his first marriage, Travis had never been tempted to remarry. Now, he wanted it so badly he could hardly sleep at night for thinking about how to ask her, how to persuade her.

He knew she would have doubts. The age difference bugged her, and then there was the baby issue. Smiling, he recalled a conversation he'd once had with Alan.

"Women always think their men should father children to pass on their good qualities," Alan said. "The fact that it's a non-issue for many of the men in question never occurs to them."

Travis's response had been that it was a good thing that women were watching out for the betterment of the species or the human race might still be living in caves. Alan hadn't argued the point—although with as much sex as Alan craved, it was a wonder he hadn't left scads of kids in his wake. So far, he hadn't, nor had he caught any nasty diseases. He was a firm believer in safe sex—and so was Travis, otherwise he might have had children with Janie. If nothing else, he'd had sense enough to delay fatherhood until he was at least old enough to vote.

If only he'd shown similar wisdom with regard to becoming a husband. Thinking back to the time of his divorce, Travis still wasn't sure what he'd done wrong. He'd been told it wasn't his fault—Janie herself had said so—but he must've done *something* to make her start sleeping with his best friend.

Maybe I need to choose my friends more carefully.

Oddly enough, Alan had never stolen a girlfriend from him. Apparently, there was some honor among cousins, even when one of them happened to be a self-proclaimed sex maniac. Then again, perhaps it was simply another of Alan's many quirks.

The horses were waiting at the gate when Travis parked the truck. They *looked* hungry, but he figured he ought to make sure Miranda hadn't fed them before he headed up to the barn.

Sticking his head in the door, he spotted her standing in front of the stove. He had no idea what she was cooking, but it smelled heavenly. The realization that this was what it would be like to come home to her every night hit him like a sledgehammer, momentarily robbing him of breath.

"Hey babe, have you fed the ponies yet?" To his surprise, his voice sounded perfectly normal. Then again, he probably wouldn't have sounded quite so ordinary if she'd turned and smiled at him before he'd asked that question.

"No," she replied. "Tabitha wanted to see them, so they each got a few pats on the nose, but no food. I bet they're pissed."

"Tabitha was here?"

"Yeah. I'm guessing she wanted a private conversation with me more than she wanted to meet the horses. Needless to say, it was an interesting discussion."

"I'll bet it was." He hesitated, not sure if the details were any of his business.

"I'll tell you all about it when you come back from the barn." She nodded toward the living room. "Levi is in there watching TV. Hopefully, he won't hear us."

"That bad, huh?"

"I wouldn't say that, exactly. I wanted to be sure she understood the whole picture. I was a little blunt, but she took it well."

"Do you think she really loves him?"

"I don't know. Maybe. Levi sure seems smitten with her. I've never seen him act like that."

Travis knew the feeling. "Hold that thought while I run up to the barn real quick. Dinner smells great."

She chuckled. "Hope you like chicken nuggets."

"I *love* chicken nuggets." Hell, he'd love anything she fixed for him, just because she was the one doing the cooking.

Boy, am I head over heels or what?

With a shrug, she added, "At least they're the homemade variety. Levi always wants the same things when he comes home. Chicken nuggets on Friday and Pizza Hut pizza on Saturday. His first time driving solo was to get pizza. So now I don't have to cook *or* drive into town on Saturday nights. I wonder if he'll still come home when he—" Her hand flew up to cover her mouth as she broke off with a sob.

Crossing the room in a few quick strides, Travis took her in his arms, holding her close to his chest. If there was one thing Travis had learned—and he'd probably heard it from Alan—it was to simply hold a woman and let her cry. She leaned into him, her whole body shaking while he stroked her back.

"What's wrong with Mom?"

Travis glanced up to see Levi standing in the doorway. "I think she's afraid if you get married, you won't come and stay with her anymore."

Miranda took a deep breath and stood up straight, wiping her eyes. "I'm okay, Levi. No need for you to worry."

Given her aversion to showing any weakness, her abrupt mood change wasn't too surprising. Travis had no doubt that she'd often kept a stiff upper lip when she'd really wanted, even *needed*, to break down and cry. After all she'd been through—the death of her husband, raising a special needs child—he wondered how on earth she'd done it alone.

One day at a time.

"Mom, I'll still come to see you if I marry Tabitha. And you have Travis now. He'll take care of you."

Miranda froze, again pressing her hand to her mouth. In an instant, she regained control, assuming the same calm demeanor she'd displayed when Levi had first spoken. Swallowing hard, she lowered her hand and nodded. "Everything will work out. We'll be okay." Turning back toward the stove, she picked up a fork and turned over the chunks of chicken in the skillet.

Travis touched her shoulder. "Anything I can do?"

She shook her head. "Just the horses. Dinner will be ready in about twenty minutes."

Food was the last thing on his mind at that point, but she'd already broken down once. Deeming it best not to make matters worse by encouraging her to talk if she wasn't ready, he gave her a quick kiss on the cheek. "Be right back."

Her eyes still focused on her task, she nodded, her lips pressed tightly together.

He smiled at Levi. "Want to give me a hand with the horses?"

"Um, sure. Let me get my boots on first."

Although Levi frowned and muttered as they walked to the barn, Travis kept quiet, waiting until the boy spoke directly to him. He was in the tackroom filling the feed buckets when Levi finally broke the silence.

"Was Mom really crying?"

"Yes, she was."

Levi shook his head slowly. "She *never* cries—well, hardly ever."

"I think she cries more than you realize. She just makes sure you don't catch her at it."

Frowning, Levi picked up a feed bucket. "This is for Kira?"

"Yeah, and that one is Arwen's."

Levi carried the two buckets out to the horses, returning just as Travis dumped a scoop of grain into the last pail.

"How come she doesn't let me see her cry?" Levi asked.

"Maybe she doesn't want you to worry."

"Well, I *do* worry." Levi scowled. "She takes care of me and the horses and all those sick people at the hospital. One of them hit her once and gave her a black eye."

"I bet she cried then."

"No. She said it just made her mad."

"I can see where it would."

Levi stood there for a moment, chewing pensively at his lower lip. Taking a deep breath, he leveled a stern glare at Travis. "You're not going to hit her, are you?"

Travis felt his jaw drop. "Why would you think that?"

"Guys hit Aunt Tracy all the time." He shook his head. "I don't understand that."

"Neither do I," Travis said. "And, no, I'm not going to hit your mother. Ever."

"Good. I'm not going to hit Tabitha. Even if she *won't* marry me." With that, he snatched up the remaining feed buckets and stomped out of the tackroom.

Travis stared after Miranda's son with increasing admiration. Every time he talked to the kid, his respect for him doubled—along with his appreciation of Miranda's parenting skills.

His gut told him that Tabitha would be very fortunate to have Levi as a husband.

Now, if only *he* could be as lucky when it came to having Miranda as a wife.

꽃꿎

"Oh, Mom, these are so, so, *so* delic-i-ous!" Levi exclaimed as he dug into a plateful of chicken nuggets. "You are *such* a good cook! Mm, mm, *mm!*"

Travis did his best not to smile, but lost it when Miranda giggled hard enough to trigger a coughing fit. He was considering the Heimlich maneuver when she finally recovered.

"Thanks, Levi," she said between giggles. "I'm glad you like them."

Levi's own laugh was a wonderful, deep-throated chuckle. He

held up a hand. "Okay, okay. You may stop laughing now."

"I'm trying." Miranda gasped, clutching her side as she succumbed to another peal of helpless laughter.

Sure as hell beats watching her cry.

Levi grinned at his mother before turning his attention to Travis. "I need you to teach me how to kiss a girl."

Travis had already swallowed the sip of tea he'd just taken or he would've spewed it all over the table. "You want me to *what*?"

"Teach me how to kiss a girl," Levi said with a trace of asperity. "Didn't you *hear* me?"

"Yeah, I heard you. I just couldn't believe you asked me that."

"Why not? You've kissed girls before, haven't you?"

"Well, yeah…"

"Then show me how."

Since Miranda looked like she was about to rupture something in her effort to control her mirth, Travis thought it best to postpone the kissing lessons. "Maybe we should finish dinner first."

"Okay. After dinner then." Levi resumed his attack on the chicken nuggets without further comment.

Meeting Miranda's eyes across the table, Travis suspected she wouldn't be able to stop laughing long enough for a decent kiss, particularly with her son watching. "Then again, maybe I should *tell* you how to do it, instead of showing you."

Levi looked up expectantly. "Okay. How do you do it?"

Now that he'd put himself on the spot, Travis had absolutely no idea how to explain the actual procedure. "That's a pretty tough question, Levi. Kissing is one of those things you do without thinking."

"Levi's always asking hard questions," Miranda said. "Like the meaning of abstract words that are almost impossible to define— concepts and ideas, rather than concrete terms."

Travis laughed. "You mean like 'abstract'?"

"Yeah. Try explaining that one."

"I can't," he said. "It's too abstract."

"See what I mean?"

"What are you two talking about?" Levi demanded. "I just want to know how to kiss Tabitha."

"Okay, Levi," Travis said. "It's like this. You put your arms around her, lean in real close, and gaze deeply into her eyes. If she doesn't back away, you get closer and closer until your lips touch. Then you close your eyes, open your mouth just a little, and start kissing her. If she *really* likes you, you can try sliding your tongue into her mouth, but don't do that right away."

A snicker from Miranda reminded him that he'd followed up at least two kisses—one she remembered and another one she didn't— by putting his penis in her mouth. Levi obviously needed to take things more slowly.

Levi grimaced. "I don't think I want to put my tongue in her mouth. That's kinda gross."

"Like I said, it's something you work up to. You might ask her how she likes it and do it that way."

"Good idea! I'll ask her." He paused for a moment. "If I kiss her the right way, will that make her want to marry me?"

"Maybe not." Travis winked at Miranda. "But it's a good start."

Chapter 29

Travis followed up his instructions on how to kiss a girl with a suggestion that only added to Miranda's worries.

"You need to take Tabitha out on a date."

"Good idea," Levi agreed. "I could take her out to dinner."

"Where do you think she'd like to go?" Travis asked.

Miranda picked up Levi's empty plate. "Bet I can guess where *he'd* like to go."

Travis shrugged. "Pizza Hut?"

"Nope. We only get pizza as a carryout." She glanced at her son. "Chinese, right?"

"Of course!" Levi replied. "I *love* dumplings, fried shrimp, and crab Rangoons."

"Does Tabitha like Chinese food?" Travis asked.

Levi frowned. "I'm not sure…"

"You know, Levi," Travis began. "If you're going to impress a lady, you have to take her where *she* wants to go, not just the places *you* like."

"Oh, really?"

"Yeah. Really."

"I'll ask her," Levi said. "But there's lots of places I'm not very good at driving to."

"He hasn't had much experience driving into Pemberton," Miranda explained. "The store where he works is on the outskirts of town."

Travis nodded. "Tell you what, Levi. You ask Tabitha where she'd like to go, and I'll help you practice getting there."

Travis obviously meant well, but the thought of the two of them in a car together scared Miranda more than she cared to admit.

What if I lose both of them in an accident?

Letting Levi learn to drive had been difficult enough, and she still worried about him—especially when he had to go someplace he'd never been before. Fighting back a wave of anxiety, she began loading the dishwasher, trying to convince herself that her irrational fears were just that. *Irrational.*

Levi got up from the table. "I'll go call her right now."

Feeling numb all over, Miranda watched him head off to his room. Picking up the skillet, she set it in the sink and turned on the water. She hadn't realized how long she'd been standing there, staring out the window until she glanced down and saw that the skillet was already overflowing.

Travis came up behind her, placing his hands on her shoulders. "You're awfully quiet. Is something wrong?"

"No, I just—well, yeah." She blew out a pent-up breath and shut off the faucet. "I never *have* gotten used to the idea of him driving in town. He knows his way around better than most people, but it still makes me nervous."

"I figured that, which is why I offered to coach him."

She didn't know whether to thank him or not. "It's been so hard to let go. It seems like only yesterday I was wondering if he'd ever graduate high school. The whole driving, job, and apartment thing happened almost overnight. Now, all of a sudden, he's talking about dating and getting married. I'm not ready for that."

"But that's what you wanted for him, isn't it?"

"Yeah." She tossed the scrubber into the skillet and squirted it with detergent. "Guess I should've been more careful about what I wished for."

"No. You wished for exactly the right things. Levi's a great guy, and Tabitha will be very lucky to have him."

She closed her eyes, shaking her head. "If only I knew more about her! I've only met her the one time, and she wasn't here very long."

"Maybe we could go out on a double date sometime."

"That's not a bad idea." For a moment, Miranda wished she could see into the future—then she realized that if she'd known Kris would've died so young, she might not have married him, and Levi wouldn't exist.

Scary thought. "Although, come to think of it, we haven't actually been on a date ourselves."

Travis chuckled. "We did kinda skip that part." Turning her around, he lifted her face to his with a knuckle under her chin. "So, how 'bout it, Miranda? Would you like to have dinner with me sometime? Chinese? Or maybe Italian?"

"Oh, God, no. I'm so sick of potstickers and pizza, I could scream."

"Mexican?"

"Perfect." Since Levi had never developed a taste for Mexican cuisine, Miranda didn't get it very often. Standing on her tiptoes, she gave him a quick peck on the cheek.

Travis obviously wanted more than a mere peck. Draping her arms over his shoulders, he pulled her into his embrace, the evidence of his growing desire pressed firmly against her stomach. Her anxiety evaporated, only to be replaced with the heat of passion as he captured her lips in a deep, bone-melting kiss. The instant he slid his hands down to cup her bottom, she realized they had an audience.

"Tabitha said yes," Levi announced. "We're going on a date on Sunday night."

"That's great," Travis said, moving his hands to a more discreet position.

Miranda leaned into him, her entire body shaking with silent giggles.

"And guess what? She likes Chinese food too." Levi arched an eyebrow. "Um, Travis…does Mom always laugh like that when you kiss her?"

"Sometimes, but usually not."

"Are you sure you're doing it right? I don't think kisses are supposed to make girls laugh."

Miranda had almost regained control of her mirth when she made the mistake of glancing up at Travis, whose attempt to keep a straight face was enough to set her off again.

"I'm sure," Travis replied.

"Yeah, *right.*"

Levi's smirk was her undoing. Clutching her side, Miranda doubled over with helpless laugher.

"Bet Tabitha doesn't laugh when I kiss her."

"I hope she doesn't," Travis said. "You be sure and let us know how it goes."

"I will. I'm going to watch TV now. You two keep practicing."

ଊ⊃ଓ

Travis took Levi out for a drive on Saturday morning, and after several round trips to the Chinese restaurant, he was able to report that Levi should have no problems going solo.

"He's already a good driver. Just needed a little practice."

"Tabitha will be with him too. I can't help wondering how the date will go. He's not very talkative whenever we go out. He pretty much wolfs down a plateful of potstickers and fried shrimp, and he's ready to go home."

Travis grinned. "Yeah, well, you're his mother, not his girlfriend."

"True."

"So, what are you up to this afternoon?"

"I'm going to try to get the lawn mower started and roll the yard. The grass is already getting green. It won't be long before it needs cutting."

"Sure you're up to that?"

"Yeah, I did some work on the rose beds yesterday, and I tried to start the trimmer. I changed the spark plug, which usually gets it going again, but no such luck. Anyway, I feel almost normal, until Levi makes me laugh my head off. I thought I was going to rupture something last night."

"Me, too."

She was a little surprised that Travis didn't fuss at her for trying to start the trimmer, but all he did was offer to take a look at it.

After lunch, Miranda sent Levi out to scour the yard for fallen branches while Travis laid the trimmer out on the table on the deck, dismantling it completely. She changed the oil and replaced the spark plug on the lawn tractor, only to discover that the battery was dead. After hooking it up to the battery charger, she went to check on Travis's progress.

"Any luck finding the problem?"

"A good cleaning and a few adjustments should get it running again. It's pretty clogged up."

She rolled her eyes. "I'm not surprised. I can do routine stuff, but I'm no mechanic. If I took it apart like that, I'd never get it back together."

"Sure you would. It's not rocket science. All it takes is a little time." He glanced up at her and winked. "Which is something you don't have."

"No shit. That's why I'm having such a hard time sitting still. There's so much that needs doing."

He dug a huge wad of oily debris out of the trimmer. "Ever feel like you've bitten off more than you can chew?"

"Constantly. It's even worse with Levi gone. He was a lot of help." She heaved a sigh. "Wish I could stay off work another two weeks. I might even get caught up."

"You know if there's anything you need me to do, all you have to do is ask."

Placing her hands on his shoulders, she leaned down and kissed his cheek. "Seems like half the time, I don't even have to ask. Thanks for all your help."

She was beginning to wonder how she'd ever managed without him. It would be so easy to give up and let him do more. Unfortunately, she had an idea that if she ever started backing off on her chores, she'd lose the necessary strength and energy and never get it back. Case in point, she'd never been unable to get that trimmer started. Ever. Her only consolation was that Travis hadn't been able to get it started, either.

"When do you have to go back to work?" he asked.

"Next Sunday night. Hopefully it'll be peaceful. Lola and Dana have both promised to do any heavy lifting for me, and Lola is dying for me to come back. Sheila's driving her nuts. I don't work again until the following Friday, which is St. Patrick's Day—

unfortunately."

Travis snickered. "What's the matter? Are you that fond of green beer?"

"No, but a lot of other people are—too fond. We always get at least one drunk. It's never fun."

"I don't suppose it is," he said. "How about if I come over Saturday morning and feed the ponies for you? Then you can tell me all about it."

Quite often, Miranda had been so exhausted that the mere thought of doing the barn chores made her want to lay down and cry. She didn't, of course. She'd always put on her boots and done the work with the promise of her bed dangling before her like a carrot. Coming home and going straight to bed would seem like a vacation. There'd been no one there to listen to her vent since Levi moved out, and he hadn't always understood what she was talking about anyway. Travis was bound to be a much more effective sounding board. "You're gonna have me so spoiled."

"I'd spoil you a helluva lot more if you'd let me."

"Ah, yes, but as soon as I did, I'd get complacent and you'd disappear." Her flippant rejoinder stopped her cold.

I can't believe I said that.

Travis looked up at her in surprise. "What are you talking about? I'm not going to disappear."

"That's what Kris always said. But he did, and with my luck—"

"That's what this is all about? You're afraid I'll get killed?"

She shrugged. "Hey, I've already lost one man."

"Which means your odds of losing another one are astronomical. I'm not going anywhere, Miranda. You can get that through your head right now."

His words were like an echo of what Lola had said when Miranda talked to her on the phone the day of her accident. She'd been so sure that Travis was sincere, but what did she know? What did *he* know, for that matter? What did anyone know? Her knees suddenly weak, she sat down heavily on the chair opposite him. "It could happen, Travis. You aren't immortal."

"Neither are you. Anyone can have a fatal accident, but Kris was a Marine. His chances of dying were a lot greater than yours or mine to start with. Besides, you can't live your life worrying about everything that might happen."

"You've let your divorce keep you from marrying again. There's no difference, really."

"I never remarried because I never fell in love. Please, don't let your fears come between you and a second shot at happiness—or mine, for that matter. I'm happier now than I've ever been." Taking her hand, he gave it a gentle squeeze. "I can make your life a whole lot easier too, and yet you still resist."

"But I'm such a–a *jinx*. I loved Kris, and he died. I had his child, but he wasn't normal. I wouldn't trade Levi for anyone, but Kris never really came to terms with his autism. In a way, I think he was relieved when I couldn't get pregnant again. Like he didn't want to take the risk."

"You're not a jinx, and Kris didn't die because you loved him. Nor is it your fault Levi is autistic. It doesn't work that way."

"Yeah. I know. It's just so hard to…" She paused, shaking her head. "I do the best I can, but it's never enough."

"It's okay to admit you aren't Superwoman. I promise I won't love you any less—and I do love you, Miranda. With all my heart."

She couldn't possibly have heard him correctly. Swallowing hard, she gave him a tremulous smile. "Not sure anyone less than Superwoman could hang onto a guy like you."

Travis had always known he'd be the one to say it first. What he hadn't anticipated was that she wouldn't repeat it back to him right away.

No. I knew that, too.

"A guy like me? Believe me, I'm nothing special."

"Oh, yes, you are. You're freakin' perfect."

"Yeah, right. If I'm so damned perfect, why did my wife cheat on me? Why did Christina think I was boring? Why couldn't Shelley trust me? No, I'm not perfect. Not by a long shot."

She waved a dismissive hand. "That only proves how imperfect *they* were."

"You're absolutely right. They weren't perfect—at least, not for me. But *you* are."

"I would *so* like to believe that."

Her voice was so soft, he barely heard her, and her wistful smile nearly broke his heart. Nevertheless, he wanted her to believe it beyond a shadow of a doubt.

"It's true, and if I'm perfect in your eyes, it's because you bring out the best in me. Whether you love me or not is entirely up to you, but please don't rule out the possibility."

"I won't." She frowned, shifting in her chair. "If only it didn't seem so…sudden."

"We may have only been together for less than a week, but we've known each other for a long time. I fell for you from the very beginning. Even knowing I couldn't have you didn't stop me. I'm right here, and I'm *not* going to disappear."

The little beagle came up on the deck and nudged her hand. She stroked his head in silence. "You're right," she finally said. "That's why I don't—or *won't*—let anyone help me. Any man, that is." She blew out a shaky breath. "For me, it's almost the same as letting them love me. I've been so afraid to fall in love again, and protecting Levi wasn't the only reason. I was protecting myself, too."

He gave her a few moments to let the idea sink in. "I'll give you as much love as you can stand, Miranda. All you have to do is let me."

His heart sank as she slowly shook her head. "Love is so risky. I've taken care of dozens of overdoses over the years, and at least half of them were depressed because of a love affair gone bad or the death of a spouse. That's why I'm so concerned about Levi. What if they get married and have an autistic child? Tabitha might decide she doesn't want any part of it and leave them both. What then?"

"I don't think she'd do that. If she loves Levi, she wouldn't think any less of his child."

"Yes, but she's seeing Levi the way he is *now*. She doesn't know how hard it was to get him to this point." Her voice trembled and tears ran down her cheeks. "Teaching him to read was a constant struggle, and helping him with his homework was a nightmare.

There were times when we both got so mad and frustrated, I had to leave the house for a while. I don't think Tabitha has any idea what she might be setting herself up for."

"Maybe not, but there's always the chance that their children might be normal. He loves her, and he loves kids. Doesn't he deserve the same chance as anyone else?"

As quickly as they'd filled with tears, her eyes hardened with anger. "It isn't that simple. You weren't here when he was little. You don't know what it was like. Hell, even Kris didn't know."

Obviously he'd touched a sore spot. "No, I wasn't here, and I don't know what it was like, but I have met Levi, and I think it would be a mistake for you to refuse to let him marry Tabitha without giving her a chance—without giving *him* a chance."

"Levi is *my* son. You have no right to tell me what to do with him." She turned away, biting her lip.

"No, I don't have the right to tell you what to do—with Levi or anything else." This wasn't only about Levi. There was a whole lot more at stake here than that. "I told you once before that I wouldn't try to run your life and whether I stayed or left was your call, and I stand by that. But I do have a right to my opinion."

Miranda's eyes widened like she'd seen a ghost, and for a moment, Travis thought he'd gone too far.

"You've never said anything of the kind," she whispered. Blinking rapidly, she added, "If you had, I might have...I don't know...maybe *annihilated* you."

Chapter 30

Travis might've been waiting his whole life for a woman to pounce on him, but Miranda had been waiting her whole life—the latter part of it, anyway—to hear a man say exactly what he'd just said.

It's your call...

Travis peered at her as though half expecting her to start speaking in tongues. "But I *did* say it. After I finally figured out that Levi wasn't your husband, I said a lot of things, doing my damndest to convince you we were meant for each other. Are you saying you don't remember that, either?"

She shook her head. "No, I don't."

"And here I thought you'd only forgotten the sex. No wonder you were acting so strangely at the hospital! In my mind, we'd come to an understanding—you have to see why I'd think that—and then—oh, God." His eyes widened in utter mortification. "I brought you home and practically shoved my dick in your mouth during lunch. You must've thought I was—well, I don't know *what* you thought. Why the hell didn't you tell me to go fuck myself?"

"Because aside from the fact that I'd wanted to get my hands on you for ages, it seemed sort of...familiar."

"Sucking my dick?"

"Well, yeah. I'd be lying if I said I hadn't fantasized about it. Among other things." With a coy smile, she added, "I have a pretty vivid imagination, and I'd dreamed up all sorts of sexy scenarios—when I wasn't telling myself I was too old for you, that is. Then there was the whole control issue. I never *could* stand the idea of some man telling me what to do—having to take orders from doctors is bad enough. I'd been avoiding men like the plague for that very reason."

"And you think that was the missing piece?"

She nodded. "Already nuts about you and then having you tell me you wouldn't try to run my life? Oh, yeah. That would definitely do it."

He still seemed cautious. "And what about now? Does it still have the same effect?"

She glanced toward the yard where Levi was still busy picking up fallen branches. "Yes, but I think I can control it—for the moment." Frowning, she rubbed the side of her head where only a slight bump lingered. "I kept trying to figure out how come I felt like I loved you, but I didn't know why. Sounds sort of silly, doesn't it?"

His lips curled into a slow, provocative smile. "Not as long as you love me." Chuckling, he added, "We certainly pick our moments. If this was a movie, we'd be in some secluded spot where we could fall into each other's arms and make mad, passionate love. But I'm sitting here fixing your weed whacker with gas and oil all over my hands."

"Good thing mine are clean." In the space of a heartbeat, she surged to her feet and closed the gap between them. His lips were as soft and inviting as ever, and cupping his face in her palms, she tasted the sweet, warm essence of the man she loved. Somewhere deep within her heart, the missing piece of the puzzle settled into place. Come what may, she was in love with Travis York. Nothing could change that now. "I love you so much it scares me."

"There's nothing to be afraid of, Miranda—not when I feel the same way about you. You're wonderful and sexy and beautiful. I love your strength, your fierce independence, and the way you seemed willing to let Levi do what he had to do without complaining." He smiled sheepishly. "Of course, the fact that he turned out to be your son, rather than your husband made a difference."

"A *huge* difference."

"Yes, but you were still willing to allow Levi his freedom, and that made an impression on me. I've never wanted a clinging vine. Given my history with other women, I think you understand what I'm talking about."

"Yeah. The jealous, possessive, controlling type doesn't appeal to you anymore than it does to me."

He nodded. "You were so right for me—I used to spend nights lying awake, trying to figure out a way to get you to leave your husband. It was a terrible thing to even think about, but at least I didn't go through with it. My cousin, Alan, helped me with that." He paused, chuckling. "You need to meet him sometime. He's a little…different. Anyway, finding out that Levi was your son didn't help me a whole lot. You'd never given me even the tiniest bit of encouragement."

"Are you kidding? Of course, I didn't. You were this hot, handsome younger man—maybe not as young as I thought you were—but I still never dreamed you might want someone my age. I'd made up my mind you could never be more to me than eye candy. Couldn't quite convince my heart, though."

He snorted a laugh. "Maybe so, but your brain was pretty much in control. I don't know if you remember this or not, but even when I told you how much I wanted you, I don't think you took me seriously."

"And then you said the magic words."

"Yeah. Wish I'd remembered them before now. I mean, I tried. I guess when the woman of your dreams pounces on you for the first time, it tends to make the details of how you got there a little fuzzy."

"I suppose it does."

"You still don't remember everything that happened that day, do you?"

She shook her head. "No, but I don't think I need to." Smiling, she kissed his cheek. "I trust you to remember it for me."

A blush crept up his neck. "As if I could ever forget *that*."

∞ℂℛ

Miranda seemed surprised when Levi decided to go back to his apartment after dinner that evening. Travis, however, had expected it. "He's got a hot date tomorrow night," he said as she closed the front door. "He needs to prepare."

She sat down beside him on the sofa. "Prepare? All he has to do is take a shower, get dressed, and go pick her up."

"That's not how I heard it. He's going to get his car washed and clean it out before the date. I think he's going to get her some flowers, too."

"Sounds like you two had a private chat during the driving lesson."

"Oh, yeah. He's quite a talker when you get him behind the wheel."

"I know. It's weird. When he's a passenger, he hardly ever says anything. Just listens to music or plays video games—or talks to himself. He hardly ever initiates a conversation unless he's driving."

"You know, he's really serious about Tabitha. I almost hate to mention this, but he was trying to come up with baby names."

"Oh, God. I am *so* not ready for that. I hope Tabitha has sense enough to wait a little while—at least until she finishes school. He did say she was studying to be a chef, didn't he?"

"Yeah, but he's ready right now. Boy, when he makes up his mind to do something…"

"Believe me, I know. He never acted like he wanted to learn to drive until he got sick of dealing with the people who were taking him out twice a week. Half the time they didn't show up, and he didn't like their cars or their driving. After that, there was no stopping him."

"He, um, asked me a few other things, too."

Miranda looked like she was about to cry. "Oh, don't tell me it went beyond kissing."

"Well, yes, it did. He's got a general idea about how to make babies, but he did ask me a few questions concerning the, um, finer points of how it's done."

"And what did you tell him?"

"That I needed to talk to you first. After all, I'm not his father."

"I'm sure you'd be better at telling him than someone else." Frowning, she stared at the floor for a long moment. "Was that something you were looking forward to doing someday?"

"I did think about it when he came over on Monday night. Honestly, I don't mind talking to him about it, but, like I said, he's your son."

She shook her head. "That's not what I meant. You do realize if you stick with me, you'll never have any children of your own, don't you?"

Travis had wondered when she'd finally get around to that. "Yes, I do."

"And it doesn't bother you?"

"Let me put it this way. I'm in love with *you*, Miranda, not with any children we might or might not have together. If fathering children was my only goal, I'd have done it by now. Besides, I can't think of a better son than the one you have, and I'd be honored to have him as a stepson." He paused, chuckling. "He's one of the coolest guys I've ever met."

Miranda ducked her head, shielding her eyes with her hand, but she couldn't completely hide the tears rolling down her cheeks. With a sob, she fell against him. "I love you so much."

Travis wrapped his arms around her, planting a kiss on the top of her head. "Could you say that again?" he whispered. "No one's told me that for a very long time."

Pulling away, she sat up, wiping the tears from her eyes. "I find that so hard to believe—like the time you told me your life was lonely and incomplete and that you weren't happy. You're the most lovable man I've ever known. I don't understand why you aren't taken, why you don't already have a wife and a whole passel of kids."

He smiled ruefully. "I'm glad you think I'm so lovable, but there have been plenty of others who would disagree. I had to meet the right person before any of that could happen—and that person is you."

She inhaled a shaky breath. "Promise me you won't disappear. I keep feeling like I'll blink and you'll be gone."

"I'll do the best I can to be here for you. This is where I want to be, and I'm so glad you were here for me to find."

"Pinch me," she said. "Hard enough to leave a mark. I have to know this is real."

"No." He pulled her into his arms and kissed her. "You're

going to have to settle for kisses. I'm not about to leave a mark on you. You're perfect just the way you are. Besides, you get hurt often enough without any help from me."

"True. I'll have to be more careful."

"You do that, Miranda. I want to keep you around for a very long time."

"Yes, and don't forget, I've got nearly ten years on you already."

"Oh, hush up and kiss me."

"My pleasure."

ഇറങ

Miranda's first night back at work went smoothly enough, or would have if they'd been busier. A quiet night with soundly sleeping patients gave Lola and Dana more opportunities to pump her for information. Dana giggled and teased. Lola, on the other hand, was positively gloating.

"Told you he was interested in you," she said with a knowing smile. "You wouldn't listen."

"Have a heart, Lola. I had a concussion. He remembered everything, but I'd forgotten all of it."

"That *would* be weird," Dana agreed. "Sort of like waking up—"

"—in Vegas married to a complete stranger?" Miranda finished for her. "Yeah. A lot like that, only I didn't even know we were married. Well…not married, exactly, but you get the idea."

Lola sniffed. "So, when's the wedding?"

Miranda snorted a laugh. "You mean mine or Levi's?"

"Yours, of course."

"I'll let you know when he asks me."

"Sounds to me like it's a done deal," Lola said.

Since there isn't much nurses *won't* discuss with each other, Miranda had told them both everything she could remember. "I'm still waiting to be asked."

Dana giggled. "Bet he does something really romantic."

"You mean like flowers, candy, and a ring?" Miranda scoffed. "I doubt it. Besides, Levi already did the proposing for him."

"But you haven't said yes, have you?" Lola pointed out.

"No, but I didn't refuse, either. Still, we've only been together for two weeks. Don't you think it's a little soon to be talking about marriage?"

Lola frowned. "Usually doesn't take me very long to decide."

"And you have such a terrific track record," Dana said with a snicker. "Not sure you're the best source for reliable statistics."

"I never said it was the right decision," Lola said. "It's just that I make up my mind fairly quickly."

"And we've seen the results of using that method." A call light went off and Dana got to her feet. "I'll get that."

"It's my patient, Dana," Miranda said. "I'll get it."

Anything to escape this inquisition…

₮ℋ

Miranda thought it best to skip her riding lesson on Tuesday morning. Travis would've helped her hitch up the trailer, but hauling herself up on top of Kira using anything less than a stepladder still seemed impossible. She'd just gotten back from the barn when Christina called.

"Hey, girlfriend, I've got a meeting in Pemberton later this afternoon, so I'm headed your way. Want to meet somewhere for lunch?"

Miranda had an idea Christina would be fishing for the latest on Mark, but for once, she had news of her own. "Sounds great. I've got a lot to tell you."

"Really? What's up?"

"Oh, the usual. Broken ribs, a concussion, a new boyfriend. Levi's got a girlfriend, too. He's even been on a date."

"Hold on, back up for a second. You've got a boyfriend? Really? Anyone I know?"

Ordinarily, this would've been unlikely given that their only mutual male friend was Mark. Travis was the lone exception. "One of your rejects, actually."

Christina gasped. "Not that little Travis guy?"

"What do you mean, little? He's taller than I am." At roughly five-ten, Christina was taller than a lot of men—Travis, included—which was something Miranda hadn't considered when she'd been matchmaking. *Yet another reason never to try that again.*

"Never mind. Not important. So, you're saying you're hurt?"

In Miranda's opinion, Travis was the most important thing that had happened to her in years. She started to argue, but figured that a boyfriend discussion would eventually lead to Mark, and she really didn't feel like rehashing the same old shit. "Slipped and fell during that ice storm we had weekend before last. Travis was here and has been helping me out ever since."

"Helping?" Christina scoffed. "Not sure that makes him a boyfriend."

"Yeah, well—trust me, he's been doing a lot more than that."

"And you don't think he's boring?"

Miranda bit back a scathing retort, opting for the simple truth. "He's probably the least boring man I've ever known." Closing her eyes, she counted to three. "Where do you want to meet for lunch?"

After they'd agreed on a time and place, Miranda switched off the phone, grumbling. She should be thanking her lucky stars that Christina hadn't liked Travis, but she couldn't help resenting her attitude toward him.

The hottest, most perfect man in the world, and she thinks he's boring.

೮೦೮೩

Miranda arrived early and was waiting at a table sipping her tea when Christina arrived with a potted shamrock and what appeared to be a permanent pout. "I figured what with broken ribs and a concussion, you could use a little luck."

"Thanks, it's lovely, but I'm not sure I need it. My luck is better than ever."

She frowned. "Wish I could say the same. I take it you're happy with Travis?"

"Extremely. You really missed out on a good one."

"No, if you're happy, I'm fine with that. Just don't know what you see in him."

Evidently, she'd never received the naked waiter treatment.

Christina sat down, flipping her hair back over her shoulder. "I, um, don't suppose you've heard anything from Mark, have you?"

Miranda's only surprise in being asked that question was that it hadn't been the first thing out of Christina's mouth. "Not lately. If you're looking to get him back, I think it's pretty hopeless."

She heaved a sigh. "I was afraid of that. I'm sorry to keep badgering you, but you're the only one I can talk to about him."

"You mean that in all the time you were together, you never met *any* of his friends—or his family?"

"Yes, but they'd probably take his side. You're more…neutral."

She had a point. Mark had actually been Kris's friend, with the result that Miranda had been much closer to Christina in recent years. "I'll talk to him, but I can't promise anything."

"I know you can't. And I know I should forget him, but I can't seem to find a reason to. At least, not yet."

"I take it you haven't met any hunky lawyers since the breakup?"

"Tons of them. Too bad they're all such cocky bastards."

"I suppose the criminal element doesn't appeal to you, either."

Christina's chuckle didn't quite fit with her demeanor—seeming more akin to gallows humor than genuine mirth. "Have *you* ever fallen for any of your patients?"

"Point made, but what about victims or their families?"

Christina arched a brow. "Need you ask?"

"Okay, I realize neither of us sees people at their best, but *I* haven't been looking. You, I presume, have."

"Not really—except to compare them to Mark, and they all come up lacking."

Mark was a handsome devil—even Miranda couldn't argue that point—but he was no Brad Pitt. She smiled to herself. *And he's certainly no Travis York.*

In the end, although she knew it wouldn't do a damn bit of good, she promised to talk to Mark.

With plenty to report for once, Miranda carried most of the conversation during lunch. Christina seemed happy for her and Levi, but her underlying gloom persisted.

Seeing no point in putting it off any longer, Miranda called Mark as soon as she and Christina parted company. As she'd expected, Mark was happier than ever and had no intention of going back.

"She'll get over me eventually," he said. "All she needs is someone new."

"Easier said than done. I tried to fix her up with a friend of mine, but she's still comparing every guy she meets with you."

"I wouldn't lose any sleep over it. She'll find someone. She's too beautiful not to."

"I hope you're right. I think she's finally figured out that her work isn't everything."

"Wish she'd done that sooner," he said with a wistful note to his voice. "We probably would've been married with a couple of kids by now. As it is, well…"

"Yeah. It's too late."

He paused for a moment. "Do you think I should talk to her myself? Somehow, I think it would be a bad idea. I mean, I've already asked Brittany to marry me."

"And?"

"She said yes."

This isn't going to be pretty. "I'm very happy for you, Mark. And you're right. It probably wouldn't be a good idea for you to talk to Christina right now. I'll tell her." Miranda sighed. "I've done it before. I can do it again."

"Thanks, I'd appreciate that." Clearing his throat, he went on, "So, how are things with you? Still raising horses and nursing the sick?" The shift in his tone from subdued to brisk spoke volumes. As far as he was concerned, Christina was ancient history.

"Among other things." Feeling like a broken record, she wound up repeating most of what she'd told Christina. "I love him to pieces,

Mark. He's the one—it's that simple."

"You don't know how much I've wanted to hear you say that. I feel the same way, myself." He laughed. "Ain't love grand?"

Miranda couldn't have agreed more, but she also had to tell Christina that Mark was gone for good.

Chapter 31

"I like crab!" Levi announced when he called on Thursday afternoon. "We went to Red Lobster last night. Tabitha taught me how to crack it. You dip it in butter sauce and it's delicious!"

Miranda had been lucky to get him to eat fried shrimp. Getting him to try crab was right up there with winning the lottery. "See? There are lots of good things to eat besides pizza and potstickers. If Tabitha is going to be a chef, she'll probably want you to taste all sorts of new things."

"I'll try, as long as it doesn't have too much pepper."

"She can't ask for more than that."

"Um, Mom, I called to tell you I won't be coming home this weekend."

Miranda smiled to herself. "I kinda figured that."

"Travis said he'd be spending the weekend with you, so you won't get lonely."

"Actually, I think he's just going to come over to feed the horses in the mornings for me."

"No, he told me he was going to be there all weekend. He told me when we were practicing driving to Red Lobster."

"Is that why you aren't coming home?"

"Oh, no. I'm going to work Saturday and go out with Tabitha on Sunday." He paused for a moment. "We might be going out tomorrow night, too. It's St. Patrick's Day, you know."

"Yeah, I know. I have to work." Generally speaking, Levi was one of the more dedicated homebodies Miranda had ever met. To the best of her recollection, he hadn't wanted to go out that often in his entire life. Carryout, yes, but going out to a restaurant? Rarely. "Seems like you're going out an awful lot. That's a little different for you, isn't it?"

"Yeah. I like going out with Tabitha. She talks to me and makes me laugh."

Looking back on all the relatively silent dinners in various restaurants over the years, Miranda couldn't help being impressed. Evidently, finding the right dinner companion made all the difference in the world. "Still thinking about getting married?"

"Not right now. Tabitha says we should wait a while."

Miranda sighed with relief. "That's probably a good idea."

"Travis thought so, too."

Good for Travis. "Did he tell you that when you were out for driving practice?"

"Yeah, but he comes here to buy gas all the time. I call him, too. He gave me his cell phone number."

"I see." Apparently, he'd found a new friend in Travis, which was…encouraging. "What do you two talk about?"

"Oh, all kinds of things. Guy stuff."

Miranda went off in a peal of laughter. "That's interesting. So, do you like having a man to talk to?"

"Oh, yeah. And since he's going to be my stepfather pretty soon—"

Miranda's heart took a nose dive. "Hold on there, Levi. He hasn't asked me to marry him. You *told* me to marry him. It makes a difference."

"You mean he hasn't asked you yet?"

"No, he hasn't."

"Well, when he does and you say yes, you'll get married, and I'll have a father again."

"It isn't that simple." *If only it were…*

"Why not? You love him, don't you?"

"Yes, but—"

"And I know he loves you."

Miranda's jaw dropped. "Did he tell you that?"

Levi snorted a laugh. "No, but I'm not stupid."

"No, you aren't. You're a lot of things, Levi. Stupid isn't one of them."

"Don't screw it up, Mom. He's a keeper."

Never having heard Levi use that particular term, Miranda was puzzled, especially since Jade had said the same thing.

No, it wasn't the cat. She'd only *imagined* that to be Jade's opinion. *Kira* was the one who'd actually said it. *Freaky.* "What did you say?"

"I said, he's a keeper. You know…like when you catch a fish big enough to keep?"

"Yeah…" Scratching her head, she tried to remember if Levi had ever been fishing in his life. She didn't think he had—although he might've done some fishing with the Scouts. Her son's reports on what he'd done at camp often amounted to more general statements like "We had fun" rather than specific activities. "Where did you hear that?"

If he said Kira told him, Miranda was going to have a stroke. "Travis said that about Tabitha."

"Ah, that explains it."

Thank God.

℘ℂ℞

On Friday night, Travis had half a mind to fake a heart attack so he could spend the evening in the emergency room—perhaps even getting to see Miranda—anything to liven up a St. Patrick's Day spent with Stuart.

"Sure you don't want to go out for a beer?" Travis asked.

Stuart frowned. "We've got beer. It's even Guinness."

"I know, but we could sit here watching TV and drinking Guinness anytime. We should be out wearing green and looking for leprechauns."

Scowling, Stuart settled back in his recliner, the one piece of furniture he'd hung onto in the wake of his divorce. "I'd rather stay home."

"You'll never find a sexy Irish girl that way."

Stuart grunted and aimed the remote at the television. "I told you, I don't want another woman. Ever. One was enough. Besides, women hate me."

Travis fought the urge to grit his teeth. "Women don't hate you—although they'd like you a lot better if you'd quit acting like a pissed-off grizzly bear."

"Don't you have a girlfriend now?"

Travis grinned. "Yes, I do. As a matter of fact, I might have a wife pretty soon, and I have a feeling she won't want to live here. If I move out, are you just gonna sit here watching TV for the rest of your life?"

"Maybe. I'll buy the house from you."

"You're already paying me rent," Travis noted. "I'd consider that as equity and give you a good deal."

"Fine. Tell me again why you aren't out partying with this new girlfriend of yours?"

"She's working tonight, and I'm going over to her place in the morning. No point in being there all by myself."

Stuart responded with another grunt and began flipping through the channels. He'd settled in to watching something about sharks on the Discovery Channel before he finally spoke. "You're really thinking about getting married again?"

"Constantly."

Heaving a sigh, Stuart shook his head. "Good luck. I *never* intend to get into a mess like that again as long as I live."

"Famous last words," Travis said with a snicker. "I'll remind you of this moment when I'm the best man at your wedding."

"Ain't gonna happen."

Travis popped open a Guinness and took a long drink. "Yeah, right."

ഇന്ദ

Miranda groaned as Adrian wheeled the stretcher into the unit, bringing up the first drunk of the evening. Rick was about thirty, with short hair, a slender build, and a blood alcohol level that would've made St. Patrick proud.

"He wants his catheter out," Adrian said in an undertone. "I told him it was up to you guys."

"No problem," Miranda said. "He's awake enough to pee on his own."

"I would have peed for them downstairs if they'd given me a minute," Rick moaned. "But they stuck that thing in my dick anyway."

"Don't worry, we'll take it out, but let's get you in bed first," Miranda said. "Lola is going to be your nurse tonight. We'll see what she says."

Lola nodded her consent as Rick pulled back the sheet to check out the damage to his penis. "Oh, my God! Look what they did to it. Why'd they want to do that?"

Miranda wasn't sure which was funnier, his lack of modesty as he displayed the horrific thing that had been done to him, or the fact that he was wearing metallic blue boxers decorated with umbrella-toting yellow ducks.

"The ER docs get a little impatient with guys who can't pee on demand," Miranda explained, doing her damndest not to laugh. "Believe me, the nurses would rather not do it." She'd heard more than one nurse warn the doctor that if he wanted a particularly creepy guy catheterized, he would have to do it himself.

Unhooking the catheter bag from the stretcher, she let the side rail down.

Rick scooted over to the bed. "I would have peed if they'd just given me a chance. They shouldn't have done that to him."

Adrian giggled as she rolled the stretcher out of the room. "Have fun, girls."

"Yeah, right." Miranda pulled up the side rail and went and got a towel, a 10-milliliter syringe, and a pair of gloves. "Okay, Rick, let's take this thing out."

He gazed up at her with grateful, bloodshot eyes. "Thank you. He's never going to be the same."

"Oh, yes he will. We haven't lost one yet."

"Will he still work?"

"You'll be able to pee," Lola said. "Not for a while, though, because your bladder is empty."

"That's not what I meant," he said. "I mean will he still be able to fuck?"

Miranda couldn't help it. Despite sore ribs and the ethical dictates against laughing at one's patient, she let out a giggle. "I promise he'll be fully functional."

"Oh, good," Rick said with a sigh. "My penis is my best friend. I wouldn't want anything to happen to him."

While Miranda had always assumed most guys felt that way about their dick, she'd never heard anyone actually say it. Lola collapsed against the wall, helpless with laughter.

After pulling down his shorts, Miranda put the towel underneath his penis, deflated the balloon that held the catheter in place, and pulled. When it didn't come out, she rechecked the balloon to assure herself that it was completely deflated. It was. She tugged again.

Nothing happened. Apparently, whoever had catheterized him hadn't used much in the way of lubricant.

"Hold on, Rick. This might hurt a little." She gave it another firm tug, and his dick stretched out like a Chinese finger trap before the catheter finally slithered out.

Rick sighed with relief, gently fondling his penis before tucking it inside his shorts and snapping the fly.

When Miranda pulled up his T-shirt to hook him up to the heart monitor, she found more surprises. Two nipple rings and a navel piercing.

Lola gaped at him in disbelief. "Why would anyone want to pierce their nipples?"

Rick grinned and wiggled his hips. "It gives me a rush." He ran a finger up his arm. "Did you see my new tattoo?"

Just what it was a picture of, Miranda couldn't tell from that angle, but it appeared to be better than most, and was certainly an improvement over the World War II type that looked like a kid with no artistic talent whatsoever had been doodling with a Magic Marker. "Very colorful."

"Thank you. I think it's beautiful."

Chuckling to herself, Miranda went out to check the orders on his chart. When she returned, Rick was on his feet at the side of the bed with Lola standing next to him, holding him up. He'd dropped the rubber ducky boxers, revealing a furry little butt and balls that swung between his legs as he rocked back and forth, trying to coax urine out of a sore dick and an empty bladder.

"Come on, you can do it," he urged. "Poor little guy. Why would anyone want to do that to you? Come on, now. Poor little guy."

Lola looked like she was going to split a gut. Miranda doubled over on the bed, shaking with silent laughter.

"Poor little guy," he said again. Looking up at Lola, he added, "I love my penis. He's my best friend."

"I'm sure he is," Lola replied gently. "But right now, I think he just needs some sleep, and so do you."

"Okay," Rick said with a yawn. "I'm going to bed now." Leaving his boxers on the floor, he crawled back into the bed, collapsing onto the pillow with a sigh. "Can my girlfriend stay with me?"

"Sure," Miranda said. "I'll go get her."

As it turned out, there was no need to fetch her, for she came around the desk as Miranda left the room. "Go on in. He's fine, he just needs to sleep it off."

"Yeah," she said wearily. "He always does."

Lola came back to the desk, apparently deciding against attempting to complete the eleven-page admitting assessment until Rick was a bit more sober. "At least he was more fun than the usual drunk," she said. "Poor little guy."

&oesc;&cam;

Travis had already fed the horses and was waiting on the porch when Miranda got home the next morning. After a hug and a kiss that made her forget all about drunks and catheters, he made her an offer she couldn't refuse. "Why don't you get ready for bed while I fix us some breakfast?"

"Sounds fabulous." After changing into her nightgown, she climbed gratefully into bed just as Travis carried in a tray. She told

Travis the "poor little guy" story while they ate, pleased that for once, she had someone there who could truly appreciate the humor.

"He was actually talking to his penis?" he asked.

"Yeah. He was certainly one of our more entertaining drunks. Most of them are obnoxious pains in the ass."

"Sounds like you had a lot more laughs than I did last night. Stuart seemed determined to have the least amount of fun possible. Honest to God, he's getting worse instead of better."

"Could be he's going through another phase in the recovery process."

"Maybe. I just wish he'd hurry up and move on to the next one. I hate to leave him there alone in the evenings, but he's kinda depressing to be around. I'd much rather be here with you."

"I'd rather be with you too. Lunch with Christina wasn't a bit of fun. She's still pining over Mark. She asked me to talk to him, and I did, but I haven't had the guts to call her back yet. He's getting married."

"I'm sure she'll love that."

"No shit. Guess I should get it over with." Yawning, she sank back against the pillows. "I'm kinda surprised she hasn't called me."

Travis gathered up the empty plates and set them on the tray. "Don't worry about it now. Get some sleep." Leaning over the bed, he gave her a sweet, bone-melting kiss. "I'll be here when you wake up."

"Thanks, Travis. Have I told you how much I love you and appreciate you and how glad I am you're here?"

"I believe you just did."

"Good," she said as she snuggled down to sleep. "I wouldn't want to be remiss."

Chapter 32

Miranda went to her riding lesson the next week, although after a short ride, she wished she'd stayed home. "The flying lead change is gonna have to wait another couple of weeks, Nigel. Just bouncing in the saddle makes me feel like I can't breathe right."

Nigel was optimistic. "I'll ride her. Bet I can get her to do it."

Miranda knew that having Nigel as a rider would be good for Kira, but the mare wouldn't do it for him, either—which made Miranda feel a little less inept, and only irritated Nigel.

"My God, Miranda. Are all of your horses evil?"

"They aren't evil, Nigel. They're just—oh, hell, I don't know. Whether Kira ever does a flying lead change or not really doesn't matter since she's primarily a broodmare anyway. I just wish I could figure out what to do with Jadzia."

"Breed her."

"Maybe, but to what?" Jadzia was beautiful, with a shiny, chocolate brown coat, a star, and one white stocking. Unfortunately, her anatomy—relatively short legs and a long back—made dressage difficult for her.

"How about an Andalusian?" he suggested. "Or a Lusitano?"

"Yeah, right. I'd have to sell her just to get enough money to pay the stud fee. Which reminds me, are you still interested in Arwen?"

"Who?"

Nigel's terrible memory had gotten him disqualified more than once for omitting a jump in the show jumping phase of a three-day event. On one of those occasions, he'd actually been in the lead after the dressage and the cross country competitions.

"Arwen," Miranda repeated. "You know…the chestnut filly that turns three this spring? The one I brought up here and showed you last fall?"

His blank expression made Miranda wonder how many concussions he'd had before she'd started taking lessons from him.

"Did I like her?" he asked.

"Yes, you did. You even told someone else that she was already yours and that I couldn't sell her to anyone else."

He scratched his head. "I did?"

Miranda nodded.

"Okay, if you say so..."

What a trusting soul. "You said you'd give me four thousand for her when she turned three." It wasn't a total lie—she'd given him her price and he *had* told that other woman that Arwen was spoken for.

"Really?" he asked, scratching his head again. "I said that?"

"You most certainly did."

"Well, okay." he said brightly. "Bring her tomorrow. I'll find the money somehow."

Miranda hoped he wouldn't have forgotten by then. The money was a different story. Hopefully, his wife would remember to pay her. Perhaps she should send an email...

ᔆᘉᘓ

Thanks to some contrivance with Levi, Travis had already bought the ring. He'd been a little overwhelmed in the jewelry store until he spotted one particular setting, and somehow, he knew it was the right one. The only problem he faced now was how, where, and when to ask her. Should he pop the question over a candlelight dinner in a fancy restaurant, or should it be after a quiet dinner at home? Or perhaps during a stroll through the pasture? He considered sticking the ring to his dick with a dollop of cookie dough or peanut butter, but he didn't want to be too kinky or too flippant. His intentions, as the saying went, were honorable, and he wanted her to know that.

Finally deciding that a more intimate setting was best, he opted to fix dinner for her at her house and ask her then, which was probably the best tactic anyway. No point in making it obvious what he was up to. After all, a proposal should come as a bit of a surprise, and, hopefully, not an unwelcome one.

Miranda was still up at the barn when he arrived, and his plan was to have everything put away before she returned. He'd already carried in all the bags when he suddenly panicked, frantically patting his pockets for the jewelry box. He found it right where he'd put it, of course, but opened it anyway, if only to reassure himself it was still there. Fumbling as he attempted to stow it back in the breast pocket of his jacket, the box fell into a bag of groceries just as Miranda came through the door.

"Hey, sweetie. Looks like you've been shopping." Within seconds, she was right there in front of him, greeting him with a hug and a kiss. "Don't tell me you brought more cookie dough. I think there's still some of the last batch left. Used to be, it wouldn't have lasted a whole day, let alone a week."

Travis gave her a sheepish grin. "Um, looks like the Travis York method of binge prevention is working."

"Yeah, now I binge on your dick," she said dryly. "I've traded one addiction for another."

"Yes, but sucking my dick is guaranteed to prevent weight gain."

"True—aside from the fact that I can't get enough peanut butter on it for a good-sized mouthful."

Scowling, he pulled out a carton of unsweetened organic soy milk and glanced inside the bag. The jewelry box was nowhere to be seen. *Great.* "Are you insinuating that my dick isn't big enough for you?"

"I'm not insinuating anything. I mean, doling it out in tiny amounts is the whole idea, isn't it?"

"Tiny? My dick is *not* tiny. It's big enough to make you scream, isn't it?"

"Well, yeah… Why are you so touchy all of the sudden?"

Heat flooded his cheeks. He arched a brow in an attempt to disguise his reaction. "I'm not being touchy. It's just that I've got plans for this evening."

"Really?"

"Yes, really. Could you just help me put the groceries away?" He knew he sounded a bit snappish, but he still had a chance to retrieve the ring while her back was turned. Unfortunately, she went for the very sack it had fallen into.

Crap!

From her crestfallen expression, he had an idea he'd hurt her feelings, or at the very least pissed her off. Averting her eyes, she began emptying the bag, setting lettuce, tomatoes, cottage cheese out on the table.

"This stuff is a lot healthier than what you usually buy," she remarked. "Are you going on a diet?"

"No, I'm not going on a diet," he replied, unable to keep the irritation out of his voice. "I don't live on cookie dough, you know."

"I didn't think you did. These things seem more normal, though. I hadn't realized I was out of so many things."

"Just stocking up." He reached blindly into another bag and pulled out a package of rib eye steaks.

Her eyes nearly popped out of her head. "Oh, my God! Steaks cost a fortune nowadays. I've quit buying them altogether."

"Me, too," he admitted. "But like I said, I've got plans for the evening."

She stared at him for a moment, then glanced at the bag of charcoal sitting on the floor.

"Planning to grill the steaks?"

"Yep," he said. "We're also having baked potatoes and salad, and I'm making chocolate mousse for dessert."

"Chocolate mousse? Really? That stuff's a bitch to make. You've got to whip the cream, melt the chocolate—oh." She stopped short as he held up a package of mousse mix, but she still seemed curious. *Too* curious. "That would be easier, of course. What's the occasion?"

"Nothing special." Travis couldn't believe how badly he was handling this. *There goes the romantic dinner...* With an absent shrug of his shoulders, he stashed a sack of potatoes in the pantry. "Just wanted a steak."

Miranda didn't pursue the matter any further because it sounded pretty good to her. If only she didn't feel like crying. Thank goodness he'd bought some Kleenex. With her luck, he would start looking for an excuse to leave now, just when she'd admitted she loved him and was starting to depend on him. Just as she'd always feared he would...

Tears stung her eyes as she opening another bag filled with detergent, fabric softener, and paper towels—he hadn't been kidding about stocking up. Another bag contained some decidedly male toiletries—body wash, disposable razors, shaving cream, and aftershave. *No wonder he always smells so good...* A bottle of wine. Candles. Baby oil.

"Baby oil?"

A seductive grin banished his irritation. "I told you I had plans for the evening." He blew out a pent up breath and pointed to a small gift box at the bottom of the bag. "You might want to open that. I got it for you."

She eyed him with suspicion. "Okay, this isn't my birthday, and it certainly isn't Christmas." Her heart plummeted. Maybe it was *his* birthday. No—he wouldn't have gotten her a present for that. "Is it some holiday I've forgotten about? Should I have gotten something for you?"

"No, you shouldn't have gotten anything for me. Right now, this is just another day."

Although Miranda seldom wore jewelry, she recognized the name on the box, having heard countless radio ads for that particular store. Gifts for non-occasions didn't come in packages like that. She lifted the lid, gasping as the diamond inside sparkled back at her.

"And yes, you can wear it to the barn," he said. "It's guaranteed for life."

Guaranteed for life. So many things weren't—husbands included. She swallowed around the tight lump in her throat. "I hope it's got a strong, tight setting. Otherwise it'll be gone in a week."

"Doesn't matter," he said. "The stone might disappear, but I won't. You're stuck with me now, Miranda—I'm not going anywhere—not after today." His voice took on a softer, deeper timbre. "Think you could put that on? I want to see it on your hand."

She slipped the ring on her finger, marveling at the perfect fit. "How on earth did you know what size ring I wore?"

He held up another ring—the one Kris had given her. "I used this."

"I can't believe you found that," she exclaimed as he dropped it onto her outstretched palm. "I mean, I didn't exactly hide it, but…"

"Are you kidding me? Did you really think Mr. Observant wouldn't spot it in there with the flag?"

She rolled her eyes. "Of course he did. I suppose he snuck it out of there for you too."

Travis nodded. "He's quite the co-conspirator. Never said a word to you, did he?"

"Not about the ring, but he seemed to think our engagement was a done deal."

Dropping his chin, Travis gazed at her with an expression in his deep blue eyes that would've melted the heart of a much stronger woman than Miranda. "So, *is* it a done deal?"

"That depends. Levi pretty much told me to marry you, but you haven't actually asked me. I think I need to hear it from you."

"Ah, but you *did* hear it from me. I distinctly remember telling Levi that you should marry me for making brownies. However, I have no problem with repeating myself." Eyes twinkling, he got down on one knee. Taking her hand, he closed her fingers around Kris's ring. "I love you with all my heart, Miranda. Will you marry me?"

As she gazed at Travis, the memory of Kris's proposal flashed through her mind. Diamond rings were a luxury he couldn't afford, and they'd been sharing a sundae when he asked her to be his wife. She'd said yes in an instant, but her feelings now seemed so much deeper than they'd been back then. Having spent so many years without a man made her realize that what he offered was the most precious thing imaginable—far more valuable than any diamond and every bit as unlikely as lightning striking twice in the same place. And yet, there he was, the embodiment of love, kneeling right in front of her with an expression that touched not only her heart, but the depths of her soul.

Tears welled up in her eyes. "Oh, yeah. If I had my choice of any man in the world, I would choose you. I love you so much."

He was on his feet in an instant, pulling her into an embrace that left her breathless. "I promise you won't regret it, Miranda. I'll do everything I can to make you happy."

"And I'll do the same for you." From Miranda's perspective, Travis was more likely to be the one to have regrets, but as his lips melted into hers, every fear—real or imagined—dissolved into nothingness.

Travis meant every word of that declaration, but it took two to make a marriage work. If nothing else, his first marriage had taught him that. A woman didn't stray from her husband if he'd done all he could to keep her unless she'd never really loved him to start with. Miranda loved him. He was sure of that now.

What he had to remember was that love was an action as well as a state of being. He hadn't been lying when he'd told Miranda he'd never been a fun kind of lover in the past. He'd been too passive, too stagnant, and not nearly adventurous enough.

He might never know what it was about Miranda that changed him, but he understood the outcome. She'd set him free of constraints imposed by his family and upbringing and allowed him to fall in love for the first time in his life. She'd given him license to use his imagination, opening a whole new world of romance and passion. He couldn't imagine doing some of the things he'd done with Miranda with any other woman.

And he certainly wouldn't have brought home a bottle of baby oil.

Alan would be proud.

Chapter 33

Meeting a friend for lunch to tell her that her ex-boyfriend was getting married was tough enough. Topping it off with the report of your own impending nuptials was like rubbing salt into an open wound. Even so, Miranda wasn't sure she could get through the meal without spilling the beans.

"I guess that's that," Christina said with an air of resignation. "At least one of us is happy." She paused, scrutinizing Miranda through narrowed eyes. "And you *are* happy, aren't you? You look like you're about to burst."

Miranda blew out a pent-up breath. "Travis asked me to marry him."

"And I suppose you said yes."

"Are you kidding? Of course I did."

"Sure he won't bore you to tears?"

"Not a chance." Miranda saw no point in trying to convince Christina that Travis was possibly the least boring man in the world. As far as she was concerned, Christina could go right on thinking that. "By the way, I'm shopping around for a maid of honor. I'd ask Tracy, but she's a little iffy on the whole marriage idea right now. Even though she'll be at the wedding, she's got some bizarre superstition about maids of honor being the next in line. I always thought it was the one who caught the bouquet, but what do I know?"

Christina's transformation from radiant to bleak happened so fast it was almost comical. "Mark won't be there, will he?"

"No. Just our families and a few close friends."

"I'm very happy for you," Christina said with a wistful smile. "But Tracy isn't the only one down on love. I…I'm not sure I can do it. Besides, it might be a little awkward since Travis and I dated a few times."

Christina was obviously grasping at straws, but Miranda wasn't about to let her off the hook. "I doubt it, unless someone decides to slap you silly for passing up such a great guy." Not that Miranda would do any such thing. In fact, she felt like getting down on her knees and thanking her friend for being such an idiot. "And yes, there are several others I could ask, but right now, I'm asking *you*."

Christina opened a package of creamer and stirred it into her coffee, a thoughtful expression on her face. "You really love him, don't you?"

"Yes, I do, and I think it would be good for you—and Tracy—to see that there really is such a thing as a happy couple." Miranda paused, drawing in a shaky breath. "I don't want to see either of you waste as many years as I did—although, I have to admit, I'm glad I waited."

Christina's laugh was a bit weak, but at least she laughed. "Not sure you gained much with that argument."

"This isn't a legal debate," Miranda said. "This is a friend asking a friend to stand up with her at her wedding."

Teeth tugging at her lip, Christina nodded. "You're right. Just don't spring Mark and his new wife on me. I couldn't take that."

"No worries. He won't be there." Miranda chose not to mention that he'd be halfway across the country on his honeymoon at the time.

"You won't try to fix me up with any of the guests, will you?"

"Absolutely not," Miranda replied, throwing up her hands in protest. "I haven't met any of Travis's friends yet myself—or any of his family. We're having dinner with his parents in a few days, but I probably won't meet anyone else until the wedding. It's not like we've planned this for months, and you of all people know how hard it is to work around everyone's schedule."

Christina heaved a sigh. "Tell me about it. One more stipulation. Please *promise* me you won't toss your bouquet anywhere near my direction."

Although she couldn't vouch for Travis's side of the family, anyone Miranda had invited would probably rather catch pneumonia than a bouquet. "I promise. In fact, I may not toss it at all."

"Okay, I'll do it."

Miranda might've gotten the answer she wanted, but she hadn't forgotten who she was dealing with. "Could I have that in writing?"

℘◌℘

When the day finally arrived, Miranda rode with Christina, Levi, and Tabitha to a small chapel where a friend of Travis's was waiting to perform the wedding ceremony. Even Christina giggled when Miranda started humming "Chapel of Love," eventually bursting into song.

After the first chorus, Levi spoke up, as Miranda had known he would. "Uh, Mom. Could you please be quiet?"

"Nope," Miranda replied. "When you and Tabitha get married—*if* you get married—you'll probably be singing too."

Levi shook his head. "Not *that* song."

"Yeah, well, I think it's perfect."

The redbud trees were just past their peak and the white dogwoods were in full bloom as they drove to the ivy-covered chapel nestled in the woods.

As Levi escorted Miranda down the aisle, she saw the familiar faces of her friends and family and those belonging to a number of strangers, but it wasn't until she reached the altar that her eyes fell on the man standing beside her future husband.

Stuart was about a head taller than Travis, with a broad-shouldered, muscular build, curly black hair, and ice-blue eyes. A square-jawed he-man type, he had the kind of beard that was still visible even when he'd shaved close enough to take off the top layer of skin. Miranda suspected that Christina had already spotted him, which might account for her slight stumble as she preceded Miranda down the aisle. Nevertheless, when Stuart handed the ring to Travis, there was no mistaking Christina's softly uttered *ohhh...* as she got her first close-up view of him.

"You see what I mean?" Travis murmured as he took Miranda's hand. "I can't figure out why he thinks women don't like him."

"Probably because the sight of him stuns them speechless," Miranda whispered back. "And I never would've guessed you two were brothers. He doesn't look anything like you."

"Different mothers," Travis said. "*His* mother's family tends to be taller."

Miranda would've bet that wasn't the only difference, but there wasn't time for further discussion, because Joel, the Justice of the Peace, had already begun the ceremony. As she promised to love, honor, and cherish her darling Travis, she realized how different this marriage would be from her first, and not only because she was marrying a different man. She'd spent most of her married life going it alone for months at a time. Travis would be with her day in and day out, and she could hardly wait for the rest of her life to begin.

She would sleep with Travis on her nights off and dream about him when she slept during the daytime. And on the weekends when she had to work, she would come home and wake him with a kiss as sweet as the first one they shared as husband and wife.

Oh, yeah. Life is good.

ഇരു

Travis placed her hand on his arm and gave it a squeeze as they walked back down the aisle. "Happy?"

Miranda leaned closer, resting her head on his shoulder. "You have no idea."

"Somehow, I think I might."

He certainly understood the contrast between the way he felt now and how he could've felt if things had turned out differently. As he'd stood waiting for his bride, for one horrific moment, he realized how close they'd come to dismissing each other as potential lovers. One chance phone call from Levi had turned the tables, just as one slip on the ice could have ended everything.

But she was here beside him, alive and well, and if she couldn't remember that pivotal moment in their lives, he'd do his best to help her relive it every time they made love. He was already well on his way to loving Levi like a son. He'd get to know her friends and become part of her life. Hell, he might even have a beer with that crazy x-ray tech, Rodney.

When he introduced her to Alan, he realized something else— he was proud of her. She was beautiful, intelligent, and sexy as hell. His only hope was that she was as proud to be his wife as he was to be her husband.

"You're a lucky man, Travis York." Alan's words reflected Travis's own thoughts as they shook hands. He nodded toward Stuart. "Get a load of that."

A glance at Stuart had Travis following his brother's starry-eyed gaze to where it rested on an obviously smitten Christina. He gave Miranda a nudge. "Check it out."

A quiet giggle escaped her. "They remind me of that old hair color commercial. You know, *the closer he gets, the better you look?*"

Travis shrugged. "Must've been before my time."

"Oh, you are in *so* much trouble," Miranda said with a menacing glare. "Just wait until I get you home…"

"Will my punishment involve leather and whips?" Travis asked, waggling his brows.

Alan grimaced, clutching a hand to his chest. "You two are killing me."

"Hang in there, Alan," Travis said with a wink. "Your time will come."

₧ℂ⅃

"Okay, Miranda," Nigel shouted. "I'm ready to be impressed. Go for it!"

Miranda approached the crossover point of the figure eight and straightened Kira before changing the bend, sliding her new outside leg back and shifting her weight to that side. Giving a slight squeeze with her other leg, she felt the mare strike off on the new lead.

"Yes, yes, *yes!*" Nigel screamed, jumping to his feet to dance a jig. "I can't stand it! That was bleeding perfect!"

With a huge grin, she cantered Kira around the circle.

"Now, do that again," he called out.

Dammit! There's always a catch.

Leaning over the gate, Travis gave her a firm thumbs up. "Come on, Miranda! You can do it! Like he said, that was perfect!"

Perfect? How many perfect things could one woman possibly do in a lifetime? On top of marrying Travis, she'd gotten Nigel to buy Arwen so she could breed Jadzia to an Andalusian. Levi and Tabitha were still dating and falling more in love with each passing week—although she really couldn't take credit for that. And then there was the whole Stuart and Christina romance...

Nope, can't take credit for that one, either. Still, after achieving so many seemingly impossible goals, what was one more flying lead change?

"Yes, yes, *yes!*" Nigel screamed again when Kira gave a nonchalant bounce onto the opposite lead. "One more time!"

Miranda shouted with laughter as Kira gave a snort. "Sure, Nigel. No problem. It's a piece of cake!"

About the Author

A native of Louisville, Kentucky, Cheryl Brooks is a former critical care nurse who resides in rural Indiana with her husband, two sons, two horses, four cats, and one dog. Her **Cat Star Chronicles** series was first published by Sourcebooks Casablanca in 2008, and includes *Slave, Warrior, Rogue, Outcast, Fugitive, Hero, Virgin, Stud,* and *Wildcat.* Look for book 10, *Rebel,* in 2014. She has one self-published e-book, *Sex, Love, and a Purple Bikini,* and one erotic short story, *Midnight in Reno.* She has also published *If You Could Read My Mind* writing as Samantha R. Michaels. As a member of *The Sextet,* she has written several erotic novellas published by Siren/Bookstrand. Her **Unlikely Lovers** series includes *Unbridled, Uninhibited, Undeniable,* and *Unrivaled.* Her other interests include cooking, gardening, singing, and guitar playing. Cheryl is a member of RWA and IRWA.

You can visit her online at www.cherylbrooksonline.com or email her at cheryl.brooks52@yahoo.com

www.ingramcontent.com/pod-product-compliance
Lightning Source LLC
Chambersburg PA
CBHW051415170626
46809CB00006B/2171